S0-ADT-002

SHE SURRENDERED TO PASSION

"Why won't you let me go?" Evangeline cried. "Why would you risk so much to keep someone who loathes you? I will not be a wife to you. You are nothing to me."

His reply was so soft that she had to strain to hear it.

"You have no idea what you mean to me."

A tremor seized her. Not of rage. Of wonder. Of inexplicable hope. And of desire.

He pulled her close to him. His body was hard, unyielding, and—contrarily—hers felt suddenly frail. She couldn't keep her legs from trembling. Even her breath quivered.

"You are mine, Evangeline. No one takes what is mine."

Those words, spoken with rough certainty, increased her helplessness. Desire shone bright in his eyes, and hers began to close. He was going to kiss her. She should have rebelled against it, yet she found herself leaning upon him, her lips moistening, preparing for possession . . .

HEARTFIRE ROMANCES

SWEET TEXAS NIGHTS   (2610, $3.75)
by Vivian Vaughan

Meg Britton grew up on the railroads, working proudly at her father's side. Nothing was going to stop them from setting the rails clear to Silver Creek, Texas — certainly not some crazy prospector. As Meg set out to confront the old coot, she planned her strategy with cool precision. But soon she was speechless with shock. For instead of a harmless geezer, she found a boldly handsome stranger whose determination matched her own.

CAPTIVE DESIRE   (2612, $3.75)
by Jane Archer

Victoria Malone fancied herself a great adventuress, but being kidnapped was too much excitement for even Victoria! Especially when her arrogant kidnapper thought she was part of Red Duke's outlaw gang. Trying to convince the overbearing, handsome stranger when that she had been an innocent bystander when the stagecoach was robbed, proved futile. But when he thought he could maker her confess by crushing her to his warm, broad chest, by caressing her with his strong, capable hands, Victoria was willing to admit to anything. . . .

LAWLESS ECSTASY   (2613, $3.75)
by Susan Sackett

Abra Beaumont could spot a thief a mile away. After all, her father was once one of the best. But he'd been on the right side of the law for years now, and she wasn't about to let a man like Dash Thorne lead him astray with some wild plan for stealing the Tear of Allah, the world's most fabulous ruby. Dash was just the sort of man she most distrusted — sophisticated, handsome, and altogether too sure of his considerable charm. Abra shivered at the devilish gleam in his blue eyes and swore he would need more than smooth kisses and skilled caresses to rob her of her virtue . . . and much more than sweet promises to steal her heart!

Available wherever paperbacks are sold, or order direct from the Publisher. Send cover price plus 50¢ per copy for mailing and handling to Zebra Books, Dept. 3055, 475 Park Avenue South, New York, N.Y. 10016. Residents of New York, New Jersey and Pennsylvania must include sales tax. DO NOT SEND CASH.

WILD SAVAGE LOVE

DANA RANSOM

ZEBRA BOOKS
KENSINGTON PUBLISHING CORP.

ZEBRA BOOKS

are published by

Kensington Publishing Corp.
475 Park Avenue South
New York, NY 10016

Copyright © 1990 by Dana Ransom

All rights reserved. No part of this book may be reproduced
in any form or by any means without the prior written
consent of the Publisher, excepting brief quotes used in
reviews.

First printing: June, 1990

Printed in the United States of America

For Carin
A belated Wedding Gift.

Many thanks to a wonderful editor,
for trusting my instincts and
giving constant encouragement.

Prologue

The Colony of New York, 1684

There was a chance she still lived. For eight years, they held no hope. Though her body was never found, they accepted the awful truth that young Evangeline Carey had died in the tragedy that took her parents. The news had been devastating but not unusual in the savage clime of the colonies. It was but one of the many hardships all had to endure, that risk that fate would find the hair of a loved one adorning the belt of a native warrior. Yet, she had been so young, only ten, a baby. Alas, youth provided no charm against butchery at the hands of heathens, and as months slipped away after the brutal discovery, the threads of hope raveled until all that remained to cling to was memory.

It was that vague memory Emma Webster ransacked as she stood anxiously at her husband's side on the gentle slope before Fort Orange. The journey upriver from New York had been wrought with expectant promise, however, as she considered the group before them, a crushing disappointment welled anew in her breast. How could they have

7

thought her brother's child would be among them. Why, these unfortunates were nothing but . . . but savages, themselves.

When word had come that the Right Honorable Francis Lord Howard of Effingham, governor-general of his Majesty's dominion of Virginia, Colonel Thomas Dongan, governor of New York, and the magistrates of Albany had demanded that the Christian women and children prisoners be restored to them during treaty negotiations, a flood of bereaved had gathered near the placid orchard in Albany. Parents and relatives traveled as far as one hundred miles from back settlements in Pennsylvania and New England to identify their children or wives, if they could. Faithfully, the kidnapped children were brought forth to be recognized, and the shrieks of joy from mothers long deprived overwhelmed the silent suffering of the Indian women who had their surrogate children wrested from their arms. Those frightened children clung to the only mothers they knew, until torn away amid wails of protest, then cried as if they would perish when delivered to the English strangers. Some had been among the Iroquois so long that they only responded to their Indian names, spoke only native dialects, and knew only the freedom of their Indian garb. The young ones were so completely savage they had to be bound hand and foot, regarding their white saviors as barbarians, and their deliverance as a frightening captivity.

"Well? Is she among them?"

Her husband's terse question served to increase Emma Webster's turmoil. She knew he considered the trip one of pitiful futility, yet had indulged her teary request. Now, in the face of her indecision, his impatience had little check.

"I'm not sure. Oh, Uriah, 'tis been so long. She was just a babe." Determinedly, she studied those left to be claimed, seeing little difference between captors and captives. She struggled to look beneath the deceiving layers of paint and grease, willing herself to find some sign of her brother in one of the pathetic faces. She would be seventeen, a young woman, not a child. She would be tall like her father, slim like her mother. Just when she was about to concede the impossibility of her hope, her attention was held by a silent pair of women standing on the outskirts of the group. She hadn't paid them notice before, assuming they were both Indian mothers come to part with their prisoners. Yet something about the younger made her gaze return with careful, almost fearful scrutiny. The braided plaits, the doeskin garb, the dashes of vermilion stripping her cheek, chin, and forehead could not disguise the piercing gray of her brother's eyes. Emma's fingers tightened on her husband's sleeve until he followed her rapt stare.

"'Tis her," came a near whisper. "'Tis Evangel-ine."

Uriah Webster's doubting frown deepened in concentration before he, too, saw the unmistakable likeness. There could be no denying the truth. He acted upon it with grim purpose, approaching one of the soldiers standing sentinel over the proceedings to exchange brief words. Then he returned to his wife's side to wait in stony silence.

At the soldier's advancement, the young woman who had been Evangeline Carey stiffened and took up the arm of the woman beside her. The girl's calm expression could not belie the desperation of that grasp. It grew more frantic as the Englishman spoke. Her head gave a denying shake and those irrefutable gray eyes fastened upon the couple across the stretch

9

of green. That look conveyed a chill of loathing that lodged cold in Emma Webster's gladdened heart. Then the Indian woman touched the girl's arm and spoke softly. For a moment, it seemed as though Evangeline would join the others with their torrents of tears and useless struggles to resist separation from their savage acquaintances. Finally, resolutely, she stood away from her companion, and with head held high and proud, walked up the incline to where the Websters waited.

Chapter One

"Where is she?"

Emma Webster's reddened eyes appeared above the fluttering handkerchief to regard her husband in an appeal of despair and defeat. Her voice, never strong, quavered like frail gossamer in a breeze.

"In her room. With door locked." That last was rendered with a miserable sigh and the threat of renewed tears. The thin bosom rose and fell precariously. "Oh, Uriah, what are we to do? I never thought . . . I never thought it would be so difficult." Finding his silence an encouragement, she poured out the rest of her upset in an emotional flood that had her weaving upon the backless bench on which she'd collapsed. Guilt and grievance colored her outburst with equal degrees of unhappiness.

"She fights me on the smallest thing. One would believe I am her enemy, and not those heathens who abducted her. She refuses to eat. She shredded the articles I gave her to clothe her nakedness. Only this morning, the moment my back was averted, she tried to flee through an open sash. Only Jamal's agility kept her within, and he had to drag her, kicking and thrashing, up the stairs. She howled on the opposite side of the door for nearly an hour in that godless tongue." Her eyes squeezed tight in remembered horror, then opened to peer beseechingly into the stern face above her as if to seek the answer there. "I do not understand it. She acts as though *we* are the kidnappers. Why should she hate us for rescuing her from her captors, from the very creatures that murdered her mother and my dearest brother?"

Uriah Webster was not a man of great compassion, and his wife's misery woke none in his breast. He was of a notion to remind her curtly just whose idea it was to take the girl into their home, but that would only bring on more tears and he'd seen enough of those weepy tirades since his niece had come under their roof nearly two weeks ago. All had, thereafter, been in tumult. He had enough to weight his brow without the added complication.

"If the task of Christian mercy has proved too much for you, my dear, perhaps the clergy could find some means of providing for her."

Tears were abruptly blinked away. "We could not do that. Evangeline is our responsibility. She is my brother's child."

"Is she, Emma?" His patience was notably thinning. Just once, he thought in annoyance, he would like to enter his home to find harmony as of old, a peace in which he could savor a bowl and a brew at his leisure, wherein his wife would greet him docile and silent, before scurrying off to wherever it was she spent her time in the big house he'd provided for her. Now the rooms seemed too small, and there was no escape from the upheaval. His voice was testy. "Can you honestly avow that the wild thing upstairs is Joshua's daughter?"

"Uriah," she gasped. "The poor dear cannot be blamed for what has befallen her. It all must be such a shock to her. We cannot in all conscience turn our backs from our duty.''

Her moral indignation made him smirk. Had she not been moments before begging him to remove the problem of the uncontrollable girl? ''What are we to do with her, Emma? Can you see her seated in our pew with us on Sunday? Will she be attending Cyrus's maturity ball in her native garb?''

That thought made the fragile woman blanch, yet instead of surrendering before the insurmountable task, Uriah had to credit her conscientious fortitude. Complaints forgotten, she began to contemplate their situation.

''No one has seen her yet. I have waved away all polite inquires by saying she is in too delicate a state to receive. I cannot have our neighbors know that our newfound niece is a—'' She paused, at a loss, and her husband supplied an ending for her most bluntly.

''Savage.''

Emma didn't disagree, as he thought she might. Instead, she sighed and nodded. ''There must be some way to reach her, some way to tap the memories she must hold of the past.''

Uriah reacted to that with a start and a brusque, ''I fear there is nothing to reach. She is one of them by choice. Will you continue to hold her by locks and force?''

''I must, for now. Don't you see?'' Her gentle brown eyes lifted, asking for understanding, for forgiveness. ''I cannot allow her to go back to what she was. She is all I have left of Joshua, and I will find some way to preserve his memory through her. With time, with love and care—''

Uriah made a harsh noise. She went on determinedly.

''She will come to realize that what we do is for her

13

own good. It will just take time for her to get used to us and our ways again, for her to return to herself."

"Do what you must, Emma, only see that she does not disgrace us. I will turn her back to the wild before I will allow that to happen. I will not endanger our son's chances, to tame a beast that may never be broken."

Emma Webster said nothing as her eyes lowered meekly beneath that ultimatum. She would work harder. She would be more tolerant. But she would not surrender the soul of her beloved brother's child to the ungodly.

Uriah closed the door to the drawing room, as if he could also shut out his troubles. If only it were that easy, he thought grimly. For once, the surrounding luxury of wainscotted walls hung with embossed leather failed to soothe him with the balm of success. He sat and brooded, oblivious to the finery about him, for he took no joy in what he might yet lose.

He had struggled too hard and been too clever to let his plans waver now. Dodd's betrayal had hit him at a bad time, and now he was not only out the profits the man had stolen from him, but pressed to find a replacement. He could not afford another error in judgment. He had gone from meager tradesman in England to a monopolistic merchant in the colonies, and he was not about to yield one inch of that advancement. If trade was his means, power was his goal, and he had achieved much since taking over Joshua Carey's business. The fur trade held an infinite potential of profit, however, it was not without its risks. Uriah's thick auburn hair gained heavier streaks of silver each time he watched his capital being packed off into the woods in the fall, each time he began the agonizing wait until spring when pelts appeared in return. His supplies from England were subject to interruption by war, piracy, navigation disasters, and the competence and honesty of exporters. To that end, he strove to cultivate political affluence as a buffer. Those lofty bedfellows aided in the licensing of traders—so heavy fines could be levied against those not in his own employ—and saw that he had imperial influence to secure decrees from the crown to his own advantage in a combination of law and larceny. He maintained a large stock of trade goods, and pumped fortunes into his warehouse inventory to have supplies on hand before his competitors. Soon, Cyrus, his son, would increase that advantage with his own law practice that would someday extend into the political realm, but that would not solve immediate problems.

Albany was the hub of trade, drawing the traffic of the north from the St. Lawrence Valley via the Richelieu River, Lake Champlain, and Lake George. Merchants set up trading houses there to entice the Indians to bring in their furs, and also hired traders to pass along merchandise to Indian customers at these remote posts. A good trader could cheat the Indians without getting caught, but would also cheat his benefactor, as Uriah had learned in Dodd's case. He had no desire to return to the raw edges of Albany to see to his profits in person. He'd worked too hard to become prosperous enough to indulge his aristocratic tastes and fancies. He would leave the hand-soiling to others. To find the right other was foremost on his mind when interrupted by news of his unwanted niece's most recent uprising. She was becoming a tedious distraction and an uncomfortable threat beneath his roof.

As he could only deal with one dilemma at a time,

he unfolded the letter he'd received only that day and reread the application. The man was obviously unsuited. Uriah needed someone with experience in Indian trade and diplomacy, not a recent arrival from England with an impressive education. He was about to cast the neatly penned petition aside, when he drew it back for yet another look. Experience had singed him once. Perhaps loyalty, intelligence, and honor would serve him better this time. Perhaps what he needed was an individual he could mold into his own likeness, one who would look to the future instead of grasp greedily at what the present offered. Dodd had been a skilled cheat and steeped in Indian politics, yet the man had cultivated the brain of a muskrat. He'd never understood that greed and ambition were two separate things, and that gain and gratification were a world apart. Perhaps what he needed was a man a world apart from temptation. He glanced at the name and post at the bottom of the single sheet, and dipped his quill in the ink pot. After shaking sand over the wet scrawl of his words, he folded the missive and carefully penned the name Royle Tanner upon it.

Evangeline Carey sat cross-legged upon the ugly yarn carpet that covered a small square of the floor in her new prison. She was still, her back as straight as a forest pine beneath the cloaking elegance of long hair which fell in blue black ripples to brush the rug. A calm had settled, and she could see clearly for the first time what she must do. She regretted the unworthy show of passions that had ruled her throughout her captivity. That was the fear and loneliness directing her actions. Now it was time for thinking. She would remain quietly seated until the path was shown her. Resistance was no good. Their number was greater, and she was alone among them. They watched her now like an animal snared. Escape could only be gained if that guard lessened. And she would escape. Desperation and determination mingled to lend strength to that promise. And she would hold to it, to see her through the remaining time among them.

Thoughts of freedom made her think of her family, not the Englishmen below, but of the Woodland People who loved her. Never had she imagined they would give her up. Many times bounties had been offered for the return of prisoners, and yet she remained safe with her family. This time it had been different; her father, He-Raises-the-Sky, had told her. If she and the others were not surrendered, the English would unite and destroy their people. She went because she could not bring them harm. She went because she had no choice. Never would she knowingly dishonor her father by betraying his oath. He was an educated man, educated in the white man's ways, and had seen her unwittingly prepared for the day in which she would walk once again, as he knew she must, among her own kind. A wistful smile touched her soft lips as she remembered the words spoken to her by She-Walks-Far. "They come to collect our flesh and our blood," she'd said. "Though you may go, we will always look upon you as one of our own. May they use you kindly and make you content to live among them." Content? Those tender lips curled to reveal strong white teeth bared in contempt. Never. Never would she sit placid among the soft white men and women, when her heart longed to race free and unrestrained. These pale strangers were nothing to her, and she could not comprehend their want to keep her where she did not

17

belong and did not wish to be.

Again, the loneliness assailed her like a great enveloping ache to the soul. How she missed her home, the companionable closeness of her relations, the crisp scent of the forest, and sounds of the wild. Here, all was a confusion of frightening unknowns, of noises without purpose, unfamiliar smells, confined spaces. It made breathing labored and movement uncomfortable. A white man's world, not hers, and the sooner she was gone from it, the better. Evangeline, they called her, a name she could remember only with the vagueness of a childhood dream. For most of her years, she had been Eyes-Like-Evening-Star, yet that, too, had been taken from her, the way the white woman below had tried to take her clothing. Foolishly, the woman had thought that by changing her garments, likewise she would easily alter habits and attachments, as if ashamed of what she was proud to claim. No external change could transform what resided in heart and soul.

She continued to sit, ignoring the rumble of a stomach long without food, of a heart long without happiness, and planned. She would have to escape this house, these cautious eyes, and to do so, would have to gain the beginnings of their trust. As long as she fought their will, they would cage her with their locks and wary looks. Pride rebelled against the thought of submitting to these inferior beings, of humbling herself to the tortuous confines of their manners, however, she crushed it with determination. She would do what needed doing to earn her chance at freedom.

A tap at the door brought an impassive mask over her features, and she regarded the fragile woman who entered with a steady stare. The woman, whose dark

18

eyes seemed to always be asking something of her, hesitated, uncertain, then stepped within.

"I came to see if you required anything," she said in a faint, yet kind voice. Her kindness was wasted on one who saw her only as her captor.

The erect posture never faltered to betray inner thoughts that screamed out all the things needed; home, family, freedom. Instead, quite civil, she asked, "I should like something to eat."

Emma's breath caught with delight, for the girl had refused all sustenance since her coming. "Yes, of course. I can have a tray brought up to you or," again the hesitation edged with hope, "if you'd like, you can dine below with us."

The disgust that suggestion wrought was concealed behind the level gaze. "I will come down."

Emma's excitement over the small victory was tempered. It was the first night of Cyrus's homecoming. He knew, of course, of Evangeline's presence in their home, but not the facts of the situation. Looking at the comely girl in her half-naked state brought an unusual firmness to the gentle woman. Taking the risk that she would lose the tentative hold she had gained with her niece, Emma said softly, yet unyieldingly, "You may come down if you dress presentably. I will provide you once again with suitable wear. If you choose to put it on, we would be most happy to have you sup with us."

There was a long pause, and Emma feared all was lost, when the young woman said in a measured tone, "I do not wish to offend you at your meal. I will wear whatever pleases you."

A tremulous smile quivered upon the pale lips, and a dampness suspiciously akin to tears glistened gratefully. "Will you? Oh, Evangeline, you do not know how much it pleases me just to hear that."

"I regret if I have burdened you with sorrow, Aunt."

That dutifully rendered title brought the spill of wetness down Emma Webster's pinched cheeks, and her handkerchief fluttered ineffectively. Her wish to embrace the girl in heartfelt relief was checked by the directness of Evangeline's gaze. Though it was no longer hostile, neither was it welcoming. That would come in time, Emma was certain. With this first concession, she felt all was truly possible, and that soon she would have her brother's child back in her fold.

Silence fell upon those at the table as they turned to regard the young woman approaching. Garbed in a fitted gown of pale yellow damask, with her long hair pulled back into a simple plait, Evangeline Carey was a picture of demure femininity. She paused within the door frame, her poise faultless, her carriage enviable, the image of a properly reared colonial miss. The Websters, Emma in particular, wished there was truth in that fleeting illusion.

"Evangeline, how pretty you look," she coaxed hopefully. "Won't you join us? We were about to take prayer."

The young woman hesitated, eyeing the stool one of the solemn servants readied for her, then she moved gracefully to assume it. Immediately, the charade of her gentility was exposed. The back of her damask gown hung open from shoulders to the beginning curve of her buttocks, and the sheen of well-tanned skin left no doubt that nothing lay between the damask and the supple form beneath it. Emma recovered from her paralyzing horror and quickly moved to the girl's aid.

"Here, let me help you. I'd forgotten that you'd be unused to our attire."

"I could not reach the hooks, and it was more comfortable this way," Evangeline stated without a blush or trace of modesty.

"I will have someone maid you, until you are more accustomed to doing for yourself," her aunt remedied rather breathlessly as she secured the last hook of propriety. To her continued dismay, she noted bare feet peeping from beneath the sweeping hem, but to save the girl from further humiliation out of ignorance, she chose to say nothing as she saw her safely seated.

Evangeline sat stiffly on her stool, as the others bowed their heads and Uriah began an unintelligible mumbling. He was speaking to one of their gods, she realized and listened curiously. She could recall uttering similar chants, but words and meaning failed her. What lingered, oddly, was a sense of comforting peace. She shook off that poignant fondness, wanting nothing to link her to the people she was forced to endure, or to their puny gods. Instead, as their heads lifted at the end of the ritual, she studied them. Her aunt held no mystery to her. She was weak and quickly dismissed. The man who called himself Uncle was big, powerful, and threatening. He was used to intimidating by his presence, and though she was not afraid, she was wary. His eyes were the color of winter ice, just as cold and hard, and held no hint of welcome for her. At least he was honest in his dislike of her. The pale woman did not want her here either, yet she hadn't the character to accept the strength of her feelings. She lived for others, not herself, and Evangeline despised that submission.

The only one she didn't know at the table met her candid gaze fully. His stare was warm, and though its implication was unknown to her, she did not think the heat due to his joy at discovering a member of the family. This was Cyrus. He had the large look of his father, but it was his mother who influenced his manner. It was decidedly womanish and weak, and she was repulsed. Her attention turned to her plate.

Evangeline frowned, for this dish—like all the others brought to her—resembled nothing she could identify. It was the way of her people to eat everything without distinction—bear, cats, dogs, snakes, frog—for to show any delicacy in the choice of food would be seen as offensive in the eyes of its spirit, but this clump upon her plate, disguised beneath heavy sauce, had no natural look about it. Her nose wrinkled and she sniffed, hoping to determine some clue by its odor. She leaned closer. When her nose was a scant inch above the plate, Emma said in a strained tone, "What is it, dear? Have you no liking for quail?"

Evangeline straightened and regarded her plate with one delicate brow lifted. "Quail?" She sounded dubious. "Yes, I like quail." Gingerly, she probed the mass upon her plate and raised a piece in dripping fingers to pop into her mouth. After a moment of loud chewing, she nodded, and applied herself two-handedly to the task. Her aunt averted her eyes and swallowed hard.

Cyrus watched his cousin with unfeigned interest. In spite of her appalling manners, he found her a rare and comely wench. The sight of her smooth, delectable flesh was not one he'd soon forget. Tanned all the way down. Bringing it to mind now had him shifting uncomfortably. Though his mother had

22

told him to treat her with the respect due family, those carnal thoughts led him to consider instead the profligate nature of the Indians. He'd heard they were quite amoral in their relations, and the odds that his fair cousin was still a virgin after having been in their hands for seven years were as slim as his mother's chance of passing her off respectably in their community. No, Evangeline Carey was not a refined New England miss to demand his proper court and gentle wooing. She was a savage, and that knowledge fueled his already well-tempted lusts into an excited shivering. Having had her share of native lovers, he wondered how she would take to a true gentleman, and how long he would have to wait to find out. A wild beauty like her was ripe for bedding. What a mistress she would make, he decided in a lather of anticipation, imagining that blue black hair wound about him. Yes, he was most glad to have Cousin Evangeline under their roof.

As the meal continued, Evangeline listened to Uriah and his son converse over business, while Emma sat meek and silent. She puzzled over the woman's attitude. Did she have no opinions? Did she have no interest in how her affairs were handled? Why would she let her man talk so freely about her money, without consulting her for permission to spend it? She had seen She-Walks-Far counting every pelt, not out of distrust for her husband, but to honor him by her attentiveness. It was a woman's duty to see to her possessions with careful scrutiny, and Evangeline looked forward to the day when she would manage her own household. Or would she? The uncertainty of her future returned the grim nature of her thoughts. She had no possessions of her own, only the Websters' charity, and that sat ill with her pride.

"Who has seen to my property these last seven years?"

The unexpected question stunned all into immobility. Then Uriah tested the request with caution. "Property? What do you mean?"

"The things belonging to Carey. They are mine now."

The blunt speech over her departed brother's effects had Emma reaching for her over-taxed handkerchief, but Uriah showed no trace of sentimentality. "And what do you know of your father's holdings?" he challenged softly.

The man's eyes were like steel, and Evangeline wondered over his anger. Hadn't she the right to ask such a thing? "I know nothing. I but assume he had a home . . . land. What has become of it?"

"My dear, if you are worried that you'll not be provided for, don't trouble yourself," Emma soothed in her own simple scope of misunderstanding. "We are your family and will see to you. You'll be well dowried when the time comes for you to marry, and until then, you'll lack for no comfort."

The gray eyes stared at her incomprehensively. Why did she talk of such silly things? "I have no want of your gifts," she stated with near disdain. The insult was clear, and Emma paled. "I am concerned with my own possessions."

Uriah sat back in his chair and regarded her unblinkingly. His words were deliberately clipped so there would be no misunderstanding. "Your father began the trading house I now own. I bought him out when he decided to risk all on a venture into the Ohio Valley. He was carrying everything he owned when he and your mother were massacred by the same barbarians you now hold so dear. In effect, you

24

have nothing."

Beneath the warm glow of her tan, Evangeline grew chilled and white. With an equal amount of control, she retaliated, "My family had no part in the death of the Careys."

"Then who did, girl? We saw them free of their hair. You cannot tell me it was not the work of your precious savages."

Her reply was quelled by a strangled sound from Emma. "Uriah, please," she moaned in anguish. "There is no need for such talk. Can't you see the child has suffered enough."

"I cannot see that she's suffered at all," he answered. "In fact, all I see is an unholy pride in the vile doings of her preferred people. I wonder if our scalps rest safe with her beneath our roof."

"Oh," the frail woman cried, clutching her breast that such ugly passions should come to light, and of all places, at the table. "How could you say such a thing?" She rose and went to put protective arms about the rigid shoulders of her niece, not noticing how ill-received her gesture was.

"'Tis my house, and I'll say what I please, woman. You'd best remember that," he roared, until the fragile figure trembled like a leaf in a merciless gale. Quickly, beaten, she slipped back to her own stool and hunched there, eyes downcast. Through it all, Cyrus continued to fill his plate and ogle the swell of yellow damask.

Purposefully, Evangeline lifted the knife at her plate edge and examined its honed sharpness. Her calm gaze rose, and a small smile played about her lips. "I should not worry too much about my rest, were I you," she said, "nor about my remaining." With that, she set the stool aside to stand, and beneath the varied stares, Uriah's fierce, Cyrus's lusting, and

25

Emma's remorseful, she strode lithely to the stairs, preferring her solitude to their company.

Once in her room, the damask was quickly dispatched, and Evangeline, in the superior comfort of her own flesh, stood at the window. It wasn't a long drop to the ground. She could have made a jump easily had the sash not been nailed shut in anticipation of her thoughts. Her undisturbed demeanor hid the anger within her heart. How dare he cast such slurs upon the goodness of her people, people who had never caused her a mite of the grief she'd known since coming within these oppressive walls. His words troubled her, and she knew not why they should. What did it matter if she was a pauper in their world? She had no intention of staying, after all. Still, she couldn't keep from mulling over what was said, and for the first time in many years, tried to remember her father's features. She could not, and it didn't sadden her. Her father was He-Raises-the-Sky, and every plane of his dear face was etched upon her memory. She would look forward to the day of their reunion, not brood over the man who lived well off what another had started.

Evangeline frowned and chastised herself. She'd allowed her face to slip again, and they had seen through to her heart. They had read her scorn, and she'd revealed her desire to flee. They would be cautious. She could not let her true feelings escape, if she were to have that chance. She must play the humble part they felt was due. If they thought she was dangerous, even worse things could happen.

In the stillness of her room, the sound of the bolt shooting home in the door echoed with futility.

26

Chapter Two

The companionable noise of the tavern was a welcome relief to Uriah Webster. Warm, inviting scents of gentlemanly smoke and beer drew him in like an old friend's embrace. As he walked through the crowded taproom, he was hailed enthusiastically by several of the grogshop's regular clientele, with whom he often met to share a newspaper or discuss shipping news and prices, sweetened by a glass of ale. On this day, he merely lifted a hand in greeting and strode to the quiet corner table he'd requested. He settled his large frame behind the ready bowl of beer, and sighed his gratitude at being out of the house. His wife was entertaining some scheme as well as the good Reverend Bentley, and he was best free of whatever she planned. Seeing the pious reverend shouting damnation down upon him each Sunday was quite enough association to suit him.

After taking his first sip of the molasses and sassafras brew, the merchant consulted his extravagantly expensive timepiece, withdrawing it from his waistcoat with a grand flourish so the movement might catch the eyes of others, in order for them to admire the heavy gold piece and its owner. It was exactly one o'clock, he noted with the beginnings of a frown. He was late. A bad start to one who worshipped time and punctuality. He had begun to replace the watch when a soft voice intruded.

"Master Webster?" At the inquiring look, he concluded, "I am Royle Tanner."

Uriah measured the man with a practiced eye. This was not what the cultured letter had led him to expect. Here was no fine gentleman, but rather a commoner with a shabby look about him. His coat, though spotless, shown bright with long wear, and the edges of his neck cloth showed signs of fraying. The fair hair capping his head was his own, and the hand he extended was not smooth from leisurely studies, but coarse, his grip strong. That grip and the direct manner in which he leveled his gaze did much to overcome the initial poor impression.

"Please, seat yourself."

Once that was accomplished, Tanner said, "I thank you for meeting with me." That was it, no effusive gratitude, no gush of words, simple and to the point. Uriah began to smile. He motioned for the barmaid to bring round another drink.

"So, you wish to be in my employ."

"If I can give what you want, and you offer what I need."

By gad, the man had a candor that was almost unnerving. It wasn't prompted by arrogance, Uriah discerned, as much as a comfortable confidence. Not aggressive, but assertive, and that intrigued him into asking, "And what is it you need, Master Tanner?"

If Uriah had expected him to cite a monetary figure, he was pleasantly taken aback. "Prestige and respect. That is what I require foremost. Then prosperity, for which I plan to work very hard to achieve." His words were soft, but extremely well

28

spoken, conveying a gentility at odds with his appearance. A gentleman fallen upon hard times, perhaps.

"Noble goals, sir, and you feel they are attainable through me."

"Yes, or elsewhere, but I prefer to start at the top. I have little fear of heights."

Or of appearing too brash before a prospective employer, obviously. Uriah was not certain whether he was in fact offended instead of flattered. But he was interested enough to continue. "And do you know what it is I do?" The man's answer had him agog with its audacity.

"Not completely, no. I do know that you are wealthy, and you are in need of someone to act on your behalf. I am at your disposal."

"Indeed?" His heavy brows gave an incredulous lift. "And how do you figure a wealthy man such as myself can benefit from taking on a scholar direct from England, who has no idea of how my business is conducted, who is a stranger to our country and to the field of my endeavor, who, in fact, seems to have naught to offer except a monumental supply of presumption?"

The calm gaze never flickered, nor did his quiet-spoken reply. "Indeed, sir, what else is there? What more does a man need than the determination to succeed? 'Twould seem ambition outweighs knowledge, if one means to prosper."

Uriah frowned, dubious to that bold statement. "So you give no credence to experience?"

"I did not mean to imply such a thing. Experience cannot be overlooked, but in itself is not everything. Which would you give greater value—a slothful man of experience or an industrious one keen to learn?"

That the man would think to question him during

29

their interview was impertinence to the extreme, yet Uriah found himself weighing that answer, and before he could come to his own, the soft-spoken man continued.

"I am not a stupid man. I am quick to learn, and never forget what I am taught and by whom. I mean to make a mark for myself, and can only see the man willing to aid in my task as better off for it. I am not afraid of hard work nor of starting at the bottom, as long as the climb upward is clear. I have little patience with failure, so you needn't worry that I will succumb to it. I ask you to take a chance, not a risk."

Uriah leaned forward, and that intense attitude put the other at ease. With huge hands splayed before him, the merchant stated, "I am in trade, Mr. Tanner. The very business is a risk, so I cannot afford to doubt the competency of the men beneath me. What I need is a man who will take those risks for me, one who is adventurous, fearless, and shy of scruples. When I entrust my goods to that man, I have to be confident that he will return with a profit. Mere cleverness may not be enough."

"Yet it is an advantage that not all can boast of."

Uriah settled back with a thoughtful smile. "True enough." He said nothing for a moment, continuing his probe into the depths of the man's eyes. What he saw there was inspiring. "So, you would like to work for me."

"Yes."

"At any position I feel suits you."

"Yes."

"Perhaps you will, Mr. Tanner. Perhaps you will."

"And when will I know?"

"I will see you contacted."

"I shall hold myself ready for your reply until

week's end, then, you will understand, I shall have to start looking elsewhere."

"I believe you stated that you were not a patient man." That was said with a small smile, and was met with complete sincerity.

"No, I am not."

"Fair enough. By week's end."

Evangeline paused just outside the entrance to the keeping room, not so much as to gather her courage, as to struggle to draw a decent breath. The clothes her aunt insisted upon were slowly strangling the life from her. Pressing her palms to the constrictive hug of stays about her naturally trim waist, she squirmed within the garment to settle it more comfortably. While she scratched and tugged and cursed in her own tongue, aware of the discreet eyes of the house servants that watched her, she also became aware of the conversation progressing within the room. Emma had only advised that there would be a visitor come to make her acquaintance after the midday meal. She listened curiously to the man's moderate tones, and wondered who this important guest might be. Her aunt had been quite adamant about keeping Evangeline isolated to this point, so she could not help puzzling over the change.

Following their talk was difficult. Her natural thought process was not of the same language, and her skills in English were stale from disuse. The man she could understand, for he spoke slowly with distinction, but her aunt's words flew about like a hummingbird, darting, lightly, flitting, very hard to keep up with, not that Evangeline was much interested in her shallow thoughts.

"I believe the Indians are redeemable," the man

31

was saying. "They live in a state of savagery too degenerate for religion to take root. Therefore, it is our duty to weed out their barbarous habits and replace them with a civilized, Christian order of living. They are much like children of the human race, with passions unfettered by reason, little better than animals, really. That is why they must be reduced from savagery to civility."

A white missionary, Evangeline thought with contempt. Though several who had tried to convert her people had a genuine interest in their humanity, most, like this one, sought only to conform what frightened them and threatened their ideals. Another sign of weakness, she concluded. So this was the special visitor Aunt Emma had been anxious for her to meet. In her anger, she thought to return to her room and refuse them both the pleasure of goading her, but her pride would not allow her such a cowardly retreat. She straightened her posture to that befitting the daughter of a chief, a daughter of the Iroquois people, and walked bravely into the unfriendly room.

The white preacher came up from his chair with a thin smile, as thin as the ribbons of hair that were meticulously swept across his shiny pate. He was garbed somberly in a coat with huge hanging sleeves that extended past the hem of his drab jacket. His eyes were feverish with piety.

"Miss Carey, I have looked forward to meeting you. What a brave and exceptional child you must be to have survived the ordeal amongst the heathens. Mistress Webster has encouraged me to come to help steer you back upon the Christian path, from which you've in innocence strayed. I am humbled before such a task."

Evangeline stood stiff, her expression stoic. She

saw no humility in the man's zealous stare. She had seen such looks in the faces of men about to torture others to the point of breaking. Well, she would not be easily broken to the will of the white man's god.

"Shall we begin our visit with a prayer of thanksgiving for your rescue?"

Emma's head obediently bowed, however, when it became obvious that Evangeline meant to remain unyielding, the Rev. Bentley took her arm. If she had thought him weak, it was only in spirit. The strength of his grip dragged her with uncompromising vigor to her knees, and held her there by sheer force while he murmured gentle platitudes. As soon as she was freed, she struggled up in a malicious tangle of skirts to resume her combative stance, her head thrown back and gray eyes chilled with defiance. That sight didn't seem to disturb the righteous smile of Rev. Bentley, however, her aunt saw an end to her hopes and was ready to weep in frustration. The situation had to be salvaged, the gentle woman thought a bit frantically and fought to appear calm.

"My dear, please join us. Take this seat next to me. I was about to pour tea."

The abject pleading in her gaze moved Evangeline to do as bade, and she settled on the uncomfortable bench at the woman's side. Awkwardly, she accepted the thin cup of tasteless liquid from her aunt and held it in her hands while warily taking the measure of the preacher.

"I asked the good Reverend to speak with you, Evangeline. Your parents were fine, God-fearing people, and they would want me to see to your soul." Emma's words were faint, almost apologetic. In her own heart, she prayed Rev. Bentley could perform some miracle upon her wayward ward to calm the storm that had settled within their home. To her relief, the look the young woman gave her was not of resentment, only one of brief and unemotional acknowledgment.

"I thank you for your concern, Aunt," Evangeline pronounced crisply. "There is nothing wrong with my soul."

The reverend spoke up quickly, the soothing words serving to tease an irritated bristle of defense within the girl. "You were among the heathens for many years, taken at a tender age. You can well understand Mistress Webster's concern for your spiritual well-being."

Evangeline said nothing, the impassive set of her features masking a mounting resentment toward his smug manner, and toward her aunt for burdening her with such an intolerable position. What did the man expect of her? What her aunt expected, what they all expected—for her to fall prostrate, begging them to save her from the evil influence of the savages. Such lies would never pass her lips, for to make such claims would be the greatest untruth. She had no want to be enfolded by Christianity. She wanted to go home. Alas, that was not possible for the moment, so she would endure the silly little man's fervor to appease her gaoler, in hopes that it would further her own cause.

"You have our deepest sympathy, my child. What horrors you must have suffered at their hands." He wet his lips as if anxious to hear of them, but the girl was silent, thinking in her own mind that none compared to this. "I have heard the confessions of tortured souls who feared they would never be worthy to walk among their brothers and sisters again. I would encourage you now to hold no such thoughts. Your ordeal is over, and God and His people are ready to embrace you as a lost member of the flock. You have only to open your heart to them and repent of your sins, to be washed clean of their unholy stain."

It grew harder to listen to his pious babbling with a stoic grace as she had been taught. Clinging to her control, Evangeline raised the frail cup to her lips and sipped the hot tea. It scalded her mouth and left a bitter taste, much like their guest's words.

"After all," he continued, "you've been exposed to a pagan culture, and that taint is bound to have had its effect. What you've been raised with is counter to all civilized ideals, with men as the epitome of slothful indulgence, while women labor for them."

"That is not true," she said, still maintaining her aloof demeanor. "Our women are far from slaves to their men. The man builds the home, repairs it, cultivates the soil, hunts, and delivers all to his wife. Women are treated with respect for their ability. Your white man's sense of chivalry tells a woman she is weak. I do not wish a man to rise when I enter the room. Rather he give me the right to my own property and to the children I bear and the choice of who rules me."

Though Emma cringed at the proud way Evangeline spoke of her relationship to her red captors, Reverend Bentley smiled again, conveying his condescension. "You are mistaken, child. A woman is a frail creature of God and in need of careful nurturing. One has only to look to the shocking mode of dress of the heathens to see the moral decay such notions encourage. Indian women are bred no better than harlots, as slaves to their passionate natures and carnal wants." The fervor in his gaze grew lurid with intensity. It traversed her slender

35

physique as if he was picturing her in a similar state of undress, naked to navel and middle thigh. He was sweating. "Such young, wild, and alluring creatures, yet their dark beauty conceals tainted blood, the refuse of Adam's lost posterity, defiant of subjection to Jehovah in their lust for sinful liberty."

Blushing fiercely, Emma tugged upon the preacher's sleeve and murmured, "Reverend, I do not feel this is proper—"

The reverend cleared his throat and dabbed his forehead with a great snowy handkerchief. "I apologize if my bluntness has offended your delicate sensibilities, Mistress Webster, but you have no idea of the depths of corruption of which we speak. Has the child been asked—has she been questioned about her virtue?"

The poor woman's features went from crimson to parchment in an instant. Her brown eyes bulged with surprise and mortification.

"You must know that when news of her captivity is made known, that question will be foremost on our good citizens' minds." He patted his parishioner's hand sympathetically. "Of course, if the improbable could be proven true, such talk could easily be hushed by a word from my pulpit. Alas, if her chastity is no longer intact, none will hold blame to you, Mistress Webster. Perhaps, in time, when the scandal quiets, a respectable match could be made for her, if your husband is generous."

That was too much. Evangeline lost her struggle for composure. Her teacup was thrust back at her aunt, threatening to dose her with the remains as she struggled to balance both upon her knees. "I need not prove anything. I am not ashamed of what I was and still am, and you, with all your silky words, will not convince me that I should be." She stood with an impressive majesty, but was not allowed a graceful retreat. Her hand was seized up between Bentley's damp palms and fervently pressed.

"My child, you must see the sinful path your pride and independent nature paves. It is my duty to see you duly mortified and humbled before our Creator. It is my obligation to draw the dregs to salvation."

Evangeline wrested her hand away and spat, "You do not seek to raise inferiors, but rather to reduce them to your level. What hypocrisy. I have found my life among the Indians to be morally superior to your English civilization. You speak of souls but are preoccupied with the flesh. I will not have you preying upon either." With that, she stormed from the room, leaving a sputtering Rev. Bentley and a near-to-swooning Aunt Emma who hastened to make her apologies.

As Evangeline gained the stairs, her fiery gaze touched upon Cyrus, who lounged at its turned post, having obviously overheard the converse within the near room. Again, she was aware of the warmth of his look, not too unlike the zeal of the reverend when he invoked the image of next-to-naked maidens. This time she felt threatened by the unknowns of it. Though she did not want to pause, his words held her upon the first step. His smile spread slowly, with intimate innuendo.

"I do not wish to see you changed, Cousin Evangeline," he said smoothly. "I appreciate you for what you are, for your beauty, for your savagery. Remember that I should like to be your friend. You can trust me. Come to me if I can be of help to you."

His words confused the message of his eyes, and she retreated a step in bewilderment before turning to

37

finish her ascension. Once in her room, she fell to her knees before the sealed window, unconsciously using the position of supplication taught her in another life, and prayed to her own gods to save her from the barbarians below.

"Oh, Reverend," Emma sniffed in her handkerchief. "I do not know what to do. At times I wish I was free of my Christian duty to the girl. Please forgive me for making such an unworthy vessel. You must think me awful."

"My dear Mistress Webster, I think you admirable indeed. What a bastion of good will you present to the community, such a self-sacrificing example of charity."

The sugary words served to mollify her, and red-rimmed eyes peered gratefully over the damp linen. "'Tis my fondest wish to be thought so. Alas, I no longer have the strength for the daily struggle. I have not your confidence that she can be won over. She is so strong-willed."

"Such haughtiness is the devil's influence. It must be driven from her, if we are to win her back into our fold. Gentle Mistress, you need not be ashamed that you are ill-equipped for such a battle. I, however, have been prepared by my calling for such trials, and will gladly confront the vile forces that work to control her soul."

Emma's puny bosom heaved with relief. She'd known she could depend upon the good Rev. Bentley. He had called her contributions to the church saintly, and vowed she was its most stalwart supporter. When she approached him with the uncomfortable business of her niece, he'd been quick to become her advocate. She was more than willing to turn all into his capable hands. "What do you suggest?"

Having waited for such an invitation, the reverend gave his narrow smile and patted her hands a second time. "First, I must caution you to be brave. 'Twill take a measure of fortitude to carry out God's will. Can you do that, sister?"

"Anything. Anything you feel will be of benefit."

The gushing sentiment made his smile widen to the point of near cheerfulness. "I knew you would be courageous. If we are to win back your niece, we must strike first at her pride. Humility will open the way to the Lord, but a haughty heart denies the truth. As you said, her will is strong. Confrontation serves only to strengthen it, as you have seen. We must bring a meekness to her manner. Then she will be ready to see the path to righteousness."

"Meekness?" Emma was overwhelmed by futility. Never had she seen an individual less prone to meekness than Evangeline Carey.

"Faith, Mistress, faith," the reverend urged firmly. "The task is not as impossible as it might appear. I have dealt with such as your niece before, and have known success. What I need you to do is apply a small dose of the tonic I will supply to her food, without her awareness. It will calm her and make her malleable to your wishes. A tranquil mind offers an open heart."

"This tonic—"

Reverend Bentley held up his hand to still her uncertainty. "I would never condone anything that would harm the child. 'Tis a mild medicine that will soothe her nerves, and make her receptive to your good intentions."

39

It was almost too much to hope for. Emma wetted her lips and tried to summon even the slightest protest to this heaven-sent plan. "If you are certain . . ."

"Very certain. 'Tis the only way."

And that was enough to remove all doubt.

Chapter Three

Royle Tanner stood in the hall of the Websters' fine house and saw into his own future. This was how he was going to live.

He had lingered long on the street, studying the magnificence of the grand structure, but that revering appreciation in no way prepared him for the splendor within. He had never set foot in so elegant a building, and self-consciously he rubbed his shoe leather on the back of his worn stockings to attempt a shine upon the dulled surface. How it taunted him to appear so threadbare in the face of such opulence yet he didn't regret his coming. Now, his dreams had a mental focus, a picture they could fix to when he thought of what it would mean to be successful. To be successful was to be just like Uriah Webster, and as Royle squared his shoulders beneath the loose fit of his coat, he had no doubt in his mind that he would be.

From his position in the foyer, Royle had an enviable view of the surrounding rooms, and what he couldn't see, he could well imagine. The house, with its first story of brick and sloping second story of overlapping cedar shingles—like many in the area

that sprouted up along with its citizens' affluence—
took its impressive design straight from the architec-
tural manuals of England. Those books gave
colonial craftsmen the details to recreate doorways,
mantels, windows, cornices, pediments, and pan-
eling, bringing a look of Mother England to threaten
the outward influence of the Dutch with their
stepped gable brick houses. A great chimney stack of
stone rose through the center of the house to feed four
wide, low-ceiled, broad-windowed rooms, flanked
on either gabled end by two more rooms of equal size.
The lower rooms were handsomely wainscotted and
painted white, as were their cased ceiling beams. The
windows were diamond-paned with leaded window
sashes, brought from Holland for their superiority.
The twelve by twelve square had glass so full of knots
and streaks that no object seen through it appeared
entire, but broken into distorted parts. Royle had
never been on the inside looking out through such
fine ground glass, and admired the view from his
elevated vantage point. Yes, his home would have
such clear panes, so he could look out to see others
admiring from the other side.

His covetous study was interrupted by a gliding
movement within a far room. Curiosity claimed his
gaze, and fascination, his attention, as he watched a
comely miss clad in lavender silk cross the doorway.
Briefly she glanced his way, and her beauty gave him
pause. There was a wistful dreaminess to her
expression he found most appealing. He began to
smile, but she looked away as if she hadn't seen him.
Granted, there was little in his appearance to hold
her gaze. What a striking young woman, he thought
to himself before she too quickly disappeared from
his sight. He wondered if she could be Webster's
daughter, and was craning rather precariously for

another glimpse when a disapproving rumble in the throat of a liveried man servant called him to task. Ah, well, the lovely Miss Webster would have to wait for another time.

"Master Webster will see you now, sir, if you will come this way."

Wishing his own attire was half as elegant as the hired man's before him, Royle strode from the wide hall into an adjacent parlor where stiffly portrayed likenesses of Webster and his wife stared uncomfortably from above a fancifully carved mantel. The opposing walls were hung with costly Flemish tapestries, and the wood floor beneath his feet was graced with several fine carpets from the Netherlands. Conscientiously, he stepped aside so as not to crush the nap, then addressed his host, who was garbed in negligent elegance as befit his stature. A dressing gown of printed India cotton covered Uriah Webster's breeches, shirt, vest, and cravat, and a dapper cap concealed a head shorn to baldness for the sake of his wig's fit, yet he looked no less commanding than when decked in his best finery.

"You sent for me, sir."

"Seat yourself, Tanner, and we will talk," Webster began without formality. "I have given thought to our discussion of the other day."

"And?" Royle forced himself to lean back into his chair to give the impression of ease, when he would have rather perched upon its edge. He was well aware of his own shortcomings in qualifying for a position with Webster, but his confidence was monumental. He refused to be discouraged by failings easily overcome. Nor would Webster be if he was a man of vision, and all the trappings of success about Royle told him that was so.

"I have some questions, so that I might know you

better. If you don't mind." At Royle's prompting, he asked, "Where are you from in England?"

"London."

"Oh? My son recently returned from an extended stay in the city. Perhaps he chanced upon meeting some of your family."

"Not likely, sir." There was a tang of something close to sarcasm in that reply, but it was quickly smoothed over as he concluded, "I have no family living." To give his thoughts ease from the uncomfortable topic, his gaze flitted to one of the impressive bookcases. It touched upon several expected titles, Mather's *Magnalia*, Raleigh's *History of the World*, *Mythologial* an anthology by Natalis Comes, and Camden's *Remains of a Greater Work Concerning Britain*, as well as Erasmus and several Tudor and Stuart writers. He longed to feel the fine leather of their bindings and breathe deep the smell of exclusive knowledge. Someday, he too would own books, a library of them, wall to wall, floor to ceiling, and he would read them at his leisure, instead of devouring their words when he should have been tending his duties.

"You are an admirer of literature, Mr. Tanner."

He was called away from his daydreams at the cost of a faint flush. "Forgive me. 'Tis not often that I've seen such a fine collection of works in one place."

"I can afford to collect fine things now, but that luxury came at a price. What price are you willing to pay, sir?" The veil of hospitality was cast aside, and Uriah Webster's stare reached into the soul of Royle to test his mettle.

"To achieve what you have, no price is too great."

The intensity of that claim made the merchant nod. Yes, he understood such hungry ambition, such blindness to all but a goal. He had been such a man, and before him was another, and he thought Royle Tanner would do very nicely in his service. "Let me tell you a little about what I do and what I will ask of you."

Now, Royle did lean forward in his seat, fingers clenching the edge and features etched with sharp attention. A buoyant expectation rose in his chest, but he forced it back lest he be distracted from his purpose.

"The fur trade is a bit of a misnomer. What it encompasses is the exchange of goods between the Indians and the manufacturers of Europe. I am the middleman who attends the needs of both. Think of trade in the colonies as its own little war; the English against the French, each Indian tribe against the other, all to make a profit before the wealth of furs is gone. Eventually we will spread further west into the rich reserve of the Ohio Valley, and Albany is in the midst of two such routes into the interior. 'Tis in a position to receive trade diverted from the St. Lawrence system and in the center of the Iroquois Five Nations. Their castles stretch out along the Mohawk Valley and Finger Lakes region, giving them a base from which to raid traffic on the St. Lawrence, Susquehanna, and Connecticut systems to divert peltry to Albany. They are industrious traders, those savages, in their lust for the flintlock and bottled rum.

"To make myself a profit, I engage a small corps of traders, usually sturdy, shrewd fellows with little or no capital of their own. They borrow my stock on credit to carry to remote posts, where the goods are passed along to Indian customers, and then acquire furs from local hunters who provide them directly from the distant areas via the overland routes, no questions asked. Scruples are something best left to

45

these not eager to succeed." He glanced at the man opposite to find his eyes gleaming. No, Uriah thought, he didn't think a little thing like conscience was going to stand in the way of Royle Tanner. Good. He smiled slightly and continued, dangling the final enticement. "As a merchant, I will reap two most gratifying profits from the same transaction, from the price of charged goods and on the price of furs accepted in payment. Goods from England yield one hundred percent advancement above their first cost, some even two, three, or four hundred percent. That is the profit I will pass along to you, if we do business together."

"And will we? Be doing business together?"

"I think yes, but I've yet to decide how best to make use of you. Why did you leave England, Mr. Tanner?"

The unexpected question took Royle aback, and for a moment, he floundered under the humiliation of the truth. Then he decided to be straightforward, in hopes that Webster would respect him for his honesty, if not his background. "The colonies offer a poor man who is industrious and thrifty the opportunity to improve his status. I had no future in London. My education could not best my pedigree. Here, even the unskilled can acquire land and gain a competence, and the ambitious can rival the blooded. Trade is the means to attain prestige. You are trade, and so, I am here."

Webster did not look displeased by that confession. In fact, his own prospects had he remained in the Mother Country had little better appeal. He had made his way in America, and he had no doubt that Royle Tanner would as well.

"You say you have no family. No wife?"

"I have naught the means to provide for the type of

woman I will one day wed. When I am prosperous, then I can offer for someone like your fair daughter."

"Daughter?" Uriah looked blank, then said, "Oh, you must mean my niece, Evangeline. You have met her then?"

"No, I am sorry to say. I happened a glimpse of her just minutes ago. She is very beautiful, if I might say as much."

Uriah stared thoughtfully toward the door and murmured, "Yes, I suppose she is." His gaze returned to the young man opposite and leveled with speculation. "I am hosting an affair to celebrate the birthday of my son Cyrus at the week's end. I would like you to attend as my guest, after which we can come to terms over your future in my employ. Would you find that to your satisfaction?"

Thinking of the opportunity to once again see the lovely Evangeline, Royle said quickly, "Very much so."

Darts of light from the multitude of candles set the length of the dining table flickered upon pieces of sterling. The irregular flashes of brilliance seemed a continuation of the dream Evangeline had found herself in these last days. Or was it weeks? A cold terror began to rise within her when she realized that she did not know, but even that emotion was oddly muted. Here she sat trussed in her civilized finery before an elaborately spread meal with her white captors, and she knew not how she'd come to be there.

What was happening to her? All she wanted to do was seek the peaceful sleep for which her body yearned. Movement seemed so tiring, thought an exhaustive struggle against the balm of lethargy.

47

There were times, like this one, when she seemed to awake from her continual stupor, when things sharpened about her, and she could almost claim awareness, but that clarity soon dimmed, and with it, the want to question. It was so much easier to drift and respond to gentle suggestions that guided her through each day with a puppet-master's skill. Her soul was calm, her sleep deep and undisturbed, she was in harmony with the world around her, and all took so little effort.

What was happening? Evangeline forced her thoughts to focus, to emerge from the muffled contentment that was somehow not real and very frightening. The idea that she might have contracted some strange white man's disease gave her the strength to rise above the soothing waves of numbness. Couldn't those about her see that something was amiss with her? Her anxious gaze touched upon the trio conversing lightly as they supped. They all seemed relaxed, accepting her in their midst as if nothing was awry. That in itself was a puzzle, for never had they behaved so naturally when in her presence, treating her like one of their number to be smiled upon in passing and spoken to in pleasant tones. But they did not speak to her; not exactly. They spoke about her, around her, as though she was an object, the way they did with their servants, and her pride roiled to rival her bewilderment.

It was difficult to sit quietly and pretend she wasn't shaken by how abnormal this casual scene appeared. Her stomach tightened into a knot of panic as she pushed her food slowly about her plate to give the illusion of eating. Why could she remember so little of the passing days? What had she been doing? Why were thoughts of escape abandoned? It was as if she was a shadow of herself, a shape without substance, and she became deathly afraid. Somehow, it had to do with the Websters and the suspicious way they acted, as if she was no longer a threat to the harmony of their home. How had they managed to tame her body and subdue her mind? She looked at the dish of lobster before her and to the mug of beer that accompanied it. Instinct made caution rise, and she vowed to touch nothing more from their table until she puzzled out the cause of her languor. She must keep her wits about her. She must escape before they plunged her once again into the indifferent darkness of mere existence.

"I have been giving great consideration to our niece," Webster was saying to all but her. She continued to stare at her plate as if unaware of his words, while clinging to them intently. "I think 'tis time we found an eligible match. She is, after all, seventeen and of a marriageable age."

Emma's startled gasp echoed the jolt of surprise that stunned her. "Marriage? Oh, Uriah, you cannot. She is not yet ready for such a step."

"Nonsense. Look upon her, the soul of demure womanhood. What more could a man ask for, and with the dowry I plan to offer, I guarantee none will look farther."

"But Uriah, 'tis not right. What they will see is not what they will gain in the bargain."

Evangeline could imagine her uncle's cold smile as he said, "'Tis not our worry, now is it, Mistress?" That would be followed with a quelling glance to seal any further protest into silence. And it did still her aunt's words, but not the horrified thoughts that careened through her own mind.

Marriage. To some pale Englishman! Her heart shriveled in disgust and cried out for Cayenderongue. Had her pride not demanded that she hesitate, she would be even now the woman of that handsome warrior, and he would never have allowed them to wrest her from him. She would have his strong arms about her as they lay upon a mat of luxurious furs, instead of the dreadful promise of some pallid white man's passions beneath the confining roof of civilization. It could not be endured. Escape took precedent over all things, and her desperate gaze lifted to search for possibilities.

Suddenly she thought of her cousin. She remembered his words to her on the stairs. Could she trust him? Could he be made to help her escape the waiting yoke of an intolerable union? His small, secret smile seemed to offer such a hope, and as her eyes lowered once more to her untouched plate, new confidence supplanted uncertain fear. She would plead the wretched misery in her heart and the impossible harmony of her within their house. Cyrus was a proud and proper gentleman. He could not wish his friends and followers to know his roof housed a savage. He would delicately shrink from the embarrassment. With his aid, she would gladly remove the source of future humiliation. She would slip back into the forest and permanently out of their lives. And wasn't that what they all wished? She would ask her cousin for help.

After the evidence of her uneaten meal was removed, Evangeline remained silently seated until her aunt directed a question to her. She made her reply heavy and somnolent.

"Will you join us in the parlor, Evangeline?"

"I thank you but no. I would like to go to my room. I am very weary."

"Yes, of course," Emma responded without surprise, and Evangeline was quickly forgotten by all but Cyrus, who intercepted her stolen glance of urgency.

It took him only moments to find some excuse to leave the company of his parents to follow her path up the stairs to her room where the door stood open in silent invitation. It was an invitation he had known would be forthcoming sooner or later, and he was smiling as he closed the door behind him. Evangeline regarded him with an intensity that flamed his loins with the expectation of what was to come.

"Wide-awake tonight are we, cousin?" he drawled. "Good. The meek corpse who has been dragging about the house had little to recommend it. You, on the other hand—" He left that purposefully open to her interpretation, but she was too agitated to grasp his subtle meaning.

"You offered me your help. Will you help me now?"

He grinned wider at her eager petition. "The thought of wedlock not to your liking, eh, dear cousin? I have an offer you might find more to your taste. Yes, of course, I will help you avoid that trap."

She was so relieved, her guard lowered without taking warning that his offer was but another cunning snare. All she could think was that her days of captivity were at an end, and soon she would be free and among her people. All Cyrus could think was soon the lovely wench would be his mistress, and his mother and father could object all they liked, but once the damage was done, they would have to accept it. Sweet Evangeline would be warming his bed. They might even be grateful that he was about to save them the dowry cost. The anticipation of her beneath him was payment enough for him to risk their displeasure.

Evangeline took a startled step back as his hand

51

brushed warm upon her face. His hungry look made her insides contract, as if she'd bitten into a beguiling fruit, only to find its pretty skin disguised a rotten center. Her retreat didn't discourage him. His hands were quick to secure her arms, to draw her up against the velvet and lace of his chest.

"How could you think I would let them sell you to another when my need for you is so great?" His voice was thick, and she trembled at hearing his lust disclosed. "I will not let you suffer an undeserving husband who won't appreciate your nature. With me, you can be yourself, and our passions will tame you."

His mouth sought hers then, and Evangeline thought she would gag as it fell wet and soft upon her cheek when she wrenched her head to the side. His grip grew hurtful upon her tender flesh.

"Of course, I should have guessed you'd want our love play to be the way you're used to having it. I shall be happy to oblige you, my little savage." Excitement rumbled in his tone when he thought of the struggle and conquest of her tempting body. What a find she was, this wildly passionate creature of the pagan woods. His desire surpassed his good sense, and he knew he must have her now. He'd meant to return to her room once all were slumbering in ignorance, but his urgency to know her ruled caution. It would be a quick, silent mating, then he could return later for a more lingering enjoyment, as he would the nights that followed until he established her in her own residence. Then, his visits would have but one glorious purpose.

The groping feel of Cyrus's hand upon her bodice woke Evangeline to his intention, and with a certainty she knew she would prefer death to his vile maulings. Never would she willingly submit to commerce with a repulsive white man, not as long as she had strength to fight him. And the strength of that fight was something Cyrus had not prepared for. He'd expected her to be eager after being long without a man, and anxious to accept his favor. Instead, he found a wild cat within his embrace, one with sharp claws and snapping teeth and surprising physical power. His delight at her tenacity was quickly transformed into determination when he realized it was no coy game she played, but a real resistance to his plan. His passions were too far gone to recognize her denial. He would have her even if he had to take her this time by force. His conceit would not let him believe that once the fact was accomplished, she would object to further relations. She just needed to be broken to her new role in life, and if she didn't want it to be gentle, so be it.

A sudden elbow thrust into her ribs robbed Evangeline of breath and, momentarily, of fight. Cyrus took advantage of that weakness to fling her to the narrow bed, but before he could fall upon her to claim his victory, she was rolling and scrambling lithely to her feet. She faced him, panting like a cornered animal, eyes wide and bright. Had he been less dulled by lust, he might have seen her look was not one of fear, but of challenge.

Evangeline's movements were too quick for him to grasp all at once, but their outcome was unmistakable. A crockery mug was snatched up from the bedside stand and dashed with one deft gesture, leaving a jagged shard attached to its handle. He had time to avoid the arc aimed for his throat, however was too slow to completely escape a seer of agony that ran from chin to ear. His high, womanish shrieks mobilized the household. Jamal, the burly black downstairs servant, caught Evangeline up in one arm

53

as she tried to dodge past him, and easily tore the makeshift weapon from her hand. She squirmed and shouted native curses upon his head, while the Websters rushed to their reeling son.

"She attacked me," he moaned, clasping a blood-ied hand to the wound she'd hoped would prove fatal. "Like an animal for no reason."

Evangeline's protest went unheard over Emma's wailings of distress and outrage. The sight of her dear son's ravaged face was enough to harden her heart to any Samaritan duty.

"Do what you will, Uriah," she wept. "Only take her from my house."

Chapter Four

Tallow candles placed in candlesticks and in the candlebeams hung from the ceiling created an intimate aura about the large group gathered in the Websters' grand parlor. It was a homecoming and birthday celebration in one, for the Websters' only son, and no expense was spared. Servants stood ready to replace any cup should it show signs of depletion, and a trestle set to one side groaned under the weight of offered delectables. Wealth was displayed in a gleam of pewter and silver glitter upon that table, and in the richness of cloth upon the backs of hosting family. To Royle, it was seeing his heart's desire all in one room, and it had him trembling.

He knew at once that he was not of the same stature as this crowd. They were of the better sort, and he, of the lower, and as such, he didn't consciously dress above his station, nor could he afford to. His coat and breeches were of respectable wool, and his vest, an old brocade over which an unadorned lawn stock flowed. He sported no lace nor velvet nor satins, and he wore his hair natural. There was nothing offensive in his look, yet it typed him clear as plain and poor. On this night, more than any other he could remember, he resented that fact. And on this night, he swore that would change.

As he accepted a noggin of rum, his covetous stare lit on the cause of the revelry—Cyrus Webster. He was in the midst of a bevy of ladies held enchanted by his courtly manner. Or by the promise of his inheritance. Royle assessed him candidly and saw nothing to impress him beyond the extravagant attire. The younger Webster had none of the power that radiated from the elder. Cyrus Webster wouldn't be an obstacle to his ambition.

Uriah was in deep converse with several prominent gentlemen. An acknowledging nod in Royle's direction was given, but he made no move to break from his talk. Royle could wait, and he slipped into an inobtrusive corner to observe the doings of his betters as a curious outsider. He knew no one among them and couldn't imagine any of them eager to make his acquaintance. He determined it better to stay out of the way. His resolve of patience was rewarded by the appearance of Webster's niece.

She was more lovely than he remembered. In the near celestial glow of candlelight, she was an earthbound angel. Evangeline. Even her name so attested. His enraptured stare followed her gliding figure about the room. She moved like a dream, slowly, without effort, with nary a ripple to the pale blue silk of her petticoat. Her eyes, when they touched upon him, likened to the gown; still, placid waters, cool and unintentionally inviting. By the time her gaze moved on, Royle was dry-mouthed and damp-palmed. A house like this one and a woman like Evangeline. That was what he would have.

"Mr. Tanner."

Royle nearly leapt in guilty surprise. Once composed, he turned to his host and executed a proper bow.

"Good evening, sir. I am honored at the invitation to your fine home. I trust I am not taking you from your guests."

Uriah chuckled at the man's effacement. For though their acquaintance was limited, he knew such humility was difficult for the straightforward younger man. Yet, it spoke well of him.

"Not at all. I should like to conclude our business. You do not appear comfortable in this company. Shall we withdraw to my rooms?"

Royle flushed painfully. Though it was tactfully said, his host had drawn an unflattering parallel between himself and the other guests. And the rightness of his observation hurt. He muttered an appropriate phrase and followed the bewigged, satined, and ruffled gentleman from the room. He made another swift promise to himself. Never would he embarrass his benefactor again. If he had to go without meals, he would dress to harmonize with this fine home upon his next visit. If there was one.

The odor of leather, tobacco, and books enveloped them as the doors were closed in their wake. Royle took the seat he'd occupied before. Webster made him wait as he shuffled through papers and seemed to ignore his presence. Then, he sat himself, and gave his petitioner a long look.

"I want you with me, Tanner."

The simple statement went to Royle's head like a bowl of kill-devil. It swirled and swelled and it took a moment for him to regain his coherency. He wanted to shout. But when he spoke, his words were carefully measured.

"Thank you, sir. I think we will do well together."

"Aren't you interested in your position and pay?"

"Oh," he replied distractedly, as though neither

57

were of any consequence. "Yes, of course."

"I am not one to waste talent, and you, Mr. Tanner, have shown me a glimpse of brilliance."

A tap at the door interrupted that promising speech, and Royle ground his teeth in annoyance until it opened to the fair Evangeline. His chest swelled. His posture straightened. Though she didn't glance at him, he didn't care. Soon, she would notice. Soon, he would be worthy of it.

"Aunt sent me to see if you required any refreshment."

What a lovely voice she had, well-modulated, quiet, a mere whisper of sound. She was everything he desired in a life's mate, a woman who would grace a home such as this with her modest comportment, who would bring peace with her tranquil spirit, who would be regarded well for her gentleness. Her beauty was restful, her manner submissive. She was a vision, an impossibly distant dream. Yet dream he did, and with such single purpose that he could scarcely swallow the huge lump of devotion that crowded his throat. He wasn't the type to fawn over a woman, but for this one, he would grovel. Had he been an equal, he would have begged an introduction in order to claim her yearned-for deference. As it was, he stayed silent.

"A bowl of beer for Mr. Tanner and myself, if you please."

The ethereal Evangeline withdrew.

Royle's infatuation did not go unnoticed. Uriah leaned back in his chair, observing the dazed features with a small smile of knowledge. "Some refreshment first, I think, and then our business."

In a fog of longing, Royle didn't think to object to the delay.

"I hope you'll find a liking for our beer," Webster

was saying. "Water could never take the place of beer to a true-born Englishman. 'Tis made mostly of molasses, well boiled with pine, and passes for a very tolerable drink." Noting the other's distraction, he supplied, "The best way to tell a good from a bad housewife is whether the family drinks beer or water. Only a slothful and careless wife would inflict water upon her husband. Evangeline has the makings of a rather fine wife, wouldn't you agree?"

The glazed stare came up and focused with a blink. Ruddy color fused up from the simple stock. "I am sure you are right, Mr. Webster."

"She is my wife's brother's child. We are her guardians since the tragic loss of her parents. A rather awesome responsibility, the welfare of such a precious miss. She is of age now, and 'tis my duty to direct her to a suitable mate. 'Tis not a duty I take lightly."

Royle said nothing, not wondering about the strangeness of the topic, since it involved the desirous Miss Evangeline. How he wished he was of a cut to be considered. But a newly hired man was not established gentry. That much had not changed by crossing an ocean.

Then she returned, drifting in on a breeze of faint lavender, bearing the two mugs of beer. Again Royle was captivated, and again Uriah did not fail to notice.

When the calm gray eyes brushed him, Royle smiled and murmured a soft, "Thank you," but she didn't respond. There was no slight in that failure, so he wasn't wounded by it. She didn't recognize him, and so, he realized with some chagrin, it should be. She left the room as silently as she came, and only then could he regain his concentration. He waited respectfully for his host to take a drink, then gratefully followed suit.

"Your application is opportune," Uriah began, and Royle warmed to the change of subject. "I find myself in need of a shrewd, intelligent individual, one eager to advance himself and my interests. I have a trading station in Albany that needs such a man to govern it. What say you, Tanner?"

"When would you like me there?"

Contrary to the casual tone, the man's eyes sparked with eagerness, and Webster's smile widened. "As soon as we come to terms." It was like dangling raw bait.

"Whatever you think agreeable."

"You may find these terms—shall we say—a bit unusual."

"Go on." Caution could not best impatience.

"I was recently cheated of a goodly profit by the last manager of that post, and thusly am wary of trusting another." He held up a hand to stave off Royle's protestations. "I have taken your measure and found it just, but you can appreciate my position. I stand to lose much."

"And gain much."

"True. I seek a man not only to do my biddings, but to grow with my future plans, and to be a voice in what I do." Again, that quick fever took the gaze opposite, that hunger he believed in beyond simple words. "The man I choose could advance into partnership in time. You have seen my son. He is not of the right cut for such a challenge. I want a man bound by honor, but also of stronger bonds."

Royle knew the beginnings of a frown. What could be more binding than blood or honor? Uriah Webster told him.

"I want a man bound by obligation. So that loyalty will not be tested and found lacking, I plan to

60

sweeten the offer so no sane man would ever think to fail my trust."

And what, Royle wondered, could make this honeyed treat sweeter. Already, he was reeling at the unexpected heights to which he'd climbed. What, indeed, could make that heady air more intoxicating?

"The man I hire will be family."

Royle came spinning down through the clouds, as if shot from the heavens in full flight. Had Webster brought him here just to taunt him with what he had in mind for another? Disappointment and ire twined into one bitter knot, but he spoke of neither.

As if he didn't see Royle's sudden disheartening, Uriah posed his plan with ill-concealed smugness. It was a well-thought plan, one to rid him of many vexations in one answer. Royle Tanner.

"The position has a prerequisite. 'Tis one you shouldn't find too abhorrent. With the appointment goes the dower of a home in Albany, one thousand pounds this year, five hundred pounds next and, of course, the hand of my niece, Evangeline."

After several rums in the closest grogshop, all seemed no less a dream to Royle Tanner. The future handed him was by far more stunning than the potent drinks. In the early evening, the most he had hoped for was a meager position to grant him a start in the colonies. Uriah Webster had not only placed his foot on that coveted ladder to prominence, he had boosted him nearly to the top.

At first, Royle had been afraid to think or speak, certain all would evaporate in a mist of imaginings. Even now, the reality had him shy of total belief, as if waking would find all had been a cruel jest. So he stayed awake and tried to comprehend what had befallen him on this wondrous night when dream came to life.

How could Uriah Webster understand the significance of his act? How could he know the single-minded determination that carried Royle across an ocean? The impetus of his entire being had focused upon that one ideal, and he was as desperate as he was determined. For he daren't fail to succeed. Anxiety and ambition had gnawed at him more ravenously than hunger during that long crossing, as all he knew was left behind in lieu of all that could be. A promise drove him, a promise to a dying man, a promise to himself. Uriah Webster had asked what price he was willing to pay. He could well have answered his soul.

Royle lifted the nearly empty blackjack to his mouth, and let the warm liquid settle within him by slow, satisfying degress, the same way the truth did. His struggle was over, his promise kept. In the end, how easy it had been, so easy, he doubted it. So easy, it overwhelmed him.

He remembered little of what was said after that staggering revelation. Marriage to Evangeline Carey. A dowry that neatly wrapped his future into a single, priceless gift. Knowledge shivered through him along with the want to weep with gratitude. He settled for another drink. In three weeks, after the banns were duly posted, he would tuck the dainty hand of Miss Evangeline into his, and make her Mistress Tanner. Then he and his fragile bride would travel to his new position, and their life would begin amid affluent luxury. A soft sound escaped him, a small disbelieving laugh at his own fortune. *Papa, you would have been so proud.* Then the mistiness did come to his eyes, and impatiently he blinked the moist memory away.

"'Pon my word, I do believe I saw you earlier at my home."

The intruding statement brought Royle from his musings. He glanced up to the primped and proper figure of Cyrus Webster, a figure nearly supported by two fellow revelers.

"Your eyes did not play you false, sir." Though, in likelihood they did now behind the glaze of rum.

"I do not believe I know you." The pale eyes squinted, and Cyrus leaned close, then looked to his companions for compliance. They shrugged and tried to tow him onward. The fellow didn't look the sort they wished to have converse with, not when there were willing wenches to be had. Cyrus resisted to his feeble capacity, somehow compelled by this stranger who invaded his home and his celebration. "Who are you, sir?"

"I am Royle Tanner, an employee of your father."

"Indeed. That is news." He wobbled into a chair, and there his disgruntled companions left him as they tottered up toward the plank where the taverner awaited with fresh cheer.

Royle took a drink while he struggled with an upbringing that would have him showing humble respect. Cyrus and those like him had always been his betters, those who commanded and controlled, those to be carefully cultivated. On this night, he had been elevated to nearly the same plane, and knowledge of that ascension had him awkward yet eager to experience the thrill of power. He forced himself to lean back in his chair, adopting the same negligent pose the other used. Such an indolent attitude was foreign to him, as was the idea of treating Cyrus Webster as an equal. A sudden flush of prideful confidence made him determined that the indolent aristocrat see him as such.

"I am not only newly employed, but soon to be in the family."

The arrogantly stated fact made by this rough-edged man brought a degree of coherency to the languishing gentleman. Cyrus frowned, instinctively pulling a haughty face. "Family, you say. And how is that to be accomplished?"

"By wedding your cousin."

Now that he'd boldly bragged of his fortune, Royle wished he'd not spoken. The other gentleman's features flushed bright, then grew pale as parchment, as if suddenly stricken by some malady. "Evangeline?" It was a disbelieving croak.

Royle nodded. Was he at liberty to boast of that claim? He couldn't believe Webster would not have told his son of his plans. Yet, Cyrus's pop-eyed stare told of his ignorance. He felt of a sudden foolish and regretted his unworthy need to flaunt his success. He was a simple man, a direct man, and such a pompous display shamed him. It was the drink, he decided, and the intoxicating change that had uplifted him.

Cyrus had recovered himself. An odd expression played about his features—regret, amusement, resentment. He lifted his mug.

"Let me be the first to welcome you into the family," he drawled. It was a cold, insincere welcome, yet Royle drank to it. Cyrus eyed him with speculation. "So, how long have you known the fair Evangeline?"

Royle felt color heat his cheeks as he muttered, "We've yet to be formally introduced."

"A groom-to-be with no knowledge of his bride." Cyrus mulled over this news with great enjoyment. The malicious light that came to his eyes and twisted his thin lips brought a defensive prickle to the back of Royle's neck. His chuckle caused that tingle of like-rebellion to stiffen his spine. "I sense this is my father's doing, am I right?"

"The arrangements were his, yes."

Royle had been too enthralled by his luck to question Uriah's methods, yet now he did so. He replayed the sentiments offered and pondered them. Uriah had expressed his need to see his niece well settled. How had he phrased it? She had suffered the loss of her parents and was longing for a protection they could not provide in their home. He hadn't thought it odd that security would prompt wedlock. The principle objectives of marriage were wealth, social position, and love, in that order. Laced with dowries and jointures, nuptials resembled business arrangements more than plighted troths of affection. He'd been too overcome by the idea to wonder what he could offer in this exchange. Now, he wondered.

It was singular enough that a man would cast a stranger into a ripe position of trust. For that same man to bestow his niece was more than curious. Yet Uriah Webster was nothing if not shrewd. Whatever motivated him, it was not unsound thinking. And though he was wise enough to recognize the oddity of the situation, Royle was not one to question. Not when showered with such bounty. Only a fool would pursue that which he had no intention of changing. For whatever reason, Royle was grateful.

"You will be staying in New York?" Cyrus was asking. He fingered the newly healed cut along his jawline as he spoke.

"No, Albany."

Cyrus vented his frustration by assessing his companion with a critical disdain. "You should fare quite well in that uncivilized terrain. Myself, I should perish without distraction. After touring Europe for two years, I confess to boredom in these

65

rural strongholds."

Royle allowed himself a smile. He was familiar with men like Cyrus Webster. The wealthy and cultivated shipped their heirs to London to acquire a veneer of English manners. After soaking up the best influences of the Mother Country, the young bloods could boast the honor of having been several times drunk in London, could move a minuet in the latest fashion, become a connoisseur in dress, and adopt elegant expressions such as "Split me, Madame," "By Gad" and "Damme." All very beneficial things to bring home and put to practical use. For ones so eager to escape the rigid tiers of social class in England, the affluent of the New World were quick to ape their manner. Royle mused over the hypocrisy as an outsider. Bettering himself would not alter what he was, he was convinced of it.

"I'm not one to sit idle and wait for entertainments. If I've the time, I should probably read."

Cyrus sniffed and looked down his long nose. "I could give you my copy of Cheever's *Accidence*, but I suppose 'twould be beyond you." He boasted his Latin grammar school text the way he would a pedigree, expecting to humble the rough-hewn commoner to awe.

"That would be most kind. I would relish another chance to reread it. 'Tis been too long since my Latin has been tested."

"Then perhaps you would prefer Horace or Virgil." That was thrown at him like a dare and deftly fielded.

"Rather Ovid or Cicero. Or Homer and Hesiod in Greek. Those are my other favorites."

"You seem to have an impressive background in the classics, Mr. Tanner." It was said begrudgingly but not without respect.

66

"My father valued education above all things. He said the mind could open any door." Royle paused and took a drink, lest his voice be effected by the sentiment washing softly through him. Vulnerability was not something one displayed before a stranger, one who could prove to be a rival.

"A wise man." Cyrus, sensing he could win no further points off this unexpectedly capable opponent, stood and bowed his good nights before weaving his way to the bar to join his friends in their quaffing and carousing. Royle remained at the table long after they sought upper rooms with a bevy of tavern beauties, and pondered over his good fortune, taking him away from his past.

Evangeline, too, began to see the good fortune in the happenings of that night. Once her fate was settled, the Websters seemed to ignore her in her tiny prison as they saw the banns posted. She was left to herself, and in the absence of her numbing tonic, her thoughts sharpened and began to spin.

She didn't dwell on the terror of days that passed without her knowing, or upon the fact that she was to be tied to a man she couldn't remember having met. What did either of those things matter, after all. What she clung to with a determined desperation was the hope that once she was out from under the Websters' roof, her escape could be more easily accomplished. One man could not be as difficult to evade as an entire household pitted against her. One pale Englishman would be no match for her. And soon, she would be free.

She had ample time to think upon her fate while sun and stars washed by her window to the world. Though her training amid the Iroquois would have her show a stoic face, inside, she had no such reign over emotion. She attributed that weepy, frightened spirit to her contemptible white heritage. Try as she would, she could not overcome that inner weakness. That staining blood had her in an anxious confusion, when she needed to be calmly plotting. It had her aching with lonesome misery, when she could be steeped in thoughts of vengeance. She wanted to be strong. She willed herself to be brave. But it was so hard. Her surroundings held her captive with their strangeness and isolation. The people below had condemned her unjustly, though she cared not for their belief. She fought equally against her desire to strike out in anger and her wish to curl into a protected knot of anguish. She could do neither. She only had to endure.

Her time among the whites had not opened any doors of fond memory, though her ease in behaving like them at times surprised her. She hadn't been a babe when she'd been embraced by the Woodland People, so naturally some of her early training would linger in the far recesses of her mind. And there she wanted it to stay. She wanted no link with these civilized savages, no bonds that would taint her as one of their imperfect race. When she was free of them, she would flush that memory from her in the purifying waters of the Canajoharie, and go to her people clean and untouched by their lies and treacheries.

In those lingering days of captivity, she contented herself with thoughts of how she would resume her life, while meticulously braiding her long black hair. She thought of Cayenderongue with his prideful stance, and of her brother Warraghiyagey of the laughing dark eyes and warm embrace. Her heart swelled with memories of He-Raises-The-Sky, comparing his compassionate logic with the irrational behavior she'd known from those claiming to be family. They had made no effort to embrace her for what she was. Had they opened their arms to her in love, she might have responded in kind. She was not cold or unfeeling. She had nearly wept on that day at Fort Orange to see the agony of joy on the faces of those mothers who thought never to see their children again. Had they greeted her with sensitivity or understanding, she might have been persuaded to attempt an adjustment to this life He-Raises-The-Sky had sent her to. But they had not. They cared not who or what she was, only what they could make her into. They wanted no part of Eyes-Like-Evening-Star, only of the child Evangeline who lived in memory alone.

And when she feared she could no longer contain the agony of loss and uncertainty, she recalled the quiet words and gentle presence of her mother. That still yet powerful figure restored her well-being and instilled her with hope of a tomorrow. With all her heart and soul, she wished to be the woman She-Walks-Far was, to command and deserve the same respect, to know the same unqualified love of a mate, to have the joys of children and the strength of destiny. Those thoughts were the charm that kept her in harmony with herself during those desperate, lonely days and longer nights, that and the remembered scent of the forest, and blanket of the sky.

Soon those things would be hers again, and she would cling to them for the remainder of her years. Nothing would ever tear her from the bosom of her family again, no power of earth or heaven. An honorable death would be preferred to the torment of captivity. If she knew with a certainty that she'd never breathe in the damp, earthy strength of nature, she would gladly sever her ties to this world, in favor of another where she could roam free.

And when the day of her wedding came, she drank deeply from the sacrificial cup they brought her, welcoming the misty threads that twined about her mind. For when she awoke, she would be free.

Chapter Five

The ceremony itself was a bleak affair. Hands were clasped before the magistrate, who murmured pronouncements to make them man and wife. For Royle, it was the significance rather than the ritual that made the moment so impressive as he stood beleaguered by emotion with small, cool fingers curled within his own.

With his own meager coin—for he'd refused to use Webster's for such a purpose—Royle purchased clothes to fit the occasion. Frugality warred with sentimental extravagance upon choosing his garb, and in the end he settled upon a compromise; velvet but no wig. Standing beside Uriah Webster, he indeed looked a son-in-law to do him proud. He felt uncomfortable, yet undeniably regal in the slate gray coat—he'd selected the color as a salute to Evangeline's eyes—with its great turned back cuffs of dark blue and heavy red braid, breeches and vest. Frills filled the opening over his chest and spilled about the backs of his damp hands, one holding his bride and the other a new tricorne with a jaunty plume. The garb made him dignified, the vows, humble. And within the man beat an ebullient heart, full of what he'd accomplished and what lay before him.

'Twas an irony that the first words Evangeline spoke to him came minutes before the binding ceremony. When Royle saw her approach, all meek and pale upon the arm of her aunt, he was taken by the need to know if this was her will. As much as he desired all that she would bring him, he would not take it over reluctantly tendered vows. He wanted the position in Uriah Webster's family. He coveted the fortune he would control. He lusted for the power both would entail. Yet, conversely, he longed for the personal happiness of a home. Oh, he knew love was out of the question. The woman had scarcely set eyes upon him. However, he would know if she objected to the joining of their futures as one. Would such a frail and sheltered creature be appalled at the thought of uniting with him? The new suit of clothes was impeccable, but what of the man within? It was plain he was not of her class. Would she resent wedding beneath her? Would she be able to love and honor him in time, to be satisfied with what he could give? Did she look upon marriage to a stranger with revulsion, or with a resigned sense of duty? He would know these things, even if the answers could tear apart his desired future.

And when he asked her softly, "Be this your will?", Emma Webster had gone alarmingly pale and was seized by a fit of trembling. But Evangeline's voice, though fragile, was clear.

"It is."

And thusly the vows were made.

The wedding party, consisting of the Websters and the Tanners, adjourned to Broad Street, where a feast of crabs, oysters, game, and roasted meat awaited. A punch of rum and water flowed freely, but for all the celebratory air, Royle came aware of a tension to the scene. He tried to dismiss it as excitement, but the eddies ran too dark and deep. It wasn't the melancholia of losing a loved one, or even the wear of stresses over the occasion. It was something hidden in the evasive eyes of Emma Webster as she nervously guided Evangeline from his side, and the lack of any feeling at all in the placid stare of his bride. The sense of uneasiness increased as an undeniably pleased Uriah presided over the meal. Evangeline left hers untouched. Nerves, he wondered, or something more akin to distress. She was very pale and her gaze never lifted to his. Modesty or distaste? The sweetness of the celebration turned sour.

After the voider was passed, he was relieved when Uriah suggested they adjourn to his study while Evangeline made herself ready to leave with him. Discomfort fled in the company of knowledge; that of books and of success.

A quick toast was raised to welcome him into the family and business the earlier vows had bought him. Uriah adopted an easy attitude toward him, one that was fatherly and almost warm. Warmth was a quality Uriah Webster could not display as genuinely as wealth. He wore it like his elaborately curled periwig, for effect.

"I am happy to have you at my side, Royle," he began, and those sentiments were genuine enough. "You have done me a great service this day, and I will return it."

Cyrus's hints that his father manipulated all returned to trouble Royle. A service? Was that how a guardian viewed the transfer of responsibilities for his ward to another? Uriah's next words did much to relieve him of his discomfiture.

"You see my niece has no assets of her own, no dowry left by her family. Her father lost all in the raid

73

that took his life. Yet Evangeline is blood, and I could not let her go without. She is too proud to take what we would gladly give her. She's been told that the benefits signed to you this day were a legacy from her father, so she can live in ease without suffering from conscience. I sense you are a good man, Royle, and a wise administrator. I know you will see well to her needs and properties. I also know you will understand why there is a clause in the nuptial contract that returns all to me should your marriage know no fruition."

Royle was very still. The conditions of this union were becoming more and more like a complicated bit of business. He was getting the future he desired, but not completely untethered. Could he blame Webster for making stipulations? Hadn't he earlier questioned the man's want to trust so completely? Such precautions were not only sound but shrewd. Uriah was risking nothing. A good businessman. Royle's admiration swelled.

"I have no objections, sir. I plan to earn my own keep, not live off the legacy of my bride." He was honest in that summation, for that was his plan. Uriah had given him a start, not an end. He meant to redouble the investment made.

"I have placed Evangeline into your care. I need not entreat you to use her kindly. The loss of her parents dealt her a cruel blow from which she still suffers. I beg you use patience rather than force to overcome her troubles."

Again, Royle felt that shiver of warning, that premonition that this bargain was not all it seemed. Was there some flaw in the character of his bride that warranted Webster's words, and provoked that anxiousness in his good wife's gaze. Yet when Royle beheld his lovely Evangeline, he could not believe it so. Never had he viewed such an image of feminine perfection. How could he doubt what his eyes told him? This woman would grace his home and his arm, toting his influence and success to all who saw them together. Her presence would establish him where reputation alone would not serve. She would provide a dignified dressing, and he cherished her and what she would do for him.

"You have no need for worries, sir." That was said simply, from the heart.

A smile spread slow upon Webster's face, an infinitely smug gesture of satisfaction. "Very good. Now, to business."

That was a more competent realm for both of them, and each relaxed into the talk of profits to be made. Soon, whatever hesitance Royle might have felt about the arrangements fell before the knowledge of what he stood to gain. Prestige. Power. Success. Anticipation made him breathless. Imaginings brought a lump of emotion to lodge in his throat and burn in his eyes. No woman had ever effected him so potently, and certainly not his pristine bride. His want for fame had him hungry, and Evangeline was but a part of that appetite. What he felt for her was a distancing reverie. It was the way he felt about books and the fine things that adorned the Websters' home, things to be admired and safeguarded from harsh use. What he felt for her was not the basic need to achieve that growled through him with disquieting demands, with passion, with desire. None of that driving emotion settled upon his bride. Nor did he wonder at its lack.

Darkness began to seep into the corners of the room, filling the spaces not reached by the dying light of day. Royle was somewhat surprised to find the time had escaped him, and thought guiltily of his waiting wife. He was unused to considering another. That would come naturally in time, he supposed, but for now it felt awkward. And pleasant. Noting his distraction, Uriah stood.

"'Tis too late to start for Albany this night. I have made arrangements at a fine hostelry and for a guide to wait upon you at first light. 'Tis unlikely that I will see you again before you leave, so I will wish you well now and will await the profits I know will come."

Bolstered by his confidence, Royle grasped the large hand and tested its strength. His own was not lax in comparison.

"See to Evangeline and secure your future."

Those words would gather meaning by morning light.

Evangeline awaited in the parlor, swathed in her cardinal. The bright cape lent color to her wan features. The weariness etched upon them stirred Royle to make an apology, yet she received it with scarcely a blink. When his hand touched her arm, she rose obediently.

At their eminent parting, tears came to Emma Webster's careworn eyes, the first sign of affection or genuine feeling he'd experienced from the woman. Evangeline accepted her embrace, but did not return it. For a moment, the older woman seemed overcome by emotions too strong and sundry to explain. She looked to Royle with what could only be a pleading gaze, and he was stunned by its intensity. It was if she was abruptly aware that she had turned her niece over to a stranger.

"Be kind to her, Mr. Tanner. She is my brother's child." The words trembled with feeling, then Emma Webster brought a well-wrung handkerchief to her mouth and stepped away. Again, Royle was touched by a feeling of privilege and pride, and vowed he'd not fail in either.

Cyrus said nothing as they passed him at the door. His gaze was eloquent. It sparked with a mocking amusement. The gash along his chin quivered in his effort to conceal his mirth.

It was a cool night, saved from darkness by lanterns lit at every seventh house. Alone with his new bride, for the Websters did not linger long at opened door, Royle felt the awkwardness of companioning a woman with whom he'd exchanged only a brief phrase. This night's end would see them in intimate terms, yet they knew naught of each other. What was she like, this protected innocent? Did she have opinions, passions? What kind of helpmate would she be? Did she know how to cook a decent meal, mend a seam, to read? Would they find anything in common with which to fill solitary evenings in discourse? How odd that he should think of these seemingly trivial yet vital questions after the vows were spoken. Had his ambition crowded him too closely to consider them before? Indeed, to consider Evangeline herself as other than a means to a desirable end? It shamed him to recognize that this was so. He had wed a stranger to secure his future, and now the enormity of what that would mean day to day settled close about him. Too late to suffer conscience now.

His bride moved gracefully at his side, neither slowing him nor depending upon him for support. Her hood was pulled close about her face. He could not judge her expression even as they passed by one of the lanterns that pooled inadequate light upon the street. She was an enigma, this woman to whom he'd bound himself, and he was uncertain as to how to approach her. She seemed content with the silence, so he let it go unchallenged. They would have years in

77

which to speak.

Curiosity over his bride gave way before enthusiasm concerning his new standing. In one evening he'd been elevated to a most glorious plane, one of affluence and responsiblity. He would be his own man, in charge of his own destiny, and would never begrudge another his existence. Never. That knowledge firmed the set of his jaw and lent a stern light to hazel eyes. Never would he adopt a subservient manner and pretend he was less than his father had raised him to be. A new life had spread itself before him, one filled with promise and expectation. He was anxious to begin, to seize his future, and control his lot.

The slight brush of a slender shoulder against him made him aware once more of the figure at his side, of his wife Evangeline. His future was her dower to him, and he was as much responsible for her as himself. He'd never had someone depend upon him before. It was a humbling feeling, one that urged a warm protectiveness within his breast, and he was determined to do his best for this lovely creature entrusted to his care. She was the first fine thing he'd ever owned, and he meant to cherish her in that position. He might not be able to furnish her with all the benefits of the Websters' gracious home—not yet—but he would. He would wreath her in luxury, and she would grace him with sons.

That idea of heirs brought a new discomfort, the thought of easing into familiarity with a delicate stranger. As they stepped into the inn Webster had appointed for them, he was more acutely aware of their circumstance as man and wife, and wondered if Evangeline suffered from those same thoughts. He doubted that she knew as explicitly of what was to come as he. The image of her quaking internally with the unknowns of it quickened a tenderness inside him. He vowed she would have naught to fear from him. Though when her cloak fell back, she didn't look afraid, only weary.

As they climbed to their room, that exhaustion grew more apparent. She seemed to stumble, and he was there to support her with a gentle hand. He did not release her as the door to their chamber opened to generous accommodations.

A mature fire in the grate bathed the room in warmth. While Evangeline hesitated at the door, Royle was drawn inward where a cordial waited in welcome. He was in dire need of that inner warmth as well, for the night stretched out long before them, and he was not so much weary as wary. Drink in hand, he turned to his bride.

She had taken off her cloak. The white sarcenet of her gown heightened the illusion of piety and chastity, and Royle was struck asunder as he wondered how to proceed. Finally, he found his voice. It was low and rough with consideration.

"The day has been long and you look done for it, Mistress. Do not feel bound to entertain me. Pray make ready for bed. I shall sit for a time by the fire."

He was trying to be sensitive to her feelings. He expected her to be shy with a man, especially with one unknown to her. Foremost, he did not want her to be afraid of this night that would mark the start of their life together. He was willing to give her all the time and privacy she desired for comfort's sake, figuring she would feel more secure when safe beneath the covers of the poster bed.

She showed no signs of maidenly reluctance, standing there in a soft glaze of firelight. Slender fingers moved surely up the hooks that restrained her bodice, and then it was Royle who awkwardly turned away from the sight of casually bared shoulders. He was quick to pour another cup and careful not to glance behind him. He'd thought of her only as something priceless and pure, but what he considered now was not nearly so virtuous. Those gleaming shoulders had been gently sloped and remarkably bronzed. They looked smooth, so smooth to the touch. He swallowed in a gulp, and the burn going down collided with the burn rising.

A rustle of linens gave him some ease. He was able to sit before the flames without imaginings running wild with thoughts of her standing nearly naked behind him. She would sleep, and he would cool the unexpected overwarming of his reason. He drank and reminded himself to go slowly, lest he scare her into denying him one of the innate pleasures he linked with matrimony, that of a warm and willing bedmate. In that area, too, they had years in which to explore, rather than ruin all with immediate and inappropriate lustings. He hadn't wedded to slake his primal wants.

It was then, upon the seditious lull of spirits, that the reason for this hasty union returned to him. And with it, Uriah Webster's warning. A fruitful union lest all be lost. He shifted slightly in his chair to view the gently contoured terrain of the counterpane. Beneath it lay his wife, and with that title came every conceivable right. She was his to do with as he willed. He controlled all that she was, all that she had, all that she would produce. A wife was to approach her husband as she did her Maker, with reverence, love, and fear, as if he was her god on earth. 'Twas her duty to surrender herself up for his conjugal rights, yet he could not bring himself to demand that she should. Not to a complete stranger. Not yet.

Although, a quick conception would anchor his

hold on all he'd yet to savor.

Restless with his musings, Royle drew his clay pipe from the bag thoughtfully left by the fireside. Another of approximately the same modest size stood beside it. Evangeline's. Just one bag. He puzzled over it while he pulled in the soothing smoke and exhaled aromatic clouds. One would think a woman of quality would travel with an entourage of staff and wardrobe. Perhaps the rest would follow. He dismissed his curiosity and let his thoughts play agreeably over what his future would hold. They came full circle at last to linger upon the woman across the room, and the potential of what was to come narrowed uncomfortably into the next minutes when he would join her upon their marriage bed.

Royle rose and tapped his smoked-out pipe against the hearth. It was late and the new day would come soon. He had no further excuse to linger, to postpone the journey across the room where breathing sounded soft and coaxing. He sighed at his own reluctance. One would think him an untried maid. Still, he was in no great rush to shed his vestments down to a single shirt.

The chill of the room away from the hearth was replaced by a downy warmth as he slipped into bed. The mattress was yielding, and no sooner had he settled then there was a quiet mutter opposite, and Evangeline rolled to press flush against him.

She was naked.

Royle lay still as he could under the circumstance, certain it was an unintentional contact; almost hoping not just as fervently. Then her slender arm rounded his middle, and she snuggled close. His breath escaped shakily.

Had she been content to remain unmoving, he might have convinced his alerted body to seek sleep, but, agonizingly, she continued to shift and wriggle as if in quest of comfort. Cautiously, he encircled her, and let his big hand open wide upon the sleek skin of her back. She was so warm. Instead of protesting his overture, she encouraged it, murmuring softly and nestling her cheek upon his chest. The gesture was so trusting, he cursed himself for entertaining lewd ideas. But cursing could not stop them from coming.

The need to chart more of her supple flesh defied earlier vows. He let his palm wander slowly over the curve of her spine, to where her shoulders fanned, then down to the tempting swell of firm buttocks. Though he'd prepared to halt his trek should she give the slightest objection, she remained still in his tentative embrace. Her compliance fed his growing urgency, making it most difficult for him to argue prudence over the need to know his wife.

He cupped her delicate chin in one large palm and canted her head upward. He spoke her name. Her eyes were open and showed no trepidation, no denial. No desire, either. They were cool, glassy ponds reflecting the distant flicker of the flames. Very slowly, he bent to claim her lips.

The mouth he'd envisioned as sweetly provocative was lax beneath the persuasion of his own, without welcome or response. The stab of his disappointment gave before understanding. Then, he realized, she most likely would not know what to do. Her inexperience heightened his own awareness, not sensually, but with a sensitivity to her tender youth. He might have withdrawn then without regret had she not nuzzled her cheek against his, then gently brushed it with her lips. He didn't require a more formal invitation than that.

Then Royle was faced with the unknowns of how to court an innocent, a well-born innocent at that.

How much would she knew about the joining of man and woman? Was she ignorant of the entice-ment she offered? After she'd presented him with the naked temptation of her body, could she be so innocent? Would she allow his touch or shrink beneath it as too personal an invasion? He longed to touch her, to acquaint himself with her every curve and moist hollow, yet was not convinced that she was ready for that degree of intimacy. The women he'd lain with were well versed in the act of love. They had coupled with him, if not enthusiastically, then at least skillfully. He was sure such art was not taught side by side with embroidery, and where else would his virtuous bride learn of such things. She was a lady of delicate constitution. Did ladies enjoy the basic pleasures as did their lesser-born sisters? Or would this carefully nurtured child do her duty with distaste and loathing? Enough debate. She was his bride, in his bed with her arms about him. Her eyes displayed no untoward fear. A child could be created between them on this very first night. She was his and he would claim her.

A second lengthier kiss was greeted with no greater response. Her mouth remained cool, immobile. When he attempted to slip his tongue between her slackly parted lips, they thinned in vague resistance. Though mild, it was enough to insure his retreat. He didn't kiss her again. Instead, his hand began to stroke along her satin curves in hopes of waking passion beneath that supple skin.

He'd expected her to be soft, pliant beneath the gentle knead of his fingers. She was a lady of leisure, one used to pursuits no more strenuous than threading a needle or summoning a maid. Yet when he ran his palm along her arm, the texture was firm. When he caressed her thigh, the muscle there was well defined, rock-hard. The unexpected contrast had him intrigued. And his desire fanned hot.

It should be quick this first time, he decided. There would be pain for her, and he wished it done and forgotten. On later nights he could teach her of passion and response. This one would be an initiation into womanhood, into wedlock. A bargain sealed and delivered.

He'd never planned to be aroused by his fragile bride, not to heights of desperate urgency, certainly not to ecstasy.

He was as gentle as he could be. He thrust quick and sure to accomplish their union, and when she received him with scarcely a flinch, he'd hoped . . . oh, how he'd hoped, that she'd lose all restraint and fly with him. Yet while he worked himself into a purposeful frenzy and spilled the wish for his future within her, Evangeline lay still beneath him, almost as if she slept.

He rolled from her, too stunned to feel anger. As he lay there listening to her calm, unaffected breathing, a disquieting dread settled about his heart. He had wed himself to a frigid bride.

And when at long last, night paled into dawn, Royle wouldn't have expressed surprise to find his bride cowering beneath the covers, or scorning him for letting his base instincts have full rein. He woke slowly, body lethargic from its unpromising first acquaintance with his wife. He lay quietly for some time, eyes closed, feeling her warmth beside him. For a man used to a solitary bed, or at least to waking in one, it was a strange, comforting heat, and it stirred a renewing fire within him. His wife. He thought on that and what it meant. Surely, he couldn't give too much credence to their first night together. He couldn't expect her—an untried maid—to act a lusty

84

bedmate with a stranger who'd given her his name. A tender courtship was what they needed, for it had been denied them under the odd circumstance of their marriage. He would woo her gently, with only a tad less determination than he'd applied to obtaining a position, and he would begin now.

His arm circled her middle and urged her close against the increasing evidence of his interest. Patience, patience, he chided that burgeoning need as it swelled and looked for encouragement from the yet slumbering figure. He felt her wake in his arms and was aware, crushingly so, of her immediate stiffening. While he pondered how to tactfully greet her as his bride, she inched away from him and slipped from the bed. Aware of her undressed state— oh, how well he was aware of it—he forced himself to remain unmoving, supposing she sought privacy in which to clothe herself for their first meeting. He didn't want her to feel at a disadvantage, so he waited, listening for sounds of her donning her garments. Silence. Then, a subtle dip to the mattress. Thinking she meant to rejoin him, he'd almost begun to smile as he opened his eyes. What greeted him, stunned his reflexes and nearly cost him his life.

Royle Tanner never expected his docile wife to wield a blade with deadly accuracy. Nor did he expect that slicing arc to seek his naked throat with a vengeance.

Chapter Six

The future came in a dream. And all was maddeningly out of her control. Like a dream, the edges of the vision were vague and shifting, but the focus was too clear. Though she did not like it, she could not deny what it showed.

She awoke within that dream all wrapped in warmth and heavy contentment. There were no sounds, just teasing tugs upon her memory. The pungent scent of smoke that was not of the fire. It clung to the fabric beneath her cheek, and recognizing it brought a poignant relief. The scent of tobacco, of liquor, of man. Her father. Convinced that all before had been the nightmare, she held tight to that securing strength and would have wept, if not for the confusion of his kiss. Not her father.

The dream had taken a disturbing turn, yet she was not afraid to follow. There was safety even in the unknowns of it. The scents placated her. The gentle touch quieted her. Even an instant of pain soon became a comforting bliss that filled her strangely in a way she'd never known. She was surrounded by love, engulfed by passionate magic. A name was spoken like a caress. It was an old name, yet one she remembered as her own. And then she saw into his eyes, and she knew her future was there within lush green and amber depths, as mysterious and inviting as a forest glen. A peaceful haven was offered therein, and it was so easy to surrender to that serene escape.

The rest was blurred to all but the sensation of belonging. That tranquility lingered throughout her heavy slumber, and though she would yet cling to it upon waking, a reality intruded too harsh to be ignored.

A man lay with her. She did not know him. He was sleeping, his arm carelessly curled about her trim waist in a possessing fashion. His hair was yellow, his skin white, and he was dressed in English linen.

For a long moment, she lay still, her chest trembling with the effort of it. The fog of past hours would not lift, she knew, so she pieced together what she could from the circumstance in which she found herself. Her furtive gaze slipped about the room. This was not the Websters' house, yet the sounds of the settlement were the same. She was free of confining night wraps, so she knew Emma Webster was not about. How then to explain this pale Englishman who embraced her with such familiarity.

Her husband.

A quick breath of panic and horror escaped her, then she forced them to come slow. She had to think. The Websters had shown good their threat. They had given her to a stranger to be rid of her presence under their pious roof. They had sold her. It was not the first time, so why did she feel so bitter and betrayed? They had tricked her, stolen her reason. Why should she hold surprise for any vile thing they did.

A fluttering movement distracted her gaze to the window. A gentle breeze tossed the curtains through the open sash. Hope bounded within her. Freedom.

The man's arm proved not only heavy, but determined to keep her close. She struggled with her desire to throw it savagely aside, but she could not risk waking him. Her escape must be quick and silent as the waning shadows. Before he woke, she could be far away. And once she reached the forest, he would never find her, nor could she believe he would want to look.

Carefully, she lifted his hand by the forefinger, and wiggled to one side until she was clear of its reach. Only then was she aware of the discomfort. Her body throbbed from a deep, vital ache. Her femininity felt bruised and torn, yet it wasn't until she observed the crimson smears upon her thighs that she understood. And with understanding came rage.

Fury, uncontrolled and volatile, boiled. He had known her. Anger collided with a strange kind of grief over what had been ripped from her without her knowledge. Had she struggled and shrieked against the violation, she wouldn't have felt so ashamed. But she had lain beneath this white man to whom she'd been sold, and had put up no fight to keep that which was precious to her. And in her failure to protest, there was a sense of permission. How could she go back to her people and take on the brave of her choice, while soiled by the knowledge of what had occurred upon this bed, beneath this man? She couldn't pretend it did not happen, though in her disjointed memory, it had not. The only evidence was physical. And though she could thank her gods she'd have no scars of remembrance, it was too late to remedy the damage done. Too late to claim her previous purity. However, a need for vindication surged, and with it, a wild passion to draw equal blood for that lost, to avenge her misuse and salvage her pride.

Blazing eyes cast about and lit with satisfaction upon a tray left at the bedside. The loaf of bread was dry, the cheese no better, but the knife beside them on the board would serve well enough. Eager fingers curled about the hilt. She would cut out the heart of this animal who had dared defile her. She would carve him like the Websters' Sabbath turkey, until bones were laid bare. She would strike at him for his careless use of her, and for the humiliation that she'd borne it and yet lived.

And when the blade streaked like lightning toward his pale neck, the man's eyes came open—and the world shuddered to a halt. The truth struck more searingly than had the knife found its mark. His eyes were gold and green. The eyes of the man in her dream. Her destiny.

In that instant of hesitation, he caught her wrist and rolled to imprison her beneath his weight. She could see surprise in those wide lush eyes, and she wished she could have cut them out before they opened. His breath rushed fast upon her flushed cheeks, and she resented each one he drew. Fingers compressed steadily about her wrist until the knife fell from her numbed hand. He was quick to knock it to the floor. Then there was only the sound of their hurried breathing and the exchange of intense stares.

"Are you mad?" That was the first thought that came to him in explanation of his rude awakening. Was that the reason the Websters had been so quick to wed their niece to a man not of their society? Were the eligible suitors all frightened away by lovely Evangeline Carey's insanity? And he was furious to think how he'd been cheated.

The words that spewed from her curled back lips were foreign to him, but he understood their meaning quite well. They were filled with the same hatred that smoldered in her glare. How had he ever seen that gaze as placid? What on earth was wrong with the woman that she would so speak in tongues? Terror possessed him that he should find himself married to a devil incarnate.

"Get off me, animal, dog, vermin." She followed with several other phrases he was sure were equally colorful, had he been able to understand them.

"Not while you're yet eager to have my throat."

She ceased her thrashing immediately and lay deceivingly still, while perfect breasts rose and fell in shallow pants in an effort at control.

"You hurt me," she claimed flatly, and he laughed.

"You expect sympathy? Woman, you meant to kill me."

"I wish I had," she spat up at him. Her pale eyes glowed with a fire he'd not seen in their depths before. It stirred him irrationally. "Then I would have had my revenge, would be free of you, and gone home to my family."

"Had you wanted to return to the Websters so badly, I would have taken you with less than knifepoint to convince me."

"They are not my family."

That cold claim struck at the heart of him. Royle was shaken by what it could mean. Not her family. Whatever had he involved himself in? His hold upon her wrists unconsciously eased as his mind spun in unsavory directions. My God, had they kidnapped the girl? Had they bartered him with some servant wench? Just what the bloody hell was going on?

"Who are you?" he demanded curtly.

Her chin thrust up proudly. What a beauty she was against the spill of ebony hair. He had thought as much before, yet now, it was of a different sort, wild,

90

defiant. Exciting.

"I am Eyes-Like-Evening-Star. My people are Caniengas of the Five Nations. I am Iroquois."

Royle snorted his disbelief. "You are no more Indian than I am."

The pale eyes flared hotter with resentment. "Fool. You are like them. You do not see beyond the outside. I am Caniengas in my heart. It is not my fault that I share your despised pale skin. I would change it if I could."

This was not the first conversation he'd thought to have with his bride. Since waking, she'd tried to stab him, had cursed him, had told him incredible tales. Either she was mad, or he was. Sanity seemed to have fled the moment. He had to think, to speak to her rationally, yet that was difficult while he straddled her naked form. Such lurid thoughts about the person of sweet Evangeline Carey would have shamed him. Not so with this pagan creature. Here was the all the passion he could have wished for when bedding her. A shame it was bent toward hatred rather than desire.

"I am going to release you, so we can dress and speak in a civilized manner. If you will act as such, so you will be treated."

"Release me," she growled. Contempt colored her stare. It was a milder emotion than the violence of moments before, so he felt safe in abandoning his cautious hold. He backed slowly off the bed, ready to seize her in an instant should she give him cause.

With inborn dignity, she slid sleek legs to the floor and stood before him. She stood proud, unembarrassed by her undress. And his sweeping glance could see no reason why she should be. She was perfect. Her body was slender yet subtly defined by a strength he had tested earlier along long shapely limbs. Her

91

small breasts were high and taut, her waist trim above the feminine flare of hips. And she was bronze. All over. That sun-warmed color was rich and equally measured from rebelliously offered features to tiny bared feet, unflawed by naught but a colorful tattoo, bracelet-fashion about one slim ankle. That all-over-tan held his thoughts mesmerized for a long moment, wondering with erotic fancy how she had come by it. Before his warming fantasy could linger on the image of her stretched naked in the sun, she slipped into a modest chemise, and the illusion came to a convulsive halt.

Pulling himself from his lustful daydreams, Royle tugged on his breeches, stuffing in his shirt with quick, jerky motions. His eyes never left the strange exotic woman that was by some quirk of fate his wife. When it became apparent that she was not going to don any more of her clothing, he gestured to one of the fireside chairs. She assumed one on the precarious edge, ready to take to flight like a restless game bird startled in its roost. Cautiously, he took the other.

Evangeline assumed a haughty pose from which to study her new white captor. She was not impressed. This man would never hold her. There was no strength in him. He was fragile and small compared to the men of her tribe, with his delicate fair skin and soft white man's body. She saw his look, the lust in his eyes, the satisfaction in them when beholding the proof of what he'd stolen smeared upon her thighs. If he thought to have some power over her because of that unfair domination, she would gladly prove him wrong. He may have conquered the momentary weakness of her female form, but overcoming the tenacity of her will was quite another thing. The fact that his inferior seed had filled her was a source of shame and fury. An Indian never cared to lie with white people, even when enjoying sovereign power over their bodies in captivity. It was the coarse lustful thinking of the whites that created tales of red barbarians eager to deflower their pale daughters, when in truth a noble warrior found nothing attractive about them. And looking upon her defiler, she could see their logic. The Websters wouldn't have believed her chaste, even if she had told them. They had believed her wanton and much used at the hands of her captors. And apparently, they felt that gave them the right to follow suit. Rape of the unwilling was a white man's trait. And how she despised this yellow-haired man for it.

He was watching her. The confusion in his eyes made him weak and fed her strength. He had not known. That knowledge gave her a grim pleasure. That made him a fool as well. Her uncle had given him a changeling for a bride. He had taken her in the belief that she was of silk and society. What a shock reality must be. She could see him studying her just as intensely now. He was not good at concealing his thoughts. They were displayed nakedly upon his colorless face. Dawning horror. Disbelief. Denial. This one would find no pleasure in the challenge of having a savage wife. She would not be long in his company.

"Now, how came you to the Websters?"

"They stole me from my family." She took delight in seeing him recoil from that idea. Let him suffer for her situation. Let him twist in guilt at what he had done. She would not let him go unpunished. Not after the unchangeable part he'd taken in her captivity.

That savagely offered bit of fact didn't make sense to him, though her bright eyes would claim it so. He tried again. "Why would they do that?"

"Because I share the unfortunate blood of her brother."

"Then you are their niece."

"Yes."

"But with them against your will."

More emphatically, "Yes."

"Why did you not leave them?"

"I was kept prisoner in their rooms." His doubtfully raised brow made her bristle. "I was awaiting the right time to escape them."

"And I offered that escape."

Before she could answer, Royle surged to his feet and began to pace in agitation. Everything was crumbling to leave only dust and dreams. By God, it was beginning to make an ironic sort of sense. Cyrus Webster's smirk hit home as he recognized the joke at last. The Websters had saddled him with an unbroken savage. He gave a laugh at his own gullibility. It was a bitter, raw sound. Now he understood Uriah's want to get Evangeline out of his home and into the wilds where she would not disgrace his name. And he also understood that having her by his side as his wife was more detriment than blessing. No fashionable home was going to open its doors to a laborer's son and his untamed bride. What a laugh Webster must have gotten upon hearing of his ambitions. The wily businessman had assured that his new man would not be quick to move from wilderness to town life. He had been nicely and neatly trapped into doing Uriah Webster's bidding, and the jaws were sprung by his own blinding greed.

Evangeline watched the man stalk about the room in typical white wastefulness. An Indian never walked back and forth upon the same path in a fruitless use of energy, not when they could remain

94

quietly seated. She studied the expressions artlessly displayed upon his face, seeing frustration, anger, and chagrin among them. Her own feelings would never be so transparent. He finally stopped his promenading and simply stared. She found she could not comfortably meet those eyes from her vision, and settled her gaze instead upon his mouth, waiting to hear what lies it would speak.

"You seemed content enough with your lot when I saw you at the Websters'." Sarcasm was sharp in his words, but she couldn't guess how it concealed his disgust at having fallen prey to her charade of gentility.

Her own reply housed secret shame. It exposed her vulnerability to her enemy, and showed she could be bested by tricks and deceit. But she would have him know the ugly circumstance behind her actions. She would have him understand how unwilling she had been in all that had befallen her. "It is because they placed something into my food and drink to steal away my will."

Every new revelation drew a worse picture. Not only had he married under false assumptions against the will of his bride, she had been drugged into complaisance. The vileness was staggering. The complications complex. He turned to find the keen gray eyes upon the open window, as if measuring the distance. His voice was low, edged with steel.

"And you thought it would be easier to escape from me."

Her gaze flew up to his in brief surprise that he should guess so well then, it was quickly masked. "Yes. Why should you want to keep me now that you know the truth of what I am?" That was smugly said, with much satisfaction, as if realizing the joke, he would be glad to be rid of its reminder.

95

His answer crushed her fleeting hopes. "What you are is my wife."

She, too, came to her feet, and his posture was immediately defensive. Fool, she thought fiercely. How could he make such a claim? Well, she would set it right. "Not by my laws. You are nothing to me. I do not wish to remain with you. It is that simple with my people to dissolve a marriage. It is done."

The calm green eyes narrowed with careful thought. He spoke quietly, with great emphasis. "The only thing that cannot be undone transpired between us last night." Her bright flush of either rage or shame did not keep him from continuing. "You are my wife because my laws sanctified it and my seed consummated it. That will not change because you will it, or because either of us wish it was not so. What's done, is done. You are mine and I will not relinquish you."

The small, firm breasts heaved with agitation. Her mind worked furiously. If she could not bully him, perhaps he would come about with gentler persuasion. He drew a quick breath when her entreating hand rested lightly on his chest.

"Please. You do not seem a cruel man. You cannot know how I suffer in this captivity. Let me go back to my people. I am not who or what you thought me to be, nor do I wish to be wife to you. Do not make their mockery into a misery as well. Let me go, I beg you."

He stepped slightly back so the contact between them ended. There was no softening betrayed in the set of his features, yet she had not struck far from the mark. She was so lovely, her delicate face etched in poignant supplication, pale eyes muted with abject pleading. Yet he had felt her strength and was not about to fall before another ruse. His pride was already battered beyond repair. It wasn't that he felt

96

no sympathy for her, for he was as unfortunately ensnared as she. A dangerous pagan bride was not the sort of helpmate he'd envisioned. He empathized with her plight, but could not be moved to aid it. Vows had been spoken. A bargain made. The future was still there before him, slightly tarnished now, yet the promise remained. He may not have received the bride he expected, but the dowry stood unchanged. To have it meant keeping her. And to his thinking, there was little choice.

"No."

She was upon him before his senses gave warning. A shrill wail rent the air, causing his blood to curdle in his veins, so murderous was the sound. As he struggled to restrain her, sharp nails—or was it teeth—raked his shoulder. She was strong, stronger than any female had a right to be. Her body squirmed in his grasp, twisting, supple. It was like trying to hold to a slippery fish with bare hands. Elbows and knees yielded well-placed jabs. It wasn't his want to hurt her, but neither was he willing to take much more punishment from the determined she-cat. Finally, he encircled her with his arms and literally squeezed the fight from her, until she was nearly limp against him. Only then did he restore her to her feet. His hands remained cuffed about her upper arms.

"You are my wife. You may even now have my child flourishing within you." Her rapid denying shake didn't alter the fact that it could be so. "I do not care who you are or what you are. I wed you, and what you are is mine."

"No," she snarled as her recovered breath seethed between clenched teeth. "You cannot hold me, puny white man. I spit on you." And she did.

"Spit and curse and fight all you like. 'Twill serve

97

only to make things more unpleasant between us."

His determined calm enraged her all the more. She shrieked insults upon him that would have withered a man of her tribe, never thinking that the effect was spoiled as he could not understand her. Clawlike fingers sought his flesh, but his held her at bay and harmless.

"Unpleasant," she panted. "You've no idea how unpleasant it will be. I will prove a bane upon you. You will rue the day when you did not release me."

Royle shrugged. "Do your worst, Madam. You'll not take me by surprise again."

"And you'll not take me at all." The cold cut of her gaze made that meaning clear. "I would as soon die as endure your touch. I will fight you to my last breath."

His eyes shuttered and his voice was a rough purr. "You were not of the same mind last night."

His words had the desired effect. Shock drove the wind from her and shame kept her deflated. Was it true? Had she welcomed his commerce? She could not believe it was so. Yet his smile was smugly male and it infuriated her. Did he think because he'd had her once, she would be eager for more of his touch? The thought disgusted her. Her flesh rebelled against it.

"Never again," she swore with feeling. "Nothing about you attracts an interest in me. I feel only loathing."

Had he logically considered her plight, he would have agreed that she had no cause to act otherwise. Yet his pride bridled at her contempt. She was his wife, whether she cared for him or not, and as such he would not allow her that sneering scorn. He would not admit to himself that it was her vow that she found no liking in him that provoked his response.

His hands tightened and drew her up against him. Before she could read of his motive, his lips swooped down to capture hers. Parted as they were in startlement, he had a moment of complete and delicious freedom until she tore hers away.

It was a sight he would never be free of, that of her spectacular beauty as she gazed up at him. Briefly, the antagonism was gone, replaced by a wondering confusion. Gray eyes as clear and pure as morning revealed her vulnerability and moist pouting lips, the temptation she would deny. She could say what she would, but he would never again believe she was unmoved by him as a man.

Her barriers were quickly rebuilt. The anger that spurred her grew out of that instant where control was lost. The kiss was worse than the knowledge that he had known her intimately, worse because she was in her right senses and yet allowed it. And she'd enjoyed it. There had been nothing soft or womanly in the masterful claim of his lips. He'd stolen her breath, and for a moment, her reason. Even now, she could feel the firm imprint of his mouth upon her, a brand of possession, and her outrage flared. She scourged herself for that weakness and faced him as a new and more dangerous threat. More was at stake than her precious freedom.

"Force me if it makes you feel more the man but I will not welcome you. I have a beloved who will fillet you inch by inch when he finds that you have so abused me."

That brought an unpleasant flicker to his green gold eyes, and she wondered if it had been the wrong thing to say. In the rule of her white passions, she was not always clearest of thought. She had wanted to strike at him, to wound him with jealousy the way he had smitten her with fear. More, she wanted a distance between them that wouldn't cause his strange eyes to burn from a light within. She earned that wish, for he stood away to regard her with an almost cold certainty. The confidence of his words wrought a shiver to her very marrow.

"I will not force you to endure my passions. But remember, dear wife, it is a two-edged knife, cutting both ways. Denying me is to deny yourself. If I am without comfort, so shall you be. We are all each other has, Evangeline. Some day you may wish you'd not chosen to be alone."

"Never," she cried. She was more shaken by the thought of a life without companionship than she was by a life bereft of her family, but she swore she'd not seek it from this hateful Englishman. "I will not endure you for long. You cannot hold me. You cannot stay awake forever. Someday you will tire of expecting my blade in your back, and there it will be ere I get the chance. I am returning to my people. Let me go now and spare yourself the misery ahead."

"Spare me your threats, Madam, and make ready. We leave for Albany this morning. Where I go, so go all of my belongings."

Her chin jutted forward in a gesture of arrogance. Her stare was of haughty disdain. "Bound hand and foot is the only way I'll leave with you."

"As you wish."

Chapter Seven

The days were all gold and green as warm sunshine and surrounding forests replaced civilization. Their boat made good progress up the Hudson, and Evangeline might have enjoyed the gliding passage had circumstances been different. It was hard to take pleasure in things when trussed like the lowest criminal. Had she not already seethed with hatred for her captor, this outrageous indignity he forced her to suffer would have been enough to spur loathing for any man. But he was not just any man. He was the man who refused her freedom. He was the man who soiled her chance to return to her people yet proud. He was the one who made her suffer for his own loss of face before the treachery of her uncle. He was furious to discover what he had wed, yet too arrogantly prideful to amend that mistake. He would keep her to spite them all. And she vowed upon the honor of her mighty ancestors that he would regret it.

Royle had taken her at her boldly offered word. When their guide—a near toothless Dutchman named Croix—came for them, Royle had marched her down to the boat launch, a firm grip on her arm. Once she was settled on one of the broad seats, he deftly bound her wrists before her. At her astonished look, he'd smiled grimly and remarked she should think twice before leaping over the side in an attempt to swim to freedom. Then he dismissed her, seating his hateful person on the plank ahead. She spent the first hours of the journey measuring his broad, overly clothed back for a good spot in which to house her blade.

Travel on the water was leisurely and soothing to the spirit. The sounds of the bow breaking the glassy surface and of paddles rhythmically dipping complimented the quiet. It was hard to maintain a fever pitch of fury in that serene clime. Evangeline allowed herself to relax. There would be time aplenty to plot revenge, and the beauty of the land was a calm distraction. Each pull of the paddles took her farther from the confinement of New York and closer to her family. Her people were the Keepers of the Eastern Door, and their influence spread from the Mohawk Valley to Montreal. Their canoes commanded the Mohawk River, Lake George, and Lake Champlain. Soon, their familiar faces would mingle with those of the whites. Soon, word that she was back among them would be carried to her family. Then her days of captivity would end. Her mouth took on a contented curve as she entertained that thought. More hours passed as she considered the terrible tortures her loved ones would have in mind for the man who had defiled her.

Meals were taken in the boat. To her annoyance, she was made to eat with hands yet bound. The men controlling their craft paid no note to her fettered state, as if it was a natural occurrence for a finely garbed lady to travel in such restraints. Perhaps these white men needed such measures to hold their women, or perhaps her captor had paid them well to be blind to her situation. Either way, there was no help for her there. The placid waters they slid along did not encourage thoughts of escape, though at times, the shore was temptingly close. She was a strong swimmer, but had no desire to test that strength against man-made shackles. Hope was not so lost to her that she would consider suicide. No, she would wait. Her time would come. Pensively, she gnawed the meat and bread she'd been given, and indulged in daydreams of how it would feel to have a knife at the pale throat of her keeper.

They took to the shore sparingly, and during those respites, she was given a limited privacy to see to her needs. The chance to flee never came, and each time she was shepherded back into the flat-bottomed boat, it was with silently muttered curses and promises of retribution. They continued on into the night as the moon was full and bright upon the water. With hands bound before her, it was difficult to gain rest, for each time her body sagged with weariness, she had to struggle to catch herself upon the seat. Finally, exhaustion claimed her, and she was lost to the world of dreams. None of them were so frightening or fateful as the one binding her to her hated enemy. She slept in innocence of her situation, but the benefits of that slumber were overshadowed by the circumstance of its passing.

She awoke to the pink of dawn, comfortably cradled against the side of her captor. Her cheek was nestled contentedly into the folds of his coat. Her arms had gone about him as awareness stirred, holding her close to his side so she rode the rhythm of his breathing. One of his arms curved behind her back to form a sturdy bolster, the other supporting her relaxed shoulder. A movement as gentle and teasing as a woodland breeze disturbed her hair. And

103

as she drifted closer to wakefulness, she realized it was the leisurely stroke of his hand upon her loose tresses. He was holding her tenderly, like a child, like a treasured loved one, and to awake in such a cherished position cast her senses into a sensual panic. He felt good beneath her cheek, beneath her arms, beneath the contours of her body. He felt right. And it frightened her near to death that he would.

The warmth and consideration of that embrace was lost in her exaggerated outrage. She jerked away as if burned. Her eyes stared icy fire.

"Forgive me for wanting to prevent you from falling over the side."

His mockery made her spine stiffen. To accept kindness—even the merest token of charity from him—was bitter gall, and then to have him laugh! To have even taken pleasure in his loathsome embrace brought home her disgrace, until she could not bear it with pride. How dare he take advantage of her—again!—while she was unaware. The man was a cunning devil bent on destroying her will. But she would not falter. She would have his fine yellow hair lifted and stretched upon a hoop. It would make a symbolic ornament on the wall of her long house. That thought pleased her, and she returned his smile in grisly humor.

Instead of resuming his seat, he remained beside her. She edged closer to the side, not only to provide a more comfortable distance, but also so she could observe him through canted eyes without being obvious. She would take the measure of this white man who provoked such unsettling currents within her. He was not exactly ugly, she decided. His strong, regular features might actually be pleasant, if not for his coloring. Pale men didn't interest her. Her preference ran toward deeply bronzed flesh, jet-colored eyes, and hair like raven's wings. And then, there was his clothing . . . so much of it. He looked half-strangled in the layers of fabric wound tight from toe to neck. At least he refused to sport the false scalps as they did in the Webster home. She studied him carefully, wanting to find a weakness or flaw that might disgust her. Other than his fairness, she could decide upon no singular objection. Though his treatment of her was unfair, it was not cruel or even unkind. He'd taken pains to see the thongs did not abrade her wrists, and saw the boat to shore several times just so she might stretch her legs. She would not, of course, thank him for these small favors. She owed him nothing but her contempt. Yet this was not the worst captivity she'd endured. She was comfortable and made to feel unafraid. Still, she could not bring herself to feel gratitude.

He caught her in her interested study and had the nerve to grin as if he'd won some concession over her. Immediately, she turned her head away with a haughty disdain, but the sound of his low chuckle robbed her of her victory. She sat for a moment, chafing in her annoyance, stewing in her hatred, while he lounged casually at her side, seemingly unaffected by either fierce emotion.

Curiosity over her fate precluded her denial of it. She was about to phrase a question, when she realized she didn't know the name of the man beside her. She searched her limited memory, but could seize upon no ready title. Finally, she swallowed her pride and asked.

"What am I to call you?"

He smiled faintly at the stiffly posed request. "I suppose dearest is out of the question. You might try husband."

Her scowl said that was just as unlikely. She forced

105

herself to pursue the matter. She would have preferred to turn her back to him. Or to shove him over the side.

"I mean what are you called?"

His brows lowered into a furrow of displeasure when he understood. His reply was clipped. "Tanner. My name is Royle Tanner. That makes you Mistress Tanner."

She had no response to that. She bit her inner cheeks to prevent an outburst that would claim she'd no intention of adopting his name in English fashion. That was not her way. In marriage between her people, the woman did not assume the man's name, but instead was known as that man's wife. Children similarly took a name from their mother's family. There was great respect for both those customs, and she had no intention of degrading them by becoming known as Tanner's Wife.

She kept her reasonings silent, knowing that if she spoke her mind, the tentative talk between them would turn unfriendly. It was not warm now, but at least it was civil, and she meant to make use of it.

"Where is it we go, Tanner?"

Her use of his surname brought a further tightening to his expression, but he didn't deny her an answer.

"We are going to live in Albany. 'Tis where I will work, and where we will have our home."

He was watching her closely now. She chose not to betray herself by commenting on the last part of his claim. Instead, she asked, "And what is your work?"

Pride seeped noticeably into his answer. "I will run a trading house there."

Evangeline's face lost all animation. She stared at him through eyes flat and void of emotion. Her voice was equally colorless. "You mean you will be one of

106

those to strip my people of their land and their dignity.''

Royle made as if to answer, but he knew not how to refute her cold claim. He was relieved of the task, for her fine profile was given him as indication that she wished no more discussion. Not knowing what in his words had so offended her, Royle merely scowled. She hadn't bothered to learn his name, and now she spurned his ambitions. In what he thought a justified pique, he moved forward to his former seat and tried to forget the aggravating woman behind him, in his eager planning for what lay ahead.

However, after several attempts in which thoughts were fragmented at best, Royle reluctantly turned his musings toward the problem foremost on his mind. Evangeline. She had thrown his life into chaos, offering his heart's desire at a fearsome cost. What lay ahead with her as his wife? No man wanted a bride who had to be shackled at his side. No man wanted a companion he could not turn his back upon for fear of having a knife thrust into it. No civilized man chose force over devotion to keep a woman. Yet how could he let her go? He was shackled to her by the subtle terms of Webster's clever contract. No wife, no chance. And he rebelled against the loss of the latter. Yet it went deeper than the threat of lost fortune. He had wed her, had held to her hand before the law of man and God, had lain with her and known her as a man does his wife. She was his. It was that simple and that complex.

All he'd ever had in earlier years had been either cast-off or borrowed. Even the clothes upon his back he couldn't claim as his alone. Often the food upon their table was due to charity. He'd been forced to humble himself and his wants for all those years, upon the promise that one day he would come into

107

his own. That day was now. In his control, he could boast of profits from his labor, of a future free of debt and degradation, of belongings not handed down, mended beyond recognition, or salvaged from another's discards. And in his bed was a woman bound to him by his name who'd known no other before him. He was possessive of the position and of the lady. Never mind that she was not what he'd expected, she was his, and no one was ever going to take what was his from him.

A shadow was cast upon his determination. She had spoken of one beloved. Was there some man among the savages that held her heart captive as he held her body? Greedily, he wanted both, to be the first and only to claim them. Practically, he faced the fact that neither was certain. She'd vowed to escape him at first opportunity. To run back to her pagan lover? He felt an unfamiliar tightening in his gut, a burning, twisting agony of rage to think of her racing into another's arms. He would stake her out like a wayward hound if he had to, until she was broken to his command. If she couldn't be made to love him, at least she would obey him. He'd had a kitten when he was a small lad, one he fed from his own meager plate, one he loved with every ounce of affection he possessed. Yet every time he'd tried to pick the tiny thing up to cuddle it close, it bit him. His father explained that it was because it was a wild thing, and that it was its nature not to trust even a caring hand. Still, he had suffered its scratches and needlelike teeth in hopes of winning its devotion, until it ran away. And he had cried over the loss of that nasty little beast. He learned his lesson. He should have kept it tied.

*   *   *

Although Albany was the center of trading activity in the north, it was a rudimentary settlement at best. One main thoroughfare paralleled the Hudson, and another climbed the low hill to the fort. Before the English took control, it was called Beverwyck. That Dutch influence remained in the stepped construction of the finer homes, but comparison to New York ended there. When he'd arrived in New York, Royle had been pleasantly surprised. He'd expected to find a wilderness overrun by Indian and wild animals. Here that preconception was closer to the truth. The attempt to imitate the comforts of the homeland were less successful in Albany. The gable ends that faced the street were made of fine brick, to give the impression that the whole house was of the same construction, when, in fact, the remaining structure was made of cheaper plank. All in all, Albany presented a picture much like their own, a glossy exterior concealing rougher stuff.

As the boatmen brought their craft up to the landing, Royle slit the bindings on Evangeline's wrists. It would not do for his new neighbors to see him lead his wife to their home bound like the veriest criminal. The consideration with which he aided her from the boat was not so much a courtesy as it was a means to maintain a firm hold on her. He needn't have worried. She seemed content to walk up the wide rambling unpaved street at his side. Those who would observe her would be struck with the same misconception that Royle had been so cruelly shaken from, of a refined, well-bred lady, and they would envy him her company. He hoped the illusion would last for them longer than it had for himself.

He had anticipated owning one of the stately Dutch homes, and his disappointment depressed his enthusiasm as they were led off one of the side streets into an older area where homesteads were farther apart and not nearly as new or nice. He stood in the street to appraise the building their guide showed them to. In comparison to the Webster's dwelling in New York, it was a shoddy second. Not one to bemoan his circumstance for long, Royle determined that it would do. For now, at least. It was his, and that made it above reproach. He led his bride across the threshold.

The interior was not as rough as first glance would intimate. Exterior walls and partitions were of heavy timbers squared by an ax and chinked with moss. They were lined with hewn two-inch planks and unevenly coated with plaster. Walls were further warmed by hangings of bear, deer, otter, wildcat, and fox skins. Windows were high-placed and deep-seated, with oiled paper instead of glass, and barred. That would solve one problem, Royle thought grimly as he glanced toward Evangeline. She stood stoically in the room's center, eyes straight ahead, as if refusing to acknowledge her surroundings and their significance. He continued his perusal.

A great stone chimney rose through the center of the house, boasting wide-throated fireplaces in each of the two first-floor rooms. The room in which they stood had served as common room and kitchen, until the lean-to addition was built to take that duty. Now it was made to act as a sitting room for social gatherings. Furnishings were homemade of lumber locally cut and sawn. Pieces were simple, heavy, and few; stools, long benches, and a settle. Lime-plastered walls were a restful green. In his earlier delusions, he would have pictured his beauteous wife attending his important guests in this setting. Now he considered that possibility with rueful doubt. He could not imagine entertaining visitors while his

110

half-wild wife stalked behind them measuring their scalp locks. The loss of that cherished dream quirked an anger in him, at his savage bride, at his unjust fate.

A tug on her arm prompted Evangeline to follow Royle into the rear of the house. The common room was where they would spend most of their time together, and Royle was glad to find it a welcoming space. Its furnishings were more refined, speaking more of comfort than function. A trestle table was centered in the room, surrounded by a chair for its master and a few stools. Ladder-backed chairs hung on the wall by pegs, to accommodate important guests. A settle was angled inviting toward the fire, and a corner cupboard housed a supply of wooden plates and trenchers. A row of iron pots and kettles adorned the fireplace, with a flintlock rifle in their midst. Evangeline's gaze lingered there, and Royle made a note to see it was not primed.

The rest of the room was filled with the usual necessities; water pail, wash benches, chest for corn meal, barrels for salt beef and pork, and a gateleg table where the women would eat when serving the men at the standing table. Royle's gaze settled upon the jack bed built into one corner. Its head and one side were supported by the wall with one outer post. Several big goose feather pillows suggested a comfortable repose, and the trundle beneath it hinted at additions to the family. He thought of the unexpected luxury of her skin, the excitement of having her struggle within his arms. His mouth went suddenly dry.

Seeing the direction of Royle's preoccupation, Evangeline moved nervously to one window. It was narrow, its bars set deep. She touched one of them pensively, then turned to catch Royle's frown upon her. Her chin hoisted a notch, daring him to comment. He did not. After all, he might term this their home, but to her, it was a prison, and he, her keeper—and she meant to escape them both as soon as possible. Her look warned him not to readily accept her momentary acquiescence. This comfortable hearth and tempting bed did not a harmonious marriage make. It called him back to her earlier vow to fight him at every turn. Her lack of resistance now was merely a gathering of new strategy.

The tension of the moment was broken by the arrival of two men from the boat, bearing their bags and Evangeline's dowry chest. It had been a surprise addition, left at the dock in New York by the Websters. Royle thanked the men and their guide, and then it was the two of them alone.

"Aren't you going to open it?"

Royle gestured to the intricately carved chest. Women were supposed to covet these dowry gifts, and he hoped Evangeline no different. They had not spoken since he'd revealed his occupation. He was anxious to establish some sort of communication between them on this, their first day in their new setting. It may have been naive of him to think it, but he yearned to start anew with her. The situation needn't be as bad as he'd assessed at first. There was no reason she could not be made into a respectable wife, into a loving mate. The lure of that untried bed coaxed forth those thinkings. She then made it quite clear that it was not only a naive hope, but an impossible one.

Cool gray eyes touched on the box, then lifted away in disdain. "I want nothing of theirs or of your world."

Or of you, hung between them unspoken. Royle repressed his want to give her a firm shake. Patience,

112

he reminded himself. That was what he'd promised the Websters. Their words returned with new shades of meaning. He'd vowed to be tolerant and kind, to have consideration for her sufferings of the past. He'd no idea at that time what that would encompass. However, a vow was a vow, no different than the one he'd spoken before the magistrate. No different than the one he'd said at his father's bedside. And above all, Royle was an honorable man.

He knelt by the chest, sliding a discreet glance toward his bride. She was looking, though she pretended not to. He nearly smiled. No, women weren't all that different. He made a show of rummaging through the contents with interest, and eventually she eased to one side so she could peer over his shoulder to see what the box yielded. There were large linen napkins and Holland board-cloths of fine quality and whiteness, several luxurious mantles of velvet and brocade, a set of good Delftware, and a half-dozen silver porringers, a niddy noddy reel, canvas and floss for feminine pursuits. On the practical side, spices from the Orient, salt from Spain, and a pure clear sugarcone imported from the West Indies. Then, the most precious gift of all. Evangeline puzzled over the rapt expression on her husband's face as he drew out three bound books. His fingers caressed their covers, then, impatiently, he looked to their titles. Cicero. He grinned and made a note to thank the pompous Cyrus Webster when next they meet. The other two volumes were more pointed in their selection, *Practice of Piety* and *Call to the Unconverted*, books directed toward the Indians to guide them into the Christian fold. He raised a brow, then looked to Evangeline. He didn't think she would be open-minded on the subject matter.

"Do you read?"

Her answer was evasive, but an answer. "There is nothing in the white man's word that appeals to me."

Evangeline dismissed the contents of the chest. Useless items, every one. She turned away so he would not see the sudden shift of her expression to heartsickness. These were not the gifts she'd dreamed of receiving as a bride. They were meant for another, for the type of woman Royle Tanner should have wed. She knew not how to use any of them. As a maiden, she had spent time as all young girls did, imagining the bestowal of gifts from her beloved. She'd pictured it as a time of great tenderness and sharing, of gifts from the heart, one to the other. This was a cold gesture, as meaningless as the marriage she'd been forced to suffer. And she was desolate. Why these empty symbols of another world should hurt her so, she didn't understand. Yet hurt she did, and it was a deep, hollow ache that touched cruelly upon all her young dreams and hopes. Moisture gathered in her eyes in a moment of weakness she would not allow. She blinked determinedly to deny it. Like all the other troubles, denial did not change fact.

A brisk tapping upon the door intruded upon her misery, and was followed almost immediately by the bustling figure of a woman.

"I saw you arrive and thought I would give you time to settle in before I came to welcome you," the newcomer claimed in boisterous tones. "I am Eva Loockermann, your neighbor across the vay. Mine is the brick house there." She gestured briefly, then regarded Evangeline with a broad smile. "How good it is to have another woman so near. One gets tired of only having one's self for company."

Royle rose from his knees and gave them a dusting.

114

Eva Loockermann's bright blue eyes ran from toe to crown in unabashed appreciation. Her grin grew even wider, and the pleasure in her gaze increased.

"I'm Royle Tanner and my wife, Evangeline."

She seized his hand for a vigorous pumping. "Pleased to meet you. Vill you be staying long?" The flirtatious cant to her eyes conveyed her wish that it be so.

"I am managing Uriah Webster's trading station."

Unlike Evangeline—who tensed at the mention— Eva grew more animated. "Vonderful! My late husband Jacobus came to this country in the uniform of the West Indies Company. Such a dashing figure he vas. But you are not from Nieuw Amsterdam."

"London."

The blue eyes took the measure of Evangeline's silk gown. "And your lady looks not the type used to this rough life. You'll be needing help and time to adjust, I think, and I am just the one to help, yah? I brought a meal for your table, as the hour is late and you'll be vanting to settle yourselves." She motioned to the kettle set beside the door. "'Tis just spoon meat, nothing fancy, but filling. It only needs be brought to a boil every day to keep it presentable. I be baking bread this night and vill bring you some hot on the morrow along with a morning draft."

"You're very kind," Royle murmured as Evangeline stood silent.

"'Tis nothing. We are all neighbors here, and do for one another when we can. I have also a spark for your fire, so you might not be cold on your first night." Her gaze slid to the prominent bedstead and lingered with longing. Then she looked back to Royle and smiled. "I should go now before my welcome be worn. Good evening to you, Royle Tanner and Frau Tanner." She was gone in a swirl of starched petticoats, and the room seemed all the quieter for her absence.

"A fine lady," Royle remarked. Evangeline surprised him with a withering glance and a haughty tip of her nose.

"She meddles in things that are not her concern."

He puzzled over that for a moment. Had Evangeline been a proper English wife, he would say her reply smacked of feminine jealousy and possessive pride. But that was not the case, and he forbade himself from being encouraged. His tone was dry when he said, "I did not know you already had plans for our dinner, that you would resent her offer of food."

"She should keep to her own house," was all his bride would say.

Royle did smile then, and busied himself with putting away their wedding gifts. Their clothing they would leave in their bags until he could purchase suitable chests for storage. As Evangeline did not see fit to do so—for all her curt words—he saw to the fire and to their evening meal, which was eaten in silence upon the Holland cloth and Delft. He felt festive, even if his new wife was determined to sulk. This was the beginning of his prosperous life, and he was pleased.

Evangeline munched begrudgingly upon the hearty stew, refusing to enjoy its flavor. As autumnal hours brought a quickening of darkness, she remained still upon her stool, trying to keep her worried gaze from stealing to the bed. Though she'd no memory of their wedding night, she knew well what had transpired between them. Yellow-haired Tanner had claimed the rights of a husband, and she was not ignorant of what that would mean this night and on those that followed. She had vowed to resist

116

his touch, to fight him should he attempt to force his stolen priviliges. Her pride insisted upon it. Her frail heart feared a return of those strange flutters of weakness that came with his kiss.

While she fretted and fidgeted at the table, Royle picked up one of the books and settled himself before the fire. He seemed oblivious to her distress, though on occasion she would catch him peering at her over the pages. Finally, weariness and dignity provoked her from her seat. In the deep shadows of the room, she shed her hated white garb, then, contrarily kept on the concealing chemise. No sense in tempting him should his thoughts not be turned in that direction.

She crawled up onto the high bed and sank into the husk-filled mattress. The plump pillows elevated her into a half-reclined position, to fit within the short bed frame. The covers were cool. She chafed bare feet together to warm them, lest he be prompted to consider other ways to inspire heat. Then she pretended slumber, and covertly watched the man before the fire. When he rose, she instinctively shrank into the yielding bed, covers clutched as if to ward off his attack. Wary eyes followed him as he first checked the rifle against the stones, then locked away several sharp knives into a slat top desk. Curiosity overcame her fears as he gathered several pots and strung them together. He seemed satisfied with their noisy clatter, then proceeded to string them upon both doors. Any attempt to open them would result in a deafening din, loud enough to wake even the soundest sleeper. Evangeline grimaced. He was protecting himself and his property, of which he considered her a part. Then he came to bed.

Swathed in his loose-fitting shirt, he slipped beneath the ready warmed sheets. Evangeline held herself tense and waited. If he moved toward her, she was ready for flight or fight. Minutes stretched out and her muscles grew sore and trembly from the strain. Finally, he made a low sound. It was a snore.

The breath left her in a shaky sigh. And so she passed her first night in the dubious comfort of her marriage bed.

Chapter Eight

It was the brightness of the day as much as the sound of voices that startled Evangeline upon waking. The hour was mid-morning. Never had she slept so far into a day. The hushed conversation she heard in the room beyond her canopy of pulled bed curtains was between Royle and *that woman*. She felt an unfamiliar prickle of annoyance shorten her temper and prod her into thoughts of throwing back the curtains in a rage to toss the interloper from her house. She did not. It wasn't her inbred reserve that held her. It was surprise. *Her house*. Why would she consider it so, and why did the idea of the jolly female entertaining the Englishman cast her into an agitation of anxiety and ire?

The woman's laughter filled the air, and Royle's was heard in response. His was a low, husky melody of sound, one she'd not witnessed before. It created a strange stirring within her breast, just as the she-creature's caused a tightening in her belly. She was excluded from their merriment, tucked away and forgotten in the imprisoning bed, and she resented their amusement and the intrusion upon her calm. Her thoughts weren't of her control, nor were the odd

119

feelings. It was the exposure to this irrational race, she decided. It was coloring her actions and seeping into her mind, weakening both with unworthy sentiments and dismays. That realization was coldly sobering, serving to starch her backbone with disavowing pride. What did she care if the white man chose to converse with one of his own kind? It relieved her of his unwanted attentions at least, and of the awkwardness of being in his company alone. Better they not be alone.

Evangeline confronted a new dilemma, that of leaving her bed in dignity. She refused to creep from behind the curtains in her rumpled state, to the knowing looks of that woman who would undoubtedly draw her own intimate conclusions about how the newlyweds had passed their first night. Such thoughts of modesty and embarrassment had never plagued her before, and her displeasure soared. Curses for both parties came to her lips.

Before she was forced to commit to some action, a new voice was added, that of a man. After pleasantries were exchanged, the men withdrew to the front room, leaving her with only the sound of the other woman clanking about Evangeline's kitchen.

"Oh, there you are, my dear," Eva cried in genuine welcome as she spied movement amid the curtains. "I hope we did not wake you vith our talking. I sent the men avay so you could have some time to make ready."

Evangeline placed bare feet solidly on the cold planks. Her narrowed eyes betrayed her irritation, but the jovial woman was too busy bustling in an efficient frenzy to make note of it.

"There is fresh bread on the table and chocolate, too. I hope you like it. 'Tis my favorite in the mornings, yah."

Since it was obvious the woman was not going to leave her in peace, Evangeline rose and shrugged into her dress of the day before, having little care for its wrinkled state. She was fastening the hooks when the scent of warm bread teased her appetite. As much as she would have liked to shun the woman's charity, that tantalizing aroma would not permit it. She dropped onto a stool and broke off a goodly piece to chew with surly fervor. The chocolate, being close at hand, was quickly consumed. It was a foreign taste, one she took to readily for its rich appeal.

"Vile the men be talking business, I thought we could get acquainted. I be Eva and Royle—I mean Mister Tanner," she amended as plump cheeks went rosy, "tells me you be Evangeline. Such a lovely name, and so fitting for such a pretty miss."

Evangeline didn't refute the name. What good would it have done, for the woman was already chattering happily. Eva Loockermann was a picture of exuberant goodwill, with her continual smile and merry blue eyes. What she lacked in height was compensated in proportions. Evangeline marveled that Eva could stir the stew without her ample bosom interfering. Her features were broad and unassumingly cheerful, the kind a man could look upon day after day to find ease of spirit. Her pale yellow hair was tightly pulled away from a face flushed with joy and exertion and covered with a quilted cap. Striped petticoats were worn short enough to display a length of dashingly clocked stocking whenever they swayed. Movement set a series of ribbons in motion as they dangled keys, scissors, and a pincushion from a narrow girdle that drew the eye to a waist as narrow as breasts and hips were bold. Having seen Royle eye those attributes with interest, Evangeline began to picture Eva's pale hair fluttering from a lance.

121

"You have so many fine things, Evangeline. I hope you do not mind me putting away your clothes. They were so crushed inside that bag, and I happened to have a spare chest vich you can use until you find one to your liking. The one with all the pretty bows is such a becoming gown. I'm sure your husband would take much pleasure to see you vearing it." Eva's gaze went meaningfully to the deeply creased silk Evangeline wore and she stiffened. How dare the woman presume to tell her what Royle found pleasing! How dare she believe the illusion that Evangeline cared at all what he thought!

"This one pleases me," she stated crisply, and with that, she rose and went to join Royle in the other room—before she did the woman bodily harm.

The scent of Royle's pipe reached her before the men's voices, and it held her on the threshold. Inhaling deep of the pungent smoke, she was lost to a moment of poignant longing. For what? She didn't understand the strange quiet misery that twisted her soul and brought the odd wont to weep. It wasn't Royle or this place. What then? She closed her eyes. The wave of melancholy, sweet and sad, overwhelmed her. Desire and need rose strong, compelling her to go to the man on the stocky chair, to put her arms about him and let her head rest upon his breast, to seek comfort there. She rebelled against those frightening feelings. Was it the dream forcing her to realize her destiny? Logic told her that she would find no security here, yet a power beyond reason argued opposite. She stared at the yellow-haired man. Panic swelled to combat the longing. How could the Fates link her to such as him, not of her kind, not of her world? She tried to draw strength from that denial, and the task left her shivering.

Oblivious to her presence, Royle pulled on the clay

mouthpiece and exhaled a bluish cloud. It momentarily concealed the redheaded man across from him. Listening to Barnabas Maxell stirred Royle's blood with excitement and challenge. So much to learn, so much to accomplish. He was anxious to get started, to plunge himself into his own endeavors and to see fruit yielded from the seeds of his effort. This was a new start for him. No one here in Albany knew any different than the image he presented, that of a prosperous trader in the employ of an influential man. They would look upon the fine clothes he wore and assume they established his rightful status. No one would guess him a common laborer's son, no better and probably much less than most of them. He would be respected fairly for his accomplishments, not for his heritage or the lack thereof. Here, he could become anything, and that knowledge was savored and stored away to be relished at a later time. He had stepped beyond the dim back streets of London, toward the future his father held up to prod him to do his best. And he would make it all worthwhile. He would not fail.

It was then he saw the faint movement, the shimmer of silk he would always associate with the apparition of Evangeline Carey. His notice drew the other man's attention and they both stood, the other awkwardly but with no less respect.

"Mister Maxell, my wife Evangeline."

Royle reached for her hand and waited. Would she rebel and spoil all his carefully nurtured dreams? Would she call him sham before these residents of Albany by refusing to comply to the illusion he'd draped about them? He waited, breath suspended, hand outstretched, and then hers was compliantly given. As he drew her into the room, her fingers tightened briefly within his. There was a desperation to it that made him seek her expression. Her wide gray eyes held his rapt. What was it about that intense stare? Not fear. Not exactly. It was a hint of vulnerability, of resistance, of surrender. What? She seemed to reach out to him with that entreating gaze. To what purpose?

Then it was gone. When he would have gladly postponed his future to explore that potent look, it was shuttered away behind opaque eyes. Her fingers slipped from his as she settled upon a low stool at his side, the image of a dutiful wife. That impression was troubling. That he missed whatever she'd tried to convey plagued him. He sensed an opportunity that would not come again, but circumstance had snatched it away.

"I be just plain Max, Mistress Tanner," their guest announced as he resumed his seat with an ill-concealed grimace of distress. There was an odd twist to the man's leg, and it was obvious that it gave him discomfort.

Royle brushed fingers along Evangeline's shoulder, hoping to recapture what had passed between them. Her subtle shift of movement made objection to both touch and overture. She was once again on her guard.

Knowing the topic would force that wedge deeper, Royle said softly, "Max is from the trading house. He's come to explain my duties."

There was a slight stiffening. Nothing more. But it was enough. Irrationally, he was annoyed that she would despise his work. He had hoped to share his pride, his accomplishment, but she wanted no part of either. So be it, he decreed. He would revel in it alone.

"I was just telling your husband some of the basics, Ma'am, things you'd like find not to your interest."

"But I am interested," she intoned flatly. "Please

124

go on."

Barnabas Maxell looked between them. Instinct told him the picture was askew. Common sense told him to mind his business. He cleared his throat and continued his tutelage. On first glance, he'd doubted that this naive Englishman had the stuff to take on the raw wilderness. Now, his opinion grew more favorable. Tanner had a direct stare, a forthright speech, and both would benefit his dealings with the Indians. He just might do well. His predecessor had been slick of word and manner. Insincerity bred distrust, and rightly so in his case. This one, if taught well, could go far.

"Webster's got hisself a sweet piece of business here, if he can get a good man in control. Albany sits on the pulse of the Five Nations and smack in the middle of all roads to the interior. A smart man could make that work for hisself. 'Tis more than trade, furs for white man's knowledge. 'Tis trust that will gain more than shrewdness. Not even Webster hisself understands that, but me, I know these people. You gots to know them, too, if you want to make good here."

"The Indians, you mean." Royle was uncomfortably aware of Evangeline at his side. He wished he knew of the thoughts that spun behind her quiet gaze. There was nothing tranquil beyond her outward appearance. That much he understood very well.

"Aye, the Indians, and there be a lot of them in these parts, Iroquois mostly. They be the ones you'll deal with up front. Don't let yourself be fooled by the look of them. They may appear to be savages, but they be a savvy lot. Sometimes I think we don't come close to being as civilized as them that rove the woods. They can be your brothers, or they can be your worst nightmare."

Royle allowed himself a wry smile. Evangeline sat very still, listening intently to the bent little man.

What Barnabas Maxell went on to describe rivaled the most sophisticated society. He told of a formalized government, of a democracy of elected leaders. Decisions made by the Iroquois councils were discussed in the royal courts of England and France. Chiefs were taken abroad and courted by all nations, vying for strategic position in the New World. They held the balance and control in any plan for expansion into the interior. That power lifted them from the realm of simple savages. They stretched across New York, controlling the Mohawk Valley, and with it the gateway to the furs of the west, and from that position, they exploited trade, playing the English at Albany against the French on the St. Lawrence. Though the Treaty of Albany had them pledged as allies to the English, they weren't above bargaining for the best profit, not unlike Uriah Webster and those of his cut.

"Tomorrow be soon enough for me to take you to the post," Max continued. "I can better show you there what you'll be doing. 'Twill give you time to settle in here with your missus. I hope she'll not be finding us too backward for her tastes. Things be right rough, but we make do. Not all them of quality can adapt, though. Webster and his family were never cut out for the life. You treats nature and her people with respect, and you'll get by fine. Then, iffen your lady gets to missing her home too much, I can always fill in for a week or so while you take her back for a visit."

Royle was at a loss. The man assumed Evangeline hailed from New York, when in truth she was closer to her native land right here in Albany. He glanced at

126

her and her quiet gaze gave him no assurance. Would she expose the truth of their relationship to spite his plans? She hated him enough. She had no reason to continue the pretense at his side. How she must be laughing at him for his bold airs, for pretending she was a tender, pampered English wife. He stewed, he simmered, he fretted until her quiet phrase put him at ease. It was simple, and not a lie.

"You are very kind, Mister Maxell."

Royle was staggered with relief. And suspicion. What would the retention of this charade cost him? Did she mean to hold it over him like some damning sword, to bend him to her will? His gratitude soured, and he gave her a piercing look which she promptly ignored.

Such a compliment from so gracious a lady fused his stubbly cheeks a ruddy crimson. "It be Max, Ma'am, and you're right welcome." He cleared his throat and hurried on with business. "The Mohawks be the ones you'll see the most. Their towns—castles, they call 'em—are along the south side of the Mohawk River between Canajoharie and Schoharie creeks. They be the boldest of the Five Nations, the shrewdest traders and the fiercest fighters. The Narragansetts gave them their name. It means man-eaters. Guess I don't have to spell out how they came by it. Most still go by their proper name, Caniengas."

Royle gave a start. His breath caught up short in his throat, and it was with difficulty that he didn't turn to Evangeline in alarm. The Indians he would deal with were his wife's chosen people. And he had led her blindly into their midst.

The day wore on lazily with both their guests in no hurry to leave. Barnabas Maxell, the wiry little man

127

with his crooked leg, had an obvious liking for the buxom Frau Loockermann, and was persuaded to stay for an afternoon meal without much coaxing. The jolly Dutch woman insisted she provide for the newcomers and happily pushed her way into control of the kitchen. Evangeline sat silent on her stool and watched them socialize. The placid smile affixed to her face spoke little of her thoughts.

She'd seen the way the color had left Royle Tanner's cheeks. Though she'd hoped the truth be kept from him a bit longer, she knew he would discover it soon. Now his guard would increase upon her, and she wondered if on this night, the bindings would be back about her wrists.

During the afternoon, she would feel his gaze upon her, those eerie green eyes that spoke other truths she would not accept. She could almost sense his uncomfortable panic. Her past was closing in about him, and he knew not how to protect from it. She could almost feel regret for his upset. Almost. He would understand now why she'd not tried harder to escape him on the trail, for this was where she was going. She was home, or close enough to it for her to feel confident. She had only to wait. She would play his game with the foolish whites of this settlement. It would be her way of thanking him for saving her from the Websters. It was the least she could do—the absolute least—before escaping him without a backward thought. Had she thought on it, she would have been appalled by this minor allowance. He deserved her contempt, and every ounce of her strength should have gone toward defying him. She should have emerged from the bed in her naked native splendor and boldly proclaimed she was no white man's wife. Yet the subtle possessive barbs that needled beneath her flesh at the thought of the

128

plump white squaw's insinuation in Evangeline's home demanded she make a stand, if a false one at the Englishman's side. She would not be ignored in favor of the woman's obvious flirtations. The attentions of Royle Tanner belonged to her, whether she wanted them or not! And then there was the wavering weakness she'd succumbed to throughout her association with this man. Her traitorous wish to welcome his touch made her pridefully determined to resist them. The strange melancholy that preyed upon her soul when she'd come into the room, held her with a frightening fascination to know its source. Was it the power of this man that so confused her reason? Or was it something beyond? Whichever, it made her submit for the moment at his side, while the puzzle of her thoughts continued to plague her.

Their visitors stayed late into the eve, supplying most of the conversation, and blind to the lack of it on the part of their hosts. When quaint tales of Holland and sterner stuff concerning Albany had been talked out, and the quantity of beer flowing into oft-raised mugs had the company pleasantly nodding, good nights were exchanged and the doors bolted behind them. It was then Evangeline came to attention, waiting for her husband's outburst.

There was no explosive accusation. He turned to her almost cordially, to inquire with disarming ease, "Why did you not tell me your people were here?"

"I did not think it would interest you," she replied. Her tone was deceivingly cool. Inside, she was in tumult trying to guess what he would do. "Was it your plan to invite them to dine with us as well?"

"With me as the main course? Not bloody likely."

They faced each other squarely, neither gaze giving quarter, neither frown willing to relent. Then Royle spun away and began his restless pacing. Her eyes followed. This time, it was *his* expression that was inscrutable, and not knowing his mind had Evangeline on edge. Would he take her back to the confinement of New York? Would he keep her bound, a prisoner in this, their home? He had no reason to trust her, and every reason to suspect her motives.

Royle knew a poorly contained fury. Bad enough his plans should go so awry with the discovery of his bride's upbringing . . . or the lack of it. Now he had to endure not only the threat of her escape, but the knowledge that any moment he could be besieged by savage natives intent upon her return. He felt helpless, and that didn't aid his mood. He paused in his anxious travels to regard her. "Is it your plan to slip away, or do you mean to wait for them to come for you?" Her chin rose a stubborn notch and he scowled. "I've already told you, I'll not let you go."

"And you have been warned that you cannot make me stay."

The stalemate gathered tension. His steps grew short with agitation. Large hands opened and closed at his sides.

"We are legally wed, Evangeline. All you are belongs to me."

"Not by the laws of my people," was her level claim.

"And they would break the white man's law and endanger their treaty by taking you from me?" He didn't know if an intrusion into their marital situation would be reason for broader notice, but Evangeline seemed to consider it as if it would. She turned very pale beneath her golden flesh, and he felt a surge of power.

Evangeline's thoughts spun. Was he right? If she fled from him back to her people, would there be

130

consequences? She had promised her father to act honorably for the benefit of their clan. To go back on that oath now sat unwell with her, especially if her people would suffer for her inconsistency. How then could this situation be endured? There must be some escape that would be good for all and cause ill to none. Then she was seized by sudden inspiration. It was most logical to her, and she offered her reasoning as if it held the solution to all. Surely he would not reject it, for what purpose was there to holding a reluctant woman to serve as wife, when others were eager for the post. She thought of Eva Loocker-mann's bright eyes, and the words came less eagerly.

"You must trade with my people if you are to profit. Without their good will, you will fail." She had his attention. It etched his features into bold, harsh lines. Encouraged, she continued to detail her proposition. "I could guarantee their cooperation. I could help you make your post the most successful in all New York. Release me from this ridiculous bond of marriage, and I will see you richer than my uncle."

He was very still now. His green eyes shone, a hard, keen emerald fire. Like all white men, he was led by his lust for possessions. That common avarice gave her a stab of savage disappointment and she was angry with him, even though that unworthy greed would gain her what she desired.

"No."

She was stunned. She was overjoyed. And then she realized what he denied her, and fury flared. Why did he have to be different among his lesser, grubbing brothers? Oh, why couldn't he let her go? She voiced that frustration, for once baring her emotions to display her desolation.

"Fool. Stupid white man. Cannot you see that I will destroy you? You don't think my people know

131

that I am here? They will come, and you will not be able to stop them. They will take your head for your trouble." She paused, panting hard. There was a vague whisper of fear in his brilliant gaze, but it in no way lessened the determination there. Foolish man. Brave, foolish man.

"For what? Why do you do this? For a wife? I hate you. I despise you and your world." She saw him flinch slightly at that attack and pursued it mercilessly. "Why would you risk so much to keep someone who loathes you, who would cheerfully see you without your hair? I will never wait upon your whims like that squaw with her plump affections. I will not be wife to you. In my mind, this marriage has been ended. You are nothing to me. How can you pretend that I matter to you?"

His reply was so soft, she had to strain to hear it.

"You've no idea what you mean to me."

A tremor seized her. Not of rage. Of wonder. Of inexplicable hope. And of desire.

That instant of weakness fueled her passions, with fear as strongly as denial. To purge herself, she acted from instinct. His surprised response was almost too slow, yet he managed to catch her as she launched herself upon him, all bared teeth and viciously wielded nails. She prided herself on her physical strength. She had wrestled village bucks up until her fourteenth year, when She-Walks-Far said without reason that it had to be stopped. The majority of the matches she had won, including against her own brother. She hadn't expected to find a matching power in this soft white man. Yet he restrained her with ease. And that defeat wrought humiliation untold and unimagined.

She was jerked close to him. His body was hard, unyielding, and contrarily, hers felt suddenly frail.

132

There seemed to be no power within her legs to still their trembling. Even her breath shivered.

"You are mine, Evangeline. No one takes what is mine."

Those words, spoken low with rough certainty, increased her helplessness. Destiny shone bright in his eyes, and hers began to drift shut. He was going to kiss her. She should have rebelled against it, yet the strange liquefaction of her bones grew more pronounced. She found herself leaning upon him, her lips moistening, preparing for possession.

Then, abruptly, she was freed.

The unexpected forced her to face her disgrace. She had wanted him, had craved his touch, had yearned to feel his mastery. Surely there could be no greater shame. Blood surged to her cheeks, staining them with humiliation, with anger. With regret. And then he spoke flatly, unemotionally, to seal her misery.

"Ready yourself for bed while I see we have no uninvited guests."

Unable to recover the pride her own weakness had stripped from her, Evangeline mutely did as told. In her pale shift, she crawled beneath the covers atop the cold, coarse linen, and curled into herself. Frustration shook through her like a sickness as she heard him string the pots at the doors and firmly latch the shutters. Then he came to bed.

Royle lay still in the muted darkness provided by their bed curtains. She had wanted him. He'd felt it, and the power of his own desire. Both surprised him. He'd grown accustomed to her hate, to her scorn, to her unexpected attacks, but the sudden softening of her tough veneer gave him a violent tumble. It unbalanced him and made him uncertain of his own powerful response. He'd wanted to seize her up, to capture her luscious lips, to demand total submission. But he feared her weakening was but a momentary thing. Had he plunged ahead with his own urgent wants, he suspected he'd find no willing woman in his embrace. And he didn't want to force her return of affection. He could savor no surrender if it was coerced. He didn't trust her reactions, nor his own around her. His mind was too fueled by the remembrance of her soft skin, of the encompassing heat of her untested body. Of the chill of her rejection. If he turned to her now to offer a gentle touch, he would be soundly rebuffed. If he attempted to find comfort beside her, he would discover a contrary discontent. Better he be satisfied that she be close at hand. Better he wait until sure of his reception. Better still, he should not tempt himself to test his earlier vow.

Evangeline listened to his breathing as it grew deep and regular with sleep. How dare he find rest when she was knotted with distress! She wanted to carve out his heart for bringing her such confusion of spirit. She wanted to seek his arms and demand to know the feel of his mouth upon hers. White man. Her man. He was the destiny revealed to her in her dreams. There seemed no answer to this turmoil of disgust, duty, and desire.

She squeezed her eyes shut and prayed to all the gods she could remember that deliverance would come soon.

Chapter Nine

The clatter of pots jerked him from his slumber with one horrible thought. She was trying to escape him.

Royle's panicked gaze flew to the door to find it undisturbed. It was then he felt her warmth beside him, curled close into his side. Her small palm rested upon his middle in a familiar, claiming gesture. Her long black hair spread like satin upon the pillows. She was a goddess in repose. For a moment, the noise at the door was forgotten as muscles wrenched tight and taut beneath that hand. He had known her once, and not at all. The need to have her now rose to an overwhelming ache. He'd seen surrender in her eyes last night, so unexpected it had unnerved him with his want to believe it true. He had vowed not to take her unwilling, and some vows were harder to honor than others. This one was becoming intolerable.

Before he gave way to the need to feel her smooth flesh fill his palm, the clamor at the door sounded again. Evangeline came awake, and her hand pulled away as if bitten. She regarded him through a narrow accusing gaze, as if she suspected him of some wrongful doings, and the coverlet hitched up high to cover the nearly bare slope of sun-warmed shoulders. Awakened, his goddess of beauty became a goddess of wrath. He was not fool enough to mistake the warning in her stare. Nor was he able to ignore the rightful indignation that it should be issued in *his* bed by *his* wife.

Unable to bear the chill of her pale eyes, and knowing he would have no time to warm them from their frosty bite, Royle rolled from the bed to tug on his breeches, then padded barefoot to the door. His expression was hardly welcoming toward the little man on the stoop.

"Expecting trouble?" Max questioned as he examined the noisy alarm in bemusement.

Royle was thankful that his attention was diverted. The flush rising hot to his face went unnoted. How to explain the device was to keep his wife in, rather than troubles at bay?

Max forgot the odd security measures when a rustle from the jack bed took his notice. The sight of Evangeline Tanner—her black hair wild about her shoulders—nearly stupefied him. Blushing fiercely, he turned back to Royle and stammered, "I thought you'd like to get an early start."

A distracted hand raked through his hair as he followed Maxell's gaze. What a picture she presented, of wild passion unfettered, of dangerous allure, of seductive invitation. A true work of art, and just as unobtainable. And just as Royle Tanner meant to own a fine collection of valuables, he was equally determined to count this pagan lovely among them. He remembered the cause for him leaving her alone upon that beckoning bed and murmured a curt, "Yes. Of course."

The little man cast another discreet glance across the room and offered a small smile. "I believe I smelled fresh bread from the widow Loockermann's. I'll await you there."

By the time Royle shut the door behind their early guest, Evangeline had slipped from the bed and was struggling into a gown. It was the one with the bows, the one Eva had claimed her husband would find pleasing. She refused to attach meaning to her choice. Yet, when he turned toward her and stopped dead, she couldn't stop a purely feminine satisfaction from warming through her. His gaze absorbed the sight of her, lingering over the snug embrace of fabric about her tiny waist, dipping along the wide, low neckline, and trailing down the full flowing skirt where uniform pleating delineated the long line of her legs. She wondered what he saw. A savage pretending to be a lady, or a woman. That she should wonder at all disturbed her.

The gown was a mistake. Fastenings ran up the back, and she could manage only the lowest. She fumbled with them, trying to decide if the wisest course would be disrobing before his ever-heating stare, or dashing across the street to Eva Loockermann's for assistance. Neither made her comfortable.

"Let me." It was a deep rumble. The thickly spoken words could have meant anything.

Rather than betray her increasing unease around him and show herself a coward, Evangeline presented her back and drew a steeling breath. She clenched her teeth and ordered her body not to tremble as the gown came together one hook at a time. When the service was done, she still was not free, for his large hands capped her shoulders. Strong fingers tightened and eased in a sensuous caress that spread a seditious languor throughout her traitorous form. He was standing close but not quite touching. Still the power of him radiated, consuming her, conspiring against her. She heard his breath rasp with curious difficulty next to her ear, growing louder as his head bent near. Her contempt for him as a white man couldn't erase the fact that he was a man, and her reactions were atuned to that basic truth. Just the thought that he meant to kiss her was enough to encourage a tremulous excitement, a yearning for . . . for what, she didn't know. She only knew that when he straightened without imparting the experience of his heated lips, she was ravaged with disappointment.

The knowledge of how close she was to yielding stiffened her flagging will. What was she thinking? He was the enemy. With a brusque shrug of her shoulders to discourage his touch—a bit too late— she stepped away. When she faced him, her expression was an impassive mask.

"What am I to do with you?" he asked softly, and her gaze grew immediately wary. Because her thoughts were already tangled amid the sheets, her gaze darted there in dismay. He smiled ruefully at her puzzlement and explained. "There's little chance I'd find you here upon my return, yet how can I engage someone to guard you lest I tell you the reason why."

"Are you ashamed to have it known you keep your wife a prisoner?"

Her retort hit hard and too near the truth. How, indeed, would he explain their relationship? They were not as isolated as he had hoped. What if someone—namely Eva Loockermann—was to come in unexpectedly to find Evangeline bound in his absence. It was one thing to restrain a willful wife. It was quite another to keep one physically disabled. Nor did he wish to explain away his reasonings for treating his bride the way one would a wild creature; the reason being, she was one. There had to be some solution to save both reputation and wife. His gaze shifted to the narrow stairs that led to the low-ceiled empty rooms of the second floor. Evangeline followed his stare and its meaning. She paled.

"Tanner, do not lock me away."

It was a simple plea, one that expressed her distress at confinement in eloquent terms. Her hand unwittingly clutched his sleeve, and it was as if she'd caught his heart as well in that desperate grip. It was the only sign of her anguish. She would not beg him. Memories of the small room at the Websters' crowded about her, and she knew she could not bear that stifling captivity again.

Royle caught the hint of panic in her voice and wondered at it. He didn't ask her to explain the fear; that it existed was enough. He would not purposefully terrify her, regardless of his own worries. His first thought was to soothe away the frightened creases marring her proudly perfect features. His hand covered hers, squeezing gently, reassuringly, and instinctively she responded with a trusting relief. After having that precious concession, he had to devise some compromise, and quick lest that tenuous warmth freeze solid with disgust.

"If I take you with me, do you promise to behave?"

Evangeline's breath escaped in an unintentional display of relief. She nodded. Any promise was worth the scent of free air and warm sun. The white man's walls were a confining prison, forbidding the elements necessary for growth, and she was like a woodland flower, withering within. Her eyes shone with unvoiced gratitude. The irony of thanking the very man who kept her from her longed-for liberties for giving her but a teasing taste of them now, escaped her.

Knowing himself a fool for even asking for her

word, let alone believing it, Royle sighed. There had to be compromises. How else were they ever to get beyond this stalemate of prisoner and captor. He didn't want a wife who needed to be leashed at all times. Perhaps if he gave her back her freedom an increment at a time, she would not be so tempted to bolt. And that warming in her gaze was reward enough for the risk he was taking. After all, it was not as though he intended to turn his back.

Uriah Webster's trading house was a goodly walk outside the boundaries of Albany. The air was so crisp it nearly hurt to draw it deeply. A snap of autumnal warning braced the morning beneath the spread of majestic trees, and a carpet of pine needles quieted their passing. It was as if the great forest slumbered. And Royle Tanner felt dwarfed by its magnificence.

With Max hobbling a few steps ahead to lead the way, and Royle's hand but a light restraint upon her arm, Evangeline, too, was caught up in the awesome splendor. The moment was untainted by the two intruders, and she forgot them in her private reverie. They wouldn't understand her kinship with nature, her respect for all she saw. They were white men. They only knew how to control, not how to coexist. This quiet, powerful wood held the secret to life itself. From its trees and streams came shelter, clothing, and food. All the elements of nature were intertwined. Each rock, bush, and forest-bordered creek contained a spirit not unlike her own. The white men trampled those souls, just as they would crush the heart of her people because they were ignorant and would not learn. How could one look to the thunder, the winds, the sun and stars, and yet be blind to the power of those gods. She was humbled anew to walk as one with them. Only the foreign bind of her swaddling clothes kept her from soaring with the trees and racing with the breezes. That, and the touch of Royle Tanner's hand.

The post squatted on the trail's edge, its rough-hewn structure nearly blending into the trees. It resembled a hastily built shed rather than a booming mercantile, and Royle's hopes knew a shiver to their foundation. This was the basis for his future? My God, it was another cruel joke played by Uriah Webster, and this devastated even more than the first. He tried not to let disillusionment weight his expectations. But it wasn't easy.

A broad porch faced the front of the building. Upon it, three men lounged with crude bundles at their feet. Royle couldn't help staring. It was the Englishman's first glimpse of the New World's native people. And he was properly shocked. They were handsome, proud, and nearly naked. Bronzed skin, toned and sleek, was uncovered but for a strip of cloth a foot wide and several feet long, looped between their legs and held for modesty's sake by a string about the waist. They wore soft leather slippers upon their feet. One of the men had hair as long as Evangeline's woven into glossy plaits. The others had a ridge of stiff black hair bristling several inches high from forehead to nape, and that was all. The rest had been shaved away. Were these of his wife's people? The thought of her exposed daily to so much virile male flesh offended his staid upbringing. And the question of how he compared in her eyes made an equally disturbing rumble. His hand tightened possessively upon her arm, and her stiffening told of her displeasure. He forced himself to relax his grip and to walk with his bride and Barnabas Maxell up the uneven plank steps. He was

141

grateful when the little man didn't pause but went directly inside the building. Then, the Indians were forgotten in favor of his prospects.

Appearances were deceiving. He would never have believed from his first look at the trading house that it could hold such a bulk of goods. Aside from a crude wooden counter, all, from floor to rafters, was merchandise. The valuable English goods included metal hardware, knives, scissors, awls, fishhooks, needles, pins, cloth, finished clothing, and countless articles of glass, iron, brass, and copper, crowded together to represent all that was desirable in the white world. Behind the counter were the most precious commodities; the casks of rum and crates of firearms. His excitement knew a hurried restoration.

The Indians had filed in silently behind them, and Royle knew a strange prickling along his scalp, as if his hair feared an imminent parting.

"I'll see to their wants, then I can show you about," Max said and took the three natives to the planked table. Their packs were placed upon it, and when untied, out spilled a luxurious wealth of peltry from rich sable to flat black. Words were spoken back and forth, a language of gutteral tones and lengthy aspirations. Max listened, alternately nodding and shaking his head until they all seemed to come to an agreement. The furs were swept behind the counter and replaced with their bargained value; two copper pots, a length of coarse wool, several cards of buttons and thread, and a gleaming flintlock. Several bottles joined the scattering of goods. Then all was bundled together, and the three left as silently as they'd come.

As much as he was interested in the details of the trade, Royle's attention was distracted in another direction. Covertly, he watched his wife. She seemed to pay no heed to the Indians, nor they to her.

Perhaps they were not of the Mohawks after all. Perhaps she was so changed in her white garb that they would not know her. Royle tried to make himself believe this. Yet he was still tense, tense and wary. He wasn't ready to begin trusting Evangeline. Every instant his hand was not upon her to insure that she stayed at his side, he feared she would run. And once in the woods, was there a chance he would ever find her? He remembered the kitten and began to grimly consider tying her to the stoutest post. What was the opinion of others, compared to nights alone in that big bed? Indeed, if she fled him, the bed would not be his to claim. All balanced on Evangeline, and it was a precarious counterweight.

Max dusted off a low barrel with his sleeve and offered, "Your missus can seat herself here whilst we talk." His perplexed gaze stated his curiosity. Why a man would want to bring his lady to such a place of business was beyond him, yet 'twas not his business in either case. The pretty Mistress Tanner would just have to content herself with her own amusements while they attended to the matters at hand.

Royle steered Evangeline to the proffered seat, and his intense gaze bade her stay. Docilely, she arranged her skirts and adopted an indifferent mien. Still, Royle was not convinced. He wondered if a discreet tether about the bottom of the barrel would be enough to secure her. Then her cool gray eyes lifted, and he was ashamed to his very soul for considering such thoughts. She had given her word, and her gaze affirmed that promise. He would keep himself conspicuously between her and the doorway.

Max hoisted the pelts back to the counter and spread them out, inviting Royle to examine them.

"Beautiful, are they not? Get used to the feel of them and the colors. You must be able to tell a

143

superior skin from one of little value, and believe me, they will test that knowledge daily until they respect your judgment." He coaxed Royle's hand down to the first skin. It was sleek, almost velvety to the touch. "This be beaver, the one they be hungry for in your country. They be nearly played out in these parts, and in much demand. 'Tis why our Mohawk brethren tend to regulate what comes into this territory from the interior. That way, they can take the best for themselves. We don't care who brings it or how it gets here, just about the quality of the skin. Next to beaver in value be the otter, here, raccoon, mink, fox, and bear. Think of them the way you would your Pine, Oak, and Willow Tree silver, like coinage in the hand. Instead of shillings, six-, three-, and twopence, this is what buys what we sell."

Royle handled each fur, noting the different textures and variations of color. Each was a prime example, and his admiration for the hunters of the woodland grew.

"Furs be but a part of native trade. They also bring in produce; maize, meat, fish, and fowl. 'Tis galling that these wild savages reap the fruit of the earth without working up a proper European sweat." He chuckled to himself, and Royle looked uncomfortably to Evangeline. If she was offended by the reference, her calm expression did not betray it. Then, she never betrayed much.

"They bring us furs and food to trade for the superiority of our European tools," Max continued as he sorted and stacked the pelts. "A steel hatchet don't shatter like stone. Woven cloth be better than animal skins. A copper kettle is easily carried and long of life. And then, there's the firearms. Most of them can't hit the side of a building, but the noise and smoke scare the devil out of their enemies. Even

144

the savages have their preferences, so you have to know their likings. The cogs of all the gunlocks have to have a good hold, otherwise they don't want them. In cloth, they prefer sad colors, deep blues and reds mostly, and they'd rather a good coarse blanket or length of broadcloth than fitted clothes. That way it can double as a coat and bedclothes. They don't have much regard for our fine English clothes. A woven garment is too quickly shredded by the rough life of the woods, and has to be washed and ironed to be proper. The Indians would rather go naked. You won't find a one of 'em who'd wear fitted trousers. Once in a while, you'll sell a shirt which will go unwashed on their body until it disintegrates. 'Tis almost better for the sake of delicacy that they keep to their robes. Unless they be part of one of the praying towns where good Christians have forced them into modest notions, cloth goods aren't of much use. Their young go sleek as otters 'til their thirteenth year. The men dress like them you just saw, and even their womenfolk go about bared above the waist except in winter.''

Royle couldn't keep his gaze from canting to the figure sitting serene and proper in her swathing of good English clothes. Had she gone about in abandon with her beauty displayed for all to see? He thought of her golden skin. Tanned all over. Embarrassment for her flooded through him, along with a forbidden thrill of excited jealousy. Heat rose to his face, and contrarily filled his loins. He made himself look away, though it was some time before he gained complete control over his labored breathing.

"This be as good as gold among the Iroquois,'' Max was saying, and Royle diverted his passions to the examination of a smooth white shell. His brow furrowed in curiosity.

"Wampum," Max explained. "Native shellfish from the coast. The Indians use the beads for decorations, gift giving, to ratify their treaties, and even to send messages. They give each color a meaning; white, purity and peace; black, war; covered with clay, grief. The way they're strung tells a story, if you know how to read it. A shortage of the shells makes them a good substitute for coin.

"On the Indian side, trade be seasonal according to produce and hunting, but their demand for English goods and wampum is year round. Mister Webster developed a credit system to tide them over from season to season. A profitable one it is, too. Land be the collateral for goods received on promise."

Evangeline's contemptuous words returned and Royle felt an uncomfortable pang. Was it business they were doing, or an excuse to steal valuable land for expansion? He looked to his wife with the beginnings of a frown to find her steady eyes upon him. He expected accusation, but was given a flat, inscrutable stare. Could it be the blame was of his own making? He dismissed it and her gaze. This was his business, after all. He didn't make the terms. He wouldn't be forcing the woodland people to put up their property. It was an exchange, a simple barter of faith. He reminded himself of how much Webster risked with each venture, and of how much he himself stood to lose. No, there were no victims here, just the universal components of trade. He girded himself with that knowledge, but Evangeline's words kept returning upon a staining whisper.

"I'll be here at the counter every day, if that be your pleasure, so don't feel you have to learn it all at once. I've manned this post for nearly two years, and will continue with your blessing."

Royle took note that reassurance was needed and

146

gave it quickly. "There's no one I'd rather have with me." It was an easy vow to make. He knew of no one else. He was also relieved that all the responsibility would not be his. These natives were a foreign people to him, and he felt shy around them. Until they sensed his confidence, it would not do for him to interfere with what Max handled so efficiently.

"What am I to do?" An odd question from one in charge, but one that needed asking. Max smiled at his honesty. Here was one who wouldn't be blundering his way through on charm and ignorance.

"Listen and learn. That be your best teacher next to experience. 'Til you feel comfortable bartering, there be a stack of scribbling to be put in the books. I ain't no good at that sort of thing. 'Twill get you familiar with prices, stock, and whatnot."

Royle nodded his agreement. Books and figures. Here was his element, and he was eager to apply himself. While Evangeline continued her indolent study of the hanging merchandise, he established himself on a corner of the counter with quill and homemade ink, and began to piece together the shambles of the record ledger. In his zeal, the time escaped him. Lunch was a hurried affair of dried meat and stale leftovers of bread from Eva Loockermann's kitchen. He chewed as he ciphered, and before he realized it, the sun had made a path from left to right across the rudely planked floor as noontime slipped into late afternoon. Alarmed, he looked to the barrel where Evangeline had been seated. To find it vacant dropped the bottom from his stomach. His gaze darted about the cramped quarters until he spied her at the far wall, scrutinizing her reflection in a display of small mirrors. Relief made him giddy, then guilt seeped in to take its place. How could he have expected her to remain like a statue while he pored over his books. Come evening, they would have to arrive at some arrangement, even if it meant trusting the Widow Loockermann with the secret of her past. He couldn't keep her bored and restless at his side day after day. Perhaps the jolly Dutchwoman would take on her instruction in the art of proper homemaking.

The thought of Evangeline awaiting him in their home with dinner set and a smile of welcome upon her lovely face did odd things to his concentration. Figures other than the slender one clad in plum-colored silk were edged from prominence in his mind. He let himself wander pleasantly through desirous daydreams, until called to attention by the knowledge that he was no longer alone.

The two of them had come to the counter as quietly as the breeze. Their black eyes touched on him only briefly before turning to Max and talk of trade. Both wore the scanty dress of the three who'd come in earlier. The taller of them wore a band of skin dyed black about his high forehead, from which a row of quill feathers rose to rival the bristle of his hair. The smaller but by no means slighter man had ornaments of shell and stones to decorate the nearly bald pate. In addition, he wore a pair of what would almost pass as trouser legs had they been joined at the hip by more than just thongs attached to his narrow waistband. Still, the garment managed to expose more than it covered.

Royle glanced nervously to Evangeline but she appeared unaware of them, still lost to whatever she saw in the glass. The Indians never once glanced her way. Nevertheless, Royle didn't draw an easy breath until they'd gone. No, he determined, he couldn't bring Evangeline to this place each day and face the eventual threat of her being recognized. Another solution would have to be found. Uneasily, he turned back to his work.

The day had been a dismal one for Evangeline. Expectations had soared upon seeing members of the Bear Clan, then died away when they did not know her. Was she so much changed? Royle's wary gaze said plainly that he would not be a lax keeper, so she dared not signal them in any way. She'd had to let them go, and with them her first chance at escape. But there would be others, she told herself. Someone would surely recognize her within the smothering English clothes, and take word back to her family. And they would come. She had to believe they would come, if for no other reason than to see if she was well. Then she wouldn't let them go without her.

She watched in disgust as her husband learned the ways of stealth and lies within the trading house. She had to bite her lip to keep silent when she wanted to shout the truth out loud. The fur trade her naive Englishman was so anxious to be a part of was tearing the lives of her people asunder. The lust for rum and the flintlock impelled hunters to kill more game than the land could support or replenish. How long before the means of their existence went the way of the beaver? Dependence upon the white man for his firepower and firewater seeped into every aspect of their lives, making warriors hunt for pelts instead of for food and clothing, even changing the way they made war, until traditional motives of revenge and honor became the desire to control trade centers. Mortality grew with the greater killing power of the guns. Liquor given by the white man destroyed the emotional reserve that was a cultivated part of their character. And then there was the ruin that came with the white man's credit. Royle Tanner would be killing her family and friends by slow degrees. And her resentment smoldered. The fool. Was it that he did not know or just that he did not care? She could accept no excuses for him.

And in time, if she remained with him, would she become just the same? That frightened her to the soul. The white man's way of life was as treacherous as their word. In distress, she moved to the tin glasses hung upon the wall to search for signs of change. Her features looked much the same, though some of her color was faded from being long within doors. The stifling gown looked disturbingly natural upon her lithe form. She thought of her own acceptance of it upon her back and was angry. When had she stopped fighting and let change steal in to alter what she was?

She was still glowering at that meek reflection when another passed close behind her. She caught a glimpse of dark, compelling eyes, and she was seized by an urgent trembling. She daren't turn around for a second look. She didn't need another to be sure. Long minutes crept by as she delighted in familiar voices, yet was forced to remain silent. Her whole body vibrated with anticipation. It screamed for the release of her joy. Her heart beat madly, each pulse singing her excitement.

She stayed where she was long after they'd gone, to make certain her composure was intact. Then, quietly, without raising her eyes, she resumed her seat and waited.

Chapter Ten

"'Twill be dark in less than an hour," Max announced as he went round closing shutters and latching them tight. "I for one have an invite to a sit-down hot meal and am anxious to get to it." His rosy color hinted that the offer was from the Widow Loockermann. His restless manner was that of randy buck in new clover.

Evangeline hid her smile. She had an odd liking for the brusque yet sweet little man, and was of a mood to wish him well. He had uncommon sense among white men and an insight to her people. Perhaps learning from him, Royle wouldn't be such a bad representative. And with the ample charms of Eva Loockermann attended to, she wouldn't feel so unsettled about her white husband. Her gaze turned reluctantly in his direction. He was still bent over the books, fading daylight gleaming gold upon the crown of his head as his quill scratched industriously. She'd avoided thought or sight of him all afternoon, and now both collided in a raw constriction within her breast. It made breathing hard, reason impossible. There was no logic in the fleeting pangs of loss and regret. One couldn't lose what one never held.

"I want to finish this page, Max. 'Twill take me hours to sort through this mess again in the morning. I'd as soon be done with it now. You go on." He didn't look up. Had he, he would have puzzled over the taut expression on his wife's face. Had he, he might have been forewarned.

Max shifted with uncertainty and impatience. He felt responsible, yet was eager to reach his destination. "Are you sure you can find the way?"

Royle did glance up then to allow a brief smile. "I won't fall off the path if that's what you mean. I'll see you in the morning." He waved a dismissing hand and Barnabas Maxell grinned his thanks. When he was gone, a quiet settled over the dim room save the scraping of the quill. Finally, that too stilled and Royle closed the heavy ledger. He straightened and gave stiff shoulders a limbering roll.

Evangeline went to the bottle she'd seen Max dip into throughout the day and poured a cup of spirits. When she placed it before him, Royle gave a start and looked up in surprise at so considerate a gesture. She found she could not meet those green eyes that spoke of a fate denied and betrayed. She'd meant the act as a simple kindness, yet his gaze bespoke of a significance which reached far deeper, and she was as uncomfortable with his false assumptions as she was with him. Nothing was simple when passed between them. To her distress, he complicated things further.

"I thank you for your patience today. It could not have been easy for you to sit idle for so long." The tenderness, the praise in his low voice was a subtle attack upon her defenses. And when he sighed wearily and let his fair head loll loose upon his shoulders to ease their tension, there was something so personal, so sensual in the movement her resolve came close to collapse. Her hands trembled in their want to touch him, to feel the tight power of his shoulder muscles, to gently knead away their distress. But the pull was too strong, the temptation too great. From an application of relief, her fingers would be drawn up to his yellow hair, and then there would be no relief for her. Already, she taunted herself with unwise desires that could know no happy end. It was better this way, she told herself firmly as she took a reluctant step back. Better for them both.

"It's just that there's much I have to learn, so I might understand things better." He looked up then and his expressive eyes froze her retreat. His words spoke of the Iroquois. His gaze spoke of her. Both were sincere. Both made her hesitate in the clutch of possibility.

"Yes, you have much to learn," she agreed quietly.

His hand fell over hers, capturing it completely, and the warm contact was so unsettling, she tried to withdraw in confusion. He wouldn't release her. It was a firm, gentle restraint.

"Then teach me, Evangeline," he encouraged with an intensity she could not break from. "Help me understand as only you can. I would not have you suffer for my ignorance." He referred to generalities and to intimate particulars. It was the latter suggestion that had her trembling. She was lost in that eloquent gaze, lost to the tide of charmed emotion whispering that she might believe him, he might be willing to breech the differences between them. Confusion fluttered about her heart, trying to best the reason she held to. The warmth of his hand surrounded hers. She felt smothered by it and afraid. Yet part of that fear was due her want to yield to the promising potential of touch and gaze. Part of her wanted to yield to both, to melt into his arms, to look for tenderness in the taste of his mouth, to seek the mysteries of his body that memory denied her. Part of her screamed that she flee in terror of her soul.

"It grows late, Tanner, and the woods are dark when the sun gets low. We should leave now." Panic gave her words a breathless quality, husky and inviting. "I am weary and yearn for home."

Home. He seized on her use of that term like a man drowning. Dazed as he was by elated hopes, he foolishly assumed she meant the roof they shared. And then he, too, was impatient to be gone. The book was quickly stored, and Evangeline steered to the door by the touch of his hand. Dimness had already grayed the shadows of the wood, but it was his expectations that had him blind. He turned to secure the door and felt the razor edge of a blade at his throat.

His attacker wasn't Evangeline. The angle was too high, the pressure too great. Even upon swallowing, he would feel his own blood. That wasn't the case. He had nothing to swallow. His mouth was suddenly very dry.

Words were exchanged behind his back in low, heavy gutterals and answered similarly by his wife. She was demanding his death, he knew. He tried to pray, to prepare his soul, but the words wouldn't come. He thought to fall to his knees, but his body was taken with the paralysis of fear. Then one fact overwhelmed his fear and even the imminence of his own death. They were taking Evangeline from him.

When he was slowly turned—knife blade still adhered to his neck—he was aware of two things immediately. His assailants were the pair from earlier that day. And Evangeline was not surprised by the turn of events. Fear rose anew, laced with anger. This wasn't a terror over his own situation, but a

154

certainty that she was lost to him. And the anger was directed at his own gullibility and toward her betrayal. That he should be hurt by it was an irony. She'd told him frankly that she would flee him, and smugly he'd not thought it possible. More the fool. He deserved to feel the blade if for no other reason than the weakening of his heart that softened reason. He should have been better prepared. He should have remembered lessons learned.

Evangeline would not look at him. Her gaze went to the woods and to the freedom beyond. Then his low promise intruded to snatch away her uneasy triumph.

"I will not let you go, Evangeline."

She met his steady stare and quailed beneath the authority of that bold and untenable claim. Her color failed and gray eyes rounded in an agitation beyond his power to make good that vow. That look was rich with unguarded emotion. Then it was gone. She spoke a command, then turned from him so as not to witness its completion. The blade left his throat and he waited for the sureness of it plunged to his heart. It couldn't be a keener pain than the one already residing there. A powerful blow took him on the temple, and he went down like a felled oak. From the rough planks of the porch, his last sight was of the shimmer of silk as Evangeline walked away.

There was no hurry. Their first campfire was lit within hours of the trading house in confidence of no pursuit. Only a fool would blunder into the forest if not one with its secrets.

Evangeline hunched close to the warmth of the small blaze, staring into the happy darts of flame as if she could find contentment there. She couldn't. Her soul should have been alive with the expectation of seeing her loved ones again. She should have been rapturous in her embrace of freedom. She shouldn't be looking back, haunted by the green gold eyes and their dauntless promise. *I won't let you go.* She shivered as if that oath was spoken on a chilling wind. Never mind that she was safe with family. Never mind that he was probably nursing an aching head in the confines of their distant house. No, she told herself firmly, angrily. *His* house. It had never been theirs. Her home was near Schoharie Creek, upon the flats into the setting sun. Her next night's rest would be taken upon furs, not upon white man's cloth. Her morning meal would be provided by nature, not by a meddling squaw with eyes for her man. No, she reminded herself even more forcefully. Royle Tanner was *not* her man. The one who would have that claim crouched across the fire, its brilliance dancing in his black eyes.

I will not look back, she told herself and struggled to make that true. The past months would be forgotten, hidden away as were her memories of a life before the Caniengas, insulated from pain the way the nightmare among the Shawnee was. Her future was here at this welcoming fire, not in some mystic dream. She would make it so.

But still she could not blot out the anguish in the Englishman's gaze, that moment of abject misery before anger, before pride, before betrayal interfered. And that look reached down deep into her soul with icy fingers to strangle any joy she should have felt. Why should she care for his distress? What right did he have to force guilt upon her when none was due? He had wronged her. He had kept her prisoner, knowing full well of her desire to be free. He knew she would escape him. She'd told him. Why had he looked so shocked, so poignantly surprised? She owed him no apology. She owed him not a second of the remorse now torturing her. She didn't even owe him his life, yet she'd insisted it be spared. She wondered at the wisdom of that now. As long as he lived, she would feel his threat, this power throbbing on that single fateful phrase. *I will not let you go.*

She didn't hear her brother's approach until he spoke softly.

"He follows."

Those two words struck a consuming terror into her heart. And a traitorous joy.

Girding herself against both emotions, she looked up at the young brave and said lightly, "He will not continue for long. He does not know the woods. The trail will grow cold before him. He will tire and return to the white man's village." That conviction did not settle within her heart.

"Why does he come?"

Evangeline was evasive. Never before had she told less than the truth to those of a shared spirit if not blood. It was a shameful sign of warping at the hands of the false invaders. Her brother looked down at her, waiting for her reply, and she could not bring herself to tell him the persistent white man was wed to her in the white way. Better to sever the ties with a vague response. One that would lessen his claim and her guilt. "He wants to make me his."

"One might try to capture the stars and have as much success," claimed the warrior from across the fire. His dark eyes were warmed with amusement and admiration. There was a time when that look would have sent her soul into flutters of delight. On this night, she was too worried to be flattered.

"He will give up before dawn," she stated in hopes of convincing herself it was so. Her eyes went to the

157

darkness that concealed the way they had come. She had no reason to believe otherwise. Royle Tanner was a helpless babe in her world. He had no knowledge to sustain his quest. No true reason to push himself into certain danger. Why would he pursue her? Yet, in her heart, she knew he still did. He was a man of conviction, not caution. *I will not let you go.* Inwardly, she trembled.

"I will watch," her brother said, following her gaze. "Sleep, my sister. By the time the sun is high tomorrow, you will be among our people where you belong."

The fire ceased to warm her. Cold doubt disturbed a chill to her marrow. Evangeline curled tight within the robe her brother had given her and shivered. She closed her eyes and tried to close her thoughts. They spun wildly, provoking her with endless, agonizing possibilities.

Tomorrow she would return to her village. She would be embraced by her family, but how secure would that homecoming be? What if Tanner went to the white soldiers with his grievance, telling them her people came to steal her away? They would not believe two acted alone without the knowledge of their tribe, without the blessing of her people. Would all be made to suffer for the impulsive rescue of two warriors? Warraghiyagey came because he was young and passionate, without a caution for convention. He would be a future chief and was arrogantly aware of his power. Cayenderongue had come for another reason. He had come for her to make her his wife. Both were bold, giving no thought to repercussions, thinking only to exact a coup by snatching her away from their weaker enemies. There would be much boasting and swaggering among the braves upon their return and the telling of this tale.

But what of her father? Would he be happy for her return? Or would he see it as a violation of his word? Would he insist that she be surrendered back to the confining care and chastisement awaiting in the world she'd fled? She could picture her husband's smug confidence as she was led back in disgrace. She could imagine his anger and she trembled. She could imagine worse things, like the soft bed and seductive presence of the man she'd sworn to deny. But could she deny him? Was her pride strong enough to deny her own wants? The pleasure she'd taken in learning of his pursuit filled her with terrible anticipation. Could she be so weak as to wish recapture and return to the dangerous delights beneath his roof?

Evangeline squirmed uncomfortably with' this new turn of thoughts. Why could she not look ahead to the joys she would find amongst her people? Why could she not anticipate the day when Cayenderongue would come with gifts, the night when he would lie with her to claim his rights as husband? Because those rights were already claimed. Another had taken them. And she didn't know if she was angrier over the loss of her maidenhood, or the fact that she couldn't remember its passing beneath her white captor.

And surprisingly she did sleep, with disturbing dreams of green eyes and promises broken.

Dawn was threading streams of quiet light through the branches that made her roof when Evangeline woke at last. The white clothing had given her an unyielding rest and she tugged to bring them in line with her form. Soon they would be happily discarded for the comfort of skins.

Cayenderongue was still squatting at the fire, as if he'd not moved throughout the long hours of night.

159

It was likely he had not. He smiled when he saw she was awake.

"Where is Warraghiyagey?" she asked as she searched the small perimeter of their camp.

The brave who thought to claim her prodded the embers with the blade of his knife. "Your brother knew you had more fears than you would speak. He went to see you safe."

Dread formed a choking lump within her throat making words difficult. "What do you mean?"

With an offhanded calm, he told her, "He went to assure the white man would follow no more."

Vague eyes fell to the smoldering fire in sightless study. Her brother had gone to kill Royle Tanner.

As many times as she had thought it, wished it, even said as much, she truly didn't mean him to pay the price for his innocent involvement in the Websters' scheme, not when that price was his life. True, he had held her against her will, but that made him no villain, rather a man bound to the honor of his vow. The words spoken before the white man's judge were meaningless to her, but not so to him. Could she fault him for trying to hold to what he considered his? His color didn't change the fact that he was man and that they were prone to jealousy guard the things they cherished. Was she one of those things to Royle Tanner? He'd not said as much. They'd had little time to speak of anything important and from the heart. If he cared for her, she had just sentenced him to death for his devotion. Her soul could not bear that knowledge. She'd only wanted separate futures, not for his to come to a sudden end.

There was no time to argue if she was responsible for Royle Tanner's fate. Not when seconds could part him from the living.

Cayenderongue was startled from his languor by

160

the swirl of silken skirts passing him in a blur of color. Though he knew not her motive for traversing the same trail, he dutifully followed. Part of him hoped the white man might yet be living, so he could have a role in his demise. And it wouldn't be swift the way his friend had planned. Not after seeing the dull terror in his beloved's eyes.

That seeping terror gave wings to Evangeline's feet. To ease her passage, she kicked off the restrictive shoes and ran on bare foot atop the carpet of leaves and pine. The thrumming of her heart seemed to count off the seconds of his time left in this world. Her breath came quick with panic, and she fought to make it slow and regular so her endurance might increase. When her skirts became a nuisance, she tugged them up above tanned knees to give her stride greater reach. With each step, the torture of thought wrought a more exquisite anguish. She was cruelly reminded of his kindnesses to her, of the gentleness of his touch, of the respect he gave her when he could have been merciless. The fact that he had lain with her, that his child might indeed reside within her body, gave impetus to her flight. Could she tell her child she'd had its father slain?

If those agonies of truth were not enough, she was punished by the power of the spirit world. Her destiny had come in a dream, and she'd refused to see it fulfilled. She'd willfully denied the wishes of her soul, and now she would suffer for it. The knowledge that her disobedience had resulted in the destruction of another life would weigh upon her conscience in eternal condemnation. She would be cursed by the gods. Fate would shun her of any blessings. She might as well die with him as to endure what lay ahead.

Things she had looked upon with pride now

daunted her, as she struggled for breath against the burning in her lungs. She'd boasted of her independence, and now she would be alone. She'd bragged upon her brother's prowess in battle, and that same skill would bring about her fall. Warraghiyagey would find no challenge in the soft white man. His ability in combat was touted throughout the Nation. Her mind formed a frightening tableau of what she would find; Royle surprised, with no chance to defend himself, her brother with his blade stained scarlet, a yellow scalp brandished in his hand.

Oh, God, don't let me be too late, she cried within her soul, unthinkingly citing the name of the most powerful god she knew, the one of her childhood.

She could hear sounds of a struggle in the undergrowth ahead, of heavy male bodies crashing about in a contest of life and death. A shriek burst from her lips as she tore through the last barrier of brush.

"No! No, stop! Don't kill him!"

Evangeline drew up short, breath wheezing from her, blood roaring through her veins. And she blinked with disbelief.

She'd come upon the end of the battle with the killing stroke left to be delivered. It was Warraghiyagey who was pinned upon the trampled ground, his throat bent to the touch of the blade. Crouched over him, knee pressed into his back to keep him prone, was a Royle Tanner she had never imagined. His shirt was nearly torn from him during the throes of confrontation, and his fair skin shown sleek and damp beneath it. The green eyes that rose to challenge her were bright and hard with the killing fever. The knife in his hand was unwavering, nor was there any sign of hesitation in his intense gaze. He was every inch a warrior, and Evangeline's heart

162

staggered, then swelled with savage pride.

Hearing Cayenderongue's rapid approach, she held up her hand to forbid him to interfere. She wanted no outside confusion to cloud this moment.

"Do not slay him, Tanner. Your quarrel is with me."

Her soft plea wrought no weakening. If anything, the tension of his pose increased. Passions worked dark and dangerous upon his face. His voice was harsh with them. "You sent him to see me dead." That he would believe it so readily wounded her to the quick. How he must hate her to think she would betray him, then seek his death.

"He thought it was my will," she said, again using quiet to control his fury.

"And was it? You will?"

"No."

He stared at her, probing to bare her soul to discern the truth of that single, potent word. He was not convinced.

"Spare him, I beg you. He is my brother."

She saw the pressure of the blade lessen, but only a fraction. It was enough. Her legs began to tremble in frail relief. Just as her senses quivered with strong emotion. She felt rubbed raw between the friction of the two.

Royle's features lost none of their taut edges. He was breathing heavily. The battle had taken a heavy toll, and his muscles protested the strain. Pain thudded dully in his temple and more bitterly within his breast. Even deeper than the pain was the wanting, the hunger. He spoke slowly, without inflection, so she could not mistake him or claim she did not understand.

"You ask for much after giving little. I would place a price upon your brother's life. Tell me if you think

163

it fair."

Mutely, she nodded, afraid and gloriously eager to hear what he would name.

"A trade," he offered bluntly. "Him for you."

The warrior at her back took a challenging step forward, the move bristling with offense. "Who is this man to make such a demand?" Cayenderongue insisted in labored English.

"He is my husband."

The quiet claim had the force of the mightiest shout. It was said without shame, without regret, and Royle hesitated before continuing to state his fee.

"You will come with me, Evangeline. You will be wife to me and in every way willing. I do not ask you to bury your past, only to make me your future. I ask for what you agreed to under my laws. You will live in my house, bear my children, and remain with me faithfully. That is the price. Do you deem it fair?"

There was no faltering in her reply, for there was no sacrifice she would refuse to save her brother's life. "Yes," she answered in a whisper with the strength of binding steel. There was no indecision because there was no reluctance. The knife came away and warily Royle stood. Evangeline's eyes followed that ascension, awed, profound in their new awareness.

"Tell them you're going with me of your own will," he commanded, sharing his restless gaze between the two braves. "Tell them not to interfere."

Quickly, distractedly, Evangeline spoke the words in their tongue, answering their arguments with unwavering strength. She belonged to Royle Tanner by her vow and of her own will. The chore of concluding that statement with emotion-choked good-byes was shortened as Royle extended his hand to her. He did not come to claim her, but waited for her to make the move to him. Emotions flickered upon his face, intense desires he hadn't the control to conceal from her, all shifting and uncertain beneath the tight rein of firm authority. He looked impatient, angry, demanding with an imperious arrogance. And afraid. Deeply afraid she would not take the steps that would bring her to his side. She went to him without hesitation, because it was where she was meant to be. She was one with her destiny now, and there would be no further denials.

His fingers closed about hers. She'd expected his grasp to be firm, aggressive in its possession, and punishing to remind her of her disobedience. His grip was infinitely gentle and she felt her heart melt. It was not with a sense of martyrdom that she moved beside his cautious retreat. It was not with despair that she looked ahead to the home that awaited them. It was with a quiet joy.

Chapter Eleven

With windows shuttered against the early dawn, the interior of the house was still deep in night shadow. It took Royle a long moment with steel to flint to coax a spark, then warm golden light spilled across the room.

He was bone weary. The thunder within his head was nearly deafening. His body felt bruised and abused over every inch. Yet each sense was alive and vital and focused upon the quiet figure kneeling to tend his fire.

What would her word mean? Given under such circumstance, dare he trust it any farther than other vows to pass her sweetly treacherous lips? She had come with him for the moment, and with good reason. But would she stay? Or would he have to continue his constant vigil with one eye on the door and the other at his back? He was tired, discouraged. The events of the long evening had drained him of all but rueful thought. He'd had no time to consider his motives for rushing headlong into possible death. To save his potential business or his marriage? He didn't know. He only knew that when the braves faced him with their knives and the possibility that he'd never see Evangeline again, losing the opportunity at the trading house hadn't entered his fury-clogged mind. It was the idea that the woman he'd made his wife was being stripped from him that prompted him to such foolhardy action. Some primal male drive insisted he recapture her, she who'd never professed to care for him, who betrayed him, who was more likely to kill him then ever love him. He had pursued her with the single purpose of returning her to his home, into his keeping, and here she was. But for how long?

The light touch of fingertips upon his arm pulled him from his heavy thoughts.

"Sit," Evangeline instructed. "I will tend your hurts."

When he obeyed, she came to him with a cool, damp cloth and pressed it to his colorful temple. It was an effort to remain in the seat at that first touch, then the relief made his eyes slide gratefully closed.

He was handsome, she decided. Not in the bold, dark beauty of her people, but with a golden promise. His jaw was firm and strong. Her forefinger stroked beneath it, then up the lean contour of his roughened cheek. She found the stubble of his facial hair intriguing, for Indian males were sleekly smooth in their lack of it. His eyes hadn't opened, those deep forest-jeweled eyes that called her to her fate.

She took the cloth away from the swelling at his temple, as yet unaware of the swelling she stirred in a more virile region. Immodest hands coaxed the ragged shirt off him and let it drop to the floor. Pale skin jerked taut and jumped along the curve of his ribs as she ministered to a surface wound snaking wickedly from side to furred navel. Had the blade been truer, she wouldn't be kneeling before him. She would be kneeling over him. That knowledge made her gentle hand tremble. The humbling realization of what he'd done on her behalf, of what he'd been willing to risk to have her, quickened a curious response. Wonder overtook her, that and a fierce, consuming pride. He'd brought down a great warrior, and in doing so had conquered more than he knew.

Her dark head was bent before him, keeping her expression hidden while her healing touch spoke volumes. He'd expected her resentment at being brought back yet a prisoner. This . . . this was something very different. His heart and mind were unprepared for gentle concern. Both were eager to accept it, even over the most sternly voiced doubts. Suddenly it was imperative for him to see into the windows of her soul. When his hand cupped her cheek, her eyes lifted to meet his without resistance or regret. His were lambent with smoldering question. Her answer was an infusion of tenderness over the glitter of tears.

With a tentative determination, his fair head bent. His palm guided her up to greet the cautious part of his lips, and he found sweet welcome. Encouraged to sample, explore, and lay claim, he tasted the ripe contours of her mouth, coaxing her to receive the questing probe of his tongue so he could know a more rewarding mastery. Her soft moan bespoke of astonished pleasure, his of increasing need.

They came apart. He seated and she upon her knees, their gazes were level and locked within one another's. They looked long, deeply, almost fearful of the mounting tension that flamed between them, yet both eager to push it to its limits.

Royle's voice was thick with longing and wary expectation.

"You are my wife, Evangeline. You belong to me

body and soul."

Her response was a velvet rumble.

"And you are mine, my husband."

No properly rendered submission could have incited him with the power of that forceful claim. His fingers tightened about the back of her slender neck and impelled her forward. This was no questioning kiss. It was certain and strong, like the passions ignited equally between them. Her lips were just as urgent and insisting. Tongues dueled briefly in a fiery exchange, then hers relented before his thrusting jabs. That forceful rhythm quickening a keener desire. The union grew unsatisfying, incomplete.

Evangeline leaned away, her hands going to his shoulders to keep him from following in pursuit of more. His eyes came open, hot and dazed with desire, yet edged with watchful heed. He did not trust her. But he did want her. And that was enough for now.

She stood and with sure movements shed the hated garments, until clad in only the natural glow of firelight. His mouth went dry. The pounding returned to his head, that insistent pulse of passion rather than pain. He stared long, lingering over each perfectly crafted turn in a private reverie of possession. That exclusive pleasure thrilled him, but not as much as the thought of what was to come. Pledged to no other. Known by no other. His alone.

His palms fit to the feminine flare of her hips and as he, too, stood, they revolved about her slender form into an embrace that caught her close. With every movement, he expected resistance and was met with none. He didn't understand her sudden turnabout toward him—from captor to captivator—but it was a wonderful change, one he would question—later. Still, their gazes held, the green of the forests, the blue gray of the sky, merging freely, offering boun-- ties untried and unclaimed. Thoughts of the fragile, proper Miss Carey fell before this new image, of his wild, pagan beauty with black hair cascading down her back in abandon, her firm, bronzed body arched against him, candidly sensual. How could he have preferred that pristine purity to the raw sexuality before him? She may not have been his idea of the perfect, respectable bride, but she was his every fantasy of a woman.

Her fingertips came up between them, tracing a sensory path up chest to shoulders where they rested in a comfortable claim. "You've made me your prize," she purred with husky persuasion. "Now make me Tanner's Wife."

He needed no further encouragement. His arms tightened. Her bare feet cleared the floor. In three impatient strides, he was laying her down amid the pile of downy pillows and was frantically ridding himself of clothes. The delicious friction of flesh on flesh excited beyond restraint. Royle found her spread in welcome and ready to receive him as he settled between uplifted knees and open arms. Both hugged about him, surrounding him the way her hot, eager body was yearning to do. She was not to go wanting long. He poised and plunged and nearly lost himself before the journey was begun. She was incredibly tight, sheathing him greedily. Though this was not virgin ground, and he was thankful for the ease that gave her, it was very much new territory.

For a moment, Evangeline lay still, absorbing this incredible new feeling of fullness. If he'd not already claimed her passions, he now claimed her soul. She didn't want him to move, wanting to revel in his completion of her woman's form. He'd shown her an emptiness where she'd known none existed, and exactly how it should be filled to perfection. And then he began to withdraw, and she realized he'd yet shown her nothing at all. The first stroke of his manhood claimed her, the second set her free.

There was nothing placid about her acceptance. Evangeline didn't give, she pursued, as aggressively as a warrior in a hunt. She was toned, taut, strong, and that strength clasped about Royle to force sensation to the brink. And what sensations they were—hot, cold, sharp, subtle, teasing him, provoking him, tantalizing him until there was no control or sanity. She thrashed beneath him like a wild thing, all sharp teeth and claws, all violent passion, making it a contest, a challenge rather than a gentle mating. And her urgent demands drove him further, faster, furiously, until a cry broke from her in rapturous surprise followed by the call of his name; not Tanner but Royle. It was half wail, half sigh, all powerful, the final thread to ravel the fabric of his discipline. Then he, too, was rapture's captive.

Presently Evangeline stirred on the high bank of pillows. Her body was weighed with heavy luxury. Her soul was at peace. A languorous contentment filled her completely, the way her husband had moments before. How foolish she'd been to struggle against her destiny when the gods had been so right. They had shown her the fulfillment of her dreams, and at last she recognized their worth.

Her head rolled lazily to the side so she could examine the man next to her. Englishman, Royle Tanner, her husband. And she was very pleased, not only by the rigors and demands of his lovemaking, but by the man himself. Her gaze assessed him. She could grow used to the pale skin and the downy blanket of hair that adorned it. She would live with him in his world, not because she'd given her word, but because he had earned the right to have her with him. He was not of the Iroquois, however, he was every inch a warrior.

She smiled to herself in thinking of his bravery at the trading house. He hadn't faltered even when overwhelmed. He had come for her in a challenge of odds and even nature. He'd fought and he'd won her, and there was great pride in going to the victor. Like a token of battle, it was her right to be at his side. Without shame. Without regret.

Evangeline considered the man at her side and tallied his admirable qualities; valor, dignity, sincerity, determination, strength. All the attributes her people held in the highest respect. She remembered him crouched over his foe, ruled by primitive emotion, and her heart beat faster. Then there was the memory of his savage tenderness in claiming her for his bride, and she grew strangely restless. Her fingertips traced beside the gash that scored his ribs, a badge of bravery hard-won and proudly born. He woke at her touch and regarded her intently.

"Good morning," she offered in welcome.

"Is it?" was his quizzical return.

Uncertain of his odd humor, Evangeline abandoned talk for the moment and indulged in other interests. Boldly, her hand explored the terrain of his chest, lowering to test the firm length of his thigh. She felt him tense, could feel his scandalized reaction.

"I did not expect a white man to be so strong," she purred in praise. "It was well hidden beneath all those clothes."

Royle said nothing. His flesh had gone rigid beneath her touch as fingers stroked up inner thigh. He shifted as if uncomfortable with her direction and her directness.

"Do you disapprove, husband? Should I not

172

delight in what is mine to enjoy?" That was said half-teasing, half-sincere, and he answered simply in the same vein.

"Yours?"

"So you became when I accepted the gift of your courage."

"You accepted me? Forgive me for mistaking it. I thought you were making a sacrifice, when all along I was giving a gift. You make it sound as though you are here with me by choice." There was bitterness there beneath the light tone. So he was still suffering from bruised pride and betrayal. She would not allow those feelings to linger and sour the gentler ones trying to take root.

"I would not have come were it otherwise."

The pose of indifference slipped farther to bare his hurt. "You came to save your brother."

"No. You would not have harmed him." She sounded so sure. It rankled him that she should see so easily through his bravado. He demanded gruffly, "How do you know that?"

"Because you are too civilized."

He relaxed on a softly expressed laugh. "And is that bad?"

"Not always." Her palm began a leisurely circle over the furred expanse of his belly. His muscles tightened and quivered at that sensual coaxing. When those tempting revolutions grew ever lower, Royle's breath grew uneven and hoarse. Finally he spoke her name, but it was in protest rather than encouragement.

Evangeline came up on her elbow to puzzle over his response to her. He'd not been hesitant before or during their fiery commerce. Why now did he seek to draw away?

"Does my touch displease you?" Her words were

soft with the concern that it was so.

"It pleases me, only—" Those ground-out senti-ments broke off. He was panting. He wanted to think clearly, not to be lured back into passion's play. Yet it was difficult not to succumb when all that was desire lay before him. "'Tis only that I'm not used to a woman who enjoys her pleasure as you do."

Her brows arched high as his meaning took her. The smoldering enjoyment of the moment was dashed by a chill of offense. Lids shuttered over her icy stare. "Forgive me," she bit out. "I did not know I should lie still and meek like your spiritless English women. I shall try not to let my pleasure interfere again." She dropped upon her back and glared at the low ceiling in indignation, hurt to think he would find fault with what had caused her soul to soar.

Royle was silent. Then he gave a great booming laugh and rolled up so his forearms straddled her shoulders. She turned her head away, refusing to look upon his smiling countenance.

"I do not want you spiritless, my savage angel," he murmured throatily. "Shout your pleasure to the heavens if that be your wish. I only meant that before—" His pause brought her gaze about in question.

"It was not like this the first time?" Though her body recalled that initial union and was prepared the second time, not so, her heart or mind. She had no memories of that first coupling and mourned its loss. She was certain it had been as spectacular as this. Greedily, she wanted that memory and was sure that had she retained it, she might have sought his arms earlier to know the ecstasy of their embrace. She felt herself unfairly cheated.

Royle considered the initiation of his virgin bride. That he had feared her cold and ungiving contrarily

174

made him want to blush or chuckle. He did a little of both. His gaze caressed her and that satisfying experience prompted his fingertips to do likewise.

"No, it was very different."

Her brow furrowed and he could see her distress as she struggled with the void of memory. "You would prefer me as I was then, as what you thought I was?" A poignant vulnerability crept out in the parameters of that question, the nagging doubt that he found her wanting.

"God, no," he assured her roughly. "I had no idea what I wanted then."

Her voice was small. "And you do now?"

"I do now." His lingering kiss did much to convince her. She was content then to lounge against the bolster of pillows in her study of his features. How had she ever been repulsed by what she saw there?

"Have I pleased you, Tanner?" she wanted to know.

"Too much, my greedy wife. I seem to have fared much better at the hands of your brother." That tender taunt drew her attention to the welts and scratches marring shoulders and back. She traced one with a rueful fingertip.

"I am sorry if I hurt you."

"You did hurt me," he confessed in a low, throbbing candor. She knew he was speaking of other things and was quiet. He continued almost without voice. "And that hurt will be too much to bear if you run from me again."

Evangeline frowned, her delicate features becoming sharp with displeasure. "I have given my word, Tanner," she scolded crossly. "I have sealed it with your shaft of life. I have no wish to leave what belongs to me."

A small, hopeful smile played upon the stern set of his lips, as if he wanted, yet dared not believe what she told him. Before she could try to convince him further, he was kissing her and she was quickly absorbed by his urgency. Whatever doubts he had about her truthfulness, he would have none over her willingness. Her hands devoured his form as her lips did his mouth, and it was a feast he could not get enough of.

And when he was tempted to taste more of this succulent fare, a loud rattle sounded upon the door. He lifted up for air and awaited the return of reason.

"A minute," he called out in less than friendly tones, then was prompted from the delights of his wife's embrace by those very words. Pulling on his clothes woke aching miseries that passion had subdued. Evangeline, too, arose and dressed herself in proper English fashion. To his admiring eyes, it seemed contemptible to conceal such perfection with convention.

Barnabas Maxell was stomping about on the stoop to warm himself against the early chill. He took in Royle's disheveled appearance and chanced a knowing grin. Had he a woman like Evangeline Tanner at home beneath his sheets, he wouldn't look too pleased at the interruption either.

"Morning," he called, grinning wider at Royle's muttered reply. "Morning, Mistress Tanner."

"And welcome, Max. I am sorry I have nothing to offer you. My larder is sadly lacking. I will see it is not so on the morrow."

It was the most he had ever heard from his employer's lovely wife, and he was as flustered as Royle, himself, seemed to be. He cleared his throat and ventured, "Be you ready to go, Mr. Tanner?"

"Directly. And it's Royle."

176

Max pursed his lips, reluctant to accept that suggestion of familiarity. "Don't seem right, you being my better."

Royle's laugh was at his own expense, but genuine in its effort to calm the little man. "You speak of betters when you will be teaching all I have to know to make my livelihood? 'Twould make us more than equals, in my thinking."

Max smiled a bit doubtfully. Then seeing the exchange pass between husband and wife, he was beset by an unprecedented moment of tact and muttered, "I be just outside."

In looking to his wife, Royle was in a quandry. He had her word that she would remain. To openly challenge it now would damage the precious threads of trust beginning to weave about their relationship. Yet, if he was to return and find her gone . . .

Evangeline was not unaware of his turmoil. She could see the dark shadows of suspicion in his eyes, could smell the fear upon him. An ache began within her breast, the knowing pain that he would never treat her as a wife when out of the comforts of the bed. Then, he took up her hand, his decision made, and pressed a light kiss upon it.

"I wish you an enjoyable day, Evangeline."

Her hand hung slack in his as she digested this in surprise. Then her fingers squeezed tight. "And you, husband," was her husky return.

He hesitated, struggling with the reluctance to make good his overture of belief. Then he took a step away, and the next was a little easier, until finally he was at the door. Their gazes mingled long, with meaningful intensity. Then he had no choice but to close the door between them and take her at her word.

As the long hours of the day stretched out into endless seconds, he began to doubt the wisdom of

177

that choice. He longed for the sun to set and contrarily dreaded it. What if she wasn't waiting? Would he go after her again? He'd already pursued her into as much of a hell as he ever wanted to visit. She was his wife, not an animal to be tethered and broken to his command. If she would not yield of her own will, well, then . . .

He touched the ledgers and looked about at the trappings of success that meant so much to him. Perhaps he could convince Webster to keep him on of his own worth, and let the bargain of wedlock be nullified. New York was a long distance away. It could be weeks before his employer learned the dowry contract had been broken. Months even. In that time, he could establish himself as invaluable. He could . . .

His thoughts ended there, and he realized in no little surprise that he didn't care, at least not with the driving force of before. He didn't want the mere vestiges of prosperity; he wanted all. And he didn't want just any woman to adorn his arm to speak well of his accomplishments. Only Evangeline would do as Tanner's Wife.

And if she was gone . . .

The day was a restless agony to endure. He ached, he was tired, he was frantic with worry. Each Indian who arrived with packs of precious furs to barter gave him an uncomfortable start and made him ill at ease. Was this another of her family come to claim his hair and his bride? None of them approached him, but all were aware of his presence. Their dark inscrutable eyes touched upon him not with the indifference of before, and he could see them wondering how this puny white man in his multitude of clothes could have wrested their mighty champion to the ground.

Finally the day was done, and Royle met the path home with a curious reluctance. Feet anxious to hurry him back to his bride were strangely leadened. Anticipation was tempered with a crushing fear. And he found himself dreading to discover what awaited him.

By the time he reached his threshold, he was as breathless as if he'd run, and cold with uncertainty. He paused and felt his hopes twist tight in an agony of despair. There was no scent of a welcoming fire from within. No sign of welcome at all. He pushed open the door.

The front room was dark and chilled, unfriendly shadow clinging in heavy oppression. There was no light from the rear. No smell of a waiting meal. No appearance of a waiting wife. Never in his life had he felt such an empty misery. Now what would he do?

It was muffled at first, so he thought it his imagination. Then, more strident than before, came a string of native curses and the clatter of metal on wood. Relief made him so weak, for a moment he could not move. His heart seemed to triple its normal beat until his chest ached to contain it. She had remained freely of her own will.

In a daze of weak delight, Royle went to the kitchen to discover the source of his wife's temper. She was facing the hearth when she heard his step and whirled in a glorious rage. Gray eyes blazed from features blackened by soot. Dough-clotted fingers were clenched about the handle of a very long-bladed knife. In her agitation, she forgot her English and hurled a volley of gutteral syllables at his head.

With a careful eyes upon the blade, Royle surveyed the disaster that had overtaken his kitchen. Bowls were overturned. Flour blanketed the floorboards like a new snow, atop which the imprints of bare feet were made. Ashes, the same that discolored his bride's silk gown, scattered over the hearth. There, covering the burned-out logs, was an indistinguishable glob of paste. His brows soared.

"What's happened here?"

The rapid gutterals began again, then Evangeline caught herself and forced the angry words out so he could understand them, if not the situation.

"I was baking bread for your supper. Your white man's fire box began to put its smoke into the room, so I put out the flames."

"With my dinner?" He couldn't help his smile. It all seemed so harmlessly ridiculous after the horrors of doubt he'd suffered. Evangeline scowled at him, not amused.

"Of course not."

"Then how did it come to be on the hearth? Did you plan to cook the bread upon open flames?" It became more difficult for him to restrain the laughter that bubbled up until it hurt to hold it inside. Evangeline's irate visage—that and the foot-long blade—kept his mirth in cautious check.

Evangeline continued her tale in cold tones, furious to think he'd find humor in her struggle against the white man's foolish conveniences.

"Once the fire was out, I could not get it to take again. My bread was ruined."

"And so you sought a fitting punishment for them both." A chuckle threatened to escape, and he clamped his lips tight for a moment until his control was better. He could picture her hacking away at the offending dough before flinging it upon his hearth. "The flue was closed. That's why the fire would not draw. Let me clean up this mess. Perhaps Mistress Loockermann has some of her stew ready."

There were few things he could have said to make

180

the moment worse for his harried bride. The mention of the capable Eva Loockermann was one of them. With a growl, she lunged at him, blade swinging wide. He stayed it quickly with the grasp of her wrist, and her with an arm about her middle. She smelled a mix of the fire and leavening. It whet dissimilar appetites.

He'd expected a struggle but the fight went out of her within his restraining clasp. Abruptly, trails of wetness appeared upon her smudged cheeks, and Royle's embrace slackened with dismay. He felt her body convulse with misery, and it pierced straight through to his heart.

"Oh, angel, don't weep over ruined bread," he soothed in a husky rumble.

Her tears gathered quicker and fell faster from the uplifted anguish of her eyes. They shone in a dejection of anger, frustrated pride, and failure. "Your white man's ways make things that are simple into impossibilities," she sniffed, trying to gather her crumbling control.

"I know, angel. I know." He released the hand that held the knife so he could wash away the streaks of soot and moisture with his fingertips. The blade clattered satisfactorily to the floor. She clung to his coat, and her fine, determined jaw quivered. The feel of her in his arms—so real, so certain—overcame him. The relief and wonder of it made him tremble. His touch moved from damp cheek down the column of her throat to the silk-covered slope of her shoulder. His hand grew more unsteady.

"I wanted to surprise you," she confessed with a humbleness that brought pride to its knees. His shook.

"You did." That claim was true. Seeing her in his home at his hearth, when he'd expected to find both empty, staggered him with the power of his need. He had wanted many things in his life, but never had he needed so desperately. At his father's deathbed, his anguish was tempered by the determination to see his promises met, filling his hurting heart with purpose. Coming home to the fear of a lonely hearth had stopped his future cold, leaving a hollow so big it echoed. There had been nothing to look ahead to. And now, there was Evangeline, and that future spread with infinite potential.

"I wanted to have your supper ready for you," Evangeline told him weakly. Her eyes cast downward, unable to behold his disappointment. The cup of his palm beneath her chin forced them upward again. His voice was nearly hoarse.

"Evangeline, what I hunger for is not upon that fire."

Chapter Twelve

Evangeline stood silent. Tears dried mutely upon her cheeks, as his words effectively stemmed the tide of her emotions. Pride, battered beyond repair, was pampered and restored. And then there was the look that came over him, that inward heat flaming behind his eyes until they glowed like a forest ablaze. Instinctively she yielded to that tempting fire, using it to kindle the embers of her passion.

She came to him easily, letting her body melt upon the brazier of desire that flared his strength and controlled her will. Her ready response nursed his fears and redoubled his thanksgiving. Her lips came apart to greedily welcome the mating of tongues and hurried breath. His arms squeezed her, his hands clutched and caressed with little gentleness. The sheer force of his possession had her weak and all powerful. The helpless frustrations of the day were cast off in this arena where she could compete as an equal. She was not uncertain of his world when in his arms.

When her fingers rose in an attempt to tangle in his yellow hair, Royle made a small objecting sound. With one hand still firm on her bottom, grinding her hips to his, his other reached to the table and apologetically offered a towel.

"Wipe your hands, love, lest we spend more time in cleaning up the mess than in pursuing other pleasures."

Her lips pursed coquettishly as she wiped the dough from between her fingers. A female trained from birth in the art of flirtation could not have managed the expression better. "Are you certain you don't wish me to finish with the loaf?"

"Quite sure," he rumbled. "'Tis more than finished, anyway and we—we've just started."

The towel fell from her fingers to the powdery whiteness of the floor, forgotten as his kiss consumed her. The strength of his earlier upset and relief at proving it false lent a rough proprietorship to the gesture, making his mouth move urgently, with a desperate command of passions. She returned that tender savagery until their lips were bruised. When he began to soften the kiss to correspond with the wealth of sweeter emotions welling within him, she broke away. Her eyes were afire.

"Royle," she said so low it vibrated and growled with excitation.

Tender expression was lost in the hunger. Clothing couldn't be shed fast enough to match the building eagerness, so they went to bed in varying stages of undress. Evangeline's stockinged calves stroked encouragingly along his thighs. Her avid fingers tore the neckband of his shirt wide so they could caress the taut tendons of his throat and thrill in the frantic pulse throbbing there. His hands pushed beneath the muffling layers of petticoat to seek her rounded buttocks, lifting, anchoring them to receive the buffeting force of his manhood. She cried out, conquered and exalted by his penetrating

184

thrusts, and was gratified by his answering groan. Their union was as violent as nature and as purely physical as the basic elements of the earth, a tempest of savage thunder shaking them to their souls.

When she called out again, it was in lusty triumph, and Royle was quick to seize like victory upon the bed their passions had torn assunder.

"I shall hire you a woman to keep the house."

Royle expressed that intention in a quieter moment as they lay in the comfort of each other's arms. The keeping room was dark, the mess upon the floor and table dismissed, ruined clothing cast aside. He nuzzled his face against her throat, content and willing to offer her anything.

"I can provide you a proper house, Tanner," Evangeline objected in a bristle of pride. The languorous curve of her body didn't react to the agitation of her voice.

"I've no doubt you can, providing you know how, which you do not."

He heard her offended sniff and he smiled, tightening his arms to convey his satisfaction. He chuckled, imagining her lovely pout.

"Evangeline, one who is scarcely civilized cannot be expected to keep a home accordingly." He anticipated her ire, delighted in it, in fact. There was an innate pleasure in feeling her strong, lithe form wriggle with dangerous intent within his clasp. "I shall speak to Mistress Loockermann to see if she knows of any one equal to the post."

"Most likely, she'll suggest herself," Evangeline spat, subdued in body but not in spirit. "You should have wed the ample widow if you desired such services."

No sooner had she spoken those vindictive words when she realized their hurt. Upon wedding her, he *had* expected those things. He'd thought he possessed a woman with knowledge of stitchery and books, of proper manners and genteel accomplishments, a woman who could run a household, prepare a simple meal, and provide him with the necessary comforts. Thus far, she had failed him badly. She wouldn't wonder that he'd beat her with a stick for being such a miserable wife. She may have given him a pleasurable bed, but his happy home was lacking. What a poor bargain he had made. She cringed beneath her own shortcomings.

And then his words purred in a verbal caress to her soul.

"The ample Mistress Loockermann offers nothing I want. All I desire, I possess."

She could have wept with gratitude at his male blindness of her faults. His kindness made them no less noticeable to her, however, they were easier to bear. Royle Tanner was a good, decent man, but as a husband, he was too generous. If he did not call her to task for her weakness, she would take up the chore herself. No man wanted a lazy, incompetent wife to trust with the fruits of his labor. In the morning, she would humble herself and cross the street on her own. And she would make Royle Tanner as proud of her as she was of her strong, brave husband.

They stood together before the fireplace in the common room. The maple sticks had burned fierce and hot, leaving a fine sheen upon the faces of the two women as they scraped the embers from the hole in the chimney. Fresh loaves of brown bread were fed into the brick oven on a peel, and the iron door closed to seal the opening.

"There," Eva Loockermann said with satisfaction. "I can go to bed tonight and take the bread out in the morning, all hot and crusty. Once a week put in your beans, brown bread, and pies, and that should keep you nicely." She wiped her hands upon a clean linen apron and turned to her young pupil.

"The trick be in preserving the leaven. Keep a lump of the latest baking buried in your flour and in a cool, dry place. If it gets too cold or damp, it will not rise, and the bread will be heavy, too hot, 'twill ferment and grow sour. Timing is the next thing to learn. If the loaves be taken out too quickly, your half-baked dough will fall into a flat, solid mass not worth serving to the animals. A man, he takes pride in a wife who can yield good bread, yah."

Evangeline nodded somberly. Good bread, a prideful husband.

Eva bustled about her large, colorful room, tidying her work space before taking one of the rush-bottomed stools next to her visitor. She eyed the girl's brocade gown with spiteless envy, noting its rich detail and sumptuous fabric. "This must be hard on you, yah, coming into the wilderness to do for yourself the things you had a staff of servants to tend before." She nodded sympathetically before Evangeline had a chance to comment. "I vas such an innocent when we came across the ocean, my Jacobus and me. Such a strange, wild place this vas then. I vas glad I brought a bit of my homeland with me." She gestured fondly to her corner cupboard, where a garnish of pewter plates and porringers sat gleaming from their daily polishing with wood ashes and oil. Intermixed with them was the cheery blue and white patterned Delftware. "We came from Wyk, Holland those many years ago, Jacobus in his fine constabu-

187

lary uniform and me toting my treasures. 'Twas grateful I vas when he transferred into the lace-collar clothes of the company's civilian service. There vas no money to be made as a soldier."

"Do you miss it?"

The bright blue eyes focused on the present and on the young woman in question. "Miss what, my dear?"

"Your home?"

"At first, yah. I cried all the time. I nearly floated Jacobus away with my tears. Now, this be my home. I can imagine no other."

Evangeline digested this in silence as her gaze took in the neat kitchen and its efficient tender. "There is so much to learn," she said at last. Hopelessness crept into that single phrase.

"Nonsense, child. I can help you learn. Besides, you be so pretty, your man won't notice if the bread does not rise."

A doubtful hand rose to smooth cheek. Was she pretty in this white world? Vanity of looks was a foreign notion to her, but seemed important here. Was Royle pleased with what he saw? His eyes said yes. His touch said yes. Her concern went no further.

"Still if you be wanting regular help, you could hire a maid. Be warned, they be scarce in these parts, marrying too quick to stay long in service. I could help you find a half-tamed squaw. They are sometimes employed as a poor substitute for a trained houseworker."

"You need not. I wish to serve my husband myself."

If Eva noticed the sudden hostility in the girl's tone, she chose to turn a deaf ear to it. She chuckled deeply. "Vere he my husband, so vould I."

Evangeline's gaze narrowed. The day had been

most pleasant until mention of Royle was made. The jolly widow seemed to take on an extra glow when speaking of him, and Evangeline's warmth increased apace.

"If you be determined to do for yourself, keep all simple and filling. For breakfast and lunch, milk and hasty pudding, or milk and stewed pumpkin, baked apples, or berries. Spit your meat for supper or cook it in a bake-kettle. I can show you who to trade with for fresh game. There are always Indians about willing to take a useless trinket in exchange for a meal. You needn't be afraid of them. They are harmless, really, like naughty children."

"I am not afraid."

Eva thought that statement a trifle bold for a stranger to these parts, but she liked the pretty Mistress Tanner and was hungry for female friends. She chose to ignore the girl's odd outbursts in favor of her company.

Just then there was a clamor of footsteps, and Royle appeared over the half-door whose bottom section was closed to keep out animals while the open top allowed a cheerful breeze. Royle looked anything but cheered. His eyes took on an unnatural brilliance against his pallor. He was out of breath. Then his gaze lit on Evangeline where she sat upon her stool in the midst of a social visit, and life was restored.

The depth of his fear confused Evangeline with a mix of pleasure and resentment. Did he think because she was not within his walls she had fled him? Then irritation gave way before compassion at how ghastly he appeared, and she murmured meekly, "Forgive me, my husband. I did not mean to stay so long. I was not expecting your return this soon. I was making bread."

Royle forced down the quivering of panic and found he could expel the breath he'd been holding. Relief did crazy little things to his manner, making him act almost jaunty as he replied, "Forgive *me*, wife. You being so much a stranger to these parts, I grew concerned at your absence. I see it was foolish of me to worry."

"Yes, it was," she answered in stiff chagrin at his twisted meaning.

Meanwhile, Eva had risen to shed her apron, uncovering a brightly striped petticoat. Its short jacket drew attention to her pendulous proportions, and when her hands fluttered about a neckline which displayed the plunging crevice between her breasts, Royle's gaze was distracted there.

"You and your missus must stay to sup with me, Mister Tanner. I insist upon it. I have venison fresh today, much more than I could ever make use of."

The flavorful scent of the meat tantalized him with the knowledge that no such treat awaited him at home. His belly growled an insistence of its own. "You are most kind," he murmured.

"Too kind," Evangeline muttered.

Evangeline sat silent through most of the meal. Stoically, she watched the animated play of conversation flow between her husband and the widow. He relaxed beneath the bolster of her flattering flirtations, smiling readily and quick with compliments in return. The meat was tender, the soup was rich, the bread fragrant. Evangeline simmered in envious resentment that he should find such favor in another female's board. She studied the way Eva's eyes addressed him and tried to view him similarly. The widow could not know of the splendor beneath his too many clothes or of his dauntless bravery. What then made her gaze so bedazzled?

At the meal's conclusion, Eva rose to cater to Royle's wants. She supplied a fragrant mix from her late husband's tobacco cupboard and encouraged him to taste it upon the low brick *stoep* outside her door. While he lounged upon one of the benches, drawing contentedly on his clay pipe, Eva took up the space beside him to work the knitting upon her lap. It was a disturbingly domestic scene.

The bright blue eyes looked up from the clicking of needles to the young woman standing stiffly at the edge of the porch. "You shall have to bring your needlework over and we can pass the evening hours at our stitching." Her gaze slid to Royle, including him in the invitation. "I have a wheel in the garret, and when the weather grows too cold, we can fill those hours spinning yarn. I envy you the wrap upon your sugar cone. It makes a splendid deep purple dye for fine wool."

"I shall make it a gift to you," Evangeline said flatly, then felt a twinge of guilt when the woman looked so grateful.

Happily, Eva turned back to her yarn and to the comforting awareness of the man at her side. "It will be so nice having you as a neighbor. I am sure you can teach me a thing or two about sewing a fine seam."

It was on the tip of her tongue to tell the woman her experience with fine needlework had to do with a bone awl punch and leather lacings, when she was caught up by Royle's gaze. Such smoky promise was held in that lingering visual caress, she forgot completely about the threat of the Dutch widow. That look stripped away all but the primitive longings of her heart. Royle rose, his intense stare commanding her eyes to follow as he murmured a polite good night to their hostess.

Feeling the possessive warmth of his hand upon her arm, Evangeline knew a smug pleasure. However capable the good Mistress Loockermann might be at preparing her table, she could not entice Evangeline's husband away from the most personal aspect of their marriage.

And watching them cross the street, all wrapped up in the sexual tension flaring between one another, Eva Loockermann gave a sigh of regret and was left with only the pungent odor of pipe and cherished memories.

That night, Royle consumed her with his passion, his lovemaking so strong and vital, she nearly wept with the joy of it. And in the morning, his absence left her adrift. Kind man that he was, Royle made no complaint at being sent off without the benefit of a hot meal, just as he made no mention of cold linens at night, for they were warmed quickly enough. But Evangeline was tormented by her failure. He deserved a filling breakfast and a competent wife, and she could give him neither thing.

Alone in the large intimidating room, Evangeline knew a panic of insecurity. How long would Royle be content with a lusty bedpartner in lieu of a proficient wife? How many evenings would they spend at the widow's bountiful table, treated to the widow's bountiful endowments, before he found lingering there more pleasurable than within the walls of his own home? She thought of the things Eva had described to her as the duties of a good wife; scrubbing the uncarpeted floors, feeding the fires, hatcheling the flax, carding wool, weaving heavy stuffs for household use, making soap, chopping sausage-meat, dipping candles, even washing linen to a snowy whiteness. She was so ignorant of these things, things of no use in her own life. The pull

The Publishers of Zebra Books Make This Special Offer to Zebra Romance Readers...

AFTER YOU HAVE READ THIS BOOK WE'D LIKE TO SEND YOU
4 MORE FOR *FREE* AN $18.00 VALUE

NO OBLIGATION!

ONLY ZEBRA HISTORICAL ROMANCES "BURN WITH THE FIRE OF HISTORY" (SEE INSIDE FOR MONEY SAVING DETAILS.)

MORE PASSION AND ADVENTURE AWAIT... YOUR TRIP TO A BIG ADVENTUROUS WORLD BEGINS WHEN YOU ACCEPT YOUR FIRST 4 NOVELS ABSOLUTELY *FREE*
(AN $18.00 VALUE)

Accept your Free gift and start to experience more of the passion and adventure you like in a historical romance novel. Each Zebra novel is filled with proud men, spirited women and tempestuous love that you'll remember long after you turn the last page.

Zebra Historical Romances are the finest novels of their kind. They are written by authors who really know how to weave tales of romance and adventure in the historical settings you love. You'll feel like you've actually gone back in time with the thrilling stories that each Zebra novel offers.

GET YOUR FREE GIFT WITH THE START OF YOUR HOME SUBSCRIPTION

Our readers tell us that these books sell out very fast in book stores and often they miss the newest titles. So Zebra has made arrangements for you to receive the four newest novels published each month.

You'll be guaranteed that you'll never miss a title, and home delivery is so convenient. And to show you just how easy it is to get Zebra Historical Romances, we'll send you your first 4 books absolutely FREE! Our gift to you just for trying our home subscription service.

BIG SAVINGS AND FREE HOME DELIVERY

Each month, you'll receive the four newest titles as soon as they are published. You'll probably receive them even before the bookstores do. What's more, you may preview these exciting novels free for 10 days. If you like them as much as we think you will, just pay the low preferred subscriber's price of just $3.75 each. *You'll save $3.00 each month off the publisher's price.* AND, your savings are even greater because there are never any shipping, handling or other hidden charges—FREE Home Delivery. Of course you can return any shipment within 10 days for full credit, no questions asked. There is no minimum number of books you must buy.

between the two worlds disappeared upon the marriage bed, but here, at the hearth, it tore her asunder.

Evangeline had left the white world at a tender age, an age of pretend and play, not of preparation for adulthood. Her schooling had come at the hands of the Iroquois women, and it did not serve her here in this foreign home of equally foreign civilized manners. She could adopt the clothes, speak the words so strangers would not think her different, but she could not hide away her failings before the one man she cared to impress. Distraught tears crowded her eyes when she thought of the cruel joke forced upon her husband, the joke of a hapless wife.

"Good morning," came a bright hailing from the opened door, and Eva Loockermann stepped in to twist the blade of her misery more deeply into her heart. The good widow carried a covered basket from which heavenly smells arose.

"Has Royle already gone so early?" Eva clucked in regret. "I had hoped to catch him. I have some fresh *olijkoecks,* the donoughts they make in my country filled with apples, citron, and raisins, and some hot crullers just off my iron. I thought your husband might enjoy—"

Enough! Evangeline drew herself up into a pillar of female indignation. Her words were crisp, not unkind, but unmistakable in their message. "If *my husband* desires hot donoughts, I will make them for him. If he wishes a filling meal, he will take it at my table. When he wants to enjoy a bowl and put up his feet, he will do so before *my* hearth. If these things are lacking, he will suffer them until they improve. I thank you for your helpful offers. I appreciate your visit, but I will not accept another loaf of bread or board at your table, until I can return the gift of your friendship. It is not my way to take what I cannot return. I wish you a good morning, Mistress Loockermann."

The little woman stood in stunned silence throughout Evangeline's stern speech, her jolly face pale and bright eyes glassy with surprise. When shown the door, her animation eked back and she managed an inoffensive grin.

"Methinks your husband be a lucky man to have a wife such as you. If you've need of me, I live across the street." And with basket in hand, she returned to her home, leaving Evangeline shaky in her triumph.

The rest of her day was spent in hurried industry. Evangeline may not have known the proper white method of getting things done, but she was creative. Combining what she knew and what she'd observed, she devised her own manner of doing about her house. The floors were swept spotless, the bedding stripped and aired in the invigorating autumn breeze. Royle's shirts were vigorously scrubbed—at the cost of several cuffs and yellowed neckbands—but mostly, she was pleased with the results. She invented a use for the devises upon her cooking hearth and kindled a warming blaze as she'd seen Royle do several times. Pelts were taken from the walls and given a satisfying beating out of doors. The exercise felt good, the effort purposeful.

And with a haunch of meat roasting over the drip pan, Evangeline donned her velvet mantle and started down the path to Webster's trading house. She'd allowed herself to be neglectful for too long. The indulgence in her shortcomings had come to an end. It was time to be a proper wife, Indian or white. Royle would know her serious in the role and he would be proud. First, she would insist upon an accounting of their assets, then she would take control of them. She'd become a passive drain upon her husband's goodwill, but no more. He would discover her an efficient manager of their property, and once relieved of that burden, Royle could concentrate upon more manly things.

Purpose lightened her step and her heart rose in harmony with the woods and the wind. Even the appearance of the trading house and its sinister effect upon her people could not lessen her mood. On her way up the steps, she passed a trio of braves and spoke to them in their language. Their eyes registered surprise as they mumbled their greetings and all three turned to appraise her as she went within. She found Royle busy at his books and couldn't bring herself to find fault with his role. She knew him innocent of deceit. A few carefully placed words could bend him to the truth. He wasn't closed of ear and heart the way others were before him at this task. He was a man of honor and could be trusted to deal fairly with her people. That knowledge warmed her gaze as it beheld him, and he looked up to witness that fond regard. That, and her very presence, held him for a moment, stare transfixed, then he rose to greet her.

"What brings you out here, Evangeline?" he questioned softly, with only a very slight edge of suspicion to his tone. She chose not to fault him for that either.

"'Tis time I began to see to things as your wife," she announced.

A sensuous male smile curved his lips. "I thought you were seeing to things quite well already," was his sultry comment. That she would blush with pleasure swelled him with a virile pride, but that, he was to find, was not her point of contention.

Her cheeks still warm and rosy, Evangeline

murmured, "I mean to tend my holdings as proper for a wife. My mother has said I have a strong natural sense and should not underestimate myself. I've been lax in my duties and beg your pardon for it. I am ready to assume my place."

His smile lingered in amused perplexity. "I'm afraid I don't understand. Your place as what?"

"As head of our family."

His smile stiffened. In a manner less friendly, he demanded, "What?"

Evangeline didn't note his cool withdrawal and went on to claim, "Upon our marriage, all you own became mine. I was weak and confused, and I let you take control, for which I am grateful. Now I am strong and ready."

"And what exactly do you plan to control?"

The chill of his frigid tones finally penetrated her enthusiasm. Was he not pleased? Slowly, she explained more fully. "Among my people, it is the woman who controls the house, who owns the property, whose name is given to her offspring. Every possession of the man except his horse and rifle belongs to her upon marriage. She takes care of the money and gives it to her husband as she thinks he needs it. She is the guardian of the home while the husband undertakes more laborious pursuits."

"Such as?" he prompted quietly.

"He builds the home, repairs it, cultivates the soil, hunts, and delivers to his wife his merchandise." She said that last quite faintly for he was looking very odd. His smile was more a grimace.

"Quite a unique arrangement," Royle drawled. His eyes had a peculiar light, of wry amusement or annoyance, she was not sure.

"Then it is done," she said with a happy relief.

"No."

That quiet monosyllable stunned her. She blinked then stammered, "Surely you don't mean to deny me that which is mine by right?"

Royle spoke carefully so she would not mistake a single word. He couldn't not allow her to harbor such ridiculous notions. "I do not deny you a place in my home, at my side, with my full protection. You will want for nothing as best as I can afford it. If you've a wish, you have only to make it known to me. You'll not find me a stingy master."

"Master?" The word echoed unpleasantly, strident with disbelief, with affront. She stood taller, as straight and majestic as a mighty forest pine. Her words boomed with authority and an anger that he would *dare* question her. "I call no *man* master, especially no inferior white male who cannot even claim to be *Ongue-honwe*, of the people who surpass all others. The women of my *ohwachira* have ruled in harmony while your society has worked to destroy itself with greed. You will not strip me of what is mine."

More aware of the eyes that turned their way in curiosity than of the embarrassment her open defiance caused, Royle warned in a low rumble, "We will speak of this at home."

"We will speak of it not at all," she flung back. A tower of outrage, she whirled and stalked toward the door, past a startled Max, whose brows soared at the muttered oaths he heard . . . something about cooking her husband's vitals.

Royle surged to his feet. "Evangeline," he roared. "You will not walk away from me." Furiously, he dodged about the hanging steel traps that delivered a nasty clang to the side of his head when disturbed. He meant to overtake her, to wrestle her down if necessary, to get her to see reason. That show of force was not needed, for she drew up short just inside the doorway, so suddenly he nearly collided with her rigid back.

It was not the angrily shouted words that stopped her, nor the firm hands that gripped her arms calling her to yield. Evangeline stood paralyzed, argument and upset forgotten in a mind void of all but terror.

For up the steps before her came her worst nightmare—in the form of a man.

Chapter Thirteen

Royle expected resistance. However, when he caught her arms, Evangeline revolved so quickly and looked so genuinely distraught, his anger washed away on a tender tide.

"Royle," she whispered hoarsely. His name was barely discernible over the tremor in her voice. It was the first time she'd called him that when not in the throes of passion. He was stunned by the power of a single word to reduce him to such humbling pleasure. She came forward as if she'd have him embrace her, yet when he opened his arms, she pushed by to gain the interior of the room. Obviously, she realized she'd been mistaken but her pride insisted she not relent too completely.

Sighing, Royle followed the quixotic figure back to where she huddled atop one of the rum barrels, looking small and miserable. When he came close, she refused to look up, instead murmuring, "I will await you here."

He'd planned to spend several hours more upon the ledger, but knew he'd be finished in minutes. He wouldn't keep her waiting in such abject distress. That their disagreement would cause her this degree of unhappiness troubled him. He knew he was right in his stand. He had no reason to relent even the slightest measure. Actually, he was being damned generous with her already! But with one wayward glance at her frozen features so drawn in despair, he knew right was no substitute for reconcilement. By evening's end, they would reach a compromise both could live with, and then the reconciliation could go on for rapturous hours.

While he hurried to tidy up his books, Royle grew aware of an ugly, raggedly dressed man hovering near, paying rude attention to his wife. That Evangeline was uncomfortable beneath that intense black stare forced him to speak up in irritation.

"Was there something you wanted?" His words were coldly delivered and laced with menace.

The man's soulless gaze pierced clear through him. Never had he felt such cold disregard. The man fingered the hilt of the huge knife hung on the left of his belt. A tomahawk balanced the right. He wore soft-soled moccasins and a loose frock coat of buckskin that hung halfway down his thigh, overlapping and belted at the hip. Neither were clean.

"Non," was all he said before striding away with the same lethal grace Royle had seen among the Indians. Royle's scalp knew a similar prickling.

"Who was that man?" Royle asked of Max when the three of them were alone. He could see Evangeline's quickened interest and wondered at it fleetingly.

"Him? He be Allouez and not a man to take lightly. He is a renegade Frenchman, a sort of freelance trader called a *coureurs de bois.* They be a dangerous lot, with no allegiances to man, honor, or country."

"And what be his business here?" The man's

200

attention to Evangeline had not been an admiring leer. That he would have brushed off as harmless, even flattering. No, his look had been of some other motive, and it left Royle unsettled.

"He and his kind range into the interior and gain concessions from competing merchants to play one against the other for the best price. They know the discipline of no government nor of conscience, but they can do business in places we could never reach on our own. Most are escaping punishment for illegal doings among the French when they turn coats and arrive in Albany. It don't pay to ask too many questions."

Royle nodded, thinking of the withering stare and steady hand on the knife. No, he would not care to confront the ugly Frenchman. Not when another confrontation awaited him in the delectable form of his wife. Resolutely, he closed the books.

"I'm for home, Max. See you in the morning."

Evangeline gave a small leap when his hand fell upon her arm. Wide eyes swiveled from their study of the door to his face. The fear within them was quickly masked, but he could not forget he'd seen it. Had he frightened her? He couldn't believe her indomitable spirit took to trembling because he'd raised his voice, yet the evidence knotted tight about his heart. His voice knew a gruff gentling.

"Let's go home, wife."

With each step down the pine-carpeted path, Royle's remorse deepened. Evangeline walked so near his side, they almost shared the same footfalls. It was his habit to keep a hand upon her, just a subtle reminder to prevent her from ranging far, but on this eve she clung to him, betraying the distress her expression denied. Guilt tortured him. He had bruised her noble will, and now sought a way to

201

make amends. He would not relent. Her demands were too absurd. No man gave his holdings over to his wife. It wasn't that he thought her incapable. Still . . . it just wasn't done! The idea of having her dole him out an allowance set his male vanity up like the back of a defensive dog. Of course, he couldn't give in to her preposterous idea. But he'd no cause to bully her into this skittish shadow entangled about his leg either. Being a husband was proving more difficult and dangerous than his work at the trading house.

The scent of roasting meat enticed him at the doorway. He stopped on the threshold and observed the miracle that had overtaken his home. In the place of chaos, there was order. While things remained much the same, subtle differences were wrought to increase the feel of welcome. The settle was tilted invitingly toward the fire. Delftware was arranged upon the trestle top. Bed linens were tucked back in an unvoiced beckoning.

It was a moment before he could react. Emotion crowded close in his throat, choking off all but humbled sentiment. She'd made him a home within the confines of her prison, and he had berated her cruelly for expressing her want to share it with him. Another time, she would have lunged at him with her knife drawn. That swift, finite pain was preferable to the dull ache of culpability aroused by her meek stance.

Royle forced himself to adopt a cheerful air as he smiled down at his docile bride. "'Twould seem you've had a fruitful day. I am pleased."

He bent, planning to take her lips in a rewarding kiss. Her head dipped down, sending the gesture awry. His mouth brushed along her hairline. Her rejection stung him, and his first impulse was to crush her close, to beg her pardon, and see her quickly to bed. But he took a step back, respecting her right to be angry even at the cost of his peace of mind.

Chafing in his helplessness, Royle stepped to the hearth and tested the meat. It was done to perfection. When he commented upon it, Evangeline moved silently to see the table prepared. Throughout the meal, he lavished compliments upon her, yet each was received with a stoic grace. She seemed determined to see him twist in discomfort, and she was not disappointed.

While the removes were cleared away by the silent figure of his wife, Royle brooded into his beer. What did she want of him? An apology upon bended knee? Complete concession to her fanciful whims? He refused to cater to this blackmail of the heart. But that didn't ease his suffering. Knowledge of his righteousness didn't lessen the fact that he'd hurt her. And that knowledge was more wounding than the assertion of authority was satisfying.

And when she passed near him—a passive ghost— he could stand it no more. He surged up before her, catching her arms when she would draw back in alarm. Her features were tense with dismay. Did she fear he would beat her? Remorse teetered upon his gruffly spoken words.

"Evangeline, I regret the harshness we exchanged."

That was a calming neutral statement, and he felt pleased with his own humility. Her gaze came up, expressing such dazed surprise—as if she'd no idea about what he spoke—that he wanted to shake her in frustration. Did she think him completely insensitive to her distress? However he continued his compromising speech.

"Your feelings took me unaware. Of course, I am

203

pleased that you have an interest in our affairs. I will always respect and listen to your opinions."

With her so close, her vulnerability displayed so nakedly before him, Royle found the apology growing stiff upon his lips and he floundered. He knew how to deal with her anger, with her desires, but not with this strange quiet that had him restless and protective.

Evangeline saved him. Softly, she said, "Please, Tanner, can we speak of this another time."

He hoped his relief didn't gush too obviously, as he smiled agreeably and murmured, "As you wish."

As she made a move to leave him, his clasp strengthened, bringing her flush against the proof of his need. He found she was trembling and the last of his defenses crashed to his feet. Aching heart thickening his voice, he pulled her against his chest and whispered, "Do not despair, my angel. There is nothing we cannot resolve between us."

In answer, she made a small sound and her arms stole trustingly about his middle. That dependent gesture staggered him, overwhelming him with a tender passion he'd dared not display. Their relationship was one of fiery conquest. Gentleness had played no part. Evangeline responded eagerly to his forcefully physical demands, yet was wary of his quieter moods. Was she stirred only by the aggressive dominance of his lust? Would she find more tender sentiments a sign of weakness and be repulsed? Would she reject the evidence that he cared as well as craved? He would know. It was then that he realized he wanted more than a possession. He wanted—he needed a wife to love him.

Royle's hand stroked lightly down the ebony spill of her hair. He felt her stiffen against him, but continued the calming caress. Eventually, she relaxed and allowed it. Cautiously, as if gentling a timid forest creature, he let his touch slip beneath her cascading tresses to move more personally upon the contour of her back. She sighed. It was all the encouragement he sought.

Slowly, his fingers worked down the fastenings of her gown, parting it and persuading it to fall. She was naked beneath the heavy brocade, and that primitive state inflamed him. He forced his passion to quiet, to concentrate upon subtleties ignored between them in the heat of shared desire. Her skin was soft, like warm, pliant velvet, and he took a moment to enjoy that tactile delight. Her trembling had returned, but he wasn't concerned that it was of fright. She gave a wondering moan into the coarse fabric of his coat, unsure of his direction, unsure of her own response.

When his head lowered this time, she made no effort to evade his kiss. Her lips were softly parted, waiting, accepting with anticipating sweetness. The taste of her submission was an aphrodisiac. He drank of it until dizzy. His tongue sank deep to sample the tender treasure of her mouth.

He felt her feathery touch upon his face, the brush of her fingertips as they followed the strong jut of cheekbones and traced down to test the fervor of his pulse. Her hands moved lower, to the buttons of his vest, to the fall of his breeches, opening both with unhurried purpose. Then, her palms slid within, seeking the hem of his shirt and slipping beneath it. His body was taut. He was taken by a delicious tremor as questing fingers sought and found him. Her caress was tempting, taunting, tormenting along the excited shaft of his desire. His breath grew ragged upon her lips, threatening his leisurely purpose with the eminent eruption of goaded passions.

That was not what he planned.

It was an effort to step away, to remove her hands, and cease their devastating fondlings when so close to a spectacular end. While she stood before him, his beautiful pagan prize, Royle removed his clothing. Her gaze smoldered, admiring his physique with a candor to which he could not quite become accustomed. Whatever troubles brewed between them, they were abandoned here as they came together, man and woman, husband, wife.

They went down together atop the cushion of pillows, arms entwined, lips engaged. Passion simmered just below a boil, just testing the edge of their control. If their fervid embrace fulfilled a hunger, these tender explorations whetted an appetite for more.

Evangeline surrendered to sensation. Thought and fears had no place in this sensual haven to which her husband brought her. A quick, impassioned release would have gained her momentary ease, but this sweet temptation surrounded her with a lasting sense of security, of strength. Royle's attentiveness buoyed her and fed her reassurance. His touch was a maddening distraction, his kisses quelling any doubt. He was her protector, her warrior, her god, and he would let no harm befall her.

"Royle." She sighed his name in worship, in reverence to his strength. She arched her body toward him in offering, begging to be taken as payment for his care. His mouth left hers panting as he nipped along the taut curve of her throat. His hands enslaved her breasts, holding them captive for a torture so exquisite, she moaned aloud. His tongue laved and lolled about their sensitive tips, showing no mercy as she was wracked with an anguish of delight.

"Royle," she cried again as her hands threaded

through his yellow hair, tightening to coax him up to satisfy her wanting lips. And as his tongue plunged deep to tantalize and torment, his hand slid low to accomplish the same devastating movement within her passion-primed body. The dual provocation drove her near to frenzy, yet he wouldn't cease until she called out his name, this time in breathless celebration.

He didn't mount her then to satisfy his own desires. Instead, he continued to adore her body with gliding fingertips, to cherish her lips and breasts with his kisses. Slowly, the lambent pleasure began to build, and Evangeline was no longer content. Impatience had her restless beneath his touch. Knowledge had her eager to go on. The knowledge that he could control her with a touch held no shame. Her body was his to mold and shape and guide toward a glorious goal. She was proud of her body and of its response, and of its ability to please him with her own uninhibited delight. Finally, expressing her wants with a rumbling moan likened to a growl, she clasped him tight and tugged him over her ebullient form, encouraging him with the upward thrust of her slender hips.

And then he was inside her, filling her with his power, with his passion, with his possession. She begged him to put a quick end to her desperation, but he prolonged it with leisurely, thorough strokes. She thrashed and twisted, trying to find a limit to the sensations that just kept massing into one momentous peak of pleasure. And when it burst, the magnificence wrought of their combined passions contained a stunning power. Never had she been so humbled, so awed by a single act. Never had she been moved to such heights of joy or known such devotion to another.

Weak and replete, Evangeline gave thanks to her gods for gifting her with Royle Tanner. Then, she slept, still cradling his body with her own.

The pungent scent of burning woke Royle to darkness. That in itself he would have ignored if not for the brilliant flashes of light and growling thunder that followed. The first thought to seize his groggy mind was that the storm had struck their home and caused it to take to blaze. Panic shook him to wakefulness, that and the fact that he was alone in bed. He sat up and stared, puzzlement replacing fear.

Evangeline knelt on the boards before the hearth, tending a small fire within one of her cook pots. Her skin gleamed golden in the faint firelight. She hadn't bothered to dress.

"What are you doing?"

He couldn't have startled her more if he had shouted. Her head jerked up. Long hair swung perilously close to the low flames.

Then the scent defined and he leaped from the bed. Good God, she was burning his entire store of pipe tobacco. Grasping a ladle from the water bucket, Royle tamped out the smoldering fire, then turned to his wife for explanation.

"Woman, do you mind telling me what this is about?"

She tried to wrest the pot from him, but he held tight, his annoyance increasing as did her agitation.

"Tanner, please. I must make the offering. Hinu approaches the earth, and I must gain favor. Let me finish."

"No," he grumbled uncharitably. "Who is this Hinu who demands my favorite tobacco and turns my wife into a madwoman?"

Evangeline's gaze entreated him to understand. "He is our god of thunder. I must appease him or suffer his wrath."

Royle's brow lowered in vexation. "You act like a child, Evangeline. Get off your knees and back into bed. Try anything this foolish again, and 'twill be my wrath you'll suffer." He must have sounded impressively angry, for she scrambled up from the floor and disappeared with a tantalizing glimpse of bare bottom beneath the covers. That sight distracted him for an instant, then he went to pour the precious contents his crazy wife had tried to destroy back into its proper drawer, and he, too, went to bed, muttering all the while.

Evangeline was curled into the corner, her back to him. Royle punched down the pillows and sagged into them, hoping to be disturbed no more this night. But it was not to be. What began as a fitful trembling multiplied into tremors that shook the very bed. He heard no weeping. Nor would she turn to him for comfort. When he spoke her name, she flinched as if he'd struck her. It couldn't be borne.

"Damnation," he uttered upon a heavy sigh, then rolled up against his quaking bride, fitting her snugly to his chest and thighs. After feeling the eddies of her distress for several seconds, he asked softly, "What is it, angel?"

"You do not understand what you have done," came her hushed whisper. It was not an accusation. The words rang with mortal fear.

"What have I done? Kept you from catching your death of cold while wasting my best smoke to scare away ghosts?"

Evangeline twisted, revolving in the circle of his arms to confront him in her terror. Her fingers pressed to his lips. "Do not mock, Tanner. The

209

power of the spirits that roam the earth is strong."

He kissed those protective fingertips and said, "You speak nonsense, Evangeline. The goblins you fear are of your imagination."

Her head shook vehemently. "I have seen them," was her ominous reply.

"You've seen naught but a little lightning. Quit frightening yourself with silly superstitions and go to sleep."

"You would not speak so if you knew the spirits of the dead lived close at hand. My gods will be angry. They will send the Great Heads with huge eyes that see all, and who fly about on streaming hair to seek our destruction."

"Evangeline, stop! There is but one God, and He does not send monsters to earth to devour the disbelieving."

"There are many gods; Ka-tash-huaht, the North Wind who brings death; Gowen, the Echo God who foretells of war, and many more who dwell within the winds, the moon, and the stars," she argued doggedly.

It did no good to disagree or speak of reason. She behaved like a child, moved by the same illogical fears and notions, and so he would treat her as one. He clasped the sides of her face between his hands, compelling her to listen and believe with the intensity of that contact. His voice throbbed with authority.

"Evangeline, I am as strong as any of your gods. I defy them to cause you any harm whilst you're in my care. You are safe with me. Nothing can or will harm you. Do you understand?"

She was silent for a long minute, then very slightly she nodded.

Royle congratulated himself for quieting her fears,

and hugged her pliant body close. She snuggled to him. Her breath was warm and light upon his neck. The woman who had inspired him to such realms of passion now played soft upon his heart, and it was a satisfying feeling. And if any of her gods stepped down to challenge him, he would defend her to the last ounce of his mettle.

Perhaps he could, Evangeline thought to herself as Royle's possessive grip loosened in slumber. It still had the strength to envelop her securely. She'd seen him take down a great warrior. Could he, in fact, humble a god? His words bespoke of confidence, of certainty. Yet, he didn't believe. He'd reacted warily to the presence of evil that afternoon, but he hadn't recognized it for the terror it was. She did. She'd seen that demon in her dreams. She would never forget that face. It used to haunt her nightly. She knew it would this night.

The Iroquois parent rarely disciplined their children. If shaming and shunning was not enough, there was the sinister tale of Long Nose, sure to curb even the most unruly child. The idea of the terrible cannibal who kidnapped youngsters who misbehaved and carried them off in a great pack basket was the stuff of nightmares. Even upon first hearing that story, she knew of whom they spoke. She had seen him. She knew his face. And now he walked upon the earth. She'd seen him in the trading house. Though she was no longer a child susceptible to his threats, her terror was very real. And Royle did not understand the danger of his claim. It would take more than words of bravery to defeat a demon god.

Evangeline's hand rested over Royle's heart, taking comfort in that strong, steady beat. The pulse of life. Royle Tanner was not of her people. He had no cause to fight their battles. Yet he plunged in and made valiant vows. For her. He might not believe. He might not understand. But he was ready to risk all on her behalf, and that made him a god in her eyes.

But on this fearful night when angry gods prowled to chastise the unworthy and the unwise, Evangeline was tormented by threads of a distant memory. The scent of tobacco brought it back to tease and taunt the vague edges of recollection. She remembered the smell of pipe, the strong circle of arms dwarfing her with their power; a power she'd never doubted but would cruelly learn had limits. In her ear, she could hear a beloved voice saying firmly over the fear, "Do not be frightened, little one. I will see you safe." But he hadn't. Emotion swelled upon the roil of uncertain panic and despair, as the glimpse of her past thinned and was gone like morning mist. But the feelings remained, the shattering sense of broken trust, the terror, the horrible aloneness. And she clung to Royle Tanner, praying he would be stronger, that his vow had the power to protect.

She pressed a gentle kiss over that courageous heart, willing it her strength should a confrontation come to pass. A fierce admiration for her white husband encouraged her own thoughts of bravery. If the gods were to take on Royle Tanner, they would find a ready fight upon their hands. And if they harmed him, they would learn that her wrath, too, could make mountains shiver. And then, with her ear against his chest to hear that comforting rhythm, Evangeline was able to sleep without dreams.

Chapter Fourteen

Evangeline seemed herself in the morning, calmly serving him his breakfast and wishing him a good day from the door of their house. The reluctance he felt upon leaving no longer had to do with the fear of finding an empty home when he returned. It was the fiery kiss she granted that had him eager to rewalk the trail at the end of the day. Only to find another plague of superstition had descended upon his home.

Evangeline greeted him with no kiss, no dinner. She would not even meet his gaze. Instead, she sidled away when he approached her, quickly putting the table between them.

What is it now? he wanted to growl in supreme annoyance. He settled for a softly spoken, "Is something amiss, Evangeline?" Her reply astounded him.

"I must be apart from you."

Panic and objection soared to give his words a gruff harshness. "No, you will not." His thoughts reeled. Had he been foolish in assuming she'd grown content with her lot and with him? Had the childish episode over his tobacco provoked this retaliation? Bloody hell, she could have the tobacco. It wasn't *that* important to him. He was about to tell her as much when she continued quietly.

"I must withdraw for several days, and need to find a small hut that will suffice to house me."

Bewilderment bred irritation. "What nonsense is this, Evangeline?" Royle snapped. He tried to close the distance between them, but she slipped away, her eyes still canted downward. "Evangeline, answer me."

"'Tis necessary while I be unclean. I do not wish you harmed. When it is done, I will wash myself and all I've touched, then can be received once more within your home and bed."

Royle's puzzled frown deepened. Then her meaning overtood him. He flushed scarlet and floundered with a turmoil of emotions. That discussion of so private a matter should involve him, made him writhe in embarrassment. Her prim suggestion made him want to laugh aloud. That she was not with child—his child—was a bittersweet ache.

"There is no need for you to take such measures. I understand," he offered formally.

Her distressed gaze flew up, then quickly down in horror of what she might have done. He did not understand. How had he managed to live so long in such ignorance? Didn't he realize she was trying to protect him? In agitation, she tried to explain. "Women in their courses possess unholy power. Food is poisoned by her touch. Game is scared at her scent. A man's health can be injured with a glance. I must be apart, Tanner."

To her horror, he actually laughed, loud and long. He moved swiftly, intercepting her with a firm embrace. She cringed at his touch and tried to pull away, but he would not allow it.

"Tanner, please," she begged of him, so distraught

to think she would bring him harm that she was near to tears.

"Evangeline, look at me."

The stern demand was followed by an impelling grasp of her chin. Her head was forcefully tilted up. She squeezed her eyes closed to prevent the taint of her evil. When his fingertips stroked gently down her cheek, she trembled.

"Angel, something so natural to your sex is not going to strike me down. I've no intention of allowing you to leave my house or my bed. I've no fear of your silly superstitions. Open your eyes. I promise you I will not turn to dust at your glance."

His voice was filled with such warmth, such tender humor, such confidence. She risked a tentative glimpse. He was smiling in encouragement.

"There, you see. I've broken out into no hideous affliction. If you yet doubt my word, go speak to the Widow Loockermann about your fears. She can put them to ease."

The notion that she would accept the assurances of that woman over those of her own husband, that he would believe it so, made Evangeline's sense of loyalty overcome her fright. She could not let him think that she didn't trust his power. Bravely, she looked him squarely in the eye, praying to her gods all the while. He withstood her gaze and she marveled at his strength. Truly, he was not afraid of anything. She risked a cautious smile of her own.

Though she slept with him that night and on the others that followed, as soon as he fell asleep, she withdrew to an uncomfortable rest upon the hearth, rejoining him at dawn. Meals were served upon her table, but the hands that prepared them were Eva Loockermann's, and Evangeline made sure his were the only hands that touched each dish. She'd given the widow no explanation for her request. None had been demanded. Her gratitude toward the woman who helped save her husband's life abounded daily. And though she sat with him in the evenings, nodding as he spoke of his work, her eyes were carefully averted and her lips moved in silent prayer. It was not that she didn't trust his power, she told herself. It was just a precaution.

Royle survived the week and took her back into his bed with unfeigned enthusiasm, which she returned wholeheartedly. Days continued to pass, each making her comfort within the white man's walls a little easier to bear. Until their visitors arrived.

Evangeline was seated cross-legged before the fire, Royle's shirt spread upon her knees. Laboriously, she plied the needle as Eva had shown her to mend a tear in one cuff. Blood from her cruelly jabbed fingers stained the linen beyond redemption, but she was determined to complete her task. All proper wives knew how to ply a perfect seam. She studied her irregular stitches with a rueful smile, but a proud accomplishment eased the ache in her hands.

A knock upon the door was no surprise. Probably the Widow Loockermann come to judge her stitchery, she thought as she carefully folded the garment and rose to go to the door. Her surprise in seeing Uriah Webster and her Cousin Cyrus held her immobile. And their obvious shock at her state held them likewise.

Evangeline recovered first and stepped back to offer a gracious, "Please, won't you enter my home?"

The two of them came in warily, as if expecting her to wield a blade, exacting punishment for her betrayal. No such emotion was displayed upon her serene face. And that unsettled them.

"My husband will return shortly from the trading

house. You are welcome to take refreshment whilst you wait."

Their disbelief rankled Evangeline. Did they think the white man the only one to undertake hospitality? Her own people were generous hosts, offering even strangers victuals among them. When guests arrived, the best house was cleaned and given up for their entertainment, the prettiest maidens washed and dressed in best arrayment for the chance of honoring the visitor with the duties as performed by a fond wife during his stay. At least, Evangeline noted with a superior air, courtesy from the Iroquois was not falsely given. Silently, she poured her relatives each an ample bowl of beer and laid out a loaf of her freshly baked bread to slake their hunger. Then she withdrew and began to hope for Royle's quick appearance. They would never suspect the turmoil that twisted within her breast as she pondered their unexpected arrival. Had they come to take her back with them? Would Royle seize upon the opportunity to rid himself of a troublesome wife? Would he decry the trickery that bound them and demand a release? Inwardly, she trembled.

It would have surprised Royle less to find his wife's Indian family at his table in the place of his white in-laws. He glanced her way to descern her mood, grateful to find it calm. Before greeting his guests, he went to her to brush a kiss upon her temple, whispering as he did, "Grab no knives, if you please." When he drew back he caught the glint of wry humor in her eyes. And something deeper, a sort of desperation he didn't understand.

"What brings you to the wilderness, Mr. Webster," he asked, assuming a chair and taking the beer Evangeline was quick to pour.

Uriah Webster smiled innocuously. "Why to see

how my niece fares, of course."

But Royle's eyes had been opened to the subtleties of Webster's speech. He'd come to see if Royle still had his hair. "She is fine as you can see. Marriage has proven to agree with her." He stared at him, leveling an intense gaze. "And with me." That claim was met with thinly veiled doubt. He smiled just as smoothly. "You've arrived just in time to share our meal. Evangeline is an excellent cook. Set extra places, wife."

Evangeline snapped rigid. Never had he ordered her about with indifference, then calmly waited for her to comply. Her eyes narrowed in consideration of his yellow hair so smugly worn at his own table. Take up no knives, indeed.

Royle glanced her way. Their eyes made brief contact. Then it was clear to her. He was asking her to perform for their guests, to act the proper wife and dutiful chattel as she should. Fury at his unspoken request clogged her reason, and the blades upon her board looked tempting. Then, cold logic crept in, and with it the whisper that if her family thought her content, they would not challenge her right to stay within the home she'd made. And Royle would have no reason to be displeased.

Silently, she removed the additional settings and laid them out on the trestle top. While Royle sipped his beer and their two guests, resplendent in their fluffy wigs and velvets, watched her every move through critical eyes, she served up the meat and seafood. Food was delivered with efficient movements, then Evangeline withdrew to wait by the hearth until they finished. Royle never required her to eat apart from the table. He looked to her in question. The haughty tip of her chin was answer enough. If she was to act the docile housewife, the role would be played to the extreme. He wasn't sure whether to be proud or provoked at the zeal with which she took to her charade.

As the voider was passed, Evangeline suggested mildly that they might want to rejoin in the sitting room. After they filed obligingly from the common room, she set upon her meal, hacking it into small, satisfying pieces upon her plate. She had observed her husband as Uriah Webster spoke. The man clearly entranced Royle, the way a viper does its victim. And the look that came over his face spoke of that odd rapture. The weakness of white man's greed was betrayed when they spoke of business. She didn't like what she saw. She admired her husband's strength and honor above all things. To see them falter before another's shrewd manipulation shook her to the core. It reminded her of the difference between them, of differences she'd been trying to overlook and overcome. But there they were, yawning wide and dangerously deep, and contempt for his kind ebbed back to taint him.

The three men sat grouped around the new fire, and each accepted the refill of their mug without a word of thanks. They were absorbed in their male talk, and she, being female, was excluded. That offended one used to attending the council fires of her people, one accustomed to being heard and respected for her voice. They might choose to ignore her, but she refused to go away. Resolutely, she dropped upon a stool within the ring of unsteady light and opened the first book she could put her hands to. It was Royle's well-worn Bible. The selection gave her pause. Then, determinedly, she opened it.

The inside pages were filled with names and dates; marriages, births, deaths. She was about to flip by them when she saw listed in a small neat script,

"Royle Augustus Tanner, January 14, 1659." Her fingers stroked along that line. Beneath it, read another inscription, one more sad and finite, and in a different pen. "Hester Rose Tanner, August 23, 1665–August 28, 1665." She skipped up several lines to the notation of marriage between Royle's parents. Behind his mother's name was the same date as his sister's birth. Motherless at six. She wondered if his father had taken another wife, and then was surprised by how little she knew of her husband. He'd come from England. He was a man of learning, a man of determination and honor. Nothing more. She'd discovered more on this single page than in their first month of marriage.

Evangeline looked at Royle Tanner and saw a virtual stranger, one who was bound to her by white man's law and by her word, one whose bed and passions she shared nightly, one whose past was a vast unknown. Why had they never spoken of themselves? When he returned from the trading house, he spoke of his day, and she, of hers. When the table was cleared, their desires led them to quickly express with their bodies what was unvoiced at other times. They spoke of the present, hinted at the future, communicated passion that spanned eternity. But never had they explored the days before that fateful one that brought them together. Was he as scornful of her years among the Indians as the Websters? Was it disgust that kept him silent about her upbringing? What in his own life did he prefer to keep untold, or did he fear she would not want to hear of a life apart from the one they were trying to make here in Albany? She vowed to discover these things before the candle went out this very night, before passions were appeased, before sleep held them silent.

With the book still open upon her lap, she began to

listen to the discussion bantered about her. Every word spoken from her uncle's lips had the smack of insincerity. Every time Royle responded with an urgent eagerness, a disquieting fear twisted tighter about her heart. She was losing him, to his world, to this unscrupled man.

"Maxell writes glowing praises of your progress here in Albany," Uriah offered, dangling that compliment like a glittering lure. Royle didn't snap it up quckly. He nudged it, studied it from varying angles, cautious, careful. Living with a savage had obviously taught him restraint.

"I am pleased he thinks highly of me. 'Tis mostly his doing."

Webster smiled at that modest claim and reeled out a little more line. "He tells me you have a natural feel for the business, an aptitude he envies. He tells me you'll go far and beyond my expectations."

"I have every reason to want to excel," was his adroit allusion to their discussion in New York. Neither of them had approached the terms of his employment. They seemed to be sidestepping it most daintily.

"So you do, my boy. So you do. 'Tis why I've come to you with a proposition. I've recently put five thousand pounds sterling into a bill of exchange for my agent to make purchases in London. Those goods are intended for the Great Lakes region, where a man on my behalf will trade with the far Indians up to the reaches of Michilmackinac. When he returns in the spring, the wealth of local furs from that frontier will make two fortunes, mine and his. Are you that man, Tanner?"

The dazzling rig gave a final jerk and Royle snapped, hard, fast, like the big lake trout when tempted beyond heed for its fate.

"Yes."

Hook set, Uriah was content to reel in at leisure. "The trace goods will arrive in Albany at the end of the week. I'll arrange for men and transport over the Iroquois trail and for a knowledgeable guide. Maxell can see to the post over the winter months. Evangeline can come to New York to live with us. Cyrus has recently wed, and she would be good company for the girl while she awaits the birth of their first child."

Royle began to feel the sting of the hook. Being apart from Evangeline was something he'd not considered, not for the months it would mean. For Webster to extend such an invitation had him wary of all. Evangeline was no favored niece. This was no fond offer from a doting uncle. To them, Evangeline was a savage. She'd known treatment beneath their roof that defied contempt. Yet the bait was tasty.

"I shall have to think on it. I'll let you know of my decision in the morning. I'll have Evangeline prepare the upstairs rooms for your stay." His tone was final. There would be no further discussion on this night.

"Well then," said Cyrus, speaking up for the first time. "If business be concluded, what say we see what amusements Albany has to offer. I understand they have some tolerable taverns."

Royle, who had never set foot in one since his arrival, was quick to avow that this was so. Coats were gathered, and without so much as a farewell, they took their leave to seek entertainment beneath another roof.

Evangeline was so numbed by what she'd heard, she didn't think to mind their rudeness. Return to the Websters. Dread seeped deep into her soul. Months of staying under their roof, in the tiny airless roof, with

222

no freedom, no choice. No Royle. It would mean adopting the stuffy propriety, because they insisted upon it, not because she wished it. It would mean enduring the brimstone of Rev. Bentley and the lecherous suggestions of Cousin Cyrus. And there would be no Royle.

She looked about the room in panic. Would he force her to leave their home? Would he demand she remain in the cruel custody of a family who didn't want her, who made no effort to show her the slightest kindness, who had used her meanly for their own purposes? Surely he would not. Yet she had seen the adventure lust in his eyes. Would his desire for fortune best his desire for her? Her doubts made her tremble, for she could not be sure. She knew not her position in his household. Or within his heart.

Dazedly she moved into the common room, where focus turned to the large bed. Months without Royle. Months of sleeping alone, without companionship, without comfort, without passion. With thought of empty nights stretched out before her went incredible loneliness and despair.

And what if while he was away, he found another more agreeable female with whom to mate?

That notion gave her enough angry vigor to stalk up the narrow stairs to lay siege to the bedrooms, rooms she'd come to hope would one day house their family. She punched the pillows until feathers flew, and struck steel on flint so furiously, it took the first time. Imagining her husband curled up before a fire with some pretty Ojibway maiden was a torment to her pride. The way he lustily pursued her bode ill for his ability to withhold from pleasurable commerce through the cold months of winter.

As she muttered curses upon her husband for his imagined infidelities, another thought struck her.

223

What if he didn't come back at all?

Terror possessed her thoughts. She couldn't think of what that would mean, losing Royle, only of where it would leave her. Had he filled her with his child, she would have no strength with which to make her own way. Not knowing the white man's law, she saw only bleakness in that future. Would that leave her at the mercy of the Websters for the rest of her days? She couldn't bear the thought.

She would not let him go, and if he did, he would not give her over to the Websters. With that decision made, she went to sit before the kitchen fire, to await the return of her husband and the chance to speak her mind.

The opening of the front door caught her yawning in the early hours of dawn. She heard them stumbling noisily about the sitting room, and Royle giving slurred directions to their room. She was standing stiff before the hearth when he reeled about the corner and came up short. If he noticed her anger, it must have made no impression. Lurid eyes swept over her. His smile was smugly arrogant.

"Come into my arms, wench. I've need of a warm welcome."

He was surprisingly agile for his condition. The wooden bowl she launched at his head missed by inches. Laughing, he dodged the next two missiles as well, then stepped boldly forward to catch her up in his embrace.

"That's the welcome I've come to expect and adore," he crowed with delight before seizing her lips for a determined kiss. He tasted of rum and tobacco. His grip was strong, not gentle, and she writhed within it, spitting oaths and fire. "What will I do without you to heat me on those wintery nights?"

The fight fled her. Evangeline hung in his crushing embrace, struggling instead with distraught tears. He meant to leave her. He was actually making light of their time apart. A wrenching agony tore through her heart.

The clearing of a throat brought them away from one another.

"Pardon the untimely interruption," Cyrus drawled, "but we find we require more blankets. 'Tis drafty upstairs."

"I will get them," Evangeline was quick to murmur, eager to escape the brutish behavior of her husband and restore some calm to her thought. She ran lightly up the steps and retrieved several quilts from where her dowry chest was stored under the eaves. She was turning out into the hall when the light was suddenly blocked by a looming shadow. Arms braced on either side of her and grinning features grew near.

"Hello, dear cousin. My memory does not do justice to your beauty. It must be the care of a man that brings forth such a glow."

"A man, yes," she spat in distaste. "Not a worm such as you."

Cyrus chuckled. It was a low, intimate sound that rippled along her back like an evil chill. "Your spirit incites me to other thoughts. Like how convenient it will be for the two of us under one roof again. You, with your husband hundreds of miles away, and me, with my wife sluggish with child. By that time, any man might appeal to you. And I will be there. And this time, my dear little savage, there'll be no weapons at hand."

"I need no weapon to best you."

Evangeline thrust the quilts into his arms and brought her knee up hard to cool the inflamed source of his desires. Cyrus gave a most satisfying grunt of

225

pain and doubled over. He had produced one child, she thought ruthlessly. No need for him to make others. She pushed by his helpless form and stormed down the stairs, ready to take on the other haughty male beneath the roof this night.

"I will not go to the Websters." That was announced the moment she entered the kitchen in an uncompromising tone.

"Is that right?" Royle said softly. He'd been slumped before the fire, but now he stood. He didn't command Cyrus's height or bulk, but his was an impressive figure, one of strength, one of might. And now that power threatened.

Evangeline braced her shoulders in defiance and shook back her long black hair. "I will not leave our home. If your greed demands you leave, then go, but I stay."

Royle had consumed just enough rum to feel the authority of his gender. He adopted a rather unpleasant smirk and drawled. "You will go where I say, wife, and you will await me."

"If I *choose* to await you at all, it will be here."

If I choose. Those words made a big echo in the uncertainty of his heart. If he left her to her own devices, she would be gone in less than a fortnight. Separation would be difficult enough without the nagging fear that he would have nothing to return to.

His smug attitude was forgotten, replaced by a cool decisiveness. His tone said he would brook no argument. "You will go to the Websters. There I know you will be safe and cared for. Albany is very much a wilderness still, and you, a beautiful woman. There are those who would seize upon my absence to make mischief. I can not allow you to remain here alone."

"Then let me go to my family. I will be safe there

226

until you return."

Her burgeoning hopes were dashed by a curt, "No!"

Evangeline swayed with disappointment and frustration. She tried one last appeal. "Surely it is not your wish to see me a prisoner among those who hate me, when I could be surrounded by those I love."

His closed expression was her answer. He had spoken, and she was to accept. By all her gods, she would not. Grief and anguish congealed into an outrage that demanded retaliation.

"Send me there then. I will not remain. I will escape them and you."

In two long strides, Royle was flush before her. His hand clenched the loose fall of her hair, looping it about his wrist in one savage twist. Her head was jerked back, her eyes uplifted to the green glaze of fury possessing his own. And he told her then, low, throbbingly, with dire promise, "If you flee me, Evangeline, I will follow you to the depths of hell if need be, and I will bring you back. You will remain at my side in chains, an animal who refused its master. Spit upon all the trust and latitude I've shown you, and I will make your gods bow beneath my wrath."

And forced to look up into the cold mask of his features, Evangeline believed him.

Chapter Fifteen

She was released so abruptly, she staggered. Evangeline shrank back and stared up at the fierce visage that was somehow that of her generous husband. In the time they'd been forced together, she had hated him, challenged him, distrusted him, even desired him, but never until now had she feared him, feared clear to her soul what he could do with the power he held over her, a power that much stronger because of her want to yield to it. She was panting like a creature cornered, and in a way she was. And like that trapped wild thing, she struck out hard at what threatened her.

"You will never find me."

There must have been some tremor in those words that betrayed her, some flickering in her wide gray eyes or softening of her stance, for suddenly Royle relaxed as if he knew for the first time the extent of his control. Supremely confident, he assumed an arrogant stance. His smile was grimly pleased.

"I won't have to," he confided quietly. "Because you'll never go."

He spoke the truth.

He'd reached into her weak, female heart and saw

her failing, written there as clearly as if it had been printed in his Bible. She would not run from him. It was no longer her wish to be free.

Drunk more on the power of that revelation than on the many mugs of kill-devil, Royle pulled her tighter against him and angled her head for the possession of his mouth upon hers. She didn't struggle. There was no point. He had beaten her. They both knew it. Even in the desolation of her defeat, Evangeline was stirred by his kiss, the way it woke her to the tingling of sensation, to the anticipation of delight. And she wished she could hate him.

When he released her, Evangeline stepped away and silently began to disrobe. Naked, she slipped beneath the covers of their shared bed and lay there, shivering with cold and devastation. The mattress dipped as he joined her upon it, and for a long moment, they lay as strangers. Royle was silent, absorbed by what it was he'd learned in the past minute. Was it surrender to a stronger will, or weakness before a quickening love? Whichever, she had come to him at last, broken to his lead, tamed to his touch And he was sorely ashamed of his treatment of her. Such a moment should be treasured, not ruined with crude flaunting. What he'd gained was tender and tenacious, and he vowed to accept his mastery with gracious honor. Better he take a bite of humble fruit himself, than to let it go bitter. At last, he said two words that broke her restraint.

"Forgive me."

With a strangled sob, she rolled away from him, face to the wall. She could not forgive him. He had exposed the weakness of her will and wrested all respect from her. With his claim, he had reduced her to simple chattel, a meaningless possession meant to be used upon whims for emotionless pleasure. How could two words restore a lifetime of self-assurance, after it had known such a shredding.

Royle's palm rubbed with knowing persuasion up the satiny curve of her back. His teeth scraped the ridge of her shoulder to send shivers clear to her toes. Though her body warmed to his claim, her mind still decried it in a feeble attempt to regain a portion of dignity.

"Can you not be satisfied with what we have here?" she asked of him, and he paused in his seduction to consider her words. "Does your lust for money overwhelm your want of happiness?"

His arms stole about her, not to inflame or excite, simply to hold. His chin rested atop her head. She could feel a strange quiet descend over him, and she waited for his words, sensing they would reveal something of the man within.

"'Tis naught to do with greed, Evangeline," he corrected gently. "What I seek is not riches. You would not understand."

"No. But I wish to. What is it that puts the fire in your eyes?"

Royle was still for a moment, gathering thoughts he'd never spoken loud. Yet it was her right to hear them, and his want to share.

"You think me fearless, but that isn't true. There are nights I wake cold in the terror that I've returned from whence I came. The thought of going back, to realizing defeat, it pushes me to things I wouldn't ordinarily do, things like frightening you to make me less afraid."

That gave her pause, and a clue to the depth of his desperate passions. She forgot herself in the want to solve that riddle. "Going back to what?"

"To nothing. There is naught worse than nothing.

To be ignored, to be used, to be despised and unseen, just because no title precedes your name. Nothing is crueler than the system society imposes. Try to rise above it, and you are beaten back."

"Like being a wife."

That insightful comment wrought silence. Then he admitted, "I'd never considered it, but yes, I suppose it is." Now both began to understand a little better.

Royle continued with his story of a childhood in London. It sufficed to say he was poor. He didn't elaborate on the conditions. Those he would never share to invite her pity, but they had much to do with the singleness of his purpose. He spoke, instead, of his father, whose ambitions fed him hope in a world where none was allowed. He told of how his father raised him to believe himself an equal to all but in circumstances, and of how, to better his chances, Bob Tanner sweated through doubled hours in one job and took another on in the evening, in order to buy his son an education. With no pedigree, schools were disinterested in young Royle Tanner, even though his quick mind far surpassed their requirements. At an exorbitant cost he obtained the right to study, and to pay the price, he worked cleaning the rooms after hours, rushing through his chores so he could steal a little time to absorb the wisdom from books beyond his reach.

He endured the snobbery of the other students, the hurt of being shunned, the sting of their taunts about his meager circumstance, the humiliation of acting the servant to those he loathed. He endured it because he looked beyond the present pain to its end, when he, Royle Tanner, would be someone of consequence. He could see the toll his future took upon his father, and pushed himself fiercely to prove worthy

231

of the price. But that price had proved an early death in exchange for knowledge, and Royle had never been able to justify the payment. The only way he could come close was to become the man his father envisioned, to realize the success his father had forfeited his life to earn him. To fail in those things would mean his father had died for nothing. And that tortured him daily.

"If I take this opportunity and go to the Great Lakes, I would be my own man. I would owe no one anything, and no one could take away what I'd gained. I came to New York with but a dream. If I cannot make it come true, there's nothing else for me." She felt him quiver then, with anxiety, with desperation, and her hands pressed over the large backs of his. The thick anguish of his voice pierced through the frustration of her own wants and fears, and she weighed the two together, his dreams against the sacrifice demanded of her. It was not an easy balance to obtain.

"And what of me and our future?" she broached carefully. He was vulnerable now, with barriers down and heart opened wide. It was a good time to ask such a thing of him.

Royle's arms tightened in painful possession. "You mean everything to me, angel. You are my hope, my dreams for the future. The children we raise between us will know nothing of the stigma of class. They will be free to rise as high as the stars if they choose, and no one can hold them back."

It was a wonderful sentiment, a beautiful dream. Her eyes misted wistfully, and her throat grew thick with what she knew she must do. Slowly, she rolled to face him. "They cannot be free until you dare to grasp your dream. You must go, Royle. You must fulfill your destiny, as I have mine."

Royle pulled her to his chest in a poignant embrace, close to the frantic thunder of his heart. There he whispered gruffly, "Do not leave me, Evangeline. You are the only thing of value I've ever possessed. You are the key to all I want, to all I need. Don't leave me."

Her answer went from heart to heart. "No, Royle. I will not leave you."

And after their guests breakfasted in the morning, she made good her vow. When the men would speak of business matters, Royle drew a stool to his side and motioned her to join them. His lingering gaze said he remembered well the plight of the wife, and that he would not force her to endure the inhumanity of it. His gesture gave her a voice where none should be allowed, and she wished she was free to express her gratitude. She settled for a press of his hand, only to find hers caught up quickly in a firm joining clasp. Webster's gaze showed protest of her presence among them, but those strongly united hands defied his will. He began reluctantly.

"Have you decided, Tanner?"

"Yes. I will go."

Uriah's smile was wide and well satisfied. "Excellent. Then we must make our plans, for you and for Evangeline." His beneficent gaze settled upon his niece, and she responded with her own small determined smile. "'Twill be our pleasure to have you with us again, my dear."

What a spectacular liar he was, she thought as she smiled. Beside him, her cousin, too, was smiling, though she thought his gesture a bit more strained. She met his stare for a long meaningful moment. He flushed and broke off contact. The agony of remembrance was clear upon his face, matching the small scar for lessons learned.

"Your offer is generous, Uncle, but I decline. I will go with my husband."

Her bold claim was greeted with silence. She didn't dare look to Royle, afraid she would see disapproval in his green gold eyes. She waited in tremulous uncertainty. If he said nay to her proposition, it would mean imprisonment beneath the roof of her enemies. It would mean months apart from Royle Tanner. It would mean more anguish than she was sure she could stand. *Please, Royle,* she breathed within her soul, *please see the logic with which I speak.*

"That's preposterous," Uriah exploded. "A young woman in such wilderness? You cannot allow it, Royle. 'Tis a journey that's wearing upon the best of men, into the heart of danger. No female could make the trip."

Royle answered slowly, finally. "Not Evangeline Carey, no. But Eyes-Like-Evening-Star should have no difficulty. 'Tis a perfect solution. I wonder that I did not think of it before. My wife will come with me. She is more than equal to the threat of trouble. Only the very foolish would tangle with her when she's well armed."

The Websters could not argue that. They could not pretend she was not a savage of the woods. That lie had long since been exposed.

Evangeline did not voice her joy. Instead, she raised Royle's hand to her cheek. And when he felt the wetness of her gratitude there upon that tender softness, his emotions knew a mighty upheaval. Respect for his shrewd bride twined about new, delicately budding desires. He admitted to the strength of his possessive feelings toward her. His passions were unashamed. But this subtle, seeping fullness of the heart defied his experience. Gently, he

234

squeezed her hand.

Days passed rapidly as plans progressed for the journey into the interior. Provisions were stocked, many supplied by a tearful Eva Loockermann from her own larder of baked goods. Evangeline's finer gowns were laid out full length in her clothes chest. There'd be no place for rich brocades and soft silks upon the trail. Secretly, she was glad for it. The sturdy calico and linens were the closest to freedom she could come within the white man's propriety. Once upon the journey, she planned to approach Royle with more practical fare. Gradually, of course. Though he was becoming used to her brazen ways, she knew when to stop short of shocking him beyond reason. He was still wearing his respectable stockings, stiff shoes, and other layers of convention. Perhaps she would suggest amending his style as well. Where they were going was beyond the reach of civilization. Into her world.

And after they'd spent their last passionate night upon a downy bed, and the house was closed up behind them, Evangeline was filled with an odd sadness, as if this place among the whites had become a home to her. That morning reluctance stayed with her as they traveled overland to catch the natural waterway at Way Through the Pines, the place Royle called Schenectady.

The first leg of their journey was by horseback, along the well-traveled paths the Indians had worn through the forests over the passage of years. They made up a long wandering caravan of heavily laden animals and brusque tenders hired by Webster. Evangeline did not like the look of them. Their eyes were hard and wary. They showed no respect to

Royle. Her they perused with insulting familiarity as she sat on a cushion behind her husband. She forgot them as the surrounding land took on the appearance of her homeland. To the right, the Mohawk River bubbled and gurgled as it lapped avidly at the muddy banks. She knew every lichen-covered boulder, every copse where the reminders of countless fires marked the campsites of her people. Spotted deer bounded past trees festooned with garlands of grape vines trailing down to brush her hair. This was her land. Her people came from the local villages scattered near; the Oneidas from the rounded hill near the Great Carrying Place, the Onondagas from the country of the Sacred Council Fire, the Cayugas from their lake as slender as a maiden's finger, and the Senecas from the land near the awesome gorge of the Genesee River. Had their horse forded the river and grunted up the opposite bank, the huge longhouses of her people would rise up before them. She wondered if Royle knew how near they were to where she was raised. She thought of pointing it out to him, but thought better of it. He would only worry that she'd be tempted to stray. Odd, though she would have liked to visit her family, she had no real desire to leave the man whose waist her arms encircled. She was content to pass by, smiling in her memories.

When twilight brought irregular shadows to the wood, two (more shifting than the rest) took up a parallel path alongside their trail. Evangeline was aware of them almost at once, but this, too, she would keep to herself to savor in her heart.

They made camp that night on the river's edge about a great, friendly fire. While they consumed their meal, Royle looked to her, catching her in that enigmatic smile. His arm circled about her shoulders to draw her into his side, where his lips brushed lightly upon her brow. Then she was startled from her happy lethargy by his quiet words.

"Why don't you invite them in to share the warmth of the fire? I hate to think of family shivering in the cold."

Evangeline came away, her wide eyes intent upon him, questioning, hopeful.

"Go on," he urged.

The simple lift of her hand brought the two men from the darkness where they'd lingered just beyond the reach of the light, so close in fact, that many of the men gasped in alarm and reached for weapons. A curt call from Royle ceased the hostile movements.

"Make them welcome. They are my—relatives."

The two braves knew better than to press the hospitality of a group glowering their distrust and hatred. They hunkered down at the edge of the camp's perimeter where the fire's warmth stretched to the end of its radius. Dark, inscrutable eyes fixed upon Royle and his bride, and beneath that steady gaze the Englishman knew a shiver of discomfort. To ease it, he turned to Evangeline with what he hoped she'd view as calm interest.

"I know the smaller to be your brother, but who is the handsome one beside him?"

"He is Cayenderongue, my cousin."

Royle's relief was evident. "Oh. From the way he was glaring at me, I assumed him to be your old betrothed."

"He is."

Royle looked back to the sleek, muscular brave his wife had professed to love and knew a sinking despair. The man was every inch the glorious noble savage that Royle had read about in books. He was ruthlessly beautiful, all hard and sinewy and wild like the land. In his state of near undress, his virility was obvious. How could Evangeline fail to be aware of it? He reeked of sensual power and lethal grace. Royle had been smug in his comparison of himself to the natives of the woods, but in this case, he fell far short of the mark. He was like a sturdy domestic pack animal beside the fleet, unconquerable stag of the forest. Had she the choice, he wouldn't wonder which direction his wife would turn. He could not compete. And knowing that, he felt a wretched jealousy.

"Why are they following?" he asked. His tone was brittle, carrying the edge of his suspicion above the unsettled undercurrent. Had the handsome warrior come to claim his woman? Was it their plan to meet in the woods after his party was in ignorant slumber? Would Evangeline rush to be with Cayenderongue given the chance? The questions were poison, eating away at his confidence and foundation of meager trust.

"I do not know." Her answer was equally stiff in response to his misgivings. When his arm dropped away, the distance widened, though neither actually moved.

"Go speak to them if you wish."

Evangeline searched his shuttered gaze, seeking insight into his offer. It was too taut to be born of generosity or goodwill. Did she really want to question it at all, when he was willing to grant her such a concession? She rose and went around the fire to greet her loved ones in their tongue.

Royle sat simmering in a stew of uncertain envy. Was he being twenty times a fool for letting her go? He saw them glance his way, then resume their hurried speech. That brief look from Evangeline set his reason askew. She looked tense, worried, nervous.

Were they even now plotting to relieve him of his hair, so Evangeline would be free to return with them? To return to a future she'd planned with another, before he'd bullied his way into her life and set it all awry with his demands for compliance. Had her softening toward him been a rouse to coax him into lowering his guard? Anxiety twisted tight. Jealousy choked him. Worse was his guilt. Was he keeping her from knowing true happiness? Selfishly, he refused to consider that for long. He was not about to offer her a choice. She was his, and he wouldn't release her from her word. Not for any reason.

Unable to bear the growl of his doubts while watching the three of them converse joyfully in their foreign words, Royle sullenly pulled the blankets about him and settled upon the unyielding ground. And if she escaped him while his eyes were closed, better he didn't witness her defection. He would be on her trail at first light, and perhaps he would learn to take scalps.

He was still indulging in grim, pettish thoughts of retribution, when the corner of the blanket lifted and a familiar warmth snuggled close. She must have concluded her plans for his murder, he thought glumly and stiffened when her small hand rubbed over his ribs. When her touch drifted lower with purpose—most likely to take an unflattering measure of him in comparison to her native lover—he rolled onto his stomach, pinning her hand beneath his belly.

"Tanner?" she whispered. Her breath tickled behind his ear. When he was silent, she settled beside him, not relinquishing her embrace.

Good, he thought. Let her believe him asleep, so when she and her savage friends made their move against him, he could take them by surprise. He

239

would lie awake, listening for the soft tread of their moccasins, for the unsheathing of their steel, as they sought his heart and hair. They would not find him twice unprepared. He would be ready.

He wasn't ready. He wasn't listening. He slept the night away with his wife pressed to his back in companionable slumber. And when he woke in the morning to find the Indians gone, he was sorely ashamed of his childish doubts and of the bitter emotions that spurred them on.

But that didn't make them go away.

They took to the river that morning, moving westward to where they would meet their guide to the interior at the Great Carrying Place. The Mohawk was flecked with bateaux such as theirs, traveling with furs and provisions in both directions. Wildlife flocked to the shores; cranes, swans, geese, and ducks thronging the calm by-waters. And Indians. Three out of four canoes that they passed were paddled by natives. And Royle Tanner felt suffocated in all that majestic space.

Albany had been rustic, but this . . . this was isolation like none he'd known before. The woodlands had their own strange language, one Evangeline seemed to understand. To him it was foreign and a bit frightening. Each mile took them farther from the edge of civilization and deeper into the unknowns of the wild. The air was fresh, pungent with pine, and clean with the scent of water. Sound carried forever and echoed back in odd distortion. With each dip of the paddles, Royle was more certain he would not be returning this way in the spring. It was a subtle knowledge, one that built and roiled from whispered worry to restrained panic. He was mad to leave the comfort of what he held to reach beyond, to risk the trust developing in his house for this tenuous unease.

Watchful eyes settled upon the figure of his wife. Evangeline sat in the bow. Her hair was braided in a single coil, with dark wisps blown back from a face tipped toward the sun. She looked so free, so content. A small smile curved her lips. What was she thinking, he wondered? Dark answers plagued his mind. This was the world she loved. He could see her straining to embrace it all the way she would a lover, rapturously, in eager welcome. What would it take for her to leave it all behind and return with him to a life she loathed? After inhaling deep of independence, would she resist the shackles of society with even greater vigor? It had been a mistake to bring her, to tease her senses with what she couldn't have—with what he wouldn't let her have. The temptation of the wild would only increase as did their distance from their home. Dread and doubt became cold companions.

When they camped that night upon the shore, Evangeline was gone longer than it usually took for her to see to her needs. Royle began to pace. Visions of her fleeing through the forest assailed his mind and would not give him peace. His features were drawn with tension when she appeared at the edge of the wood. She stopped, her expression puzzled, then at once tight with understanding. She moved briskly by him without a word, to kneel before the fire with the cache of roots and berries she'd gathered not twenty feet from his side.

Chagrined at his own behavior, Royle sought to make amends. He bent down beside his wife to observe her brisk preparation of what she'd garnered. The items she held looked like nothing edible he'd ever seen.

"What are you making?"

241

"Dinner," was her curt reply.

He lifted one of the velvety berries and rolled it between his fingers. Such a tiny thing could be deadly, and he'd have no way of knowing it. No way of knowing it until it was too late. "Do you know what all of these things are?"

"Of course. My people do not go to the cupboard for food. We go to the forest. Here." She extended a white tuber bud from one of the rootstocks she'd harvested. He took it in uncertainty, but it was not until she bit into another that he dared to follow suit. It had a crisp and mildly peppery taste, not at all unpleasant. "Toothwart."

The name was unappetizing. He couldn't force another bite. The remainder fell discreetly to the ground behind him.

"These are bullrushes. I will mash the roots and boil them to make a sweet syrup. It has a much better taste than the nectar of your English flies." His brow furrowed. "Honey," she explained and he appeared relieved. "These are blackberries." He munched on the handful she gave him. They were seedy but delicious. "And these berries are from the staghorn sumac. From them, I will make you a most pleasing drink. I grow tired of your weak tea that discolors the water and lays bitter in the mouth."

Royle stood, offered a thin smile before he went to where he'd positioned his packs, and ate hearty from the dried fare that was familiar. When she approached him with cup in hand, that meal grew restless in his stomach.

"Drink," she urged gently, pushing the cup at him. He took it gingerly and looked from the odd-colored brew to the cool steel of her gaze. After lying with him nightly and crying his name in ecstasy, would she really try to kill him? Would she wait until

242

they were out on an isolated trail when she could well have slit his throat in their bed? Or had this been her plan all along? He remembered her entreaties not to be returned to the Websters. All a clever ploy to induce him to take her away from where she might be caught and punished? Who would know way out here? Who would question a sudden, fatal illness?

He made a deliberate move, trying to make it look accidental. The contents of the cup spilled out onto the ground and stained as darkly as his mistrust. He could not meet her eyes.

"I'm sorry," he murmured. "How clumsy of me, after you went to all the trouble."

Evangeline's voice was silken. "That's all right. I made more."

She returned bearing the potion. Her stare bore into his. She was angry. Because of his mistrust? Or because she'd failed the first time?

"Here. Enjoy. Or to your health, as your people are fond of saying." That last was drawled in sweet malice.

Royle took the cup and drank. At first, he didn't think he could force the liquid past the obstruction of his heart crowded close into his throat. But it went down, smoothly, silkily, with a tang much like lemonade. He gave her back the emptied cup and awaited the outcome of his act. Would it be swift and sure, or prolonged agony? As it was, the only injury came from the fleeting flicker of hurt within her eyes, the only poison, the suspicion threading through him.

Chapter Sixteen

Morning brought with it a sharper focus to Evangeline's distress, encumbering the wonderful sense of freedom that should have accompanied the long golden day upon the water. The invigorating air, the endless expanse of green land and blue sky, untainted by the smoke of white man's dwellings, should have made her spirit soar, but it grew heavy and disheartened within her chest.

What was wrong? Evangeline spent tormented hours upon that puzzle. Royle was a stranger. The budding trust, the tenderness that had been theirs in Albany, grew wavery and dispelled in widening ripples with every pull of the paddles. He did not approach her, but that distance went beyond the physical. He watched. She could feel his eyes upon her, wary and alert. When she came near, she could feel his tension, could scent his fear.

At first, she'd believed it was the wildness of the land that made his actions so bizarre. He was unused to the surrounding forest, to depending upon a nature that wasn't always forgiving. To one raised on feather beds and confining walls, she could understand why he might be threatened by this raw environment. But that didn't explain his reaction to her.

On those days before leaving Albany, she'd felt a satisfying warmth about them. There'd been a certain intimacy in their shared glances, a frequency of touch, and quiet words of the heart. She would believe he'd begun to care for her. That's what she wished to believe. But now . . .

Evangeline looked to where her husband sat huddled near the fire, his eyes restlessly scanning the forest's edge. Had she betrayed her anxiousness? Had her wariness at her brother's warning made him so alert? Did he suspect they were not alone? She couldn't believe that, for even her sharp vision hadn't caught movement there. She'd warned them to remain hidden. Still he watched, and that cautious gaze eventually came to settle upon her where she stood near the water. There was no warning, no invitation in his shadowed look, and she turned away from it as he had turned away from her.

A storm gathered strength throughout the day. Moisture hung thickly in the air, begging for release. From a distance, the first flashes of the temper could be seen. Evangeline shivered and hugged her arms about herself. A low, ominous growl of nature made her quiver. Instead of finding proper shelter, she began to pace the perimeters of the camp, her step quick in agitation, taking her back and forth over the same ground. The wasted movement went unnoted as expectation mounted in the heavens and within her soul. Her eyes were on those angry heavens when a strong, familiar scent grew upon the air. Tobacco. Royle's tobacco.

Evangeline came about. Her eyes searched and found him where he sat puffing on his pipe. She couldn't remember him smoking it since they'd been on the trail. Yet he chose tonight to enjoy its pungent taste. Tonight when Hinu would be prowling.

Royle opened the blanket to make a welcoming hollow beside him, and she didn't hesitate to seek shelter there. Both fabric and strong arm enveloped her, surrounding her, protecting her from elements real and imagined. And as she curled up to him, resting fitfully upon his knees, Royle's hand repeated a rhythm along the glorious spill of her hair, while the aroma of his tobacco wafted close and comforting.

The rumbling passed, and with it the threat of rain. Royle's pipe was cold. The hour was late.

Evangeline rose from her secure cocoon upon his lap. They were sitting close. It was impossible to avoid the stir of that nearness, that demand of passions long suppressed. Her hand touched to his face. She felt him recoil slightly, unmistakably. Then his head turned so his lips found her palm.

"Royle," she whispered. It was more potent than any caress.

"God, help me," he groaned. Whether it was an oath or a plea, she didn't know, for his lips buried in hers, slanting fiercely back and forth until her whole world rocked apace. His arms crushed her in a violent response, eager, desperate to dominate, and their meaning was lost.

He bore her down amid their blankets, his mouth hungry in its feast upon her own. His breath came in quick, shallow pants, shivering with intensity, with impatience, with need. She cursed the fact that they were not alone, and that others slumbered nearby. She wanted to shed constricting clothing and revel in his naked splendor beneath the roof of nature, but circumstance forbid it. His hands were tangled in her skirts, seeking to free a way to satisfy their urgency.

246

He pulled her bared leg over his hips, anchoring it there while his hardness probed and provoked and finally pleasured. With tenting blankets as a shield and the muffle of kisses to keep completing cries from disturbing the stillness of the night, they found a secret paradise.

Royle continued to hold her close. It was a long while before his rapid breath quieted beneath her cheek. His chest jerked briefly in an unfamiliar motion, and his arms tightened until the spasm passed. Then he slept and Evangeline was able to find ease for her troubled soul.

Dawn came in wreaths of gray shadow. The fire had burned low during the night, and its final embers cast a lurid glow upon the mist. The pleasure of waking within the circle of Royle's arms died the instant Evangeline's eyes came open. Her scream pierced the silence, shivering upon it in a crescendo of utter terror.

There, on the opposite side of the fire, cloaked in swirls of dreamy haze, was the horror that preyed upon the sleep of children, the nightmare that haunted her dreams.

No single sound could exact the same degree of heartstopping panic as the cry torn from his wife. Royle came up from the nest of blankets, sweat cold upon his face, breath frozen within his chest. Two moves were instinctive. He placed himself between the cowering Evangeline and any threat, and his hand snatched up his flintlock. This was done before his eyes were fully opened. The bore of his rifle measured a lethal spot upon the man standing at their fire. He wasn't a stranger. Royle had seen him before at the trading house. Recognition didn't ease his bristling defenses, not when Evangeline's cry still echoed about the frantic thunder of his heart.

"I am sorry if I frightened your woman," the intruder said. His voice was lilting, as beautiful as the man was ugly. "I am Allouez. Monsieur Webster hired me to guide you to the Great Lakes."

The surging pulse of his blood defied relaxation at such a simple claim. "You are early," he challenged. Behind him, he could hear a faint whimpering from Evangeline. He fought his want to turn to her as his gaze studied the newcomer.

"I reached the Great Carrying Place yesterday. When you did not arrive, I came back to meet with you. I hope you have not met with any trouble."

"No," said Royle as his rifle bore lowered. "No trouble." He stood and went to offer his hand, never seeing the tremulous one Evangeline extended to stay him. They exchanged a firm handclasp. "I am Royle Tanner. I have heard of you." He let that hang unqualified. Allouez nodded as if it mattered not what Royle had learned.

"If I might join your fire," he asked, and Royle made a welcoming gesture. "Can we be ready to leave at daybreak? I would like to make the portage before darkness settles."

"Yes, of course."

As he started to pass Royle, the Frenchman leaned close for a low aside. "There are two Mohawk braves scouting your camp. Would you have me take care of them?"

So they remained, stalking silently in the shadows. It was difficult for Royle to keep his gaze from darting to the trees. His answer was pitched softly, with what he hoped was nonchalance. "No. Leave them. They mean no harm."

The Frenchman's black eyes challenged his wisdom, but he did not argue. When he moved to squat at the fire where the others gathered, groggy at being wrested from their sleep, Royle went back to his wife. She was sitting upright, blankets hugged about her in an insulating gesture. Her eyes were dazed, devoid of expression. She didn't seem to notice him until he knelt in front of her, between her and the fire. Then she regarded him almost blindly. That bleak appeal caught at his heart, and he drew her unresisting form to his chest. Her fingers were like talons at his back.

"It's all right, angel. You've nothing to fear. You know I'd let no harm come to you."

And as Royle spoke those tender words and his embrace provided her a thankful haven, his mind worked with gripping clarity. Had she known her brother and lover still lingered in the woods? Of course, she did.

The heavily laden boats were in the water before the mist fully cleared, sending them forward into a hazy unknown. The canoe bearing Allouez was swallowed by that fog, but Evangeline's gaze never strayed from the spot in which it disappeared.

On the narrow seat behind her, Royle studied her rigid back. Her shoulders were squared with tension, and that anxious posture fed Royle's insecurities. His gaze slipped to the shore, along the untamed fringe of wilderness that could hide many things. He felt exposed and vulnerable out upon the open water, yet feared a closer danger. The blade he carried in his pack was gone. Sometime between slumber and departure, it had vanished. Uneasily, his eyes roved over his wife's trim figure, wondering where she'd hidden it, and at the same time wondering if he'd discover it point first the moment his guard was lowered. There could be no lowering of his wary reserve, or easy slumber, until they reached the next small outpost of civilization. Or until she made her move against him.

After four days on the Mohawk, their comfortable mode of travel came to an end. The small crooked stream called Wood Creek provided difficult passage until joining Lake Oneida. The narrow bends became so shallow, their goods had to be portaged over land for miles at a time. It slowed their progress to an unwieldy pace upon paths wide enough to permit single file passage, paths choked with underbrush and overlapping shadow.

It was there upon that treacherous path that Royle heard a quiet sound behind him, a sort of muffled gasp. Curious, he began to turn, as Evangeline did before him. From the periphery of his vision, he saw a bronze arm snake about his wife's middle, jerking her from the path. Before he could respond to what he'd seen and turn back toward her, a fearsome visage appeared, all smeared with paint and bristling with grease. He had time to suck a startled breath, time for his widening eyes to follow the arc of a tomahawk. Then sense and sound exploded.

From the loamy ground, he was aware of scuffling feet and short cries. An accented voice called out, "Not him." Dizzy, swaying, nearly blinded by the wetness cascading down his face, Royle staggered to his feet amid turmoil. His unfocused stare tallied over a half-dozen Indians. He'd thought there were only two. Confusion swirled his head.

On the path appeared Evangeline's brother. He held no weapon. From over his shoulder, Royle caught the hint of movement, of a rifle barrel seeking destruction. His reflexes were too slow. His feet tangled. The push meant to move the young brave from the line of fire was not powerful enough to keep the bullet from finding its mark. Together, they fell.

There was silence, deep and undisturbed but for the slow throb of his heart. A hand upon his shoulder turned him, waking all sorts of horrible demons within his head. He groaned. His eyes fluttered open.

Evangeline was crouching over him, his bloodied blade clenched in her upraised fist. The image seared through to his sluggish brain, stabbing it with disbelief and dawning horror. She'd come to finish him.

"No," he cried. It was a raw sound, ripped from his heart. Frantically, he tried to move, to roll away, to evade the fateful end of his life. But there was no strength left to save him. Only darkness. And it was cold and complete.

The attack came as no surprise to Evangeline. Her brother's warning prepared her and their close company kept her encouraged. They could not tell her what the threat was, only that whispers through the woods brought word that their caravan was in danger. She didn't speak her doubts to Royle. In his odd mood, she knew he wouldn't believe her. He didn't know who the enemy was. She kept her silence and trusted in her brethren to protect them.

Then the one called Allouez appeared to shake her confidence. Once he spoke, she knew he was not the dreaded cannibal come to claim her, yet her fears refused relief. He might not have been a true demon, but some evil worked behind his black eyes. Her skin grew cold and crept with dread whenever his gaze touched upon her. She tried telling herself it was his similarity to her nightmare that provoked her unease. But it was something else, too. Something so dark and terrible her mind could not contain it.

251

Instinct told her to beware. It had the short hairs at her nape prickling as they walked the narrow, twisting path. Her ears were atuned to the rhythm of the woods, and something there was not right. The natural joy of them was stilled, hushed, as if waiting breath held. And then she heard the sound of danger, feeling it just an instant before.

She saw the threat to Royle and tried to scream out his name, but Cayenderongue seized her tight to pull her to safety. That cry died in horror upon her lips as she watched the hatchet descend. Had it been of the white man's metal, it would have split his skull. As it was, the stone did damage enough.

Evangeline writhed in the constrictive embrace, mindless of the struggles for life going on about her as their party was ruthlessly attacked. She saw only Royle, sprawled upon the ground with the warrior who'd attached him bending low, blade in hand, intent upon his yellow hair. Her undulating wail rose from a primitive heart if not shared blood, as she jerked free of her protector, Royle's knife drawn from the hollow between her breasts. She flung herself upon the brave, plunging the blade downward with all her strength. With momentum a driving force, she toppled him to the ground, ready to strike again. But there was no need. Her aim had been true.

Cayenderongue was behind her, tugging upon her arms. Her resistance at leaving her husband crumpled upon the ground was no match for her cousin's strength. He dragged her away from the carnage, and out of sight from the cold black eyes that sought her. Forced to crouch in the underbrush, safe while her mate could yet face danger and death, made Evangeline an unwilling rescuee. She wanted to cry out a protest when she saw Royle stagger to his feet, presenting a ready target. Then her brother appeared, and her momentary relief at seeing him on the scene to save her wounded Englishman was crushed by the tragedy her husband couldn't prevent.

Fire spat from the rifle, blooming vivid upon her brother's chest. The warm, vibrant life was gone from his eyes before he reached the earth. Shock made her malleable enough to yield to Cayenderongue's restraint. She sagged in his tight embrace, stunned by the evidence of death, while greed quickly overcame the lust for murder on the trail and the men who fled were ignored in favor of their packs. The wealth of provisions were stripped from the dead as the leader of the renegades searched in vain among those who'd fallen. Finally, anger twisting his features into a mask of evil, he made a sign, and the warriors and the Frenchman Allouez melted into the forest. Silence was heavy for several long seconds, then the sound of continuation began again in nature, the song of the birds, the sigh of the breeze, the gurgle of the water. And the moaning of Royle Tanner.

"Royle," Evangeline cried, scrambling through the brambles to gain his side. "Royle, oh dear God. Royle."

She was weeping unashamedly, great wracking spasms of anguish holding her hesitant as she beheld his still form. Cayenderongue rolled him face upward, and she gave a stricken moan. So much blood! The wound to his brow was grave. Surely he could not survive it. His eyes flickered, and she came down to him, wanting to comfort him with her presence, to assure him all was well. That wish knew a harsh reception, and her heart, a cruel reality. She read the stark message in his eyes. He recognized his enemy. It was she.

*   *   *

It was death or madness. Naught else could explain the visions to which he awoke. Pain colored all in hazy distortion. Hideous creatures bobbed about him. A whirring clatter filled his aching head, and a fine mist filtered down from—from where? Hell? He was no longer in the woods. His body was cradled in soft luxury. Things of nature arched high above his head, rough bark and limbs, but in no natural order. There was no sun, no sky. The pulse of sound he'd thought from within his tortured skull took on a chantlike intonation, forming no words he could recognize. But the cadence was familiar. He was among the Indians.

Images flashed to mind, lancing him with terror and depthless remorse. The painted face in the woods. Evangeline, bloody knife in hand. He closed his eyes and tried to shut out that awful truth. Yet, if it be truth, why did he live? The presence of pain defied the fact of death. He groaned in confusion.

The rhythm of gutterals stopped. The rattles were silent. Cool palms pressed to his cheeks, inviting comfort. That touch quieted him, surrounded him with a sense of peace, and he was able to sleep.

Evangeline came up off the fur mats, consternation lining her face. She nodded her thanks to the masked spirit men who'd come to cure her husband, and they left silently with their turkey rattles and pots of ash. There was no more magic the False Faces could provide. Now it was up to her husband, and his own determination to live.

She knelt at his side for a day and a night, bathing his brow and chest when fever overtook him, and securing him in a wrap of pelts when he was ravaged by chills. She refused to think, functioning on instinct alone. To think would give audience to the probable futility of her acts. To think would return the image of her brother as he fell. To think would fill her dreams with the black eyes of the Frenchman, eyes she could remember from the terror of childhood, eyes that now haunted her with the truth. Better that she lose herself in caring for her husband, letting the repetitious tasks absorb her to the point of exhaustion. Then she could sleep in short stretches untroubled by dreams.

On the third day, she found Royle's eyes open and claiming a vague awareness. Smiling her relief, she bent close so he might see her and take comfort. His eyes focused upon her face. They were slow to show recognition. Then it came, and with it a desperate terror. The hand she reached down to lay upon his hot cheek woke a violent reaction. His head snapped to the side in weak objection, the movement costing him his consciousness. Evangeline bit her lip until the salty warmth of blood was tasted. Anguish, sharp and bitter, took her. Such hatred in those green gold eyes of destiny. Such mortal fear. That look stripped away her hopes. She was a savage in his eyes; untrustworthy, dangerous, capable of treachery untold. A hurt more vicious than the fear possessed her. He did not care for the woman who was his wife. He saw her as an object of loathing, something to be used for pleasure, something to be watched for signs of betrayal. The tenderness of his touch, the wonder of his words, were lies. He did not want her, he owned her. That made all the fragile feelings flowering within her heart a lie as well. A man she could love would not believe her eager for his death.

Royle awoke gradually from an unpleasant dream. He had no immediate knowledge of where he was, only of the figure curled tight against him. He loosed a hand from his soft bedcovers and let it fall atop the glorious raven tresses. She murmured in her sleep and nestled closer. Content that all was as it should be, he let his eyes drift shut. Evangeline was with him, sharing his bed and her warmth. It had been a dream.

To wake within the accepting embrace flooded Evangeline with wistful encouragement. She shifted to behold his face and found him regarding her with tender affection. Her heart trembled with flutters of wary hope. He wet his lips and said her name in a hoarse caress. She turned liquid inside.

"Oh, Royle," she whispered, voice failing. She stretched up to kiss his cheek. It was rough, dry, not consumed by the heat of the previous days. He turned slightly until his mouth brushed hers. Reminding herself he was yet weak tempered the surge of her emotion. She satisfied herself with a brief sampling of his lips, then leaned away, smiling through her tears.

"How do you feel, my husband?" Her words were thick, barely recognizable as her own.

He seemed to take stock of his situation. "I hurt. My head—" Restlessly fingers curled in the mat of furs, and his awareness sharpened. "Where are we?"

"In my village. I brought you here to tend your wound. I was not sure you would live."

She knew the instant he remembered. A hard opaqueness glazed over his eyes, concealing the flicker of dread behind it. The companionable moment they shared was gone, destroyed by suspicion. Her features froze in a mask as false as those worn by the spirit men who'd come at her call. He yet feared her, and it was a mortal terror, one far surpassing any of the joys they'd found together, one that stripped their relationships to barest bones. She was Indian. He was white. And in that difference, he found reason to cling to his terrible doubts. That difference made his confusion a possibility in his mind. She forced a narrow smile and a voice even thinner.

"Rest now, Tanner. You need your strength. Then we can talk."

He seemed reluctant to close his eyes while she was near him. Evangeline stood, the knowledge of his immediate relief a bitter punishment. Emotions cloaked by an impassive face, she left the house of her family and sought strength of her own among the familiar.

Chapter Seventeen

He rested. Truthfully, he was too weak to do anything else. If he thought his head ached after his first introduction to the Websters, it was a cruel misrepresentation. That had been little more than the suffering sunlight brought after a night of indulgent cheer. This was worse than dying. Movement brought waves of sickness. Mere thought provoked a merciless din like musket fire. So he lay still and tried not to wake the waiting distress.

From where he lay upon his back, he could see little of his surroundings. A ceil of bark and log soared over head. From the cross-rafters hung strips of dried pumpkin, strings of apples, herbs, and ears of corn. His bed was made of furs. Examination beyond that required turning his head, and he wasn't prepared for the effort of pain that would bring. He could hear movement and low-pitched voices, so he knew he wasn't alone, though no one approached him. He could smell cook fires and hear the muffled sounds of dogs barking and the squeals of laughing children. Evangeline's village, he remembered her telling him. From there, thoughts grew confused.

Why had she kept him alive? 'Twould seem his

wife would be better served to have finished him in the woods, or left him there for nature to do the task. Did she mean to keep him prisoner, a sort of ironic retribution for what she had endured? He didn't entertain thoughts of escape. Even if he could manage to lift his head, or even crawl as far as the door, how did he get to civilization from . . . from where? He was at her mercy. But then he had been since the moment they left Albany. That, after all, had been her plan.

Bitterness colored his reflection of how naive he'd been. It was brilliant, actually, this masterstroke of vengeance against himself and Uriah Webster. The merchant's goods were gone, as was Royle's chance of proving himself. She'd struck cleanly and cruelly to the heart of their ambitions, smiting their greed and desirous dreams in one calculated move. What did he have left to live for? he wondered, adrift on his bed of pain. There was nothing . . . and no one to return to.

Curiosity prompted him to open his eyes again when he heard a quiet stirring at his pallet side. Evangeline crouched there. As her hand reached toward him, he flinched back and groaned with the punishing effort of it.

"Do not move," she told him. "I will not disturb you long. I only want to see how your head heals."

Carefully, she lifted the padding bound about his brow and stoically examined the swelling. Satisfied with what she saw, she replaced the bandage and began to rise. Royle stopped her with an unsteady hand. She froze beneath his touch, eyes suddenly wary.

"Your brother?" he wanted to know.

Grief flashed across her expression before it was sternly blanked. "He is dead. I wish to thank you for your effort to save him. It was . . . most noble."

Royle's hand dropped away and he gave a weary sigh. He was not immune to her pain. "Why would his own people kill him?"

"His own people?" Her brow beetled. She looked genuinely perplexed. Then anger came, hot, quick, explosive, and was just as sharply controlled. "Is that what you think? That my people were responsible?"

Royle's jaw tightened in surly temper. So she would have him drag out the humiliation he'd suffered at her hands. Her look chided him for it. Did she think he wouldn't guess her part in it all? Had she hoped the insufficient blow to his head would knock all remembrance from it? He remembered all right. Never could he blank the sight of her crouched over him, blade drawn, eyes wild. Her hate for him was rawly exposed at that instant, and even now, now when his own helpless fury burned hot at her betrayal, the keenest pain was felt to the heart. What a fool he was to think she could ever cast aside her pagan ways, to actually begin to love him. He ached with that realized loss. And it made him reply as sharp as his hurt. "That's what I saw."

She stood, and for the first time, he was aware of her, of all of her. If ever he'd harbored a hope that she might return with him to civilization, it died when he beheld her heathen splendor. She stood erect and proud, rounded hips clad in a short skin skirt that went from waist to middle thigh, and exposed a good deal more where it was slit up on the left side. Small feet were encased in moccasins. A heavy black braid draped over one tanned shoulder, its end curving softly about one perfectly naked breast.

"All red men are not of the Iroquois," she snapped impatiently. "Just as all white men are not English or French. The Indians you saw were Shawnee, led by your guide, Allouez. It was their plan to steal your goods and murder all. That is why my brother came to warn me. That was why they followed, hoping they could be of help."

Briefly, her gray eyes conveyed her anger, her anguish of emotion at having to explain these things to him, at having to plead her own innocence. Had he been the man she'd thought, he wouldn't have doubted. Yet, still, he did. The uncertainty remained in his expression. There was naught for her to do but leave him to his own confusions. She would not beg his understanding. She would not plead her case. He was no longer worthy to hear it.

Royle was too weak to pursue the ramifications of what he heard. His mind spun feebly, trying to hold to what was true. Finally he slept, to wake late in the evening to silence and clear thought. That thought created new doubts aplenty . . . doubts of his actions, not those of his wife. Had he been so quick to judge that his insecurities had led him astray? He replayed each hour of their journey, twisting the events he'd believed he understood to give them new meaning, and a damning conclusion surfaced. Was he wrong? Had he wronged Evangeline? The sinister cast he'd given to her motives could have been something altogether different. Or she could be lying to him now. The agony of indecision was a worse torment than his wound. The want to trust warred with his innate self-preservation. Which to believe. The woman lying beneath him flushed with the passion of his possession? Or the one bent low clutching a stained blade?

He was on the edge of sleep when Evangeline came to him. Wordlessly she saw to his wrappings and bathed his face. Never did her eyes touch upon his. Never did her set expression betray the workings of her mind, although her ministrations were gentle. Did she hate him for his inconsistencies, he wondered. He would as soon test her motives as spend another night in torn thought.

"Am I a prisoner here?"

She looked at him then, her eyes clear reflecting pools, showing nothing beneath their surface. "My people do not make slaves of those among them." A hint of haughtiness strengthened her words.

"I am free to go then?"

She spoke without inflection, as if his fate mattered not to her. "When you are fit to travel, you will be seen back to your white man's village."

"And you?" A small question to cover a multitude of possibilities.

Evangeline stood before answering, placing more distance between them than merely the physical. "I will remain here where my word has value." He didn't need to hear her anguish intoned upon those words. Their meaning struck straight to his heart and twisted viciously. He didn't know how to respond. He didn't know how to stop her when she turned and walked proudly away. He didn't know how to end the castigating truth revealed to him in that instant. He *was* wrong, and he was to have no chance to make amends.

Sleep was elusive after that. Evangeline's words and the pain that lurked unspoken behind them provoked him to punishing reflection. He'd no right to demand anymore of her, not now when he'd failed her so unforgivably. She'd placed herself trustingly, humbly in his hands, and he'd cruelly, foolishly abused her vulnerable offering. When he returned to Albany, it would be alone, and there he would face the consequence of his failures. There was no point in contemplating the future, not when it yawned so bleak and empty. He didn't think of what he would do. He was tortured by what he had lost.

And when she did not return to him the next day, the time grew meaningless. From somewhere within the Indian village, the keening sounds of wails and lamentations companioned the ache residing heavily in his soul. In those lonely hours, the need to see her, to apologize for his weakness, to somehow lessen the horrible shame teething upon his heart, possessed him. But she did not come. His needs were attended by several young maidens, each in similar stages of undress. They regarded him with modest curiosity, while he tried to keep his gaze respectfully from noting their natural beauty. His face burned hot as they bent near, seemingly fascinated by the downy hair upon his chest. They whispered between themselves, and with much giggling finally left him to continue his brooding.

"You have a hard skull, white man."

Royle regarded Cayenderongue with some surprise. He'd not expected a visit from the handsome warrior who'd been his wife's betrothed. Had he come to gloat over his chances of yet claiming her? That thought prodded a rumble of protest through him. But what right did he have to object to Evangeline's native lover? None. Not after he'd betrayed her trust and destroyed whatever feelings she'd held for him. He had absolutely no right to harbor jealous feeling. But it simmered as bitterly as the truth of his own failings. Royle greeted him with a hostile glare.

The brave squatted beside his mat of furs to observe him with equal reserve. His English was labored, but eloquent in its expression. "You fought well, Englishman. A pity you are a fool. I might have been pleased to call you brother." He allowed a small smile to escape him. "When Eyes-Like-Evening-Star is over her year of mourning, it will please me more to take her for my bride. Since first I saw her, her eyes the color of musket barrel, her face as fair as ermine, I have wanted her. Instead, she chose you. Had you been honorable, I would have turned my thoughts to another. I am glad I waited."

A boiling fury poured up through Royle's veins, scalding the weakness that kept him humbly helpless, until exploding in his benumbed mind. The haughty brave was casually claiming what was his. No! That single objection burst forth with instinctive rage. Sometime between the moment he awoke upon the rough boards of the trading house to the knowledge that Evangeline had fled him and the moment he realized the extent of his wrongs to her, the motives that drove him had subtly shifted. When he'd pursued her into the vast unknowns of the woods, it had been outrage spurring him on, the simple, unadulterated fury that she would actually flee him, she, a possession he'd acquired at great cost and intended to keep at even greater price. Bringing her back had inflated his male pride, having her willing had inflamed his male passions. But when she'd made it clear that she intended to stay, to make a home for them both, she'd tamed her spirited rebellion into a gift so sweet, he'd trembled to take it. Her willful resistance had given away before an awakening desire for her white husband, and with each reluctant slip of her pride into treasured submission, she'd wound herself more tenaciously about his heart.

Evangeline Tanner was more than a beneficial possession. How much more, he hadn't the time to consider. He only knew that *no* man was going to stand before him and arrogantly claim he meant to take her for his own. No man.

"Evangeline is my wife," Royle declared seething-ly. There was incredible force behind that claim, and he realized he would not relinquish it without a fight, whether it be with this smug brave or with Evangeline herself. He could not just let go. And once he'd made that decision, the strength of purpose flowed back to him.

It was humbling to have to face his rival while flat upon his back. The man mocked him, sneered at his inability to prove a threat. Slowly, Royle shifted, bringing his elbows beneath him and pushing up until he was seated. His head reeled and roared, but he refused to recognize his distress.

"You had claim to her in your world, now you are in ours. She has set you aside, white man. Accept your loss."

"I accept nothing. Where is my wife?"

The bristled hair nodded to one side. "She is mourning her brother. He was buried as a warrior this morning. He was buried in a disguised grave so you English robbers would not see the noble palisades and violate it to strip the dead of its beaver skins, wampum, and belongings." His disgust was clear and heaped upon Royle as if he was responsible for all his race. "For six days, she will remain face downward and speechless in a house with no fire, with only cold food. Her grief was great. It took much slashing of her skin to release it."

Royle paled at that casual revelation. His voice was gruff. "Where is she?"

"I will take you, white man." He stood and waited, dark eyes conveying a contemptuous disbelief that he would ever rise from the mat. Royle staggered up, swaying upon his feet as the unfamiliar world tipped and rolled about him. A steadying arm braced about

265

his middle when he would have surely fallen. It took a moment for the waves of dizziness to pass. He was absurdly weak and wobbly. Yet he pushed away from the offer to support.

"I will make my own way," he growled with more bravado than sense. And he did manage to walk on his own a total of three steps. This time, when he was caught on his way to the ground, he made no bold claims, and instead clung in grateful humility to the sturdy arm so impassively given for his use.

The walk was short, just across a stretch of ground no wider than a road, yet the effort left Royle drenched with the sweat of agony and unsure of any faculty. When Cayenderongue gestured within one of the bark-shingled huts, purposefully he straightened. He would go to his wife on his own. The brave stood back, expression begrudging his admiration as the Englishman ducked beneath the skin door.

It was dark within. It took moments for his eyes to adjust, then the scene that greeted him made his own misery pale in comparison. He tried to speak, but found his voice had failed him. Just as he had failed her earlier. But he would not now. No matter what the cost to his feeble strength, he would provide her with comfort. Whether she would accept it or not.

The house was cold but no colder than her heart. All joy and hope was gone from both. Her brother was dead. Her husband was lost. Even the will to wail and mourn aloud was emptied from her as she lay prostrate upon the rough mats. A bowl of *eschionque* was within her reach, but she had no desire for the dry corn flour. Nourishment wasn't what she hungered for. Her soul cried out for a purpose, for a reason to drag herself from this depthless well of pain and sorrow. Rich stores of goods were heaped within the cabin in which her brother had lain, but she took no comfort from those magnificent gifts lavished by relatives and neighbors. No material bounty could slake the barren state of her heart. Nothing could feed her starved spirit, or so she believed until she heard the soft call of her name.

"Evangeline."

She came up off her face and turned, aware of the tears long since dried upon her cheeks and of the grief that swelled her features. Still, she was able to present a stoic front when her weaker will trembled and urged her to run to him, to admonish him for being up, to cling to him for solace, to the very one responsible for much of her tearing grief.

"You should not be here, Tanner," she said quietly.

"Have I broken some taboo among your people? If so, I am sorry. 'Twas not my purpose to intrude, only to see how you fared." Expressive green eyes touched upon the cuts she'd inflicted upon her arms and legs in the throes of her despair. She could see his struggle to say nothing of them and to hold himself away. He did not look as strong as he pretended. His color was poor; his eyes pinched with discomfort. Yet he maintained his feet and waited for her to speak.

"I am in mourning for my brother."

"Is it your will to mourn alone?"

"My mother and cousins will join me soon. They have gone to see to their families. It is permissible to leave at night if done so with proper discretion. You need not stay to keep company with me."

"Do you wish me to go?" That was softly said and could have offered many things, none of which she wanted to consider. No, she didn't want him with her, she thought in panic. She didn't wish to put her grief on display before him, or to wallow in the misery his mere presence caused. She was too weak to confront him with her anger and pride, too vulnerable to the tenderness she could see escaping his gaze. She didn't need more self-scourging. Her heart was raw enough. She couldn't look upon his sympathetic face without seeing it twisted tight with mistrust and accusation. That wound, too, was too new, too sore to be easily overlooked.

"That would be best, Tanner."

Royle nodded stiffly, dejected and dismissed. He began to withdraw, then paused to say softly, with heart-breaking sincerity, "I wish I'd had the chance to know him, as he was a part of you."

The walls of her resolution shivered. How dare he speak to her with such tender feelings, when he'd ruined all hope within her heart. How could he play so savagely upon her sorrow with his expression of regret. Where was that regret when he'd looked to her in hatred? Where was his empathy when he'd shrunk from her on the trail? Understanding that would have gone far then, was wasted now. Her lips quivered and she stilled them forcefully. The tears that had a want to spring into her eyes were fiercely blinked away. Stoically she nodded to accept his words.

Still he lingered. She wanted to shriek at him to go, while she could yet resist the effect he had upon her. She tried to force contemptible images before her to strengthen her resolve, when her treacherous heart would have her yearning for the remembered security of his embrace. She struggled to recall his hateful words in lieu of the sweet heaven of his kiss. She attempted to return to her martyred solitude, when she craved a closer union. How could she yet want him with such devastating power, when he'd proved himself a false god? He had a man's weaknesses, a man's doubts, a man's faults.

But was it man or god she wanted? That unwelcomed question shook her to her very soul. Was it husband or idol?

"I think he would have liked you, Royle Tanner." With that admission, the barriers began to crumble, releasing her grief, her numbing loss, her bittersweet hopes. She called upon her training, praying it would serve her now. A proud Caniengas could control emotion even under pain of death.

But Evangeline Tanner was no true Caniengas. The blood in her veins was not their noble blood. The heart that beat within her was not capable of such restraint. And she faltered and failed miserably.

"His warrior spirit has gone to live in the underworld with Mother of Animals. There he will know no war, no hunger, or disease. His shadow will be at peace."

The moment tears dampened her cheeks, Royle came to her, kneeling down, encircling her with his arms. Differences and distrust were thrust aside. Evangeline lost herself in that caring embrace, wetting his shirt with her grief, hugging to him in her quavering joy. The soft words he murmured went from heart to heart, lifting her burden of distress with the strength of his compassion. She felt comforted, restored, alive. And she loved the man who held her with all her might, for all his faults, for all his tender passion. And if he would have her as Tanner's Wife, nothing could tear her away from that honor, nothing short of death or his disinterest.

Evangeline pushed away, sniffing softly and brushing away the last of her tears. She was able to smile up into the worried face of her husband and ease his own despair.

"Go now, Tanner. You must rest, and I must

honor my brother with five days of great mourning."

"And then?" he coaxed, unwilling to give way to the expectation surging within his breast without due cause.

"And then, we will talk."

Royle drew the furs that had fallen away up about her slender figure, surrounding her with warmth and with the potency of his care. He touched one of the gashes that marred her supple hip. "No more of this," he insisted huskily.

"No. My grief no longer controls me."

Something else much stronger and infinitely more frightening had taken its place. Love.

With pride and poignant remembering, Evangeline watched covertly through the skin over the doorway as Royle was prodded from her longhouse before the gathering of her clans and those of Cayenderongue. He was so weak, her heart went out to him, yet he withstood all with an enviable posture. She could imagine his fear as the voices of her people rose sharp and shrill, loud and deep, in such a dreadful noise the very senses were stupified. He must have thought it his death knell, but she knew different. This live-shout was nothing like the dead-shout which came from taking scalps.

Evangeline wished she was not bound to her solitude, that she could have prepared him for what was to come. Her people assembled in two long lines between which Royle was thrust. With the prodding of those behind him, he was forced to run down the gauntlet of flailing ax handles, tomahawks, hoops, poles, clubs, and switches, where the white would be beaten from him. None of the blows were severe, more symbolic than threatening harm, though in his condition some staggered him. At the end of the trial, he was still on his feet and managed to put up an impressive struggle when dragged through the rear entrance of the castle walls to the river below.

Evangeline could not witness his baptism in the cold water, nor the divesting of his white clothing, from where she was confined by duty. Her memory served her well enough. She strained for the sight of him and was rewarded when he was paraded back within the stockade walls in native array. She'd always thought him magnificent, but never so much as now. His bared chest was pale, but no less mighty than the braves beside him. The scar of battle curving about his ribs was an obvious token of valor. He may have lacked the sleek stature of Cayenderongue, but he was no less impressive. His limbs were sturdy and strong, his flanks powerful where exposed by the scant thong of hide. Evangeline noted the way he brought a sigh to the lips of the young maidens, and wished she was at liberty to seek his side in claim for all to see. Soon enough they would know her heart.

The village had gathered about a great council fire, and its chief spoke eloquently of the ritual before them all. The oratory was slow, deliberate, and repetitious, and elaborate wampum belts were draped about Royle's bruised shoulders to verify his words. She remembered her own confusion when faced with this lengthy spew of gutterals and sympathized with her husband, who had no understanding of their significance. She did, and she wept with pride and feeling.

Finally the speech was over, and Royle was brought before a group containing Cayenderongue. His family set up a dismal howling of loss and grief, an echo of her own in days past. Then the mourning was done, and Royle was welcomed with kisses of joy and boisterous hugs from even Cayenderongue. After receiving a wealth of gifts, Royle was led before each member of the clan and introduced with great formality. Evangeline could feel his confusion, could see the strain of his injury wearing upon him, yet he complied with the solemnity of the greetings, realizing their importance if not their meaning. She exhaled a grateful breath when he was allowed to sit to a grand feast. Only then did she return to her mat and happily bow in prayer.

It was dark when Evangeline crept into her own small cubicle, onto the soft furs which held her husband in slumber. She slid beneath the warm pelts only to find him awake and curious.

"What went on this afternoon?" he wanted to know in a low whisper. "When they took me down to that river, I thought for certain I was to be cleaned for the next meal, after being thoroughly tenderized."

Evangeline laughed softly. Her reply was filled with her satisfaction. She wanted to hug him, to show him how well-pleased she was, but held herself away. She wasn't sure he would yet welcome her embrace. "It is the way of my people to increase their number by adopting their prisoners into a family who has known a loss. Cayenderongue's brother was killed by a fever last year at the time of corn ripening. His family chose you to replace him in their hearts. Once you'd been purged of your white blood and they, of their grief, you became one of their number."

"If he is your cousin, then I am of your family, too."

"No. He is of the Bear and I of the Wolf. His *ohwachira*—his clan of sisterhood—is not of my line.

There is no shared blood."

"If I am of his family, why am I still here?" Confusion made his head ache and his question terse.

"You are my husband, therefore of my family, but through adoption you are also of my people. If a Caniengas marries a Delaware women, she and her children remain Delaware and aliens, unless brought in to the Caniengas by adoption. Do you understand?"

He sighed and shifted on the bed of furs. "I think it's easier not to. I'll trust your explanation."

Simple words avowing trust, yet they struck through to the heart of her, swelling it with hope and love and longing. A small step, this slight concession, yet it could soon strengthen into a run.

"And is this how you came to be a Caniengas?"

His question was no surprise to her. It was long overdue in the asking. She'd been mulling over her own circumstance since witnessing Royle's indoctrination. No, since the trail when the past was brought cruelly to the forefront of her mind. Upon her own adoption into the tribe, she'd been advised by the gentle She-Walks-Far to forget all that came before with its power to hurt her. And she had, even upon her return to the white world. She'd kept those truths buried deep and locked away, and once they were torn open, she knew why. The memories were horrible, overshadowing the sweetness of her past with violence and terror. She could not recall one without the other, so all was pushed away.

She remembered now, there in the cocoon of furs, in the strong presence of her husband. She remembered the booming laugh of her white father and the wonderful scent of pipe tobacco that always clung to his clothing. She remembered the soft lullabies and gentle smile of her white mother. And she remembered how happy she had been, how loved, how content.

And she remembered the horror surrounding their deaths.

"We were taken in a raid much like the one that claimed my brother. A party of six Shawnee and four French took my family and the other adults away from the fire where I sat. They did not return. The Shawnee came back to the fire to stretch their scalps on hoops to dry, and when they were combing out the hair, I recognized that of my mother and father." Her voice was even in the telling, but inside she was beset with the shock and paralyzing fear of a child alone. Royle's arm opened, inviting her within its warming circle where he pulled her tight against him. She clung to that closeness to ward off the strength of remembered horror.

"I should be thankful for their greed," she continued quietly. "It kept me alive. I was taken to a French fort and locked up with other white prisoners for the night. There was much weeping and praying. None of our prayers to the white god were answered. None of us would be going back to our home and our families. In the morning, I was bought by a Seneca woman who lived down on the Ohio River, and we embarked in two canoes for her home. I thought I should die then, but I did not. I suffered no hardships, but the memory of my parents kept me lonesome and gloomy. I was not allowed to speak English, so I repeated my prayers and catechisms to keep the language alive in me. I was with her for three months, then was traded to She-Walks-Far to take the place of a son lost in battle.

"I was welcomed as daughter, as sister, as family. They embraced me, and I them, for I had no family of my own. My mother told me to put aside the past and I did, all but a dream I did not understand. In time, I began to link it to Indian legend, so I would not be afraid. The face in that dream that haunted me was of one of my French captors, the one I thought of as Long Nose, the one who calls himself Allouez."

Chapter Eighteen

"You're sure?" Royle's voice was low and urgent.

"Oh, yes," came the whispered return. "I would never forget such a thing. When I saw him at the trading house, my mind would not let me recall him, but when they set upon you to take your hair, I could not let him stretch your scalp before a fire, the way he did my parents'. 'Twas then I remembered him for his part in their deaths."

Royle cuddled her close to ease the anguish of memory, while his own thoughts spun ahead. Coincidence? he wondered. Perhaps, but not likely. He recalled the Frenchman's command. *Not him.* He was not meant to die with the others upon that trail. Why? The answer lay with the renegade Allouez.

Abruptly, Royle was no longer concerned with riddles or revenge. Evangeline was tucked into his side, and he was very aware of the sweet contours of her body. He breasts were soft and full against him, and her thigh casual in the way it rode atop his own. The degree of his own nakedness—which to now had caused him great embarrassment—seemed a blessing, for how else could he enjoy the feel of her beside him with such unrestricted delight.

Royle shifted subtly, turning toward her to increase the tantalizing contact of flesh upon flesh. His hand rested easily upon the dip of her narow waist, then he hesitated. She had set him aside, Cayenderongue had said. He had no further claim upon her. His mind argued that. She *was* his. She would never belong to another. The thought of another possessing her, lying with her, touching her— Involuntarily, his casual gesture became a selfish clutch, his embrace pulling her tight to the uncovered strength of his body. Never. Not while he lived and breathed.

She was here beside him. She had coaxed him back to health. Though her words would deny him, her actions said otherwise. She had reason to hate—a hundred times over. Yet, she pressed close, encouraging possession with the arch of her supple body. He had only to touch and she responded, to offer and she greedily accepted. She was his unconditionally, and he would remind her of that now. If only he could find the strength.

He didn't have to.

The moment his hand caressed her, Evangeline warmed and burned with desire. Her body trembled with it and grew restless in its demands. She rubbed against him. The friction of his chest hair upon her tightening nipples made her wild. Her hips moved against his to let him know of it. He hesitated. She thought it due the nature of his wound, but it was more the nature of his modesty. They were not exactly alone. Eight other families shared the same roof, and all the small partitions opened to the central fire. But it was dark and passion knew no inhibitions.

She could be patient no longer. To have him beside

her, to experience the rekindling of his trust, the renewal of his desire, made her eager to forget all hurts. When her mind would urge her to roll away, to reinforce her position of pride, her female logic argued that now was the time to anchor claims of the heart. Gladly, she listened to her emotions.

Evangeline stretched up to claim her husband's lips with the hunger of her own. She tasted his willingness upon them and provoked it to a desperation with spearing thrusts of her tongue. His hands rose to her shoulders, kneading them, caressing them, tightening as his pleasure grew. Her tempting mouth slipped away, grazing the hurried pulse at his throat, to tease through the carpet of hair that thickened and waned and thickened again. The hot feel of her mouth and flickering, taunting tongue as she tasted him—more fully once the slight barrier of his clothing was breached—had Royle feverish with excitement rather than distress. The texture of the furs tickling and caressing beneath him, the forbidden thrill of finding such pleasure surrounded by her family, the devastating effect her samplings exacted upon his body, combined to an irresistible need.

When he drew her up and tried to urge her beneath him, Evangeline's palms pressed to his shoulders, forcing him down upon his back. Her words were whispered in silky seduction upon his mouth.

"Lie still, my husband. I would not see you harmed by overtaxing your recovery."

He was about to protest when he realized her intention. Then he was more than willing to give himself into her care. Her sleek, strong thighs straddled him, lifting and lowering until he rested firm and full and mighty inside her. Her muscles clasped about him, and he bit back a groan of

278

exquisite sensation. Then she began to move, and reality was lost with each galvanizing surge. In the molten glow of firelight and seductive shadow, he could barely see her, the way her beautiful torso curved in rapture, the taut arch of her neck as her head flung back in a spill of ebony hair. He could imagine her expression as her lithe figure trembled above him, then convulsed in the throes of her pleasure. It was enough to provoke his own violent release as her body settled in spent luxury upon him.

Too soon, she was moving, sliding away and replacing her warmth with those of the furs.

"Evangeline?"

Her lips caressed his. "I must go now. 'Twill be dawn soon."

"Don't leave me," came his thick reply.

"I must, Royle. I cannot stay."

"Don't leave me," he repeated gruffly, and it was then she took his meaning. Her fingertips brushed across his damp mouth in a tender trail, stilling his doubts and pleas upon them.

"I am Tanner's Wife by your laws and my word, unless you will it otherwise."

"I don't." That was said with strong conviction, and her teeth flashed white in a satisfied smile.

"Good."

Then he was able to let her go, satisfied with the bonding of their words, content in the resumed strength of their passions. She was his once more, and secure with the knowledge, he could lose himself in much needed slumber.

The next evening found Royle not alone on the six-foot platform which served as bed, chair, and table. He and Cayenderongue were in deep discussion when Evangeline approached. She paused to allow a purely female pleasure to envelope her as the green gold gaze lifted. He was looking stronger, having cast off all signs of sickness, but it was the way his eyes warmed with welcome that crowned her satisfaction. The two men were a dawn and dusk comparison, Royle burnished gold, Cayenderongue steeped in shadowed twilight. They were the two men who'd thought to claim her, to have her for their own. They were strong, handsome men with traits to link them, as well as differences to hold them apart. Royle was a foreigner, yet he displayed the same worthy valor and haughty dignity as his Caniengas brother. And though Cayenderongue was of her people and the first with his claim upon her, she felt no ties to him. He was a warrior. And he was a trusted friend. His suit had flattered her and made her proud among the other maidens. But never had he made her feel the flurry of warm emotions parading through her as did the single glance of her white husband. Evangeline realized then that though Cayenderongue had the first claim to her hand, Royle Tanner had the first to her heart. And she was pleased with the revelation. Silently, she slipped down onto the furs beside him.

"Cayenderongue has brought me news of the Frenchman."

Evangeline stiffened at that blunt statement delivered in lieu of greeting. Her uncertain gaze searched Royle's and found only cool determined fury, then she turned to her cousin to hear what he would share.

"His party of raiders went on to Oswego to trade the goods for wampum and white man's coin," the brave stated softly in their own tongue. "There was no hope that we could catch him in time to prevent the sale, but their moves have been watched by our Keepers of the Western Door. The Frenchman, the one we seek, returns this way. Sahawhe believes he goes to the white man's village of Albany."

"Sahawhe?"

Cayenderongue gestured to Royle. "My brother," he explained.

It was the Iroquois way to rename worthy white men, so they could be identified in pictures. It was also their way to grant several names to the same individual, one to the child in honor of its heritage and another to the man in recognition of deeds. The giving of that second name was sacred and symbolic, done in love and respect. Long Feather had been Cayenderongue's true brother's name. That he would allow it bestowed upon Royle was the highest compliment. It meant the English blood was no longer a barrier between them. It made them family. She was pleased.

"And what does this mean, my husband?" she asked Royle.

His expression grew grimly serious and she knew a moment of fearful premonition. "It means we plan to intercept him and discover his purpose."

Her own personal worries over Royle's safety would never be voiced to challenge him when he was in council with another. A warrior always sought combat in which to distinguish himself, and she would not deny him that right. But she, too, had rights, those of a wife, those of a woman, and of those she would not remain silent.

"When do you go?"

"At first light."

"I will be ready."

Under Cayenderongue's gauging stare, Royle refused to state his objections; his fear that she might find herself in danger, that he might disgrace himself beside the stalwart Iroquois warriors. Instead, he asked, "What of your mourning period?" hoping to forestall her plans to go.

Evangeline would not be deterred. The women of her clan followed loyally behind their men as they went into battle, to serve then as they could, to tend them if there was need, to bury them if they had to. Though she was touched by his poorly veiled concern, she would not be swayed.

"Warraghiyagey would be proud to know he's to be avenged. He would not wish me to spend time upon my knees, when I could further his retribution."

"That is so," Cayenderongue agreed, as he stood and sealed all with those few words. "We will leave at dawn."

When they were alone, much of Evangeline's stoic facade slipped before the strength of her concern. Now she could voice the uncertainties of her heart as a woman instead of a warrior's wife. "You do not have to go, Tanner. You are not yet healed. You haven't your full strength. The trail will be long and hard."

"I'll keep pace," he vowed, with a touch of arrogance that made her smile.

"I know you will, my husband, but at what cost to you? There is no shame in admitting what all can plainly see. You were nearly in the shadow world. It is too soon to expect so much."

Royle's features firmed with determination, and Evangeline saw there would be no cause for further protest. "I will not allow others to do for me. My own foolishness lost me those goods and cost your brother his life." He waved off her objection with a crisp gesture. "No, I know it is true. I let myself be led by stupid doubts, when I should have been watching for real trouble. It's because of my weakness that all has befallen us, and I must make amends to your brother, to your uncle and—and to you, if you'll let me."

Evangeline sat very still, her uplifted eyes reflecting the tender swell within her heart, but he could not read it there in the darkness. A bursting love filled her as his words continued.

"I betrayed my promise to you by dishonoring the same trust I insisted you give me. I failed you. I hurt you, and that I cannot forgive. Nor can I ask anymore of you."

Her hands slid over his to clutch tightly, to convey the strength of her feelings and the depths of her words. "Then I will. The past is done and cannot be changed. I would be foolish myself to hold it before the promise of a future. I do not want to hate you. I don't wish to be angry. I don't wish your apologies. I only wish to be Tanner's Wife. We are different, you and I. There will be times we don't understand what moves the other, but we can learn. With patience, we can—"

His big hands curled about hers, using that clasp to impel her forward against his bare chest. The contact was all primitive passion.

"I am not a patient man," he claimed gruffly, then possessed her mouth with a proving urgency.

And there upon the luxuriant blanket of furs, he proved more. And she delighted in the lusty demonstration.

Eight of them set out at early light; Cayende-rongue, five of his clan, Royle, and Evangeline. They traveled light and fast afoot over paths Royle would not have believed would grant them passage. The supple moccasins he wore gave remarkable fleetness to his feet, and the wrap of leggings protected him from the tear of brambles. Still, he felt most naked in the daylight, as he trotted on his Iroquois brethren's heels with Evangeline behind him.

And she was most certainly enjoying the view. Her gaze devoured the strength his body displayed, caressing along the contour of muscle across shoulders and firm flank with detailing appreciation. This was how man was made to appear, all sleek and sinewy as nature intended, instead of bundled within confining garb to suffocate the skin and deny the beauty of his being. She thought with regret to the time when such a tantalizing sight would only come in the dark privacy of their bed. It seemed much more satisfying this way, so pure, so noble amid the glory of the forest and sky; innocent yet provocative in this sylvan setting. Here he was her man, her husband, and convention could not come between them. He was of her world, and she was proud of his effort to blend well. He brought her no shame even next to the strongest warrior. With pride and satisfaction, she could hold him up to boast he was hers. He was still a white man. The fairness of his skin held him apart. Skin could bronze in the sun and darken, just as a heart could change and soften. During this time, he could join with the heart of her people and see their goodness, their strength, and know, too, of their weakness. When he returned to the white world, he would carry that knowledge in his being, that oneness that would never let him forget the linking pride of his Caniengas name. And in knowing them, he would know her. Royle Tanner would serve her people well in his own way, and confidence lightened her stride and lifted her spirits. Destiny had bound her to a savior of their race. Fate had brought her the perfect mate.

It was late when they finally made camp. The Iroquois braves squatted before the low fire and ate in silence from the long leather bags they carried at their back. Seeing Royle's uncertainty over the near-colorless powder in his hand, Evangeline sat beside him and mixed the parched corn she held with enough water to make a paste, then ate it from the cup of her palm. He did likewise and was surprised to find the scant-looking fare not only filling but sweet.

"Nookick provides a toothsome and hearty meal on the trail," she explained. "Corn is parched in hot ashes and beaten to powder. 'Tis easy to carry, and is mixed with water in summer and snow in winter."

Royle mentally weighed the bag with the bulky provisions he had carried and could see the sense of it. Why tax strength needed for the journey, by the burden of foods that would only keep a short time? Their reasoning was sound and shrewd, and he respected it. When Evangeline passed him a cup of what she brewed over the fire, he took it without reservation. She did not serve the other braves in the way of the white woman, only him, and he was conscious of a possessive pleasure. It set him above the others in her eyes, and he reveled in her singular attention with a purely male contentment. He sipped from the cup she brought him. It satisfied much like coffee, but tasted subtly different. When he asked of what it was made, she smiled and refilled the cup he extended.

"Roasted corn." Noting his raised brow, she chuckled. "Corn is our main food, even when game is plentiful. It is called our life by my people. It is grown with squash and beans, and the three are known as the three sisters. These maidens are protective spirits watching over our crops."

285

Royle leaned back on his elbows to hear her speak her lore with warm conviction. He no longer argued the right or wrong of her beliefs. If her people found explanation and comfort among their primitive taboos and rituals, he would respect them. How odd indeed they would find many of his own beliefs. Who was he to judge?

"It is our custom to hold feasts in honor of the spirit controlling the crop. We've a festival at each stage of cultivation; a planting feast when seeds are sown, another when ears turn green, and a gathering celebration to give thanks for an abundant harvest."

"So prayer is the answer to your success in the garden."

Evangeline scrutinized his expression to assure herself he was not mocking her enthusiasm. He looked relaxed, interested, and not at all skeptical, so she smiled at him and enlightened, "We have a great power which fills earth and sky called *Orenda*. 'Tis not one god like the one you worship, but made up of many spirits inhabiting every object. All around us, everything has a soul of its own to be revered and respected. If your people could understand that, the difference between us would not be so wide. When we make offerings to appease both good and evil spirits, your missionaries are quick to cry we worship the devil, when in fact we worship life."

"There are things you do that label your people as barbarians." He offered that not in accusation, but as a topic of confusion within his own mind. She heard that bewilderment in his tone, read of it in his candid stare. Wanting to help in his understanding, gratified that he would wish to know, she responded easily, taking no offense or defensiveness.

"Even the taking of scalps is part of our religion. They are not mere trophies of war. The hair upon the

286

crown represents the living spirit. To lose that hair to an enemy is to lose control over one's life. It transfers the power and identity into the victor's hands. The more heads taken, the greater that power. 'Tis not something to be trifled with.

"My father He-Raises-the-Sky wanted to understand your people. He went to one of your white schools to know what it is to be brought up English. The white men at the school would not adapt to the needs of an Indian fresh from the forest. As a chief's son, he was welcomed for his use as a hostage in their hands, to guarantee the safety of the English in our territory. They taught him religious catechism, your grammer, arithmetic, Latin, and Greek, all at the prompting of a birch rod, but nothing of what it is to be white, and they cared nothing of what it meant to him to be of the Iroquois. They wanted to strip him of his pride, of his people, and so he came home to where a man is judged by what is inside him."

Royle grew pensive as she spoke with such quiet passion. How similar were his own motives to those of the unbending teachers? He had thought only to bend Evangeline to his will and ways, instead of appreciating her for the unique qualities she possessed. He'd given no credence to the wisdom she held, treating her as though she was ignorant of life. Only of the life he led, he realized. He'd deemed that life superior without ever questioning hers. Stubbornly, arrogantly, he'd insisted she make all the changes to fit his world, not caring that he robbed her of her values and sacred customs. He'd applauded himself for his sensitivity on her behalf, when his motives were clearly selfish and self-serving. How could she fail to resent him for that? Abruptly, he knew of the sacrifice he'd demanded, and the great humility and courage it had taken for her to comply. And he was sorely ashamed. He needed to take her aside, to explain what he'd discovered, to beg her forgiveness, to begin anew.

Evangeline's gaze lifted in question as he rose, skimming along the muscled thighs that topped his leggings, roaming the lightly furred terrain of his chest until she gained his features. She puzzled at his intensity. She was perplexed by her own.

"Can we walk a bit, Evangeline?"

The offer stunned her. She could see he was close to collapse. The long day had drained him of the little strength he'd managed to recoup. She knew he must be hurting and weary, yet he refused rest in favor of a moment alone with her. To protest would belittle his manhood. To hesitate would question his wisdom. What could be so important that he would risk so much? Quickly, she scrambled up and led the way down to the rushing waters.

Royle stood on the edge of the bank, staring out over the black, glassy river. His profile was etched sharply in shadow, so she could not read his mood. However, she sensed a troubled brooding, something against which he struggled in vain. He was too tired to engage in such a conflict of heart and spirit, and she sought to ease his way.

Royle gave a delicious start when her palms slid over the fan of his shoulder blades. He gave a low, completely primal moan as her fingers dug deep into the knotted muscles there, forcing them to release their tension in languorous degrees. His mind emptied of his planned speech at her purposeful manipulations.

"Better?"

"Ummm," was his heartfelt response.

"You should soothe your spirit in the water." She felt him tense once more at her suggestion, and she

288

laughed. "'Twill do you good to soak away your weariness and worries."

"In the river?" His typical English aversion to water extended to bathing. Exposing the body invited colds, pneumonia, and took many to their graves. How could she suggest such a thing?

"Come Tanner. There is nothing to fear."

To prove her words, she let the brief skirt and cloak of hide she wore drop at the river bank. Her body shimmered golden in the fading light before disappearing beneath the dark surface. Royle held his breath until she broke water some distance away from the shore, where she played about as graceful as an otter.

"Come in, Tanner."

"I don't know how to swim," he growled, as if such a thing was necessary knowledge while growing up in the heart of London.

"Just wade out then. It isn't deep."

He bent to dip his fingertips in the wetness that lapped the bank. It was cold. His skin tightened rebelliously.

Then Evangeline stood, clearing the water to her waist. Dampness glistened on her perfect torso and made her hair into a length of slick black satin. Suddenly the lure of the river became more inviting. He tested it again. Not so bad, he decided.

She had turned away, lifting her heavy hair high to wring out the wetness, exposing the long, clean line of her back until it disappeared with the tempting offer of curving buttocks. Too tempting, as well she knew. She heard his muffled oath—it was more groan than grumble—then the splash of water. Closing her eyes, she reached out with her senses and felt her body come alive with expectation. The shiver beginning with the cool tickle of water down the base of her neck became the warm caress of his hands. They spanned her ribs, filled themselves with her taut breasts to feel them bud within roughened palms. Evangeline slid back against the hard wall of chest, letting her head rest upon his shoulder. His face nuzzled the damp fall of her hair, freeing her arched throat for his succulent kisses. One hand slipped down to disappear within the water, and her gasp echoed in the night.

"You're right, angel," he murmured against her ear. "These waters must hold curative powers. I find myself renewed already."

She revolved in his embrace to face him. Her loveliness was bathed in cool, crystal moonlight. Her pale eyes shimmered with like mysteries, beckoning yet hauntingly out of reach. Enticed, he tried to span that taunting distance. His palms cradled her finely cut jaw, holding her reverently while her moist lips knew the worshipping touch of his own. And while she sighed, eyes closed in the luxury of his attention, his mouth traced down to lick the beads of dampness from her skin. Fingers twined and twisted in his tawny hair, restless in their longing. Tantalizing lips made a slow provocative circle about one aching breast, until her greedy hands directed urgently. He suckled.

And there in the water and then on the mossy shore, he went on to show her just how well-recovered he was.

Chapter Nineteen

The next day they drove themselves even harder. A tension bound them in silence, as if they knew their quarry was near. The strength Royle boasted of last evening failed him at the merciless pace. His muscles, unused to trailing afoot, cramped and complained. His head ached mightily. Only his pride kept him going, that and the want to compare well with the Iroquois in the eyes of his wife.

By the time the sun was high, it was obvious to all but Royle that he could not take another steady step. When Cayenderongue suggested a scout be sent ahead, Royle was only too happy to collapse upon the ground, dignity intact and final reserves untested. He hurt all over, and when looking at the unwinded Indians, he marveled at their stamina. He was soft, bred to studies and white comforts, while they were honed by vigorous pursuits. Even Evangeline showed no sign of being out of breath. It was a humbling moment for his vanity.

She came to kneel beside him, offering water and a paste of corn. There was no derision in her soft gaze, no pity or contempt, only an unspoken pride for what he considered his feeble effort. He ate and drank in silence, wondering at that look.

As the day waned hot and lazy, the braves stretched out in contented lethargy. A bowl, some beans, and a scattering of small bones were produced to spark interest among them. Royle watched, intrigued, as the bowl was struck, causing the bones to fly out, then much was made over the combinations in which they fell. Gambling, he understood, and he was quick to catch on to the simple rules. Though when he was invited into the game, he shook his head, claiming he had nothing to wager. A few sly words were exchanged between the braves, and they chuckled. Royle looked to Evangeline for translation.

"They say you have more to wager than you realize," she supplied a bit tersely.

"Meaning?"

"They play for blankets, furs, and pipes, which you do not have. But they also bet wives and fingers, which the winner will string as a necklace."

Royle lost all enthusiasm and much of his color. "I don't think I care to risk either of those things for the sake of entertainment."

She smiled slightly and turned to address the lounging braves. Her words brought a certain stiffening to their posture, and they went haughtily back to their game.

"What did you tell them?" he asked, curious at her self-satisfied smirk.

"I said my husband was a man of great wisdom, who knows the value of what he has, and that it would take death to part them from him."

"Oh." Just as he was beginning to believe his hair safe. He scowled his displeasure, but she continued to look smugly pleased.

Their indolence wasn't long lasting. A rustle in the

brush brought them up from the cast of bones battle-alert, Royle just slightly slower in his response. The man they'd sent ahead to scout rejoined them and spoke rapidly in their language. Royle waited impatiently for Evangeline to retell his news.

"The Frenchman and five others are an hour to the west and coming this way."

Her somber words woke an unfamiliar savagery within Royle. His lust for vengeance curled hot and tight in his belly, and fatigue was instantly forgotten. His thoughts were afire with the want to have the traitor Allouez in his grasp.

"The Frenchman must be taken alive," he told the others curtly. "The rest I don't care about, but Allouez I need. I have some questions for him."

Cayenderongue gave a slow, cruel smile. "We will see you get your answers."

They set upon the unsuspecting group just as the sun melted in bloody splendor over the great Mohawk River. It was short, savage work at close range. Expertly wielded knives and hatchets gave time for no cries from the already dead, until the Frenchman stood alone at the end of Royle's rifle. His ugly features showed no sign of fear. The black eyes held only contempt.

Royle's thirst for retribution knew a faltering as the dead were quickly stripped of valuables and hair. It was gruesome fare for even the stoutest of heart. Evangeline never blinked an eye when handed the gory trophies. He couldn't help wondering how she could maintain such composure when the reminder of her parents' demise must be a foremost torment in her mind. He feared he would never understand the complexities of thought turning behind her lovely, impassive face.

They returned with their prisoner to their own campsite, and while Royle tried questioning him, the Iroquois built the fire high. The Frenchman stood mute before the inquiry. He knew speech would not save his life, so he remained silent. Heat and brilliance brought a sheen to his huge hook nose, and danced in his flat obsidian eyes. Frustrated that he could force no answers from him, Royle nevertheless had to admire the man for his reckless courage.

"He will not talk to you," Cayenderongue told his new brother with a matter-of-fact certainty. "Let us ask the questions in a way he understands. He will speak to us. Eventually."

Royle wasn't sure what was meant by that cold conclusion, but he had to hear the secrets Allouez carried. He stepped aside and let the braves lash their captive to a tree. A tug upon his arm distracted his attention from the grim tableau.

"Tanner, come away," Evangeline said softly. "This is not for your eyes."

"I will stay to hear what he has to say," he replied. Her gaze was entreating, compassionate. Did she think him too weak to witness what would occur? He was white, but he was not delicate. In his youth, he'd faced many sober truths without flinching, as he would now. His anger over the betrayal and loss was such that he was eager to land a few blows of his own. Yet she persisted.

"Royle, please. You will not understand, and you cannot interfere. It's best you come apart with me and leave them to their work."

He frowned. What was she hinting at? Their work. No, he didn't understand. She pulled at his arm. She was strong and determined. To break free would mean a struggle. He didn't want to hurt her, and,

294

more than that, he wasn't sure he could best her. Instead, he gave and followed her down to the riverbank where they had made love the night before beneath the pagan moon. On this night, she made no attempt to seduce him under that silvery cresent. She stood in silent support at his side, her bewitching eyes upon him, watching, waiting. The gentle hand upon his arm implored and comforted. To what end? Was he a child who needed such careful nurturing? Impatiently, Royle looked out over the water. He was irritated at being pulled away from the questioning. His blood burned hot for the answers. He was slighted that Evangeline would think him too soft to stand beside her people. Hadn't he proved his bravery to her satisfaction? That she would emphasize the difference between him and the Iroquois warriors by drawing him apart with a protective attitude rankled his male pride. He would indulge her for the moment, but determined to rejoin the others at the fire. This was his battle, after all.

He was the one who stood to gain from the outcome. He should be there. He wanted to be there.

And then the screams began.

Evangeline saw her husband jerk as that first hoarse wail ripped through the woods. His gaze flew toward the hidden camp, and he took an involuntary step forward. She was quick to stay him.

"No, Royle."

"What are they—"

Another undulating cry interrupted his question. Gooseflesh broke out along his arms in a cold prickle. Never had he heard such a raw sound. It made his insides quiver and rebel. It made his mind create horrors he coud not accept.

"You do not wish to know," she told him with ominous certainty.

His round, dazed stare returned to her, and she recoiled from the horror of knowledge she saw in them. "They're torturing that man," he said hoarsely, his tone begging her to tell him it wasn't so. She gave him no such relief. She could not.

"They are getting your answers."

Frantically his gaze went back to the woods as another scream rippled up his spine. His breath came quicker, in horror, in sickness. He felt trapped by his proximity, obligated by the bounds of decency to halt the ruthless actions wrought at his request. Caught in that panic of conscience, he struck out blindly. "And you condone such barbarity? How can you? You are no savage. You were raised in a decent, God-fearing home, whether you choose to remember it or not."

Evangeline didn't shrink from the blame of his words. She could see the violence of his internal struggle etched in harsh relief upon his features. His gaze was desperate with shock and hideous dread. It begged relief from her, from the crushing guilt of association. Quietly, she said, "I accept it. As you must."

"No, I don't have to. My God, it's inhuman."

"You do have to. You cannot stop what you've started." She spoke to him brutally, to shake him from his misplaced sympathies. "Do you think he suffered from like conscience when he had my parents' and my brother killed? It was quicker, true, but no more humane."

Royle fell silent, torn between the bitter logic she offered and his own abhorrence for what was taking place mere yards away. She could not allow him to harbor any doubts over which way his heart lay.

"Do you want your answers or not?"

She saw his jaw work fiercely, angrily, in an agony

296

of indecision. Everything they were doing was against all his beliefs, against his moral stands. Yet when he replied, his voice was grim and steady. "I want them, dammit. I want them."

Then he turned away from her and stalked to the edge of the river, denying her presence and his own part in the atrocity. And she watched from her distance, feeling his distress, her heart softening for his pain, but not for that of the deserving Frenchman. She didn't suffer from Royle's anguish. She may have shared his heritage, but she'd been hardened long ago to the harsh simplicity of life. Life was cruel and unforgiving. Vengeance was not a pleasure but an obligation. He could not understand that. She hoped he never had to. And she ached for him.

Dawn's gray awakening shone with silver along the horizon before the tormented cries finally ceased. Royle had given up his rigid stance and was seated in the shadows, head buried in the wrap of his arms atop upraised knees. Evangeline fought her longing to go to him, to embrace and comfort him. She didn't think he'd receive her, for now she was of the vile godless who tortured his soul. She'd watched him suffer like misery with the utterance of each pitiful cry, until she was moved to wretched weeping. She couldn't bear his hurt, the shattering of his noble ideals at the ruthless hands of her people. She would have spared him if she could. It was such a cruel way to learn life. Yet he could not be shielded from the lesson. He was not a child, and she wouldn't treat him as such. He was a man, tormented by a reality he couldn't conceive, that he couldn't accept. And she grieved for his loss of innocence.

Silence brought up the twany head. He looked so terrible, Evangeline nearly sobbed anew. Instead she bit her lip and stood waiting.

"Is it over?" How hoarse his voice was, as if each scream had torn from his own throat.

"I do not know."

He rose and went to bathe his face in the cool waters. His insides were weak with nausea, his heart heavy with disgust. If the cries began again, he knew he could not withstand it. He'd been tortured to his limit. When he straightened, he could see Cayende-rongue reflected at his back.

"A most fitting enemy," the warrior remarked with pride for the man who'd died so horribly at his hands. "A brave man meets his death with insults on his lips."

"Is that all he told you?" Royle demanded. Had it been for nothing? Had he allowed a man to suffer unto death for no reason? Guilt choked him until he could speak no more.

"He told us enough, my brother."

Cold reason assailed him, more revitalizing than the splash of clear water. "What?" He came to his feet, anxiousness overcoming much of his despair. "What did he say?"

"That he was paid to ambush Eyes-Like-Evening-Star's white parents. None were to have survived, but he let his greed for trade rule reason. The same man paid him to take you on the trail. You were not to be killed. Only your wife."

Only Evangeline? He glanced at her, as if he could find some logic there he'd overlooked before. But there was none. Why her?

"What man? Did he say what man?"

"Death mocked us by keeping it silent. We will go home now."

Royle stood for a long while, staring into the water as thoughts revolved without meaning. He was exhausted in body and spirit. His head and his heart ached, and there seemed no help for either. A light touch upon his arm jerked him back to the ugliness of the present. He twitched away from that hand.

"Come, Royle."

Royle simply looked at her, seeing what, she didn't know. His eyes held a queer opaqueness. Evangeline felt isolated from whatever moved behind them. A quiver of uncertainty took her. Would he refuse to go with them?

"Come, Royle," she repeated and took a step away. Then another. Then she forced herself to turn and begin to walk toward their camp, straining for the sound of him following, praying to hear it. Finally she heard the slow fall of his steps, and her breath released from its suspension.

They returned through the castle gates early the next morning, to be greeted by the sight of industry at one of the longhouses. Ten families already lived within the head matron's great house, and a newly married daughter was bringing a husband under their roof. Men were busy raising an extension, lashing bent saplings to the framework of forked posts and horizontal poles, over which a shingle of elm bark would later be attached. There was much laughter and good-natured kidding toward the recent groom. It was the type of scene Evangeline had long envisioned for herself, the joy of having a man gladly prepare to come beneath her roof, to set his belongings on the platform above their sleeping mats, linking his life with her own.

When he'd been accepted into their ranks, Evangeline had harbored hopes. Royle had been receptive to her people and their ways. But this stranger who'd returned with them was wrapped tightly within himself, resisting the way of things, rejecting the truth of life. Sadly she knew there would be no such joining between her and Royle Tanner, no happy medium in which they would both be comfortable. Realizing that, her spirit plummeted, but she put on a welcoming smile for those who rushed to greet them.

They were enfolded into the gathering as heroes, with much made over the display of drying scalps. Royle was drawn into the circle of praise, and though he made no attempt to deny his part, he was very quiet, and Evangeline worried over him. She slipped away while the men grouped to boast and pass rum between them, going first to speak with her mother, then to prepare her small compartment for her husband's return. And there she waited until shadows stretched long, and the only light came from the central fire.

Finally, Royle joined her. She could smell the heavy odor of rum upon him. Her nose wrinkled in objection. Bottled rum was an evil among her people, one she held in loathing. They did not drink as the white man, lifting a glass in polite social surroundings. They drank with inebriation alone as their goal, to inflate their self-esteem, to excuse any aggression they might commit against another tribesman that was strictly forbidden. They hailed the dreamlike state of drunkenness as a likening to religious possession. But Evangeline knew different. It was an excuse for men to act on the evil of their heart, and she feared the way it changed them, and the lust for it that drove them into the power of the whites.

Another time she might have chastened her husband for coming into her bed reeking of drink, but on this night she stayed silent. It was more than the liquor that worked on Royle's soul, and she waited almost fearfully for him to speak of it. But he didn't. He settled onto the wealth of furs without a word, his eyes closing almost immediately, as if to shut out he sight of her. Evangeline chewed her lip apprehensively, not sure what to make of his snub. His coldness wounded deep, but she was determined to act as if she didn't feel it.

"Does your head still pain you?" she asked, placing her hand to the discolored split on his brow. He winced away, not from pain, she thought, but rather from her touch.

"Not so bad now," was all he offered before rolling to present her with his back.

"You stayed long before the fire, when you should be seeking your rest," she scolded gently. She felt his hurt like a physical thing between them. She longed to push it aside with the strength of her embrace. She yearned to encourage him to purge his pain with cleansing tears, anything to provide relief from the torments bottled tight within him. Yet he denied her and himself that outlet.

"It matters not. I'll be getting no rest this night," was his cryptic reply. "Cayenderongue leaves in the morning, and he wished to spend time with me first. You need not have waited up."

"I didn't mind," she murmured while thoughts spun widly. She was reluctant to voice them, fearing his answer, fearing the unknown. But she had to ask, she had to know. "And when do you leave?" She wished she could see his face, to read his heart within his expressive eyes.

"I, too, leave at first light."

Evangeline waited for him to say more, to say what her soul ached to hear, but he remained silent.

Finally, she had to prompt, "What of me?"

"What of you?"

The emotionless quality of his tone was like a slap, and she reeled back from it barely able to control her tears. Did he not care then what became of her? Had his heart turned from her in disgust?

"Do I go with you?" That was said with all the pride she could muster, for she would not let him see her frailty or her fear. What if he said no? His long pause was sheer agony.

"There is naught to go back to unless you do," was his flat reply, and she puzzled over the words he would not explain.

"I will be ready then."

Royle had no more to say to her. She sat staring at his broad back until his breath regulated in slumber. Then she lay beside him, not touching for she could feel no closeness between them. Instead, she wrapped herself in the comfort of furs and in the knowledge that she would be going with him in the morning. That was what was important, after all, and she gave no undo thought to leaving her own world to follow him back to his. Her home was now beneath the roof he chose, and she would be content wherever that might be. At last she closed her eyes and she, too, slept.

The two of them created quite a stir when they emerged from the wilderness of the outskirts of Albany, like two white savages in full Indian dress. A bearskin robe covered much of Royle's bared skin, and Evangeline adopted a short cape (with slits cut for movement of her arms) and leggings (to conceal the scandalous amount of tawny limb left beneath the brevity of her skirt). Had Royle burned off his

302

hair into a roach ridge, he couldn't have gotten a more stunned reception from Barnabas Maxell. But then, that was not due to his appearance, rather the fact that he appeared at all.

"By God, I'd heard you were dead!"

Royle tossed off his robe and opted for one of the crudely made buckskin shirts displayed within the store. "As you can see, I am not."

Max's gaze darted between the two of them in confusion. "Word had it that you was set upon by thieves, who left you without your hair."

Royle's fingers threaded through his untidy locks. "Still attached," he remarked glibly, then he grew more serious. "But the provisions, not so lucky."

"You're back and that be the important thing," Max assured him.

"I doubt Webster will see it that way," came his rueful reply.

Ignored by both men as they set to business, Evangeline slipped from the trading house and stared down the trail toward her home. Anticipation fluttered within her breast and bloomed to a poignant welcome when she beheld the familiar house. Careful not to be seen in her native garb, she ducked into the rear door and was overwhelmed by the feeling of being home. Her misty eyes took in the plain common room; no splendor of material goods would have looked finer. All she saw was hers. And Royle's.

Thinking of him drew her to the corner bed where they'd loved and fought and learned of one another. It seemed so long ago that they'd shared it in the passion of discovery. Would that intensity return tonight? Or would the chill Royle had retreated behind linger within these walls? She couldn't bear it if it did. She ached for his touch, for his passion, for

303

his care. What could she do to restore it?

Decision made, Evangeline hurried to the task. There was much to do before Royle's return, and she was determined that all be perfect when he crossed the threshold. She rushed the kitchen to life with her enthusiasm, kindling a warmth within it to make it a welcoming home, the type of home he would relish coming to, one far removed from reminders of the woods. Finally she flung open her chest and completed the final touches, just as a gust of cool autumn wind announced his arrival.

Royle stood, taking in his welcome with a slow deliberate stare. A fire crackled invitingly in the hearth. Fragrant smells wafted from the hanging pots. The table was dressed with a fine broadcloth and Delftware and a bundle of freshly picked wildflowers. The bed curtains and covers had been pulled back to suggest an easy rest. And then there was Evangeline.

She waited by the trestle table, hands folded before her in a demure attitude. She looked radiant. Black hair was swept away from her face and pinned in a glossy coronet of braids. Her slender figure was draped in an mauve-colored silk and ivory lace, all swags and ribbon and fabric roses. All proper femininity. The subtle scent of lavender teased him where he stood. Royle was reminded of the first time he'd seen her and was captivated by the hope that she would be his. Her wide guileless gray eyes said that that was now so. He remembered his dream of coming home to such an enticing hearth with warm dinner and warmer wife waiting. And so it was. All was perfect, just as planned. Except it was all wrong.

Evangeline controlled her nervous want to fidget as her husband surveyed her accomplishments. This was the home and wife he wanted, and so she would make it so. If it was a gentle English woman he desired, she would try her best to become one. She would tend his every wish, fulfill his every dream, for pride mattered not when sacrificed for love. To have him cross the room and sweep her into his arms, to feel his stirring kisses, to hear him claim for the first time what he felt for her in his heart, for those things there was nothing she would not do. She would put the past behind her, forfeit her heritage, her upbringing, her beliefs, to have him as her future. He was ravaged in body and spirit by the hell he'd been through, and now she would grant him solace. She would give him peace from the miseries he'd suffered. Her heart swelled with the wish to share her newly recognized love. It beat fast and furious for the desire to share more. With one word, she would humble herself before him. With a single sign, she would fly into his embrace. She waited, flushed with anticipations, buoyant with hope. This would be their new beginning.

And then Royle came out of his trance. He crossed the room, walking right by her. He didn't look at her as he brushed past on his way to the sitting room and the bottle of rum, which on this night offered more than the benefits of a willing wife.

Chapter Twenty

She was devastated.

Nothing he could have done would have held the power to wound her deeper.

That he passed her by as if all her efforts and all she offered was of no value crushed her proud spirit.

She wanted to weep. She wanted to wail. She wanted to kill him!

Fury rose up, instinctive and all-consuming. How dare he spurn her! How dare he ignore her! Her first impulse was to grasp the handiest blade and rush into the other room. That would surely get his attention.

But it wouldn't gain his love.

Evangeline sank down onto the nearest stool. The savageness left her on a helpless sigh. What had she done wrong? She'd thought he would be overjoyed by her reception. She'd thought he'd be too happy to push aside her pagan past in preference of this pristine image. Why wasn't he? She had no understanding of white men, and she didn't care to learn. It was only this one man to whom she needed insight. Why was that wisdom denied her?

She rose and mechanically measured the savory

stew upon a trencher and added the spoon bread she'd hastily prepared. When the pewter mugs were filled with cold beer, she called out optimistically, "Royle, your plate is on the table."

There was silence for a moment, then he replied brusquely, "Serve yourself. I've no appetite. I must draft a letter to your uncle tonight."

Evangeline's features tightened. She lifted the plate she'd readied for him and barely stopped herself from flinging it into the fire. What good would that burst of temper do? She'd still have no husband at the table, and a mess to clean up besides. After his portion had been returned to the pot, she sat before her own scant meal and consumed it in silence. Alone.

Darkness came and still Royle labored over the letter describing his failure on the trail to the Great Lakes. Finally Evangeline ran the warming pan under the sheets, careful not to scorch them. At least she'd have some heat to share, if not of the desired source. She lay awake for long hours until she heard him moving in the other room. She forced herself to lie quiet as he readied to join her on their marriage bed. When he slipped beneath the covers, more than his unshed shirt came between them. He remained stiffly upon his back, making no effort to enjoy her warmth and other available comforts. With him so near, Evangeline's senses heightened into taut expectation and grew desperate for the feel of him. It was more than the soaring pleasure of his body that she craved. It was the unique blending of their souls entwining at that perfect moment that she sought so hungrily, the oneness. The harmony of love.

Casually, as if by accident, she brushed her knee against his thigh. He rolled away in abrupt denial. It was an action so deliberate, so cold, she could not mistake its meaning. He did not want her. Evangeline sobbed within her secret heart while she lay silent and stunned by his rejection. She didn't know if he ever slept, but the room saw streaks of palest morning before she found any rest.

And when she awoke, he was already gone.

Weeks passed miserably in that same manner. Royle stayed late at the trading house and returned tired and uncommunicative. He shared none of his day with her. He shared nothing at all. Evangeline was distraught. Even when she'd been his prisoner, he'd treated her better. He'd at least acknowledge she was there.

She decided upon the problem. Having seen her in her native surroundings, Royle had taken a deep disgust to her. He wanted no part of a savage bride, no commerce with a brutal wife. His shock and horror at what had occurred upon the trail had hardened his heart toward her. It was worse than being dead. At least then her memory would have been revered.

Daily she worked to prove how different things could be. She could make him a civilized mate. Eva Loockermann proved to be her greatest asset after she arrived unexpectedly to find the young woman in tears upon her hearth. Between the sobs, Evangeline managed to tell her of her failure to hold her husband's affection. Eva clucked with disbelief, dried her tears, and taught her to make delectable meals. Their afternoons were spent together at genteel pursuits, at stitchery, at the hearth, trimming gowns, and dressing her hair. The modest home took on elements of romance, with soft candlelight, verbena packets tucked into pillows, rose leaves burned upon the hearth, and arrangements of flowers. Evangeline practiced subtle coquetry in hopes of luring his interest. All was a dismal failure. Their table was arid space, their bed barren ground.

And when Eva caught her moping over her needlework, her eyes red and swollen from tears she could no longer seem to control, she sat beside Evangeline and took up her hand. Then gave her the shock of her life.

"Does he know yet of the babe you carry?"

Evangeline winced as the needle jabbed deep into her thumb. "Babe?" she repeated foolishly, and Eva chuckled.

"Surely it isn't news to you? Then I can see it is."

Flosses fell from her fingers as her hands went to her flat belly. A child. Royle's child. She thought back frantically, not daring to give herself hope. And then she was certain. Her time of isolation had failed to come since he had forced her to remain in his presence that first month. And that was three ago.

In unrestrained joy she flung her arms about the plump Dutch woman, who enthusiastically returned her hug.

"There now, you see. All will be taken care of. When he hears of the babe, all will be right between you again."

That sentiment shook her from her excitement with uncertainty anew. She drew back and cried, "No, please. You mustn't tell him."

"But—"

"No! I must first know if he loves me for myself, and not just because he's filled me with his child."

Eva couldn't fathom her distress. "How could he not love you, child? You be his wife, and such a lovely

309

little thing."

"But he has never spoken of it," she confessed wretchedly. What she wouldn't trade to hear him speak those words. Yet he remained silent. He'd pursued her as a possession, not because of any personal value she held to his heart. It was pride not love that bound her to his house, and before she revealed this precious link, there would have to be more.

"Then he be a fool," the Dutch woman decreed with a confirming nod. "And what he needs is someone else to show him the way a man should behave when smitten with a woman."

Evangeline was about to disavow her claim, then fell silent. And thoughtful. Then she smiled. Exactly! If pride was his greatest weakness, she would hit him where he would feel it.

"Docile work for a warrior."

Royle looked up from his books to see Cayenderongue smirking down at him. His own smile came easily in return. "Yes, but it keeps me clothed and fed."

"You wear too many clothes, and nature abounds with food," came the expected challenge.

"I am but a puny white man."

"Pah." He turned and made a gesture as if to spit upon the plank floor. "You are an Iroquois and holder of a brave name. You seek excuses where there are none."

Royle shrugged. "Perhaps I do. Have you come to trade?" He closed his books and went to draw them both a mug of rum.

"I have come to visit family. How is Eyes-Like-Evening-Star?"

"She's fine and fit," Royle said distractedly.

"Good, then you will not mind if I see for myself."

Evangeline raced across the room to embrace the handsome warrior, her eyes bright with tears of gladness. From over Cayenderongue's broad, bared shoulder, she saw Royle methodically rehang his flintlock above the hearth and remove his coat. She noticed how relaxed his mode of dress had become since returning from the wilds. He'd foregone the inappropriate velvets and brocades in favor of sturdier stuff. His wrapping coat was of heavy canvas over a simple shirt. Heeled shoes of stiff leather were replaced by ankle-high moccasins. He seemed to be adapting more easily to the ways then to the people themselves.

"This is a surprise," she cried, nearly convincing herself with her enthusiasm as she stepped back from the muscular chest of bronze. She refused to meet her cousin's amused rebuke for that tiny lie. "You will stay to eat with us?" She looked to Royle hopefully, but Cayenderongue had already made himself at home under the white man's roof. He let his shoulder bags fall to the floor and went to sniff within the open kettle suspended above the hearth.

"What have you provided, Sahawhe?" he asked of Royle.

"'Tis venison, brought down fresh this morning," Evangeline said quickly. She did not add that she'd purchased it from a local hunter. That the brave would not understand, for in their society, the husband always brought home the game. To fail at that was to fail as a provider.

"Good." Cayenderongue grunted his satisfaction.

Royle stiffened at the exchange, his pride smarting

that his wife would have to protect him with vague untruths. She shouldn't make excuses for him. Yet he made no move to correct her.

The black stare came about to fasten upon the swirls and swags of yellow silk Evangeline wore. His look was frank and unflattering, as it went from the fluffy short sleeves down the outline of her corset-shaped middle to lace-bordered petticoat. "How can you move in such things?" he commented bluntly. "I am surprised, my brother, that you would allow your woman to hide her beauty beneath such unappealing garb."

Evangeline flushed. She didn't dare look to Royle for his reaction. "'Tis the way women dress among the whites, cousin. Were I to stride about in my native clothes, my neighbors would fall into fits."

"Let them. Only the fat and old should conceal themselves as if ashamed."

"You do not understand their ways."

"They are foolish ways. I am hungry."

Grateful for the change of topic, Evangeline went to dish up the meat, now self-conscious in her pretty gown. With food upon each plate, Cayenderongue ignored the ladder-back chair brought down for his use in favor of the warm stones before the fire. He sat cross-legged upon the floor and began to apply his fingers to the meal. Evangeline froze for a long second, unsure of what to do, then Royle gave a small smile and joined him upon the hearth stones.

Because her full skirts would not bend comfortably for such seating, Evangeline remained standing to serve the two men. As she moved about to refill plates and mugs, the Caniengas's dark gaze followed her. His look was puzzled and went between his host and hostess.

When the food was gone, Cayenderongue patted his belly in appreciation and declared, "You are fortunate, my brother. How I would like to have such a wife in my *ganonh'sees*." Then his black eyes lifted to the woman who served them. That warming gaze clearly said, it was this woman he wished was there. Royle was not oblivious to that unexpressed desire, and he felt the hospitable smile tighten on his lips.

Only their guest was unaware of the disturbance his remark awoke. He looked to Royle with a more serious attitude.

"I wanted to speak to you, my brother, about your place at the trading house, and the way it has been cheating my people."

Royle immediately bristled in defense. "I have seen no one cheated of a fair exchange."

"Not yet. 'Tis still good hunting for us. But when that time is gone and we come to you for goods, will you try to steal from us what is not ours to give?"

Seeing her husband grow rigid with affront, Evangeline interceded quietly. "He speaks of the land, Tanner, of the way the white man takes the land in exchange for goods."

"That's called collateral for credit, and it's a respectable means of business. No one is cheated. Even if the promise of pelts cannot be met the following season, the Iroquois are still allowed the right to hunt, fish, and gather plants and wood. I don't see the problem."

"No," she said softly. "Because you see with white eyes. To us, the land is like our mother. It feeds us, clothes and shelters us. We belong to the land, not the land to us. We do not believe in land ownership. It is tribal territory shared by all. When one makes a treaty or a sale of land, it is because they do not realize the full meaning of the agreement."

"That's not up to me. The terms are clearly explained."

"And will be quickly violated. We are not like you. The white man is greedy for personal property, with getting, when all the Indian is concerned with is living. The land will be taken from us. We will be pushed aside by white settlers, and there will be trouble."

"And you say that fault is mine? Am I responsible to educate a whole people?"

"I only ask that you understand."

Their gazes locked for an intense exchange, each searching for something that went beyond the conversation into the deeper realm of character. Royle felt uncomfortable under that scrutiny and looked away.

"This is a big house," Cayenderongue stated suddenly. "How many families live beneath it?"

"Just the two of us," Royle said a bit tersely, still unsettled over the directness of his wife's appeal.

Black brows arched. "Then you must be a very wealthy man in the eyes of your people, to waste so much that could be shared."

"Wealthy? Not at all."

"Look at what you possess beyond what you need. Is that not how you measure wealth? Among my brethren, none are poor as long as many are rich. All we possess is held in common for everyone to enjoy."

Royle smiled a bit wryly. "And in England, where I come from, only the very wealthy live as you, taking their diversions at hunting and fishing. Only the nobility could claim the fruits of the forest."

"Then we are both wealthy men and have no reason to complain."

"Yes. We are both lucky men." Royle said that

314

vaguely, his gaze looking to thoughts far beyond the company.

"You are a fair man, Sahawhe. I look to you to do what is right for all." With that, the tall warrior unwound his long limbs to stand bold and bronze before the fire. His gaze settled on Evangeline and simmered quietly. "And little cousin, should my brother cease to please you, I would gladly set aside any other to take you for myself." He grinned broadly so there was no cause for tension, but none doubted his sincerity. "If you tire of serving and wish to hold your own house, you know how to reach me."

Evangeline had no response, but the true words struck her squarely. She stood in stiff silence while the men exchanged farewells. She was still caught up in thought when Royle shrugged on his coat and gruffly announced he planned to spend some time talking business at the Gold Cross. As far as she knew, only two pursuits were found at that local tavern; drunkenness and harlots. Wondering which he sought, she watched him go through a misty veil of tears.

Solitude settled about her. Its silence was great. Hollow. Cold. Like her relationship with her husband. Like her spirit. Cayenderongue's pointed observation woke her to her dissatisfaction. Here she had vowed she would have her husband love her for herself, and she'd not the courage to act herself when around him. She had smothered her fire beneath the clutter of white ways and had allowed it to sputter out. And Royle had let the ashes of her pride lay unstirred. No. That was not true. She had allowed it, by her uncertainty, by her insecurity. She'd let the ember of life flicker out, until nothing remained to warm hearth and home. She'd become a shadowy servant, afraid to offend or disturb the mounting

315

silence, a dim caricature of the woman who would have fought for the right to speak her mind, for the privilege of holding her home. She'd tried with ploys and subtleties to earn what was hers to demand. Instead of upset with the failure of her plan to lure her husband with jealousy, she began to ponder Cayenderongue's words. *If you ever tire of serving . . .*

As she began to clear the kitchen, anger simmered, and with it, sparked a renewal of life and self.

Royle sat pulling sullenly at his beer. The noise swelling about him found no way to penetrate his gloom. He was unconscious of the normal objections he'd hold to such a place as the Gold Cross. It was the rudest form of tavern, with few rooms, a single, small parlor, and a crude shack for horses. The tapster indulged as heartily as his patrons, and the rooms let above accommodated two. Royle was interested in none of those things. He wanted to lose himself amid strangers and to thought itself. Only the latter he couldn't manage.

The mood tormenting him deepened with the persuasion of alcohol. Increasing it was the memory of his Iroquois brother's warm appraisal of his wife. He'd been wrong to interfere there, just as he'd been wrong in so many things of late. He seemed to have lost his ability for clear thought. His judgment was appalling, his motives of the basest nature; greed and pride. And his conscience could no longer sustain them.

Royle swallowed the last of his beer and waved off the offer of another. Coming to this place was another poor choice. Nothing was solved. Nothing eased. Wearily, disheartened, he rose from his seat and made his way to the door, ignoring the ploys of several of the establishment's doxies. He would find no more solace in their bartered charms then he had in the stale drink. That peace could only come from within, and it continued to escape him. He stepped out into the cool night to begin the walk home. To where Evangeline would be waiting.

When he pictured her, his misery twisted tighter. She'd become the perfect mistress of his house, the very image of that vision he'd seen from Webster's foyer. And it taunted him mercilessly, piling on the weight of guilt until his shoulders bowed beneath it. Had he been so wrong to pursue his dreams? Was there cause for the horrendous plague of shame? If not, why was he so afraid to take a certain stand? Maybe then the vacillating doubts would leave him be. He had only to best his conscience, as others had before him. He had only to look to Uriah Webster for a prime example. And wasn't he the model Royle sought to follow? How bitter that taste of truth settled.

Darkness greeted him upon his return, and for a moment he was relieved to be spared a meeting with his wife. His mood was too low to withstand it. Purposefully, he crossed the clean-swept floor, weaving with uncanny reflex between the pieces of furniture he couldn't see until he'd reached the sitting room. A low fire kindled there lit the way to his objective, the nearly empty decanter of rum. There was just enough left to ease his way to slumber, hopefully without dreams. He wanted no more to do with dreams. As his hand reached for the bottle, another stayed it firmly.

"No, Tanner. Tonight we talk."

He stared, then nerves weren't the only thing aflutter. Evangeline wore only her chemise. With feet bared and black hair loose to fan about her shoulders, she looked every inch the savage beauty. Her eyes were as crisp as a mountain spring, and her lips lushly inviting in spite of their stubborn set. Her nostrils flared at the scent of liquor and pinched tight in displeasure. It was more than Royle's wavering will could withstand.

"I've had enough of the silence," she began in a magnificent tirade. It held Royle spellbound. "No more. I've tried to hide my heritage, since you've taken a disgust to it. Well, no longer. I am a daughter of the mighty Caniengas, a member of the Clan of the Wolf. And I am not ashamed. I chose to remain Tanner's Wife, even though you did not provide for me as is customary among my people and refused me my proper place at head of the house. You did not know who or what I was when we wed, so I cannot fault you for your disappointment. I am not the docile wife you would desire, nor will I ever be. I have a voice and will be heard. I demand a say in the management of my property. I will not be ignored.

"I may concede to you on matters of home and business but I will not be denied the privileges due a wife. I will not remain if you take no joy in my company. I will not stay if you find no pleasure in my bed. If you do not want me—"

Royle's reserve exploded. His hands seized her flushed face between them, almost cruel in his intensity. He held her captive so his lips could silence her proud declaration. He drew her up roughly so she might feel his argument to her every claim pressed in bold evidence against her belly. She stood stunned as his mouth ravaged hers with urgent, demanding kisses. Such ardor she'd never expected after long weeks of isolation.

"Not want you?" he breathed huskily between

samples of her moist lips. "God, Evangeline, I'm dying for the want of you."

Protest registered somewhere amid the feverish unfurling of emotion. "But Royle—" she panted faintly.

"I haven't known what to do," he hurried on, as if he couldn't wait to unburden his words or his passions. "I've made so many mistakes. So much of what I've desired has proven wrong. But not this. Not you. I know that now. This is right."

Bedcovers that provided the only warmth on past nights were tossed aside in favor of a more ebullient heat. The chemise proved a frail barrier to hands seeking the smoothness it concealed. Opposites clashed and combined. Behind the damask curtains hung to ward off the harshest elements, a tumultuous storm began to brew, until the very foundation of the bed was shaken. A greedy tempest of desire prevailed, ruling the night and reigning supreme until near dawn, when spent, it quieted to a contented lull.

Evangeline sighed and nestled her head upon the chest of the man who'd given all she desired—save answers. And though she reveled in what she received so bountifully throughout the night, she would have the rest as well. She had to in order for all to be complete, so her anxieties would have no cause to plague her. And though it may not have been the perfect time to risk the rekindling of harsh memory, for never would that occur, it seemed the right time to ask.

"Royle, can you ever forgive me?"

The soft whisper brought him fully awake. "For what, angel?"

"For what has kept us apart these past weeks. I know you were cruelly shocked by the savagery of my people, and by my willingness to allow it. I cannot

319

change what is bred in each of us, but I've tried to lessen its ugliness in your eyes. My efforts have failed, I know. I cannot convince you that I am other than a brutal child of the wild. I can hide what I am under frilled fabric and pretty manners, but it changes not what lies in the heart of me. I would have you happy, my husband, but not at the cost of my own enslavement. Can you not accept a part of what I am? Can you give me no single bit of my heritage to hold with pride?''

"What is it you want?" His hand began a lingering caress down the spill of her hair, only to lose itself in the luxurious splendor.

"Your respect," she named boldly, then with less confidence, "and your love." When he was silent, she rushed on. "I know it is much to ask, and in your world, I've no right to make such a demand. But I am not of your world, and I need to know these things. I need to know you do not hate that part of me that exists when we are not joined in passion."

"Evangeline," he began slowly, "what you are is not what's troubled me these weeks. It's what I am."

She came up on one elbow, expression knit in confusion. Long ebony tresses made a silken curtain behind which the beauty of her bared breasts was concealed. It was parted with the deliberate move of his hand and pushed back over her shoulder.

"I do not understand," she admitted finally, when he showed a reluctance to explain.

"Nor did I." He gave her a tight smile. It was a pained gesture. "'Tis I who needs beg forgiveness of you. You placed me rightly as one of those grubbing white men always lusting for more. More wealth. More possessions. More status. Never satisfied. Never caring who paid the price. Only I got to caring so much, it was tearing me apart inside."

320

Though her gaze moistened with a sympathy for his distress, Evangeline remained silent, encouraging him with the gentle brush of her fingers along his jaw to continue.

"You can't know how it is to be driven to succeed. I wanted that success so badly I would have given anything to have it. And I almost did. It wasn't what your people did to the Frenchman, it was my willingness to see it done. I was angry because he dared interfere with my future. I wanted my answers regardless of the cost he had to pay. And every time I close my eyes, I hear his screams and feel more damned."

She kissed his mouth softly, then his cheeks, and the corners of his fated green eyes. "No, Royle," she murmured. "You mustn't let the guilt consume you. You couldn't have stopped it. What you felt came from a human heart, not from any ugliness in your soul."

He wrenched his head away to deny her consolation. "You still don't understand," he cried wretchedly. "That's not the worst of it. What torments me is what I've hidden from you out of my own greedy purpose."

Very quietly, she prompted, "And what is that, my husband?"

"I think your uncle wants you dead."

Chapter Twenty-One

"What?" The single word escaped on a startled breath.

"I tried to convince myself it wasn't so. I let myself believe that the danger to you was less important than my own success. I kept telling myself I had no facts, no reason to jeopardize my future on a vague suspicion. To challenge Webster would tear down everything I'd ever hoped to gain, and for what? For something over and done? I couldn't bring back your parents. I couldn't bring back your brother. But it was when I realized that I could yet lose you—"

"Royle, what are you saying?"

"I'm saying I don't deserve your trust. I didn't value you as much as a position with your uncle. I was willing to stay silent and keep my precious profits. Oh, I told myself I could protect you. Look what prime protection I was able to give against Allouez." His voice thickened with self-deprecation. But Evangeline was listening to none of his anguished confession.

"My uncle had them killed," she repeated softly, as if to impress that fact upon a resisting mind. "Why?" she was quick to demand. "Why would he do such a thing?''

Seeing she wasn't following his rambling confession, Royle broke off from his harsh blaming to explain, "For the same reason I was ready to look the other way. Greed. Ambition. Webster told me they were different things. I don't believe that now.''

Evangeline reached out to him with instant support, with quick comfort that would deny his guilt. She still didn't understand as she tried to hold him. He could no longer endure her tender empathy. He was unworthy of that compassion. Abruptly, he rolled from the tempting warmth of her body to the cold reality of the floorboards upon the bottom of his feet. Tugging on his breeches, he went to kneel before the hearth. The fire burned low upon it, and he tossed on another log. Sparks showered like brilliant fireflies against the sooty backdrop, then were quick to expire. Like his hopes. Then strong fingers pressed his shoulders as Evangeline came down behind him on the chilly stones.

"But you didn't look the other way," she said. "You didn't stay silent and secure with your success. You chose the honorable way.''

He gripped her hands and held them fiercely within his own. His laugh was brittle. "Not for the lack of trying. It wasn't until tonight that honor outweighed greed. Up until now, it was a fairly uneven race.''

"Does that matter now that the race has been won?''

"It should. It does," he corrected firmly. "How can you forgive so easily? You should despise me for my weakness. I thought you valued honor and truth above all things.''

Her lips peppered light kisses along his taut shoulder blades before she answered quietly, "I do.

And were you not an honorable man, you would not have walked through your white man's hell for the past weeks, or known a struggle of conscience at all. You cannot help what you are and what you were raised to be, anymore than I can. But you have risen above your weakness by telling me this truth. But is it the truth?"

The arms that rode his shoulders rose and fell with the effort of his sigh. "I've prayed to God every night that it isn't, but it just makes too much sense."

The fire had grown warm in its rekindled strength. Evangeline padded to the sitting room to take several of the rich pelts down from the wall to spread before it. She curled up beside Royle, pillowing her head against him. A shiver ran the length of her slender body, and his arm was quick to draw her tight into his side. It was not from cold that she trembled, but from uncertain dread.

"Tell me what you remember of your father."

The question took Evangeline by surprise. She stared hard into the flame, as if trying to conjure his features upon their dancing pattern. It was hard, as if her subconscious mind put up a blank of memory to keep her safe. "It was so long ago. For many years I forbid thoughts of him or my mother into my heart or mind."

She felt Royle nod in understanding, and was encouraged to go on. She continued to probe back into what her past would hide, and a dim recall emerged. And with Royle's arm about her, she felt secure in remembering. The hurt was still there, but so was a long-repressed wealth of tender feeling. Uncovering it was like receiving a precious gift. She clung to her husband and spoke softly.

"He was a good man. That I know. A man of vision and strength and much learning, like you."

Royle's heart squeezed tight. He couldn't express how that casual comparison touched him to the quick. Gently, his lips brushed her glossy crown. "What of his business?" he questioned softly. "What can you recall?"

"I was a child, Tanner. I had no place in his business dealings." Then she fell silent and pensive. "But I do remember that when I first came to the Websters, my uncle told me he'd bought the trade from my father before he died. It troubled my mind then, but I ignored it. I wanted no part of that knowledge, no part of them. But I remember it well, now, and am puzzled. I cannot be certain, but I believe he lies. He told me my father sold him everything to finance his expedition but again, it does not ring true. My father and my uncle did not get along. I can recall them arguing long and furiously after dinners we shared together. I don't know over what they fought, but I cannot believe that dislike would end with the selling of his business to his despised foe. My father loved his home. He loved his work. Mostly he loved me and my mother. He would not have risked our future recklessly. He was not that kind of man."

Royle's cheek nuzzled against the satiny waves of her hair in a comforting distraction, while his mind flew shrewdly ahead. His words were carefully phrased and direct. "And if he indeed purchased the company, he would have papers to prove the sale, and some legal representative to bear witness. Unless, of course, he waited until he heard of your father's demise to concoct that tale to his benefit."

Evangeline's summation was cold and to the point. "Unless he hired Allouez to kill my father and deliver the company into his own greedy hands."

"Have you seen such papers of sale?"

"No."

"And if no sale was ever legally made, you would still be heir to all Webster has accumulated over the years." He did not follow that supposition in speech to where his thoughts took it. If Evangeline still owned all the Carey holdings, they would be right by marriage belong to him. He would be everything that Uriah Webster was.

A supple movement against his ribs detracted from that anticipation. His hand slid easily down one graceful arm to rest upon bared thigh. He held her not with passion, but with a fierce protectiveness as another realization took precedence. If Evangeline did indeed own the bulk of Webster's fortune, it was no wonder he sought her death. And with her gone and the threat of her memories buried, Royle would be naught but a loyal employee and of no danger. That was why he was to have survived the ambush. Only Evangeline was to have perished.

And that was when he discovered the difference between himself and Uriah Webster. His ambition had limitations he would not exceed. Webster knew no such restraint. In his own hunger, Royle had never developed the taste for blood.

Evangeline's arms went about her husband's middle. Within his embrace, she felt powerful and secure. She spoke strongly, without hesitation or doubt, "'Tis time we paid a visit to my relatives in New York."

She felt Royle stiffen, and his response warmed her more satisfactorily than the baking blaze. "I'll not let you risk the danger."

The cool gray eyes lifted, steeped in confidence and love. "I am not afraid to confront he who stole from me and caused the deaths of those I loved. I will have my warrior to protect me. And I plan to go very well armed. One need not fear the snake when the sound of his rattle is known."

Wrapped in his arms, basking in his strength, Evangeline might have told him of the child. Yet she kept silent. Many of their differences may have been breached on this night, but she'd yet to hear him speak of what resided in his heart. Sentimentally, she wanted to hold to that knowledge when she told him of the fruit sown by that love. She wanted it to be a moment she could hold tenderly in her heart for the rest of her days, to make amends for their rocky beginning. And she would be able to laugh with their children when she told them how she'd once plotted to relieve their father of his hair. And, of course, she wouldn't be believed. She could scarcely acknowledge such emotion had simmered in a heart so full of love. When she had the words, she would share her joy. Until then, her secret would grow within her, a source of continual pride whenever she looked upon the yellow-haired man who'd given it life. Together they would share this little house near the woods, where the child could know of its heritage and prosper in nature's embrace. She smiled blissfully in that reverie.

Royle, too, was thinking of the future, of the house on Broad Street with its fine collections that only wealth could acquire, of an education in England for their children, of Evangeline, pampered and in silk. And of himself, looking out those clear-paned windows from his seat of success. And he, too, smiled.

His mood was dark as their small craft skimmed down the Huron several days later. Uncertainty crept in to tarnish his purpose. What if he was wrong?

Again. What if all was just an unfortunate coincidence? Webster might well have the papers to prove himself innocent. Even if he didn't he could be guilty of only greed, not murder, in his seizure of property thought to be unclaimable. He couldn't blame the man for stepping in to hold a business begun by family. Nor could he find great fault in his subtle lies to retain that business. After all, he'd seen Evangeline when she'd come to live with them. She was hardly capable of controlling such an enterprise. And why would Uriah Webster blindly hand Royle, a stranger, the means of his own livelihood? Perhaps he was doing Webster a grave wrong. Perhaps the shrewd man was preparing him in Albany to assume the reins entitled to him. Was it his own grasping ambition driving him to make accusations against his mentor when none were due? Webster's fall would precipitate his own rise. Was he being too hasty, just to gain the taste of that elevated power?

And by bursting into Webster's home to claim him a murderer, he could be risking all. Or he could gain everything.

Royle agonized over those two possibilities as their journey brought them nearer to where all had started. Evangeline sat beside him, her lovely features set to betray no emotion. However he could guess what turned behind those cool gray eyes. Revenge. She was on a blood trail, and was anticipating their destination as much as he was growing to dread it. Evangeline was never troubled by degrees of right and wrong. There was either guilt or innocence, no shades in between. She would not take into account how thirst for power could warp a man's judgment, sullying a good man with bad intent. Only the end result impressed her. And she saw Uriah Webster as the man responsible for the murder of her family, whether it was his hand that directed it or not. Because he had profited, he was culpable. And Royle was bewildered by the part of him that would see Webster protected from his wife's wrath.

He spent his days upon the golden ribbon of water and his nights encircled by his wife's warmth, pondering that strange desire. Was it because he understood what ambition could drive a man to do? Was it because he didn't want to unfairly accuse until he knew the truth? Was it because he feared to his soul what he would lose should an outraged Webster turn against him? Or, more closely guarded than all the rest, did he seek to shield Uriah Webster because he emulated all that he was and could not bear it should his idol fall. To show his mentor guilty of unpardonable sins, would he be any less soiled? No, Evangeline wouldn't understand his turmoil. She would scoff at his want to cling to loyalty in lieu of truth. She would not weigh admiration against honor or motive against result. And so he would have to carefully temper his wife's unswerving justice lest he, too, feel its brunt.

Though the circumstances were far different from her first arrival, Evangeline knew an inner trembling when she crossed the threshold on Broad Street. This time she was dressed in enviable silks instead of savage skins. This time the huge servant, Jamal, bowed to her in respect instead of restraining her within his mighty grasp. Even though she arrived as guest, she couldn't rid herself of the fear that came with having been a prisoner beneath this same roof, and she tread cautiously, subconsciously clinging to Royle's arm for support. He seemed oblivious to her distress, but was quick to offer comfort as his long fingers caressed the back of her white-knuckled hand. The gesture stated she was his wife now, and had no need to fear she'd be treated as any less. She clung gratefully to that unspoken assurance as they confronted the Webster family domestically grouped in the elegant parlor.

Surprised and, more subtly, suspicion were quickly concealed upon the face of Uriah Webster as he rose to greet them. Murmuring proper pleasantries, he heartily pumped Royle's hand, then bussed his niece's cheek with a respectful kiss. She held herself rigid lest she shrink away in disgust. His lips were as cold as the undercurrent flowing beneath his gracious welcome.

"What brings you here, though we are glad for any excuse to offer our hospitality?" That last was added to gloss over the sharpness of the first.

Then Royle's incredible reply stunned her.

"Evangeline was anxious to meet her cousin's wife. She feared by the time the babe arrived, the weather would not permit a visit. I hope you don't mind our unannounced arrival. And then, we have business matters to discuss."

Evangeline's shuttered gaze flew between the two men. She could feel her uncle weighing her husband's smooth answer, testing it, prodding it with doubt. Royle's innocuous smile never faltered beneath that careful scrutiny. Then Uriah struck him fondly upon the back and called, "Come in where the fire can warm you. I'll see your room properly aired."

Relief rippled through her, replaced by a swelling pride. Of course, her husband was being clever. One did not bait a trap by laying bare its teeth. He was covering the snare with a disguise of harmless fronds and flattery. But they would not lessen the bite of the teeth when the jaws of truth snapped closed. In

330

deference to her husband's cunning, she would follow his footsteps and adopt an unsuspecting pose. Only the gun metal glitter in her expressionless gaze betrayed her lust for retribution. But she could be patient, holding to the knowledge that it would come. And it would be sweet. And in that cold eagerness, she forgot her own claim that revenge was not to be savored for its own sake.

Emma Webster had not risen at their arrival. If anything, she seemed more determined to shrink upon her stool, as if her guests offered more threat than company. Unaware of the disturbance, the young woman at her side knew no such hesitancy. Her smile was genuine, the only sincere expression in the overly warm room, and Evangeline found it easy to respond.

"I am Faith, Cyrus's wife," she announced with obvious pride, taking Evangeline's hand in her own. "I am happy to meet you at last. Cyrus speaks of you often and with apparent fondness

Blind Faith, Evangeline amended to herself as she smiled at the dainty woman of limited vision. Then her gaze cut to her cousin to see him squirm in discomfort. She doubted that any of the memories shared between them were cherished, and that he would have his pretty wife believe it was so, placed him a notch lower in her already abysmal regard. And that cold glare let him know it.

Evangeline turned her attention away from her unworthy cousin to his bride. She was undeniably lovely, with curling auburn hair and great trusting brown eyes. Already the gentle swell of her condition was evident upon her small frame, and Evangeline felt a binding kinship. After all, this woman was in no way to blame for the sins of her husband or his father, and it would be unfair of her to treat her with

331

like contempt. She would offer the unwise woman her friendship, and be ready with her support when the truth of her unfortunate alliance was know.

"You must be very excited about the coming of the babe," she said, and experienced a similar glow at the thought of her own impending event. "I have made a small token to welcome the child."

Faith took the tiny package with unashamed pleasure. That delight became bemusement when she examined its contents. She turned the baby moccasins over in her hands and frowned. "There are holes in the bottom."

Evangeline smiled at her confusion. "That is to convince the spirits that the babe cannot make the long journey to the distant land of the dead."

Faith hid her dismay behind a hastily adopted smile of politeness. "Thank you," she said, and quickly set the odd gift aside.

Only Royle knew the significance of the gift and the wealth of feeling that accompanied the giving. His hand settled against the curve of Evangeline's back and moved slowly, gently stroking, to tell her he understood. And the look she turned upon him made his marrow molten, so intensely was it rendered. Royle froze. Never did he expect such a potent onslaught of passion in the midst of the Webster's austere possessions. The sensations were basic, so raw, so completely uncivilized. And propriety be damned, he determined to let her know her effect upon him. Lids slid down languorously until vivid green eyes were half-masked. Lips were seductively moistened. He, alone, heard Evangeline's breath escape its fragile suspension. His hand trembled, his fingers grew restless upon the snug stretch of warm fabric. By God, they did wear too many clothes.

"We were about to sit down to dinner," Webster

announced. "I'll have two more places set."

Before Royle could protest that nothing upon their ample board could whet the appetite growling through him, they were shepherded into the dining room where Evangeline was settled unsatisfactorily on the opposite side of the table. The distance was tantalizing and Royle simmered. Tension and the purpose for their presence in New York was suppressed by bold stirrings of desire. He felt starved and desperate to know the taste of his wife's passion, as if he'd not been fed nightly along their journey from Albany. It was a complex hunger, expressing his need to claim what was his beneath this roof where all else belonged to another, a need to forge a union of camaraderie between them, a need to exert his control. And mostly to renew his sense of purpose when dangerously close to succumbing to the influences around him.

He devoured all placed before him in a rush to reach the meal's conclusion so he could come to his own. However Evangeline appeared in no such hurry. She savored each bite, chewing slowly with infinite appreciation while veiled eyes studied his reaction. Between each interminable courses, she licked the juices from her fingers with the flicker of her tongue, then sucked each digit clean. She teased him blatantly, purposefully into an impatient frenzy. Never had even the most practiced flirt inspired such agitation of heart and body.

To distract his lusts and aid his digestion, Royle shifted his gaze to the delicate form of the new Mistress Webster. She was young, comely, and obviously well bred. He watched her at her modest plate, her knife decorously slanted, her gaze meekly canted, then returned his look to his fiery Evangeline who ate with relish and attacked her meat without mercy. Those smoky gray eyes were far from mild in their expressive candor. While the proper Mistress Webster murmured inoffensive platitudes, his own wife's bold outbursts were prone to shock and startle. Where Faith Webster held every virtue desirous in a bride, Royle could not find Evangeline lacking. She sizzled, she sparkled, she spoke her mind with a directness reserved for the male. And he would prefer her no other way.

The moment the voider was passed, Royle stood to ask that they be shown to their quarters, for the journey had been very tiring. Actually, it was his patience that had been overtaxed to near expiring. It quavered anew as Evangeline swept gracefully around the table to place her hand lightly upon his arm. That submissive, wifely gesture was at an intriguing variance with the mysteries her gaze foretold. Muttering brusque good nights, he led her from their company with a vigorous step.

And when the door to their upper chamber closed, he didn't need to encourage her to come into his arms. She met him with eager lips and urgent caresses. Her hands tore at his attire as hurriedly as his did her own. Hot kisses sustained them until they reached the bed. Then they weren't enough. Nothing satisfied short of the pinnacle of bliss they drove one another to find.

It was a wild, desperate mating, the joining of two forces into one, so fears could be crushed beneath the power of passion. Moaning cries and straining breaths were muffled by hungry kisses. Limbs intertwined to aid and encourage the rhythm of love. And as that tempo grew fast and furious, pounding like the war drums of her people, throbbing in her blood to incite a frantic quivering, Evangeline's silent shout of exultation against the urgent pressure

334

of his mouth brought Royle with her to claim shattering satisfaction. Then the contented circle of each other's arms was more than enough.

Royle was prompted from his sated languor when cool replaced warmth beneath the sheets. His gaze flickered open, then lingered in appreciation upon the figure of his wife standing at the window in well-defined relief. It was a sight that would always have the power to stir him; the sleek, clean line of her limbs, the proud jut of her breasts, the glossy mantle of raven hair framing the perfect cast of her features. There was a wild, basic beauty to Evangeline Tanner that left him breathless and in awe. It was the way he'd felt when he saw a graceful doe standing proud and free, half on the path, half in the woods. Huge dark eyes had gauged him as a possible threat, while the magnificent creature stood undecided over which direction to take. Then his scent reached her, and she bound into the concealing trees. There were times when he feared a sudden move would startle Evangeline back to the safety of her people, but now was not one of them. He was feeling smug in his prowess and confident in his claim. But mostly, he was missing the feel of her beside him.

"What are you thinking, angel?" It irked him slightly that he would always have to ask. She gave no clues away.

She was silent, pensive for a long moment, her slender fingers pressed against the glass. He was about to rise and go to her when at last she spoke.

"It was in this room that they kept me prisoner." The inflection of her voice betrayed none of the horror that lingered within a constricted breast. But he guessed it nonetheless.

"You need never fear that helplessness again." His promise rang strong and angry. "You are my wife and no one's captive save mine, by our vows, by your word, and because I wish it."

A small smile curved her lips at his arrogant claim and she came back to him, to sink back down onto the comfort of feathers and flesh. His arms formed an unbroken band of security, and she savored his protection. While her fingers toyed with his wonderfully furred chest, her thoughts addressed more sober fare.

"It was very clever of you to let the Websters think they have nothing to fear from us. It will make the final blow sure and justice sweet."

The regular rhythm of Royle's breathing was briefly interrupted before he cautioned, "We must be careful to give nothing away until all is certain. It is too much to risk on supposition alone."

"But we know, both you and I. We don't need proof to know what he has done."

"It's not that simple, Evangeline. Avenging yourself upon your uncle by the lifting of his hair will only deed all to your cousin Cryus. If we wish to establish our own claim, we must prove he has none."

Then her casual words gave Royle stunning pause.

"I care not for the money. I want no part of his evil empire built off the drunken weakness of my people. I seek only to oblige my loved ones who suffered for his greed."

Royle phrased himself with care, knowing she'd be repelled by the knowledge of his own grasping wants. "You'll strike the harshest blow by taking from him what he covets most, his fortune. The white man cares only about the getting. You said as much yourself."

"There is much truth in what you say," she considered thoughtfully. "If I take back what was my father's, he will have nothing. And that will hurt him. Yes?"

"Yes." She had no idea what the stripping away of wealth would do to a man like Uriah Webster. Royle reasoned he would rather she slay him outright than reduce him to poverty. He knew he would hold the same sentiment were he in that position. Then he moved on to more pleasant considerations. Like how it would feel to handle all that delicious power.

And they lay entwined together, as Evangeline drifted to sleep plotting her fiery retribution. Royle lay awake long hours planning how he would rise from Webster's ashes. For all his eager anticipation, he failed to see the irony in the words he'd spoken nights before, disclaiming the avarice now obsessing him. He hadn't prepared for the subtle temptations within this fine house; the scent of book leather, the glitter of imported carpeting beneath the feet, the elegant vision of his wife in satin across a well-laid board. The indescribable want returned with ever mounting intensity, and its ready availability was a torment to his thoughts.

His restless mind continued to spin and weave, while Evangeline slumbered in his close embrace. In a matter of days, he could well have all. Or nothing.

Chapter Twenty-Two

Uriah Webster lifted two pewter mugs from the tray his servant rendered and passed one of them to his guest. Royle nodded his thanks and let the satiny metal warm between his hands, its potent liquor untouched.

"I was, of course, stunned to hear of your travails," the older man remarked from the opposite chair. His gaze was steady and unreadably fixed upon the other as he spoke. "What a trauma for your wife. Would that you had listened and left her safe within our care."

"Do not think I haven't turned that possibility over and over in my mind," was Royle's quiet response. Yes, indeed, he had trouble sleeping, wondering what would have happened to Evangeline had he sent her here alone.

Suitably impressed by Royle's admission of guilt, Webster chose to be magnanimous. "A tragedy all around, but don't think I hold you in any way to blame."

"I thank you for that."

"The loss of the goods is a rather telling blow to my business."

"I'm sure the outcome has inconvenienced you."

That dry statement prompted a careful scrutiny, but Webster could find no reason to doubt the meaning. Tanner's features were bland, displaying confidence touched with remorse. Just the right amount of each. The merchant relaxed.

"I will survive the loss and go on."

Royle's small smile encouraged him to continue the unfolding of his plans. Tanner's calm inspired trust, and Webster considered himself fortunate to have found such a man to do his bidding. A man controllable, but not without ideas of his own. He returned the younger man's smile and let the atmosphere of mutual admiration settle companionably about them. He took in the ease of the other's confidence, the intelligent edge of his gaze, the simmer of aspiration always bubbling beneath the control. This was what he'd wished for in a son, instead of the narrow self-indulgence of his own heir; character, strength of purpose, aptness, instead of self-serving cunning. Cyrus's ambitions didn't stretch beyond the minute. Tanner's view was infinite. Had circumstance been different, he would have been embraced within the family without a thought to his less-than-exceptional past. As it was, Webster was happy to enfold him into his business.

"Would you be agreeable to another attempt at the Great Lakes?"

"I'm not easily discouraged. It is rather late in the season to attempt such a journey now."

Webster shrugged off his impatience. That was one of the reasons he cared so much for the younger man; eager, yes, but prudent. He wasn't afraid of risk, but would not take one foolishly. That was a quality that couldn't be taught. Lord knows he'd tried and failed with his son. "Yes, I fear you are right. In the spring then."

"Fine."

"And this time, I trust you will not be swayed by your wife's insistence and will do what's best for her."

"I intend to keep her safe at any cost."

Uriah smiled and took a long, satisfied swallow of his drink. He felt in the mood to impart some fatherly advice. "My niece is a strong-willed woman. She needs a stronger hand to govern her."

"She's learned to respond well to mine." A hint of smugness accompanied that claim, and Webster chuckled in appreciation.

"I like you, Tanner. You're a man who knows what he wants and goes after it. A man much like myself."

"I am flattered, sir, but there is really no comparison."

"You are too modest."

Royle shrugged. He let the man talk, part of him enjoying the banter, part of him alert for any slip. It was a precarious way to travel, one foot on one either side. Just then he felt a kinship to Evangeline and her walk between two worlds. It was an uncomfortable journey.

"My instincts were right about you. You'll go far in this business."

"I plan to."

Webster regarded him with a pleased smile, guard down and open for a subtle attack.

"In the future," Royle began, "I would like to hire my own guides from among my wife's people. The Frenchman you engaged proved almost to be the death of us."

A frown tugged at his employer's mouth and he was quick to say, "He was not my choice. That was

Maxell's doing. I have no trust of the renegades. They find it too easy to betray those they're pledged to serve.''

A lie? He didn't know, but he could find out easily enough from Maxell. Perhaps Webster hadn't been as careful as he'd planned. If it was a game between them, Royle thought it time to make a more aggressive move of his own. "Wise of you. For this one had no qualms about revealing all he knew when asked the proper way.''

Webster's features took on a rigid quality. His voice was admirably smooth. "And what did he say?''

"Some very interesting and perplexing things. It seems that he was a party to the slaying of my wife's parents. Quite a coincidence, wouldn't you agree? He suggested it was part of some plot against them. Would you know anything about that?''

"Shocking business,'' Webster murmured, shaking his bewigged head. "I'm afraid I don't. Perhaps my niece could enlighten you. After all, she survived the attack.''

"I did ask, but unfortunately she can remember none of it. She was just a child, and it was long ago. She has few memories of her natural parents.''

"Pity.''

"Yes, isn't it. I would like to speak to the solicitor who handled her father's affairs. Perhaps he can offer some clue.''

"That would have been Thomas Fisk. He also drew up the papers of sale between us, before my brother-in-law's untimely death.''

"Is he still in New York?''

"Oh yes. Quite permanently. He's buried not far from here. A terrible fire in his home, it was. He lost his life. All the documents pertaining to Joshua's business went up as well.''

341

"Including those deeding his company to you?"

"Yes. Why do you ask? If there's something you wish to know about the sale, I'll be happy to inform you."

"No. Just curious, is all. It's not important after all these years."

Damn! Damn! Royle dropped his gaze to the contents of his mug to conceal his frustration. Uriah Webster was an excellent swordsman, prepared to parry his every inexpert thrust. Was it innocence that kept him from uncovering any clues? Or was Webster too good at concealing his own trail of misdeeds? Begrudgingly, Royle yet admired him. He enjoyed the mental sparring, even anticipated it. Nothing shook the man who lorded over his ill-gotten gains like a smug deadly spider, and with one careless move, Royle could find himself ensnared upon his web. Patience, he cautioned. No good could come of exposing his suspicions. The threat to Evangeline had been successfully removed. Now, all he had to do was wait. The truth would surface eventually, and there was no better place for him to be than in the man's confidence. If he was wrong about Webster's involvement, he would suffer no repercussions. And if he was right, he would be sitting in Webster's chair. Either reward was well worth the wait.

Two floors above, within the long garret under the eves, Evangeline sat upon a stool watching Faith spin wool. In the spill of golden light from mullioned windows at either end, one, two, three steps she took holding the long yarn high as it twisted and quivered to the hum of the wheel. Then she'd glide forward to let the fibers wind onto its spindle. Over and over, she retraced the same steps with a quiet perseverance. She told Evangeline that with the six skeins of yarn she could spin in a good day's work, she would pace over twenty miles. Evangeline said nothing, though she thought it little gain for a long journey. She listened to the other woman speak of the dyes she'd make from iris, goldenrod, berries, and barks of the red oak and hickory. It reminded her of what Eva had said about the purple paper she'd saved from the sugar cone. A fine, regal blanket that would make for her baby. Perhaps she would ask the Dutch woman to teach her to walk the wheel when they returned to Albany. It would give her something to fill the hours while she waited for the birth.

"The babe must be no burden for you to do so much."

Faith smiled at her. It was a proud, glowing smile. "No burden at all. I've suffered none of the ills I've heard others complain of. Except, of course, having to loosen the hooks of my gowns."

Evangeline returned the smile a bit wistfully. Her hand went unconsciously to her own still trim waist. She may have had little in common with Faith Webster, but she yearned to talk of the one thing they shared. Childbirth was taken so naturally by her own people that it was joyously discussed. She held no fear of the process and was eager to compare experiences. She wondered if the other woman was quick to come to foolish tears, if she dreaded the thought that a thickening figure would repel her husband, if she'd given thought to any names. Silly things, woman things. However, until she told her husband of her condition, she knew she could not reveal it to another. So she bit back her questions and settled for idle talk. Anything was better than remaining in the stifling room below, or enduring

343

her aunt's nervous glances. Or risking a solitary meeting with her cousin. She couldn't believe that being under the same roof with his wife in her family situation would deter the wretch from his lecherous schemes.

"How I envy you your cabin in the woods," Faith said dreamily. "Such a paradise that must be, all alone with the man you love."

Evangeline's answer came without hesitation. "Yes, it is."

"My own family was so large we were always falling over one another, and now we live with Cyrus's parents. I'm not ungrateful, mind you, but I do so wish for a home of my own."

Evangeline nodded. Yes, she could understand that yearning. To have one's own hearth, to answer to no other, to pride one's self on the efficient management of a home. Yes, that feeling she knew, and the strength of her own longing for her hearth in Albany stunned Evangeline. But then, that was home to her now, her home and Royle's. And she missed it mightily.

The whir of the wheel died down and Faith leaned upon it, her pretty expression pensive. "Perhaps if we were to live in such a place, Cryus wouldn't have so many distractions."

Evangeline felt uncomfortable coming to the aid of her currish cousin, but she would ease the look of sadness from her new friend's face if she could. "'Tis expected for his work to keep him busy. Why there are times Royle is gone before I wake, and we have nary a chance to exchange hellos before he is asleep that night. Ambitious men are also wed to their pursuits."

"'Twere it business he pursued, I would not be minding. 'Tis the gentlemanly entertainments that claim his time; cockfights, horse racing, bear baiting, and philosophizing over mugs at Trayburn's tavern." She fell silent, then her cheeks took on hot color. "Oh, I beg your pardon. What a shrew I must sound. I truly do not object to manly endeavors, nor would I ever think to chastise my husband for his enjoyment of them."

"I would," Evangeline stated firmly. "And I have, with every piece of crockery I could lay my hands upon."

Faith's brown eyes grew round and wide. Then a naughty giggle escaped her. "Really? And your husband did not beat you for your disrespect?"

"He would not dare," was her haughty claim. For all her boldness, she knew the truth. Royle did not need to beat her. He'd discovered better means to conquer her temper. This time, her face felt the warming flame.

Faith sighed. "He must love you very much."

The answer to that simple statement lodged painfully in Evangeline's throat. She didn't trust her gaze not to betray her, so she studied the coarse twists of wool. "It is my wish that be true," she was able to murmur.

Faith returned to her rhythmic steps and the wheel to its whining. The sound and motion had a soothing, hypnotic effect, calming Evangeline like the croon of a lullaby. Had she sat as a child to watch her mother in this domestic task? How much of her childhood had been involved in scenes such as this, of quiet industry and contented companionship? For the first time, her inability to recall frustrated her and left her lacking, as if part of her life had been cruelly stolen. And it had. Never could she return to the serenity of simple pursuits, to the almost blissful ignorance of Faith Webster. It was not that she felt less complete with her life among the Iroquois, it was a sense that she could have been so differnet. Would Royle Tanner have loved her had she grown up Evangeline Carey, daughter of a wealthy trader? That she would never know didn't stop the bittersweet wondering.

"My father solved everything with a rod, never bigger than his finger, of course," Faith was saying. "'Twas his way of showing his love, I suppose, by discouraging us from the error of our own."

"Among my people, discipline is never accomplished by violent means."

"Your family? I'm sorry, I thought you were orphaned."

"My adopted family," she explained comfortably, and the other looked relieved.

"And if not by the rod, how did they manage?"

Evangeline shared the tale she'd been told, and marveled that it no longer had the power to intimidate her. The goblins of her past had been buried. All but one.

Faith gave an eloquent shudder. "How horrible. It makes me think of this perfectly dreadful man who came to the door some months ago. He quite frightened me out of a night's sleep."

The serenity of the moment was gone. Evangeline's blood turned to ice. She seized upon those innocently tendered words. What they might mean overwhelmed her with a forceful trembling. "What man was this?" It was a struggle to keep her voice evenly pitched when the pounding of her heart tried to propel it into excited panic.

"A Frenchman. I cannot remember his name exactly. It was similar to a French ditty I learned as a child, about some poor chicken loosing its head."

"Allouez," she breathed.

"Yes, that was it. He came to see Father Webster on some sort of business. It must have been important, for he would not discuss it under our roof. I cannot fathom what type of service a man like that performs."

Evangeline knew.

Both men looked up in surprise when the doors to the study were flung open. Those expressions were undisguised when they beheld her and came reflexively to their feet. Royle's was frozen in dismay, her uncle's in disgust.

"Young woman, in this house we do not intrude upon one another without invitation," he began frostily.

"In this house much goes on that has naught to do with propriety," she hurled back.

"Evangeline."

Her husband's soft cautioning went ignored. Evangeline strode into the smoky male bastion and took an akimbo stance before the authoritative figure of her host.

"In fact, things go on within this house that have naught to do with anything decent."

"How dare—"

"Oh, I dare. There is little I do not dare. You should understand that, Uncle. It is a trait we share. The only one, I hope."

She felt Royle's fingers curl about her waist.

"Evangeline, this is not the time." The edge to his words should have stopped her, but she shook them off, as she would have his hand if he'd allowed it.

"This is the time," she argued, her icy gaze never leaving her uncle's. "There is always time for truth, and I will hear it now."

347

"And what truth is that, my dear?" came the condescending question one would use upon a stubborn child.

"There is only one truth, or have you forgotten? You have stolen from me, and I will have my property back. Now."

"Tanner, have you any notion about what non-sense she speaks?" Patiently, he looked to Royle, expecting him to quickly rally to his cause. But the penetrating green eyes were half-shuttered, reflecting none of the sought-after responses. He seemed to hesitate, to weigh his answer carefully, until Evangeline, too, looked askance. The thoughtful gaze went between them, wife to employer and back. Confident in his allegiance, Webster prompted, "Well, do you?"

Royle met the exasperated appeal with a cool, "Is it nonsense?"

Uriah Webster's features went as rigid as stone. He'd not anticipated a hindrance, not from one so loyal. "You would do well to take you wife in hand, before she gets you both in difficulties you'll not resolve with pretty apologies."

"I do not apologize for her. She has a mind and a voice of her own, though neither are always expressed as I would have them."

Webster looked at him as though he were mad, but the other betrayed no sign of unstable weakness. Contrarily, his look was as strongly determined as his words. Could it be he really believed them? "A man who cannot control his wife has a questionable place in my business." That warning was not so subtly veiled, and he expected it to hit the mark. Again, annoyingly, he was wrong.

Royle smiled faintly. "I believe the question is whether or not it is your business." He tugged lightly

348

on Evangeline's arm to bring her to heel at his side. She gave gracefully this time, but he could feel her impatience to continue the confrontation. He didn't feel fully prepared for the conflict of fact or interest, yet had no choice but to take an uncertain stand. Webster was mentally circling, searching out a weakness.

"This is not nonsense. This is insanity. Tanner, remember with whom you are dealing."

"I think we're only beginning to discover that."

Webster sucked in a vicious breath. His eyes glittered. The beginnings of betrayal struck him like a savage personal blow, and he retaliated in kind. "Cross me and you'll wish you hadn't. Strange things happen to traders without proper merchant protection. They are jailed on suspicion of treason. They can be plagued by plundering savages. Or they can simply disappear."

Those words struck harder than their intended insinuations. And to the opposite purpose. To that point, Royle had wavered. Now, he firmed. Uriah Webster was not the admirable man of honor he portrayed. He was vicious, and more than willing to see his threats to completion. He was a man more than capable of seeking the murder of his brother-in-law and niece. And Royle was repulsed.

"I think we already have a good idea of what you can do. What you cannot do is cheat me of what is mine by right. When you made Evangeline my wife, you made me administrator of her possessions."

Royle felt Evangeline's recoil and the chill of her stare upon him, as if she wasn't sure who her enemy was. Now was not the time to settle the mastery of their household, if they were to yet retain one. He restrained her with the strength of his grip and willed her to be silent.

"I accuse you of nothing beyond simple greed," Royle continued. "What man would not want to take up the reins of such a prize when it seemed there was no proper successor. It was your cleverness and ambition that built upon what Evangeline's father started. And you began to consider it as your own. And then your niece returns, a savage with no respect for property or possessions. Only a fool would release a fortune into such unsuitable hands."

Royle's fingers tightened. He could feel her resistance and her resentment in the sharp twisting of her wrists, but he'd no time to soothe her vanity. Injured feelings and misunderstandings could wait for another moment.

"So," Royle continued on theory and supposition, "you decided the best way to deal with the threat of your niece was to distance her from you, somewhere isolated with someone to control her, that someone being under your control. And that was my part. Am I close so far? I think, yes. Only Evangeline remembers that her father still owned this business upon that fateful trip. Which means he never sold it to you. Which means, as her guardian, you were well entitled to the profits for all those years. But it also means that when you gave her to me in marriage, you also transferred your right to manage and profit from her father's business. I thank you for the fine job you've done overseeing my investments."

"You are very like him, you know," Uriah said softly. It had the sound of a compliment as well as a complaint. "The same bold arrogance, the same uncompromising standards. Fools, the both of you. Neither of you had the strength needed to succeed in this business. Well, I did and do, and I let no silly sympathies detain me. Honor is a fool's armor. It gives false security and is quick to fold. Joshua wouldn't listen to me. My methods were beneath him."

"And that made you angry enough to kill him," Royle concluded.

He gave a cynical laugh. "I didn't say that."

"I did."

Webster's eyes had narrowed into dangerous slits. He was astounded, and further, he was impressed. Had the stakes not been so high and he the victim of them, he would have applauded his young apprentice's initiative. What incredible nerve it took to stand bold before him with such a decree. What admirable, if foolish, skill it took to pursue such an ambitious plot. How well he had chosen Royle Tanner, and now he would suffer for that choice. He looked over the arrogant Englishman from head to foot and sneered. "You were nothing when you came to my door. You had more pride then pedigree, more bluff than business sense. I gave you a job. I took that risk, and now you make me regret it sorely. How dare you feed from my hand, then sink in your teeth when your appetite had outgrown my means to feed it. Is that how you repay my generosity? With brazen lies and slander? I have no fault with your success, only make your own place. You'll not steal mine."

Royle faltered slightly, stricken by pangs of conscience and by the truth thrown up at him. He was treacherous. He was ungrateful. He was violating every standard he had of honor and loyalty. And what greater call in life was there? Then he heard his answer spoken up crisply at his side.

At the lowering of his eyes, Evangeline was quick to resume the attack.

"What manner of man are you who can accuse another of sins you have mastered? The fact remains that what you have does not belong to you. It is mine and I will have it."

"You may find that a bit difficult, my dear. Where is your proof?"

"Where is yours?" Royle countered softly. His gaze rose, slowly, steadily to regard Webster. The regret was there, but so was a promise that no further quarter would be given. He'd chosen his side and became a very dangerous foe. "Can you prove money exchanged hands? Can you produce signed documents to varify the sale? So far, all I can link you to is theft from a dead man. Force me to and I'll look farther. And I guarantee that what I find will weigh far more in consequence than the loss of your brother-in-law's business."

The threat wasn't idle. He would see to it, but it sat unwell in Royle's belly, twisting tight and bitter. He didn't want to look any farther. He didn't want to discover proof making the man he respected—whose accomplishments he revered—a lowly murderer. Royle waited, hoping Webster would admit to the lesser guilt. From there the man could go on to rebuild his dreams. And Royle would aid him if he could. He was not immune to the call of loyalty. To turn against the man who gave him the chance to know his own dream, for whatever the purpose, was leaving a very unpleasant taste. But Uriah Webster could not go unpunished. Since the past could not be altered, Royle prayed a change of the future would suffice, that the transfer of her father's company would satisfy Evangeline.

Uriah laughed. He threw back his great head and let the peels of mirth roll forth, until he shook with the effort of them. Then abruptly his humor was gone. He confronted the couple before him as if they were a pestilence he meant to rid himself of. "You simple fool. Do you think to threaten me? Do you expect me to cower in fear of your meager intimidation? I have crushed mightier than you with one hand. Look at what I am; one of the most powerful men in New York. Wealth can overcome any sin. Do you think anyone cares how I came by my fortune? Do you actually believe that anyone would side against me in favor of a greedy pauper's brat and a woman who whored for savages?"

He began to laugh again, a harsh, ugly sound at the expense of the two before him. It strangled in his throat.

With a blood-freezing cry, Evangeline freed herself from Royle and bared the blade she wore strapped to her calf. Webster may have been a mighty oak, but he bent before her fury as she came at him like a vengeful storm, launching herself upon his chest. He stumbled back, falling hard into his chair with the snarling woodland demon fixed to him. Before he could rally his senses, his wig was torn from his shiny pate, and the blade glittered against it in deadly promise.

"I will hear the truth now or I will peel your skull like an over ripe fruit," came her fierce vow.

"Tanner!" he shouted in terror. Surely the man would not stand by as witness to this barbarity, his panicked thoughts declared.

Then softly came Royle's words. "I would tell her what she wants to know."

Evangeline's breath seethed from teeth clenched and gleaming whitely. Her eyes were frozen ponds, void of emotion save hate. The grip she had on the thick, corded throat tightened with purpose. "Lie and I will know it," she hissed into his contorted face. "The Frenchman was seen at your door. You gave the orders, just as you did years before. You had my parents slain, as you did my brother. I would kill you

353

now, but it would give me little satisfaction. My people believe in tormenting the soul until it cries out for death. Which will it be, white man? Truth or torture?"

For a moment, there was only the sound of her ragged breathing, then Webster's composure shattered.

"Yes! Yes, I ordered it done. And if that French fool hadn't been so greedy, none would ever have been the wiser."

A tormented sound intruded upon the tense tableau. At the open door stood Emma Webster, knuckles raised to her mouth, her wide eyes stark with horror above them. Just as her husband readied to call to her for help, she spoke a single, damning truth.

"You killed my brother!"

Chapter Twenty-Three

The great house was silent, almost as if its occupants were in deep mourning. Drapes were drawn tight at the windows. For once, the less fortunate weren't invited to stare within. Servants kept to their quarters, but their whispers already spread far beyond the stately brick walls. By morning, not a soul in New York would be unaware that Uriah Webster had been taken away in disgrace.

Evangeline remained at the shrouded window. She'd stood apart from the rest while the authorities purged the ugly truth from a sadly broken man. After they'd escorted him from the house, a frightened Faith led Emma from the room, her aunt's near hysterical sobs trailing behind them. Cyrus had disappeared, most likely seeking solace in the nearest tavern. That left her alone with her pensive husband.

"What will happen to him?" she asked at last.

Royle shrugged. "I don't know. He'll be punished. It will be a white man's justice, but 'twill serve."

Evangeline nodded. The fate of Uriah Webster no longer concerned her. Her code of retribution was satisfied, and honor restored. She had no want to see him and his family suffer unduly. Exposing his vileness was enough.

"What a waste of a brilliant man," Royle mused as his fingers traced reverently along the back of the chair that had held him. "He could have gotten just as far on his own talents. Alas, success wasn't enough for him. It was the power he desired. I can understand the demons that drove him, but not what made him want to embrace them."

Evangeline had no answer for him. She was watching him now, carefully, gaugingly, testing his mood. Something in his quiet disturbed her, as did his continued respect for her uncle. A man without honor deserved no admiration. He should be held up as an example of the evils of excess, not praised for his ingenuity. Royle's attitude held her puzzled. And alarmed.

"When do we go home?" The thought of returning to the sanctity of their woodland dwelling stirred an anxiousness in her heart. Away from the influence of the Websters, they could begin afresh, without the taint of memory or association. They could be happy, free. And they could find love together.

Royle gave a quizzical smile. "We won't be going back there, Evangeline," he told her simply.

She drew an anguished breath. Not going back. A tightness of loss squeezed within her breast at the thought of forfeiting their home. But the house belonged to Webster, and Royle no longer did. When he came forward against his employer, their partnership ended. Evangeline hadn't considered how much Royle stood to lose by aiding her quest for truth. He'd lost the position he treasured, the start he needed to succeed. All for her. The knowledge of that sacrifice swelled her heart with love and tenderness. She would make it up to him, she vowed within her soul. She would see he never regretted his choice.

Though she tried to sound enthusiastic, her voice thickened with emotion. "There will always be a home for us amongst my people. You have more than proven yourself worthy in their eyes."

Royle's brow furrowed, and his head cocked to one side as he tried to solve the riddle of her words. Then understanding dawned, and with it a broad smile. He came to her, sweeping her into his embrace for a hearty squeeze that left her feeling wonderfully mashed. She surrendered her lips with a sigh and let herself float on the tidal passion of his kiss. As long as they were together, as long as he was moved by this potent need for her, it mattered not where they dwelt. So she told herself as she languished beneath the urgent demands of his mouth.

He came away, slightly breathless and more than a little giddy. Restless hands rubbed over the silken barrier of her bodice, as if impatient with the material that kept her from him. He chuckled softly. It was a warm, delicious sound.

"You are a treasure, Evangeline. How I delight in you and all you've given me. You are the lioness who protects my back. You are the lamb who warms my bed. I marvel at you daily, at your strength, at your virtue, at your passion. No man has every been luckier as when you came into my life, blade bared and teeth gnashing. It's a miracle I survived those first weeks to reflect back upon my good fortune."

She blushed deeply at those teasing words, pleased and flustered by the intoxicating flow of his praise. It set her pulse upon a frantic flight, with her hopes not far behind. When she began to speak, his forefinger brushed lightly across her lips to seal them in silence.

"Silly woman," he crooned gently. "We are hardly destitute. *This* is our home now."

She was too stunned for an immediate response.

357

Surely she'd heard wrong. Her gaze searched his, hoping for enlightenment and fearing it at the same time. "Why would we want to stay here?" she blurted out.

His bright green gold eyes swept the room in an eager appraisal. "Because, 'tis ours, Evangeline. All of it. Don't you understand what this means?" His stare returned to delve deeply into hers, reading of her uncertainty and hesitation. His look gentled. His fingers stroked down her cheek to pause beneath her chin. "All that your uncle has is mine. All that he was, I now am."

Those fateful words shivered through her. A grim glimpse into the future, of her husband, Royle Tanner, within this house, obsessed with this work, becoming another Uriah Webster, terrified her beyond speech. It was like looking ahead in anticipation of a nightmare.

"No." A mere whisper rose from the torment of her soul but he heard none of the despair that trembled in that single syllable. He only listened to the pulse of his own ambition.

"If you don't wish to remain beneath this roof, we can build another, even grander, if you like," he offered in a distracted attempt at sensitivity. Evangeline pulled away, rejecting both in confusion.

"I don't want another roof. I want to go home," she stated with a touch of belligerence. The lurid gleam in her husband's eyes frightened her, as this place frightened her. Both forced a wedge to prevent the closeness she desired between them. That avaricious look excluded her in favor of another lover. That mistress was power. Couldn't he see the danger? Hadn't he learned from the tragic comparison of greed and corruption? If they remained in New York, she would lose him to that struggle, and he would lose the qualities she cherished most within him. He *would* become like her uncle, and that knowledge destroyed any hope for happiness.

"Royle, please." She placed an entreating hand upon his sleeve. "I want no part of this blood money."

He scooped up her hand and lavished it with little kisses before pressing it over his heart. The frantic pace beneath her palm only increased her disquieting reservations.

"Angel, there is no crime in taking what is ours. Webster stole it from your father. All is mine by right."

How easily he slipped from *ours* to *mine* within the frame of a few words.

"There's no need to return to the meagerness of what we were, not when we have it all. You'll no longer need to toil upon the hearth or mend shirts already beyond redemption. You'll have a league of servants to command. When something is torn, it can be tossed away without conscience. It may seem foreign to you now, but you'll come to enjoy the pampered luxury that comes with wealth. Think of what we'll be able to give our children."

That fear struck a piercing blow to her heart. She thought of the child she carried growing into maturity beneath this roof, granted every whim, protected from knowledge of life, kept from developing values to shape a virtuous character. She pictured the indolent Cyrus Webster, and protest rose hot within her throat.

But Royle had moved away, confident that further persuasion was unneeded. For who, indeed, who could find fault with living every man's dream? He stood before the shelf of books and let his fingertips linger over the embossed titles, until they trembled with the power of possession. Who, indeed, when surrounded by the very stuff of prosperity, would wish to turn away? A deep, satisfying sense that he had completed all required of him by duty and obligation settled and warmed through him, soothing the last threads of his guilt. He had attained the goal that provoked him so mercilessly. Now he had only to enjoy the fruits of that accomplishment. For the first time he could ever remember, he felt secure and content. It was a heady feeling, one he wanted to exalt in and to share.

He turned to his wife to find her regarding him through inscrutable eyes. He'd given up trying to discern her expressions and had learned to read her posture. She was standing stiff, almost angrily, but it was more than that, almost as if she was bracing against some terrible foe. Tenderness consumed him. Of course she would be frightened. This was another beginning, a new world of opportunity for them both. She was anxious. He was anxious, but it was a wonderful sort of uncertainty, hinting at wondrous exploration and discovery to come. And he was eager to begin experiencing.

Royle's determined step toward his wife was curtailed by a polite knock. A tall, slender man wrapped tight in velvet was issued in by a solemn Jamal.

"Master Tanner, I am Franklin Tibbs, solicitor for the Websters. I believe we have much business to attend."

Royle was torn between the lure of finance and the challenging opaqueness in his wife's lovely eyes. The desire to see that cool chill simmer and burn bright at his skilled coaxing was a temptation not easily dismissed. He went to her and curved his hand behind the slender column of her neck. He was surprised to find her trembling, and that evidence of her urgency excited him all the more. But the bewigged Mr. Tibbs awaited, and reluctantly Royle forced his ardor to retreat. Tonight he would make love to her on the great feather bed in the master bedroom, not in the tiny guest quarters. She would come to him swathed in vaporish silk upon a perfumed cloud, fresh from her bath and straight into his arms. And he would be an equal, worthy to claim her, just as he'd promised himself the first time he'd lost himself in the enchantment of her beauty.

"I shan't be long," he murmured for her hearing alone. "When I'm finished here, we'll pursue this discussion in a more private setting."

He leaned down, meaning to take her lips in a sample of what was forthcoming, but she dipped her head slightly so his mouth brushed her forehead. Perhaps that was wiser, for had his aim been true, he might not have ranked the stuffy Mr. Tibbs as a priority. He released her, letting his fingers glide along the line of her jaw, surrendering the feel of her with regret.

Her eyes lifted then, revealing the heart of her emotions, but he hadn't the vision to read them. He saw the need, the naked longing, her plea . . . for what? It was a question he couldn't let go unanswered.

But before he could stay her to request an explanation, Evangeline turned quietly and made her way to the door. The sound it made upon closing echoed significantly of something left undone.

Once in the empty foyer, Evangeline released her frustrations with a heavy sigh. How could the man harbor such insight and yet remain so blind, she wondered without solution. And how could she hold him so dear in her heart and wish to strangle him at the same instant?

She glanced mournfully about the cavernous rooms, so filled with objects and so void of life. It made her think of one of their burial monuments. To consider living within these walls depressed her soul into a shuddering dread. Memories of captivity and misuse would haunt them and her spirit. She would become like Faith Webster, desperately lonely within the restrictive shell of wedlock that white society imposed. She imagined waiting passively for him to return from his entertainments on the town, of not questioning his whereabouts, only accepting his absence. That was what the wife of this house would do. Convention demanded it.

However she felt no allegiance to those mores. No unwritten law impelled her to docilely serve at the cost of her own independence. No dictates would hold her in silent misery while she had the will to protest. And protest she would. To become entombed within these walls would doom all hope of happiness with her husband, and that she valued more than the opinion of her neighbors. He would see her not as a vital partner and helpmate, but as another precious possession. And she didn't want to be revered. She wanted to be loved! She wanted the basic passion they'd found rolling upon a sensuous blanket of furs, the excitement of caresses beneath the moonlight, the expression that warmed his gaze when he came home from the trading house to find her bent over the hearth. Those were the things forging a link between their souls. And those things would be lost here.

She would not quietly accept the fate assigned her. When Royle was finished behind the doors, he would find the first battle won. The next siege would begin the moment she could get him alone.

Her own restless distress made her think of
another, of her hapless aunt, suffering through no
fault of her own. No bitterness resided in her heart at
remembrances of the woman's treachery, for there
was no true evil in her intent. How she must be
devastated at the findings of this day. And now she
had to cope with the uncertainty of her future. It
wasn't fair that she should know such misery and
fright because of her husband's greed. Evangeline
determined to lighten that load of precarious doubt
and went to seek her for that purpose.

Emma Webster sat in the parlor, huddled upon a
stool in its darkest corner. Her eyes were rimmed with
red and swollen from incessant weeping. A saturated
handkerchief knew ruin in her twisting hands.
Unable to absorb anymore of her grief, it managed to
smear the wetness upon her pallid cheeks when
applied with a frail flutter.

Evangeline's good nature was tortured by the
sight. She rushed to kneel at the woman's feet,
empathy etched upon her uplifted features.

"Oh, Aunt Emma, do not mourn over your fate,"
she implored, grasping the cool hands in the strength
of her own. "You'll want for nothing. I shall see to it.
You are my father's sister, family to me, and I'll not
forsake you. The guilt of your husband will not put a
stain upon the respect I hold for you."

Emma said nothing. She sat stiffly, her tear-
ravaged face a frozen mask of disbelief. She drew a
single, quavering breath and held it suspended for
countless seconds. How beaten she looked, as though
the spirit of life had left her. But then that spirit had
always been fragile in her repressed existence.
Evangeline was angry anew at the domineering
monster who would so cruelly crush the will of

another to serve his own needs. Now her aunt need know no further boundaries. She could flower and flourish without the fear of being cut back to the roots. She could take charge of her own destiny and live with pride and independence. Evangeline was flushed with these hopes that she could offer the despondent woman, and hastened to speak them.

"You are free," she encouraged joyously. "The man who slew your brother can intimidate you no more. You can cast off his oppressive bonds and live for yourself. He will not return to steal your smile or the gladness from your heart. The demon has been driven away."

Animation sparkled in Emma Webster. She reared back on the seat and smote her niece resoundingly upon the cheek.

"Horrid creature," she cried. "Would that you speak so of my husband before me. How dare you nurture the very viper who struck him down and come to me to beg forgiveness! Heathen. Devil-worshipper. Get from my sight before I am tainted by your vile presence. I'll hear no more evil from your defiling lips."

Evangeline's head swam with the viciousness of the blow, and with the equally unexpected tirade in defense of one so unworthy. Her hand pressed to the heated mark upon her cheek as she gazed up in stunned surprise. Grief had obviously overset the woman. She was not accountable for her actions. Pity replaced shock. Evangeline made another attempt to reach her.

"Aunt, I am not your enemy. He who used you is gone. Do not be afraid."

"Afraid?" she shrilled. "How can I not be afraid? You have stolen my husband from me, my only means of protection and support. What will I do?

What will become of me?" She drew away, repulsed by the offer of her niece's embrace. "You think I would accept anything from you? Or from him, that filthy schemer. It was his plan, you know, right from the start. Mr. Webster gave him his trust and generosity, and he used it to cripple him. He abused an offer of kindness with a return of betrayal and greed."

Evangeline's brows came down to form an angry vee. Her sentiments were rapidly shifting from sympathy to outrage. "My husband took no part in your husband's fall. He undertook his own ruin when he had my father killed. You would forgive him *that?*"

"My brother is dead. He can be no help to me. I want the husband you've denied me!" She stood down from the stool, looking not so helpless when flushed with righteous wrath. "'Tis you who are a demon. You brought this plague into our house. You made our efforts into a mockery with your pagan pride. I wish you had died with them. I wish I had never thought to seek you out from amongst the savages. Then I would have my husband, and my house would be my own. Now I must suffer *him*, when I would rather choke than taste the bitterness of his charity."

Evangeline colored in hot objection to those words. Fiercely she sought to defend against her aunt's warped claims. "Tanner is a good and just man. He is a man of honor and obligation. He could not be swayed away from the truth by the seductive ploys of gain your husband thought to offer. You should be grateful for what he is, instead of spiteful in your ignorance."

Emma laughed. It was a strange, incoherent sound, expressing no humor, but rather a disjointed pain. "Ignorant? You call me ignorant? Look to yourself, girl. Open your eyes. This manly paragon you boast of is no better than the one you abhor."

When she saw the arrogant disbelief on her niece's face, Emma pursued her point with malicious glee. "Foolish creature. Why do you think he wed you? He took you to get to my husband. You were a part of the bargain between them. Unless he took you away with him, he would get nothing, no position, no house in which to live, no hope for a better future. You were a tool he used to carve out his own fortune. He used you to destroy my family. And now that he has what he wants, you vain, haughty chit, do you think he'll be half so enamored of you? Do you think he'll bother to pretend interest in a half-tamed squaw when he can buy and sell the best of New York? You will be an embarrassment to him, just as you were to us. He will shut you away and ignore you, while he lives high and fat off the money you represent.

"You flaunt yourself as so superior. In a matter of time you'll know what real humility is. You are lower than any possession, for your use has been served. Think on that, missy, when you sneer at me and what I have. At least I was not blind to my fate. You are his prisoner now, and do you think he will treat you any better?"

For a moment, Evangeline stood frozen. The woman regarded her with a gloating malice, eager to feed off her niece's pain to ease her own. And Evangeline could not allow that weakening before this vicious foe. But neither could she maintain an argument or call her ugly statements lies. Upset, trembling with the force to cripple resolve, Evangeline saved her pride the only way she could, in a hurried retreat. The sound of her aunt's taunting laughter followed her from the room and up the stairs. No sooner had she shut the door to her chamber behind her than she began to feel it was again her cell. Moaning in fright, she sank to the woven rug, hugging her arms about herself in hopes of containing the terror that all she'd heard was true.

Terms of a bargain. That was why he had pursued her. Not because he desired her return, but because of what he would lose without her. She no longer wondered at his determination. It was clear. And it hurt. Royle Tanner was not her brave warrior, risking life for honor or for his wife. He wagered for what he couldn't bear to lose, a prominent future and fat profit. Her aunt was wrong. He was worse than her uncle, because she had so wanted him to be different. She had held him up with pride and devotion. What a fool she was. She had no choice to retain what she'd never had. Royle was not of her, he was a world apart, and no wish or wanting would bring them closer.

She had boasted of her husband's cleverness, but never had she realized just how shrewd he was. He had risen from nothing with but a single purpose, until all was within his grasp. She'd been a pawn to that calculated climb, and Uriah Webster had been another. Webster suffered with the loss of his fortune. She, with the loss of her heart. Neither absence would know any restitution. Men like Royle Tanner only looked ahead.

In an agony of comprehension, Evangeline swayed to her feet. She made her way blindly to the window to stare out onto her bleak future. Trapped within these walls, she would wither and die, slowly, daily, of neglect and sorrow. Torn from her roots, torn from her trust, she'd have nothing to cling to. She reviewed the speeches Royle had made her, and his words took a vile twist in the light of knowledge. Of course he was grateful to her. After all, she was the hook that snagged his dreams. But how far would that gratitude extend? How would she live with him and the recognition of his true intent? How could she lie with him, knowing she was only a vessel for his passion, never a receptacle for his love? She would move through the days, a ghost like Emma Webster, colorless, spiritless, without hopes or dreams of her own. And she would bring up her child, his child, in this world, to emulate all he saw, to believe all the illusions before his innocent eyes, to admire his father and look down upon his mother as little more than chattel.

No! Her palm slapped the cool glass, and then her fist dealt it a more forceful blow. She would not surrender her child up to fulfill his bargain. She would not have that power and privilege torn from her arms. She'd let no white tutors and godless fanatics teach her child the corruption of the white world, to scorn her people, to cheat them, to lie. To become like its father.

Evangeline took a deep breath, filling her lungs with the desire for freedom and her soul with determination. Royle could have the wealth her father had died for, that her uncle had killed for. She didn't want it. It would only bring greater greed and dissatisfaction. What he could not have was control of her child. She would not relinquish that most important right. To protect her unborn, she would make any sacrifice, even to the limit of her own endurance. Even with the forfeiture of her rapidly failing hopes. Her family would embrace her without question. Her child would grow up a Caniengas, proud, free, with honor. Fervently, she thanked her gods she'd had the wisdom to say nothing of its existence. An heir, he might pursue. A possession that had outlived its usefulness, he would not. He no longer had the incentive.

It was so easy this time. The escape she'd struggled so hard to attain before was won by merely opening the front door. She stepped out onto the street and breathed in the air. Soon it would be crisp and vital with the power of the forest, instead of tainted by the white man's dirt and civilization. Soon she would walk free and proud. That walk began with a single step, then another toward the river. She, too, would only look ahead.

Chapter Twenty-Four

"You must eat," came the soft, coaxing voice. "It will do no good to you or the babe should you waste away in grief."

Evangeline looked to her mother, her chin lifting with a defiant pride. "I do not grieve for what I am better off without," she declared staunchly. "I have put the past behind me, following wise words given me long ago. I am not hungry, 'tis all."

She-Walks-Far placed a hand upon her daughter's arm and pressed lightly. "There is little wisdom in what moves the heart," she shared with gentle knowledge. "But you are right. You must go on. You must think of yourself and of what name you will give the child. More gifts have come. Will you not receive them now? Or at least look at them, to see if you find favor?"

The pale, tormented eyes fastened undecidedly upon the older woman, hoping to find an answer within her calming spirit. "Is this what you would do, my mother?"

The black braids swung affirmingly with her nod. "You are of the proud Caniengas. You must think of how to bring honor and strength into our clan by the choice of a new husband. The little one will need a role to follow. You will need a means to fill your empty soul. A husband is more than a provider. He is the strength that sustains your spirit. Choose wisely and have no regrets, as I have had none these past twenty winters. One day you will hold my power before the chiefs. Your decisions will select them, your strength will guide the destiny of our people. Choose a mate so you might not rule alone."

Evangeline recognized the truth of those encouragements. Slowly, she nodded. "It will be done."

"Do not wait long, daughter. Already the hurt festers to a plague upon your soul. Purge it with the love of one who is worthy. Pick well so your strength might grow from within. Welcome the gifts outside your door and the giver. I have examined his heart and found him to be true. He has loved you long and faithfully, and I would give my blessing to such a union. The decision is yours, Eyes-Like-Evening-Star. Give yourself the chance to know happiness. You have mourned long enough."

"Bring the gifts," Evangeline said softly, then stoically received her mother's hug. She offered a narrow smile when they came apart, but She-Walks-Far was not deceived. The decision brought with it no joy. Not yet.

Alone, Evangeline reclined within her sleeping booth, finding little comfort in the luxurious mat of furs. Throughout the long *ganonh'sees*, the sounds of children being hushed for sleep echoed. Soon, the small voices would quiet, replaced by the lower tones of their parents as they cuddled in pairs to speak of things shared and intimate. Evangeline had no one with which to trade the stirrings of her heart or the secrets of her soul, and resentment for those personal murmurings filled her with unworthy envy. How unfair that she should dwell in solitude in the midst of so much love. In the morning, she would accept the gifts of courtship and continue with her life. Loneliness only fed her misery, and too much time for thought bred discontent and heartbreak. Better she turn her attention to another, then to allow it to linger upon her pain. Though she might wish it, she would not die of loss and shame, so there was no hope but to go on. Her strength would renew itself. Her heart would mend. Her pleasure in life would return. And with those things, she could only pray her love of Royle Tanner would fade and be forgotten.

But on this night it would torment her, in thoughts, in longings, in dreams, as it had since her return to the Wolf castle two weeks before. On each night she would lie awake listening for his step, craving the feel of his warmth. And on each night, disappointment was her only bedmate. Tanner was not coming for her. She knew that, so why could she not accept it?

The child stirred within her womb, as it often did now when she was still. That tender flutter reminded her that she was not alone. There was another life dependent upon her, another life upon which she could turn her affection. And this precious little being would not deceive or betray her. It would love her for herself, with the selfish need of the very young for those they could not do without.

And if the babe was born with hair of gold and eyes of green, she didn't know how she would stand that reminder of her lost love and misplaced trust. Of a destiny that did not come true.

Evangeline huddled within the nest of peltry. In the morning, she would accept the gifts and the suit of their giver. It wasn't fair to her child that she be tortured by the past. And it wasn't fair to her.

A pair of giggling maidens brought the wealth of gifts to her platform and left them with great reluctance. The backward glances bespoke their wistful dreams and sighing hopes. Emotionlessly, Evangeline assessed the tokens of betrothal. They were fine, honorable presents, chosen with care and rich with intent. She would never be wanting or unappreciated, these gifts told her. Some were traditional, some curious, from the sought-after white wampum to an oval reflecting glass. One in particular gave her pause. It was a mantle of wild turkey feathers, the brilliant, iridescent plumes completely covering the warm woven cloth. Such a grand, important offering surprised her, for it was a symbol of the highest esteem. She wasn't sure how Cayenderongue had come by it, but his sentiment overwhelmed her.

When she heard her persistent suitor was of the Bear, she knew her cousin had come to make good his claim. He would care for her and adore her. This she knew. But could she love him in return, as he deserved? She would be honest with him, tell him of the frailty of her misguided heart. Then if he was yet willing, she would take him into her house. He would be good with the child. He would be patient with her. It was more than she could hope from any other. It was more than she had a right to expect.

She looked up as her mother knelt before her. Tears clouded that beloved vision.

"Have you an answer, daughter?"

The gentle question wrought a myraid of doubts. She wanted to cling to the supportive figure and bewail her circumstance. She wanted to cry out her pain, to plead for an end to her torment. If only there were herbs or medicines she could take to free her heart from the power of the despised white man. She wished she could call upon the False Faces to drive away the demon of her ill-fated love. She longed to beg some wisdom from her mother that would soothe the bitterness and return her will to live.

But none of those things would occur to save her. She could only save herself by calling upon the pride of her people, by girding the strength of her spirit.

"I will accept them," she said in a strong, unwavering voice.

She-Walks-Far tendered a knowing smile. "You will not have reason for regret. I have listened long to him speak of his love for you. I believe in my heart that you belong one to another, though you may not see the truth of that now. I will send him to you, so you might speak these words to him."

Evangeline's courage failed as quiet filled the longhouse. She, alone, remained within, the others giving her privacy in which to receive her new husband. The ache of admitting to past mistakes was weak compared to the awful pain of letting go her beautiful dreams. With the acceptance of Cayende-rongue, Royle Tanner would have no place in her thoughts or in her heart. He would be dead to her, for she would not dishonor her new husband with yearnings for another. But could she release those poignant hopes, those tender plans, those passionate memories? That would require a strength unknown before, and she quelled with fear of failing. The entirety of what she was she'd pledged upon her love. Was there anything left for her, or for another?

She couldn't force herself to look up at the whisper of his moccasins. Her gaze was frozen to the ground until the quill-worked toes stopped before her. Her heart shuddered in raw despair. Truth—harsh and unalterable—directed her mind. She could not welcome another when her soul was already bound.

Hating the hurt she would cause him, and herself for admitting the weakness that ruled her, Evangeline lifted her gaze to confront and discourage her suitor. Her eyes skimmed over the ankle-high moccasins to the pale calves above. Heart and stare leapt upward.

Speaking slowly, awkwardly, in the tongue of her people, he asked, "Will you take these tokens and thereby take my love?"

Crazy emotions upset her thinking, tearing through her in violent opposites. With a frantic cry, she sprang up to launch herself upon him, not in a grateful, welcoming embrace, but all vicious nails and native curses. The passion of her attack unbalanced him, and together they fell to the soft bed of furs. It was a struggle reminiscent of others which ended more dangerously than in death. She was strong, but he, stronger. She was angry but he, determined. She would refuse him, but he wouldn't allow it.

For a moment, the fierce spew of her words was overwhelmed by his demanding kiss. Her fight gave before the treacherous weakening of her will as his mouth shaped hers to its mold, but no sooner had her arms begun to enfold him then reason denounced her failing. Her head jerked to the side and panting oaths assailed him.

"No! I hate you. Monster. Demon. Liar."

For all her furious claims, her body betrayed the vulnerability of her heart. It arched against him, welcoming his weight, reveling in his dominance, desperate to surrender the resistance of her pride. But her dignity made demands of its own.

"Release me," she snarled.

"Not until you listen to me."

"Hear more of your lies? No. Never!"

He anchored her flailing arms with the pressure of his own, holding her secure, immobile, a reluctant captive. "You've always boasted of your fairness, of your honor. I ask that you spare me time to speak what's in my heart. I don't ask you to believe me, only to listen. Then I'll go, if that be your desire."

Her breath seethed in silence as her angry eyes searched his. The green gold depths were steeped in sincerity. But then, they always were, even upon the telling of his lies. She wished she could deny him a fair hearing. Alas, her plaintive heart would not forgo the chance to attend his words. Like a true warrior, she chose to take an offensive rather than to passively defend.

"Why have you come, Tanner?"

The rumble of his voice quickened a matching timbre in her soul. "I vowed never to let you go. Have you forgotten?"

"That part of your bargain you need no longer keep."

"Oh," he said in sudden revelation. "So that's the way of it. Here I'd thought you merely took exception to my choice of dwelling, when 'tis the impurity of my motives that's provoked your pride."

"You do not deny it?" Surprised quavered over her outrage. She'd not expected him to admit the truth so willingly.

"Why would I? You had only to ask. I am not ashamed to claim the wisest exchange of my life." His grip tightened to subdue her renewed struggles. Bare breasts grazed bare chest and the igniting friction hindered rational thought.

"You mock me," Evangeline growled, hurt by his candor, barbed by his arrogance. "You laugh at the barter of my affection."

"Affection?" He did laugh then. "By God, woman, it was all I could do to keep my hair through the first weeks of our marriage. In fact, it took quite some doing for me to convince myself that the bargain was in my favor."

She quieted then, devastated by his blunt claim. How he must have loathed the trap her uncle caught him in. How much greater that made his greed to overcome it. "Why did you comply with the terms?" she demanded flatly. "Why did you come after me?"

"Because you were mine. Because I wanted you the first instant I saw you. I fell in love with an illusion, only to discover the truth far more valuable."

Tears gathered. Her eyes shimmered like mist-covered pools. Anguish caught at her words, snagging them upon his heart. "And now you have what you desired, your precious fortune and fame. I will not protest, if that's what's brought you here. Keep your coin, only leave me in peace." It was her turn to speak a lie, for peace would never find her after enduring his closeness this last time. Her body cried out for his. Her spirit longed to encompass all that he was, and all that he would never be.

He angled his imprisoning embrace so his thumbs could brush aside the dewlike moisture upon her cheeks. "It is because of the fortune that I have come."

It was true! A sob of hurt lodged within her throat, yet she would not release it and confess her pain. That much of her self-respect she would fight to retain, to the death if need be. She would not divulge her broken heart. Let him think it was anger that drove her away. Let him believe the disgust of his greed he saw in her eyes. But never, oh God, never let him know he had ripped the soul from her with his indifference.

He continued to caress the gentle angles of her face as he pledged, "I've come to offer all my possessions, if you will have me for a husband, as is the custom of your people."

He paused a moment, waiting for a response. She stared up at him through wide, unblinking eyes. Her disbelief was so apparent, he began to feel cha-grinned. After he'd come all this way to offer up his very soul, this was not the greeting he expected. Gruffly, a bit tersely, he gave more explanation.

"The vows we took before have never been enough to hold you. Perhaps these will convince you."

An incredulous thought seized her. For a time, she could not speak of the fragile expectation. It was too much to hope for. Too much to believe over the hurts and disappointments of the past. Yet she clung to the offer of tenuous hope, a cautious want to believe. Because she loved him more than life. Because she wanted what he spoke of with all her fragile heart. So, she risked shame, she dared the Fates to fail her yet again.

"You truly came for *me*?" It was a tremulous whisper.

"Why else? I've spent the better part of our marriage pursuing you or persuading you to stay."

He sounded so aggrieved, her temper pricked her to retort, "You never gave the right argument."

"Is saying I love you argument enough, or would you prefer I beat you with a stick?"

"Say it again." It was a demand, one which cost no humbling of his pride to comply with.

He said it with his mouth, with his touch, and

finally with his husky voice. "I love you, Tanner's Wife."

"Oh, Royle."

The sobs came freely then, wetting his shoulder, then mingling saltily with his kisses.

"Why didn't you tell me of your unhappiness?" he chided gently, cradling her close to the comfort of his chest. He'd rolled to the luxurious bed so they could lie side by side. Atop her, he could only focus his thoughts toward one conclusion, and it was talk they needed between them. That was where the problem lay, not in the rapture of their loving. "Why did I have to discover it from Cayenderongue? I'd no notion as to why you left me. I thought perhaps it was because you wished to control the money. So I came to give it to you. Why didn't you stay to tell me of your fears? Why didn't you remain to hear my explanation? Do you still have so little trust in my feeling for you?"

Royle sat up then, and Evangeline came up on her elbows to watch the sundry emotions play upon his face. He was as easy to read as the signs of changing seasons, but not always so predictable. Now he appeared angry, slighted. And afraid. While she puzzled over those things, he accused, "You should have said something. You let me go on and on about how we would live, when you knew well it was not the life you wanted. You let me stoke the fires of my ambition when a word from you would have smothered the flame. What a tyrant you must think me, to believe I'd not consider your feelings at all. Have you no idea at all what you mean to me? I was so busy congratulating myself on my success, I forgot to listen to your opinion. I was selfish. I was thoughtless. I was insensitive, but, by God, Evangeline, a word from you was all it would have taken.''

His tone grew husky and rough with sentiment. "I didn't deserve the terror you put me through when I discovered you had fled. There is nothing in that empty house to hold me without you in it. There is nothing in my future without you to give it joy. How could you hurt me so? Everything I've done has been for you and for our future. It may not have been what you had chosen, but not for an instant did my thinking fail to include you."

He was silent then, and Evangeline was tortured by his confession. In one, it was elegant apology and subtle reproach, and her emotions quivered taut as a bowstring. He was blaming and absolving her, and the ripping currents between them caught her mercilessly. He claimed she was wrong for not trusting him. Perhaps she was. He claimed a word would have pulled him from his purpose. Perhaps, but she was not so easily convinced of it. She'd seen that consuming passion in his eyes. He faulted her for not speaking her mind and heart, and in that she could find no disagreement. It was the lack of truth that stood between them, breeding misunderstanding and insecurity, not the true motivations of their hearts. He said he loved her. If he'd told her that the moment he'd realized it was true, how much would have changed between them? Perhaps nothing. Perhaps everything. What would or would not have changed was not the issue. It was what they were willing to change between them now that mattered.

Softly, Royle continued to bare his heart, and the anguish of his words quickened tears as he spoke them. "When I found you gone, nothing mattered. I felt as though my life had ended. You'd taken away my purpose, my reason for wanting to succeed. None of it meant a thing without you there to share it.

There was no accomplishment in having everything when alone. God in heaven, you scared me. All I could imagine was a life without you. Do you know how that felt? How empty I was inside? Did you really think the money was all that mattered to me? Did you believe my principles were more important than your happiness? What have I done to make you think that of me? Is it something I can change? Is there something I can say? Can't you believe I love you?"

"You had never made it known. Until now," was her quiet defense. She sat up then and let her arms circle about his middle. His bare chest felt warm and strong beneath her palms. His heart beat out a powerful message. It was a language she understood at last.

"Nor have you said a word about what you feel for me. Yet I have followed you, I have relied upon you, I have risked all I have in hopes that you care."

"Can you doubt that I do?" She let herself release all the remaining barriers from about her heart, the last of the doubts, the last of her fears. It was a wonderful, lightening purge. And once the mat of yellow gold hair slipped through her fingers, she could not wait to satisfy her need for more. She traced his shoulders, stroked his furred chest, rubbed the firm swell of his arms, until she was absorbed with the wonder of how he was made. His eyes had kindled into hot green coals, yet he dared not return her caresses until all had been settled between them. She was too tempting, too lush, too exquisitely distracting. And once he took her again as his bride, he didn't want to be interrupted by questions or doubts. Or by anything short of exhaustion.

His words of answer came from a deep treasured knowledge and trembled in the telling. "I never will

381

again. Nor will I allow differences to come between us. And if it be your wish to head our family, I will bow before it."

"You will give me say over all we choose to do, over all our decisions, over all that effects our lives?"

Royle hesitated. It was a brief reluctance, but it made her lips soften into the beginnings of a smile where they pressed to the supple skin of his shoulder. "Yes," he stated nobly, with a conviction she did not doubt. His word was irrefutable. It was the same sort of bond that had carried him across an ocean to see a promise kept. "I have had my Caniengas brother show me how to string the wampum belt, so you might believe my vow."

Evangeline's smile tugged more insistently. "You would do that for me? You would surrender your right to rule in the white way? You would give me the power over your future and that of our children? You would sacrifice your pride and humble your beliefs?"

"Isn't that what I've asked of you?" he challenged softly. He did turn then, coming about to face her, only to be lost to her beauty and to the tenderness that warmed her eyes. "Do you deny me the right to make an equal sacrifice?"

Her fingertips rode the intriguing line of his cheeks and jaw, until she held his face between them. Her love for him was such that it radiated from her glance in a tender wave. "It was no sacrifice. I gave because I wished to. I gave because I love you."

His hands seized hers so he could press fervent kisses to her palms.

Evangeline smiled easily, because of how well she knew him at this minute. And it was that very sense of pride and honor he offered to surrender that irrevocably mastered her will. To strip from him the strength of manhood would make him something less in both their eyes. "You would be miserable in such a role," she chided not unkindly. "You are a man used to controlling destiny. In a dream, I gave you the power over mine. You could not be satisfied to spend the day in the forest hunting game, and I could not waste hours upon a velvet cushion being idle. Those are not the things that move our hearts. There must be a compromise between our worlds. I will not serve, but it is my wish to share."

"Then the giving will be equal. Tell me your heart's desire, and I will see you have it."

Evangeline's tone was gruff with emotion. "I already possess all I need. What of you? What of your dreams?"

"It wasn't the wealth, angel. It was never greed. It was the want to be recognized, to be worthy, and you have fulfilled that dream daily. The fine house in the city was an illusion, like the pretty miss in lavender silk, spun fancies with no real substance. Neither belonged to me. Neither was right for me. True success is holding a woman like you, hearing her speak of her love, filling her with children. Those lessons were hard-learned, but will never be forgotten."

"And the house in New York?"

"Will remain with your aunt and cousin. We do not belong among them. I've found my happiness upon a stone hearth with a woman struggling to make bread to please me."

Her heart leapt. Her hopes abounded. That anticipation lifted her spirits and gave her voice music. "We will live in Albany?"

"Close to your people and near to mine. The crossroads of our worlds. I would like to make a success of the trading house, but I need you to explain the needs of your people. I would treat them fairly and with respect. Would they trust me with their interests?"

"Why would they not? After all, you are their brother, bound by adopted blood and marriage."

Royle grinned. His hand had grown inpatient with talk, and her response betrayed a similar dissatisfaction. It became imperative to reach an agreement so they might enjoy the fruits of the bargain.

"So you will accept my gifts."

Evangeline regarded him seriously, sober expression belied by the tender misting of her eyes. "You have come to me out of respect for my ways, and by this you do me great honor. It is the custom of my people to cherish the gifts given and to return to the giver one of equal or greater value. I accept your offer and have a gift of my own to present you."

Lovingly, she lifted Royle's hand. After a brief, warm clasp of intertwined fingers, Evangeline brought his palm down to the slight swell of her belly, to feel the gift of life within.

DON'T MISS A YEAR OF

Slocum Giant
by
Jake Logan

Slocum Giant 2004:
Slocum in the Secret Service

Slocum Giant 2005:
Slocum and the Larcenous Lady

Slocum Giant 2006:
Slocum and the Hanging Horse

Slocum Giant 2007:
Slocum and the Celestial Bones

Slocum Giant 2008:
Slocum and the Town Killers

penguin.com/actionwesterns

M230AS0808

Jove Westerns put the "wild"
back into the Wild West.

LONGARM
by Tabor Evans

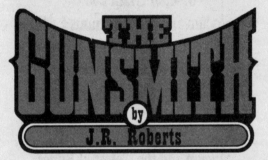

THE GUNSMITH
by
J.R. Roberts

SLOCUM by
JAKE LOGAN

Don't miss these exciting, all-action series!
penguin.com/actionwesterns

M11G0808

As soon as they were dressed, the elves began to dance faster and faster. They hopped and laughed and sang until, at last, they twirled right out the door of the shop. The shoemaker and his wife watched them dance down the moonlit path.

From that day on, the shoemaker and his wife had very good luck in all that they did. And they never forgot those who had helped them when they needed it most—the two little elves.

At midnight, sure enough, the two little elves came skipping into the shop, ready for work. When they saw the beautiful tiny clothes, they were surprised and delighted.

They began to dress themselves in the suits, little hats, and boots. As they put on their clothes, laughing and dancing a lively jig, they sang:

Now we are jaunty gentlemen,

Why should we ever work again?

The next morning, the shoemaker's wife said, "Those two little elves have done so much for us. We should make them a gift to thank them. They must be cold in their ragged clothes, so I will make two little suits and hats. Will you make two tiny pairs of boots for them?"

"Of course," said the shoemaker. So they set to work to make clothes for the elves. That night, they laid out their gifts on the workbench.

At exactly midnight, as the shoemaker and his wife watched, two little elves came into the shop. Their clothes were thin and ragged. They jumped up onto the work-bench and began sewing away.

The shoemaker and his wife were surprised to see how swiftly the two elves worked. They did not stop until all the leather was made into shoes. Then they jumped down from the bench and ran away.

SO-ADT-089

Moving Targets

Slocum fell into the easy rhythm of the horse, warmed by Suzanne's arms around him and her body pressing tightly against his. The shot that sang through the still, early morning took him completely by surprise.

"Hang on," he called to Suzanne. She lurched and almost tumbled from horseback as he bent forward and put his spurs to his horse's flanks. Barely had the horse run a dozen yards when another shot rang out.

Slocum went sailing through the air, Suzanne still clinging to him. His horse's front legs crumpled and its head hit the ground. After that, Slocum wasn't sure what happened. He skidded along the road on his belly with Suzanne clinging to him. By the time he came to a halt, Slocum was torn up and bloody and madder than hell.

He stood and the dark-haired woman slid to one side, sitting in the dirt and staring numbly at him.

"Stay down," he snarled. Slocum slapped leather. His Colt Navy came easily to his hand, but he could not find a target . . .

DON'T MISS THESE
ALL-ACTION WESTERN SERIES
FROM THE BERKLEY PUBLISHING GROUP

THE GUNSMITH by J. R. Roberts
Clint Adams was a legend among lawmen, outlaws, and ladies. They called him . . . the Gunsmith.

LONGARM by Tabor Evans
The popular long-running series about Deputy U.S. Marshal Custis Long—his life, his loves, his fight for justice.

SLOCUM by Jake Logan
Today's longest-running action Western. John Slocum rides a deadly trail of hot blood and cold steel.

BUSHWHACKERS by B. J. Lanagan
An action-packed series by the creators of Longarm! The rousing adventures of the most brutal gang of cutthroats ever assembled—Quantrill's Raiders.

DIAMONDBACK by Guy Brewer
Dex Yancey is Diamondback, a Southern gentleman turned con man when his brother cheats him out of the family fortune. Ladies love him. Gamblers hate him. But nobody pulls one over on Dex . . .

WILDGUN by Jack Hanson
The blazing adventures of mountain man Will Barlow—from the creators of Longarm!

TEXAS TRACKER by Tom Calhoun
J. T. Law: the most relentless—and dangerous—manhunter in all Texas. Where sheriffs and posses fail, he's the best man to bring in the most vicious outlaws—for a price.

JAKE LOGAN

SLOCUM'S
BAR-S RANCH

JOVE BOOKS, NEW YORK

THE BERKLEY PUBLISHING GROUP
Published by the Penguin Group
Penguin Group (USA) Inc.
375 Hudson Street, New York, New York 10014, USA
Penguin Group (Canada), 90 Eglinton Avenue East, Suite 700, Toronto, Ontario M4P 2Y3, Canada
(a division of Pearson Penguin Canada Inc.)
Penguin Books Ltd., 80 Strand, London WC2R 0RL, England
Penguin Group Ireland, 25 St. Stephen's Green, Dublin 2, Ireland (a division of Penguin Books Ltd.)
Penguin Group (Australia), 250 Camberwell Road, Camberwell, Victoria 3124, Australia
(a division of Pearson Australia Group Pty. Ltd.)
Penguin Books India Pvt. Ltd., 11 Community Centre, Panchsheel Park, New Delhi—110 017, India
Penguin Group (NZ), 67 Apollo Drive, Rosedale, North Shore 0632, New Zealand
(a division of Pearson New Zealand Ltd.)
Penguin Books (South Africa) (Pty.) Ltd., 24 Sturdee Avenue, Rosebank, Johannesburg 2196,
South Africa

Penguin Books Ltd., Registered Offices: 80 Strand, London WC2R 0RL, England

This is a work of fiction. Names, characters, places, and incidents either are the product of the author's imagination or are used fictitiously, and any resemblance to actual persons, living or dead, business establishments, events, or locales is entirely coincidental.

SLOCUM'S BAR-S RANCH

A Jove Book / published by arrangement with the author

PRINTING HISTORY
Jove edition / January 2009

Copyright © 2009 by Penguin Group (USA) Inc.
Cover illustration by Sergio Giovine.

All rights reserved.
No part of this book may be reproduced, scanned, or distributed in any printed or electronic form without permission. Please do not participate in or encourage piracy of copyrighted materials in violation of the author's rights. Purchase only authorized editions.
For information, address: The Berkley Publishing Group,
a division of Penguin Group (USA) Inc.,
375 Hudson Street, New York, New York 10014.

ISBN: 978-0-515-14571-7

JOVE®
Jove Books are published by The Berkley Publishing Group,
a division of Penguin Group (USA) Inc.
375 Hudson Street, New York, New York 10014.
JOVE® is a registered trademark of Penguin Group (USA) Inc.
The "J" design is a trademark of Penguin Group (USA) Inc.

PRINTED IN THE UNITED STATES OF AMERICA

10 9 8 7 6 5 4 3 2 1

If you purchased this book without a cover, you should be aware that this book is stolen property. It was reported as "unsold and destroyed" to the publisher, and neither the author nor the publisher has received any payment for this "stripped book."

1

John Slocum rode into Middle Park on the western slope of the Rocky Mountains, thinking it was a lovely day. And it was. A lovely day filled with bullets, all directed at him.

The first shot tore a piece out of his canvas duster. The second sent his black, floppy-brimmed hat snapping back on his head, caught and held only by the string he had fastened under his chin. The sudden bite of that string reminded him too much of a hangman's noose. Another bullet, which spooked his horse and caused the roan to rear, removed such thoughts of dangling by the neck, and replaced them with the need just to keep from getting filled with lead.

He fought his horse and got it under control, only to have a rifleman on the opposite side of the road open up on him. The horse reared and threw him. Slocum landed hard on his back and spent a few seconds staring open-eyed at the bright blue Colorado sky stretching in an unbroken dome above him. Then dust began billowing all around as more slugs sought a permanent home in his body.

The fall dazed him, and he had a difficult time figuring which way to dodge. Men with six-shooters on his left side and at least one sniper with a rifle on his right made the decision one of life and death. All he saw of his horse was a

slowly settling dust cloud down the road. The pounding he heard might have been the roan's hooves or it could have been the blood rushing in his ears. Reacting more out of instinct than logic, Slocum got to his feet and fell forward into a ditch alongside the road. During rainy season, it probably ran full. Since it was late summer, all that remained was dust, more dust, and weeds that poked at his face until he sneezed. He tried to hold back another pollen-caused sneeze, but his situation got worse by the instant.

The men—there had to be at least four—on his left were moving closer, firing steadily as they came. They worked together better than a posse. They might have been a military unit on foot, some shooting while the rest reloaded. That way, they maintained a curtain of lead in front of them and kept anyone stupid enough to be there flat on his face. Worse, the way they moved, two were always covering their partners. This tactic stole away any chance Slocum had to drop even one of them and improve his odds.

If he tried getting to the other side of the road, the rifleman would take him out. Try as he might, he could not find where the sniper hid even to throw a couple slugs his way.

Slocum rolled onto his side, drew his Colt Navy, and waited to take his first shot. He cocked the six-gun, but did not fire when he saw a hat poke above a rock twenty feet away. They wanted him to waste his ammo shooting at a hat intentionally raised on a stick. Slocum arched his back and looked in a different direction in time to see two men trying to get him in a box. He was already caught in a cross fire. They wanted to get south of him, cut off escape, and fire from all directions.

His first shot hit a man in the leg and sent him to the ground, grunting in pain. His next two bullets fell right for a kill on the outlaw accompanying the wounded man. He didn't see what happened to that owlhoot, but there was neither sound nor return gunfire.

"He got Ned! The damn varmint's done kilt Ned!"

Slocum paid no heed to the words. They were intended to make him careless. Some men might have felt elation at the idea he had shot one of his attackers. Slocum would savor that feeling only when they were all ready for a simple grave in a potter's field.

Two more quick shots added extra lead to the man he had hit in the leg earlier. He couldn't be certain, but thought he had about blown off the man's leg. Even if the son of a bitch didn't bleed to death, he wouldn't be a factor in the fight.

Slocum took advantage of the lull in the fight to fumble out a few cartridges from his pocket as the other men he faced hesitated. They had thought to roll over him and probably rob him. If he had been able to discuss the matter, he would have easily convinced them he was so broke he didn't have two nickels to rub together. Worse, he had left Gunnison owing a powerful lot of money to a crooked gambler. Slocum wasn't sure he had been cheated, but it didn't much matter. Moving on was easier than listening to the tinhorn gambler gloat about how he had drawn to an inside straight and won.

Reloaded six-gun in hand, Slocum considered his options. He could go south along the road he had cleared with his accurate gunfire and hope to find his horse eventually. There was only one problem with this sensible scheme. To do that exposed his back. If he crossed the road, the hidden sniper would take him out.

That limited his options to one. He attacked. Slocum got his feet under him and dug the toes of his boots into the rocky ground the best he could to launch himself forward. He headed for the boulder where the hat had been thrust up. He swarmed over and found nothing but footprints in the soft earth.

Slocum kept running, following that distinctive trail. He burst out of the tumble of rocks to where a pair of men argued. Neither saw him coming. He had taken them by surprise. His six-shooter blared out four rounds, two for each man. One shot each would have been enough.

Still moving, Slocum skirted the small clearing and hunted for others. The best he could tell, there had only been four trying to ventilate him from this side of the road. However, he counted tracks from six horses. Two more of the owlhoots were out there.

One had to be the rifleman. Maybe the other had back-tracked to be sure Slocum didn't have a partner riding to catch up. His guesses fell apart when he heard at least two six-guns firing with what had to be return fire from the rifle.

Slocum reloaded and made his way back to the men he had cut down. A quick search yielded twenty dollars in scrip and no clue who they might be. He tucked the money into his shirt pocket, then picked up their pistols. If he had to get himself in a protracted gunfight, by damn but he wasn't going to waste his own ammo.

A six-gun in each hand, he got back to the road and tried to locate the sniper up in the rocks. He caught the briefest flash of a man on a horse heading into the hills, swinging a six-shooter around as he rode like all the demons of Hell nipped at his heels. Slocum couldn't be certain what he actually saw, though. The only thing he knew for sure was that if it was human and moved, he would try to gun it down before it got him.

This wasn't the kind of fight where he had to worry about friends.

Sucking in his breath and letting it out slowly calmed him a little. Then he ran as hard as he could across the road and found another ditch to dive into. This one lacked the hip-high weeds, but sported brutal thistles that tore at his face and hands. Ignoring the nettles, he looked for a spot to make a stand. A lone cottonwood tree fifty feet away had to be enough.

Slocum ran. Bullets tore at him as he dodged. One grazed his cheek and left a bloody, inconsequential gash. By the time he reached the safety of the thirty-foot-tall cottonwood, he

was mad all over again. He settled down and tried to make sense out of everything around him.

The occasional slug that knocked splinters off the tree trunk made him wary, and caused him to take longer getting the lay of the land than was his wont. When he did, he gripped the two six-shooters he had taken from the outlaws and ran straight for an arroyo at the base of a hill. He got there without anyone taking a potshot at him.

He listened hard and knew the tide of battle was changing fast. The rifle fire came sporadically now, as if the sniper was hoarding his ammunition. The flatter crack of handguns did not let up. The two men going after the sniper must have a pack mule weighed down with cartridges to be so profligate.

Moving carefully, Slocum made his way up the hill and found himself looking down into a draw. When a horseman slowly rode past, Slocum stepped out and blazed away with both captured six-guns. The rider toppled to the ground without making a sound.

"You figgered it out yet, Glasgow?" The question came from higher on the hillside, about where Slocum reckoned the sniper to be holed up. "I got reinforcements. You and me and my boys. Don't like them odds, do you?"

Slocum reacted when a second rider galloped past. His six-shooters came up empty fast, and he went for his ebony-handled Colt Navy. Barely had he cleared leather when the rifleman took the rider out of the saddle. Slocum saw a tiny fountain of blood at the back of the rider's head before he crumpled forward. The runaway horse quickly took its dead rider out of sight.

"You willin' to call a truce, mister?" the sniper shouted.

"I never wanted to be in this fight," Slocum called back. He knew better than to step out into the line of fire. He thought he understood all that had happened, but he could be wrong. Those weren't deputies or lawmen of any kind. He pegged them as road agents. That didn't mean the man on

the hillside was pure as the wind-driven snow. The outlaws might have had a falling-out.

"I cain't come down to you, so you got to come to me."

"Tell you what," Slocum called. "I've got a better idea. I'll leave. You go your way, and I'll go mine." He looked over his shoulder at the road leading southward. His roan must have run itself out by now. It might be several miles away, but he could retrieve it before sundown if he got lucky.

"Then you're signin' my death warrant. Them rustlers drilled me through both legs. No way I can even drag myself along."

"Throw out your rifle."

"Why should I trust you?"

"See you in Hell," Slocum said. He had no hankering to argue the matter.

"Wait, mister, confound you, wait a goddamn minute!" The rifle clattered against a rock and slid a few feet. "My six-shooter is empty." A pistol followed. "I got a knife, too, but it's got a buckhorn handle and tossing it into the rocks'll chip its damned hilt."

Slocum was already moving, heading back around the hill and making his way upward in a spiral path to come out behind the man. By the time the man was cursing a blue streak, Slocum spotted him. He was hunched over, his shoulders and back making him appear to be a human question mark. His hands were trembling and wizened, and the only part of the man Slocum could tell that was in good shape was his mouth. Not once did he repeat a curse.

"I suppose I could let you go on. I'm getting quite an education in cussing," Slocum said. The old man twisted about. Slocum saw that he had not lied about his injuries. Blood soaked both pants legs.

"I done what I said. If you're one of them sons of bitches, go on and kill me." The man made an obscene gesture.

"I got caught in the cross fire. Who were they? Outlaws?"

"Rustlers, each and ever' last one. Coldhearted killers.

Not content with stealin' a man's cows. They want to kill the one what owns the cows, too."

"You were out hunting the rustlers?"

"Hell, no, I was out tryin' to figger why my lazy cowboys wasn't able to round up 'nuff cows for us to even have steak for dinner. I ran into them varmints. Goddamn them all."

"Probably," Slocum said. "They're all certainly on their way to Hell."

"You kilt the lot of them?"

"They shouldn't have fired on me." Slocum knew at least one had ridden off, but he wasn't inclined to worry over details at the moment.

"I shot at you, thinkin' you was one of 'em," the man said. His leathery face contorted into what Slocum guessed was a smile. "My name's Jackson Wimmer, and I own the biggest damn spread in all of Middle Park."

"The biggest?" Slocum looked skeptical, and the old man grinned even more.

"Maybe not the *biggest* but certainly the best."

Slocum had to laugh. "That I'll buy." When he saw Wimmer wince as he tried to move, he knew the old man was in bad shape. "I'll rustle up a couple horses and get you to a doctor."

"Rustle? Hell, no, steal 'em if you have to, but don't go sayin' that word round me. Makes me mad. All the time I hear 'rustlers' and it always means I lost me another hunnerd head of beeves. Horse thievin's just fine, but no rustlin'."

Slocum took the better part of an hour catching two of the outlaws' horses and leading them back up the hill to where Wimmer lay. At first, Slocum thought the old rancher had upped and died, but he proved to be of sterner stuff.

"Cain't climb into the saddle. Might be you could toss me across a saddle like a bag o' flour?"

"That'd kill a healthy man, riding like that," Slocum said. "Better if I tied you upright."

"You're a big, strappin' fella. Reckon you can hoist me into the saddle if I give you some help?"

Slocum lifted the old man more easily than he had thought. Wimmer was nothing but a bag of bones. He wobbled in the saddle but held on gamely. After he was astride the horse, Slocum did what he could for the old man's shot-up legs. From the look of it, a single bullet had entered the left thigh and come out on the right side. Other than this wound, Wimmer was in decent enough shape.

"Which way do we ride?" Slocum mounted and looked at the road with some longing. He had nothing drawing him southward, but his roan was in that direction along with his gear.

"Back north, from the direction you were ridin'," Wimmer said. Slocum looked at him sharply. There was a drop of acid in the old man's tone, as if he took some delight in putting Slocum out.

"Is there a town nearby with a doctor? You need those holes in your legs tended."

"You did a fine job bandagin' me up. You wouldn't happen to be a doctor now, would you, Slocum?"

"I do what I can but never thought of myself that way." Slocum turned away, memories flooding back on him about the time he had been forced to act as a doctor during the war. His friends had been killed left and right. The Federals had overrun an artillery position and turned the cannon against the Rebs. Slocum's entire unit had been wiped out, leaving only him. A field doctor had ordered him to help with the wounded—and not just to carry off the dead and stack them like cordwood. Slocum had assisted the doctor in hacking off arms and legs in a filthy surgery tent. He reckoned they killed more between them, the doctor and him, than the Federals had using the cannon at point-blank range.

There had always been a dozen more wounded waiting for them that day, no matter how long they worked. Slocum was no stranger to bullet wounds, but he could never think of

himself as a doctor after that endless day. He had felt more like a butcher.

"You got the look of a man able to do a lot of things purty good."

Slocum shrugged.

"You wear that hogleg of yours slung in a cross-draw holster like you know how to use it. You a gunfighter?"

"Just a drifter."

"You kin use that gun of yours and you don't shy from a fight," Wimmer said. The old man fixed him with a gimlet eye. The body might be frail, but the mind was sharp and appraising. "You kin ride and rope, too, betcha."

"Done my fair share." Slocum found himself telling Jackson Wimmer about the numerous cattle drives he had been on from Texas up to the railheads in Kansas.

"You ever boss one of them drives?"

"Trail boss on one, ramrod on another," Slocum said. "About the only thing I never did was be a cook. The way I'd've fixed chuck would have given everybody bellyaches. No work would have gotten done. Might have even gotten lynched."

Wimmer laughed at this. "A wise man knows his limitations."

"You including yourself in that or excluding?" Slocum asked.

"Nobody's ever called me a wise man. Worse. Always worse."

"You a mean drunk?" Slocum asked.

"What's that supposed to mean?"

Slocum reached back in the saddlebags and rummaged about until he found the half-pint of whiskey that had sloshed so loud it had drawn his attention for nigh on a mile. He pulled the cork and took a swig. It burned at his mouth and throat but went down good. Passing it over to Wimmer, he watched the man's eyes fix on the bottle.

"Ain't 'nuff there to git me drunk," Wimmer complained.

He drained the rest of the bottle and tossed it away. The glass shattered loudly when it hit a large rock alongside the road.

Slocum hoped the liquor would ease some of the pain etched on the man's face. Wimmer said nothing, but he was weakening fast. A man half his age would have been in trouble, yet the rancher refused to slow down or take more than a few minutes' rest.

"You got family to look after you?" Slocum asked.

"Ain't got family. Hardly have any ranch hands no more either," Wimmer said. "Cowards. The lot of 'em are cowards. They all run off when the rustlers moved in on us."

"What's the law doing about them?"

"Cain't do much. From what I kin tell, them rustlers are 'bout half white and half Ute."

"You mean breeds?"

"No, you idiot. I mean some of 'em are white men and some are redskins."

"That there's the road to your ranch," Slocum said. A neatly carved sign with Wimmer's name in white-painted lettering showed the way off the road and back into a wide valley. "Don't fall off before you get there."

"Hold on. Where the hell're you goin', Slocum?"

"Somewhere that crotchety old men don't call me an idiot."

"You prefer me callin' you a son of a bitch?" Wimmer eyed him carefully.

"Yeah."

"I promise not to call you an idiot again."

"That promise doesn't mean a whole lot since I'm riding back to find my roan as soon as I see you to your house."

"Find your damned horse, but you got a whole lot more of me to put up with."

"How's that?" Slocum saw the expression on Jackson Wimmer's face and could not figure out what it was. Something sly, but also something else, as if he was on the point of begging.

"It wouldn't be right for my foreman to ride off and never come back."

Slocum hadn't known what Wimmer was going to say, but this took him completely by surprise.

2

"So you git them beeves moved into a better pasture?" Jackson Wimmer glared at Slocum.

"Did that yesterday. Have the boys putting up a new corral right now. Your old one was falling down. It's a wonder you didn't lose more horses just from taking it into their heads to walk off."

"You might call me sir when you address me."

"I'm your foreman, not your slave," Slocum said. He stared at Wimmer and wondered how an old man with such a tongue ever put together a spread like this. It had amused Slocum, for a day or so, that the ranch carried the Bar-S name. About where that brand had come from, Wimmer was silent although Slocum had asked. Somewhere in the back of his mind, he made a small joke that it was named after him. The Bar-S for the Bar-Slocum Ranch. It had taken less than a week for this notion to fade away and no longer amuse him, mostly because there was no one to share the joke with. The cowboys working for him were as surly as their employer, and nowhere near as competent, except a couple who might prove decent cowboys someday, if they ever got off their cracker asses and worked longer than a few minutes at a time. Slocum had

looked over the books and seen that the Bar-S made money most years. Even in as lush a place as Middle Park with pastureland everywhere, making a profit was always a problem.

The rustlers added to the losses. The prior year Wimmer had lost a considerable portion of his herd to some disease that Slocum reckoned to be splenic fever. Even then, the Bar-S had broken even. Weather and disease were things Wimmer took in stride as being forces of nature, but the rustlers were another matter.

"For what I'm payin' you, I deserve respect," Wimmer groused.

"For what you're paying me, I ought to get on my horse and ride till its legs fall off, hoping never to see you again," Slocum said.

"A week on the job and already you're gettin' uppity."

Jackson Wimmer winced as he tried to shift position on the sofa in the parlor. He was pale under his weather-beaten hide, but there was no trace of fever from his gunshots. He looked to be wasting away, but that didn't come from shooting it out with the outlaws.

"You need a housekeeper to boss around," Slocum said. "Maybe then you'd let me be so I could do my job."

"I need to know what's goin' on out there," Wimmer said.

"You want to meddle. I can run this spread." Slocum saw from Wimmer's reaction that was what the old man feared most. He wanted to be indispensable. Knowing that a younger man was as capable, if not more so, rankled worse than being laid up with bullet wounds. Those shot-up legs probably wore down on Wimmer, too, with a constant reminder. The very rustlers he tried to stop had laid him up. Worse, he'd only accounted for one of them. Slocum had cut the rest of them down to size.

"You call it meddlin', I call it lookin' after my business."

"You should have done better hiring ranch hands," Slocum said. "They're a pitiful lot."

"Had better," Wimmer said sullenly. "Most of the good ones upped and left, like you're threatenin' to do."

"Fancy that. Why'd any self-respecting man take your shit and not get paid better for it?" Slocum heard a fight outside in the yard and itched to go settle it. The cowboys working the Bar-S were worse than he let on to Wimmer, but the man had to know the caliber of those who worked for him. The top hand, Colorado Pete Kelso, spent as much time drunk as he did sober, if the sober times were counted as when he passed out. For two days Slocum had tried to figure out what particular skills Colorado Pete had that qualified him to do anything more than muck the stables. Unless Slocum looked a lot harder, he wasn't likely to find the man's real talents.

"Why'd you take the job, if you think I'm such a skinflint?"

"I needed the aggravation," Slocum said. "Wasn't enough out there." He saw the small smile come to Wimmer's lips. It vanished almost instantly, replaced by a look of pure pain. "Let me get on into town and fetch the doctor. You need more looking after than I can deliver."

"No!" The word came explosively. Wimmer's watery eyes sharpened with anger and he half sat up, in spite of his obvious pain. "You do somethin' dumb like that and you can get on your horse and ride. Won't pay you, will charge you for your room and board whilst you been here."

"Don't like the doctor much?"

"Don't go pryin' where there's no cause, Slocum. You got work to do, don't you? Why ain't you out there doin' it then? Them boys'll like on to kill one another if you don't do somethin' about the fightin'."

"Because a cranky old man wanted to waste my time," Slocum said.

He left, and saw that the fight between two men had drawn quite a crowd. The Bar-S had twelve hands. Six of them, including Colorado Pete, circled the two fighting. They swung

hard and if either had landed one of those blows, the other would have ended up dead. Both men were drunk, and the fight was more of a grunting match. They grappled and shoved and mostly tried to keep from falling down.

"Don't, Slocum. Let 'em fight it out. There's been bad blood 'twixt 'em for a month," said Colorado Pete.

Slocum hesitated. The top hand might be right. Sometimes a fight settled the dust and drained off animosity that otherwise festered into gunplay. He hadn't been on the Bar-S long enough to know.

"How much have those two had to drink?" Slocum peered up at the sky. The sun was barely past noon.

"What's it to you?"

Slocum turned from the men tentatively fighting and squared off with Colorado Pete.

"I'm foreman and I asked you a question. If you're top hand, you have two choices. Answer or get the hell off the Bar-S."

"No need to get testy," Colorado Pete said, looking away. The way his hand twitched near his six-gun made Slocum wary. He doubted Kelso would throw down on him, but from what he had seen, it was more likely the cowboy might consider shooting him in the back.

"No more booze until after evening chuck from now on," Slocum said. "The next man who's drunk before then gets kicked out of the company."

"You'll lose the lot of 'em," Colorado Pete warned.

"Then I'll have enough money to hire a couple cowboys able to do all their jobs." Slocum was past caring what Colorado Pete or any of the others thought of him. In a way, he admired Jackson Wimmer, but the old man's hiring practices left a lot to be desired.

"Whatever you say, Slocum."

"Break it up!" Slocum bellowed, and got the attention of the men in the circle as well as those fighting. "You two got a lot of piss and vinegar in you. Time to turn it against the

rustlers. Both of you, saddle up. Bring along rifles. We're going hunting for rustlers."

The men pushed away from each other, wary of a sneak attack, then looked at Slocum with complete disbelief.

"You cain't mean it. We ain't deputies to go trackin' down rustlers."

"I can track. You two will do the shooting, if it comes to that. Mount up."

Slocum brushed past Colorado Pete and went to the barn. The roan stood nervously in a stall as he entered. Slocum gave it a carrot, calmed it, and then saddled. Although he took better than ten minutes, he still ended up waiting for the other two.

They eventually rode up, apprehensive.

"You makin' us kill rustlers, Slocum?"

Slocum tried to remember the man's name. He had been introduced to the whole sorry lot, but had forgotten their names as soon as he heard them.

"If it comes down to shooting an outlaw or getting shot yourself, which do you figure is better?"

"Shootin' them, I suppose."

"Don't get into no pissin' match with 'em in the first place," said the other.

"If we find rustlers and you try to run, you'll catch a bullet in the back, sure as rain," Slocum said. "I don't miss." He rested his hand on the butt of his Colt Navy. Both men swallowed and nodded. They got the message. Jackson Wimmer had not been quiet about the fight where he had been injured. He might have embroidered his own participation a mite, but he had made it clear that Slocum had been responsible for cutting down the bulk of the outlaws.

"Where we headin'?"

Slocum had pored over a map of the Bar-S for an hour and had located a high pasture that provided most of the forage for the cattle—and which was about perfect for stealing beeves if you were a rustler.

"Follow me," he said, turning his roan's face and heading down toward the road, away from the high meadow. Only when he was sure he was out of sight of the ranch did he veer away from the road and circle westward toward the meadow. The two men with him whispered between themselves. If nothing else, Slocum was forcing them to look at each other as partners rather than foes.

"You recognize him?" Slocum pointed ahead along the winding trail zigzagging higher into the mountains. A lone rider struggled up the steep slope.

"Might be Johnny Stillman."

"He hired on about six weeks back," said the second cowboy. "Came over from Denver, he said, but he didn't know much 'bout the place. Figgered he just rode through. Don't know why he stayed, other than for three squares a day."

Slocum hadn't ordered any of the cowboys to the pasture. The only good reason he could think of why Stillman rode so hard for the meadow was to warn his fellow rustlers. Stillman had always hung back, watching and not saying anything. Slocum had caught him more than once staring hard at him, as if taking his measure. It wasn't so strange for a new foreman to be subjected to such scrutiny, but there had been more in his eyes. Stillman was wondering how good Slocum was with his six-shooter and if maybe Wimmer had brought in a hired gun to stop the rustling.

That was guesswork on Slocum's part, but it fit what he had seen and had felt deep in his gut.

"You think Johnny there's one of the gang rustlin' Bar-S cattle?"

"I'm not accusing him," Slocum said slowly, "but let's say that he's got me wondering what he's up to."

"There! Up there. A lookout's spotted us!"

Slocum had not caught the movement high atop a rocky spire, but the almost drunk cowboy had. He cursed himself for being too wrapped up in his own thoughts. If he intended to stop the rustlers, he had to keep alert.

"Come on, ride like you mean it," Slocum called. He used his reins to whip his roan into a gallop. As he bent forward, he chanced a look behind. He had decided there was a fifty-fifty chance of the two cowboys joining him. It was a good thing he hadn't bet. Both came tearing after him, looking like they were spoiling for a fight.

They got it mighty fast.

The air filled with hot lead all around Slocum as two snipers in the rocks opened up on them. He kept his head down and galloped on, finally leaving the riflemen behind. Both of his cowboys cursed and pissed and moaned, but they stuck with him. He finally reached the top of the long trail and came onto the wide mouth of the lush valley brimming with juicy green grass. Two knots of brown and white cattle grazed nearby. One munched away in peace. The other, maybe fifty head, were being annoyed by two men intent on stealing them.

Slocum headed directly for the rustlers, whooping and shouting as he went. He got within a hundred yards of them before he drew his six-shooter and began firing. At that range, hitting anything was more luck than skill. He got lucky.

One rustler groaned and sagged to the side, falling from his horse. His foot tangled in the stirrup and spooked his mount. The horse lit out like its tail was on fire, dragging the rustler along.

The second rustler had already fled.

Slocum fired a few more times to keep him going, then turned to see how his men were doing. Both had the drop on Johnny Stillman, whose boot had come off and saved him from being dragged to death.

"He confessed, Slocum, he chirped like a bird and said he was guilty. Can we hang him? There's plenty o' trees up here."

"I'm partial to hanging horse thieves," Slocum said, eyeing Stillman closely as he lay stretched out on the ground.

"Not so much cattle thieves. I prefer staking them out in the sun and letting the buzzards pluck out their eyes."

Stillman went pale under his tan. "You can't do that. I got rights. Turn me over to the sheriff."

"The law's a mighty long way off," Slocum said. "The trees are just over there. You prefer getting strung up or staked out?"

"I . . . I'll do whatever you want. Just don't kill me. I got a few dollars." Stillman fumbled in his shirt pocket, tearing it as he pulled out a wad of greenbacks. "Most of a hunnerd dollars."

"Give it to them," Slocum said, pointing to his two cowhands. One reached down and snared the roll of greenbacks with practiced ease. "Count that as your reward for bringing a notorious outlaw to justice," Slocum said to the pair.

They grinned and set about divvying up the money.

"That's a start, but you got to do something else for me," Slocum said, his cold green eyes boring into Stillman's frightened eyes.

"Anything, Slocum, whatever you want."

"Who's the leader of your gang?"

"He . . . George Gilley. He's from down in Texas. I hooked up with him in Santa Fe, been ridin' alongside for close to six months now."

"Six months of rustling, all the way up from New Mexico," Slocum mused. "So you lied about coming from Denver? Doesn't make any difference to me if you rode west or north to get here. You were rustling Bar-S cattle. That's all I care about." Slocum looked hard at Stillman, then shook his head sadly. "All you got to show for it is a hundred dollars, give or take?"

Stillman's head bobbed as if it had been mounted on a spring. He opened his mouth but no words came out.

"I'd say either Gilley is keeping most of the spoils for

himself or you drank up the money mighty fast." Slocum no longer enjoyed toying with Stillman. He had as much information from the rustler as he was likely to get.

"That, whores, some gamblin'," Stillman admitted.

"If you ever want to lie on top of a nickel whore again," Slocum said, "this is what you're going to do. You're going to Gilley and tell him I will string up every last one of his gang when I catch them from now on. If one more cow carrying the Bar-S is lost, I'll come down on his head so hard he'll be sucking wind out of his asshole. You understand?"

"You want him to clear out."

"Don't care if he steals others' cattle," Slocum said. "No more Bar-S cattle get stolen."

"Wh-what about me?"

"He might kill you when you tell him what I just said. If so, he's not likely to believe I mean what I say. There might be a chance he does believe me. I'd highly recommend that you hightail it out of Colorado and find some other line of work you're better suited for."

Stillman's head bounced up and down.

"You got his horse?" Slocum asked.

"Right here, Slocum." One cowboy held up the reins. The boot still dangled from the right stirrup where Stillman's spur had cut into the leather.

"It's property of the Bar-S now. Goes to repay Mr. Wimmer for his losses. That all right with you, Johnny?"

"Yes, sir, it's all right." He had gone pale when Slocum reached across to tap his fingers lightly on the butt of his six-shooter. "You want me to go tell Gilley what you said?"

"Do it," Slocum said. "The boys and me, we got a couple gunmen on the trail leading up here to run down."

"Kin I have my boot back?" He reached for it, but Slocum used his own rein to slap Stillman's hand away.

"Get going or I swear I'll stake you out for the buzzards and coyotes to feast on."

Stillman started walking, then began to run with an un-

even gait caused by the lack of one boot. Slocum watched as he went.

"You think them rustlers will hightail it?"

Both cowboys watched Slocum closely.

"Yes," was all Slocum said.

3

Slocum rode into the town of Heavenly, looking around. He had worked for Jackson Wimmer for more than three weeks and this was the first time he had a chance to take a break. There were two saloons in town, both looking mighty inviting to a thirsty cowpoke. But he rode past them and stopped at the general store. He had accounts to settle before getting down to some serious drinking.

He created quite a stir going inside the cool, dim general store. Two women looked up, then turned to each other and began whispering. From the way their eyes boldly returned now and again to stare at him, he knew the subject of their discussion. It wasn't often a stranger came into a town this size, and when he did it was not likely as the new foreman of a big spread.

"Howdy, you must be Mr. Slocum," greeted the proprietor, coming around the counter and thrusting out a hand the size of a small ham. "My name's Gutherie."

"Pleased to make your acquaintance, Mr. Gutherie," Slocum said. "I heard tell some of the boys at the Bar-S had run up a bill."

"You never authorized 'em, I know, but they took plenty of flour and sugar a week back." Gutherie's expression hardened.

22

"They cut open the bags and rode from one end of town to the other. Turned folks as pale as ghosts by giving everyone a good dusting."

"But mighty sweet, I reckon, if they opened the sugar sacks, too." Slocum turned to the women and touched the brim of his hat. "Not that any in Heavenly need to be any sweeter." This provoked titters from the two. They came to the counter and paid their bills, taking time to look Slocum over more closely. After they left, Slocum got down to business.

"How much of a bill did they run up? My cowboys?"

"More 'n twenty dollars, Mr. Slocum. I—" Gutherie's eyes bugged out when Slocum reached into his vest pocket and pulled out a twenty-dollar gold piece. The tiny coin rang true when he dropped it on the counter.

"I don't cotton much to what they did. I've been keeping a tighter rein on them, and I only found out yesterday what they did. Please accept my apologies and those of Mr. Wimmer."

"That old coot never apologized to no one nohow," Gutherie said. His finger traced the circumference of the tiny coin on the counter. "You payin' fer them mangy cayuses?"

"They work for the Bar-S. We want to keep things friendly. I think the bill for the ranch is a considerable bit more."

"More 'n two hundred dollars."

"We're getting close to selling the herd. You'll get your money then."

"If you got any cattle left," Gutherie said.

"We have plenty now that the rustlers decided to move on."

"What's that? The marshal never said anything 'bout that."

"I came to an agreement with them. About half were from Texas. The rest were Utes off the reservation over in Utah. Convinced George Gilley to send the Indians on their way. After that, it wasn't too hard to get him to move on."

"Can't imagine how you did that. You got a way about you, Mr. Slocum. Don't get me wrong. You might charm the bloomers off the women here in Heavenly, but no

rustler worth his salt's gonna just mosey on because you told him to."

"You're wrong," Slocum said. "I doubt I could charm the bloomers off any of the fine, upstanding ladies in town. As to the rustlers, after four of them ended up with ropes around their neck and dangling from oak tree limbs, Gilley got the idea."

"You done something the marshal never could then. So Wimmer's herd is in good condition?"

"With plenty of them left to turn a decent profit."

Gutherie slid the coin off the counter and smiled.

"Good doing business with you, Mr. Slocum. That son of a bitch should've hired you a long time back."

"Then there's no problem getting more flour and sugar?" Slocum almost laughed at the way Gutherie tensed. He went on. "Cookie's out of sugar and he's threatening to use cement in his biscuits. With flour, they're bad enough."

"You needin' any salt pork? A man can get mighty tired of eating nothing but fine beef."

Slocum did laugh at this.

"The day I get tired of steak's the day they put me in the ground. Here's what we need." Slocum pulled the penciled list from his pocket. "I'll pick it up later on. Might send Colorado Pete in to get it."

"Him," grumbled Gutherie. "He's the one what dusted the whole danged town with flour."

"I know," Slocum said. "If you need me, I'll be over at the saloon."

"The Prancing Pony's the best of the lot. Cagney over at the Double Diamond waters his whiskey."

Slocum waited a moment to hear the rest. It came quick enough.

"Not that I have that big a stake in the Prancing Pony's business, mind you. Just a little."

"The Pony it is," Slocum said. He stepped out into the cool Colorado afternoon and took a deep breath. The odors

of the town hit him like a hammer blow. Heavenly had fewer than a hundred people, but it was still too crowded for his liking. Some of the reasons it seemed so crowded watched him and batted their long dark eyelashes from across the street. Slocum tipped his hat politely to the ladies—different from the two in the general store—and reflected on how mighty friendly this place was. He didn't have to guess much to know how it had gotten its name. So many pretty young ladies certainly made it Heavenly after doing nothing more than chasing cattle with smelly, cussing, unshaven cowboys as his only human companions.

He walked to the Prancing Pony, trying not to appear in too big a hurry. Ridding the countryside of the rustlers had taken most of his time since becoming foreman. After he found Colorado Pete's stash of whiskey and poured it all out, the cowboys had begun putting in a full day's work. Going without liquor had been hard for them, and it had been hard for Slocum, too. He appreciated a dollop now and then to help his digestion.

He deserved a taste as reward for finally running off George Gilley and his gang of cattle thieves.

Slocum paused in the swinging doors and looked around the Prancing Pony. With a name like Heavenly for the town, he had expected Mormons and their nondrinking ways to have a big influence everywhere. He was wrong. Either that or they adhered to a brand of religion that was exactly what he needed. A large picture of a reclining nude woman with hair so red and tits so big that it made Slocum's teeth ache stretched along the wall behind the bar. Inch-deep sawdust gave the saloon a fragrant smell instead of the usual spilled-beer-and-vomit odor found in most watering holes. The tables were neatly arranged and the chairs had been set in precise locations, waiting for customers.

"Come on in, partner," called the barkeep, a small, waspish man with a mustache so thin that Slocum wondered if he poked out eyes if he got too close with it. "You're the

first customer of the afternoon. The rest of the boys'll be in shortly."

Slocum wondered at this camaraderie. What if he preferred to drink alone? That never seemed to occur to the cheerful bartender, who'd already set up a shot glass and poured two fingers of whiskey into it.

"First one's on the house."

"This *is* a right friendly place," Slocum said. "The owner of the general store steered me in this direction. Even if he does own part of the bar, he's to be commended. The Prancing Pony is one mighty fine place."

Slocum lifted the glass in salute, downed the contents, and waited for the kick. Warmth spread throughout his belly, but no kick of nitric acid or gunpowder came. He looked at the empty glass and then at the bottle.

"I'll be switched. That is Kentucky bourbon, like it says on the label. Either that or you made your trade whiskey so smooth that it hardly matters."

"Straight from the vat in Kaintuck," the barkeep bragged.

"You gave me one, now sell me another," Slocum said. He took it into his mouth and rolled it around to savor the texture and flow over his tongue. Swallowing almost seemed a crime, but he committed it anyway.

"Mighty fine."

"You must be the new foreman out at the Bar-S," the barkeep said.

"Word gets around."

"Small town. I heard some of the women cackling like hens that there was a new rooster in the yard. That must be you."

Slocum snorted and shook his head. Seemed the only thing the womenfolk in Heavenly had on their mind was finding a husband.

"Are men that scarce in these parts?"

"Well, not exactly, but the good ones have been run off by the rustlers or left for Denver or the goldfields over in Victor.

Not too many decent ranches around here. The Bar-S is the biggest."

"What about yourself?" Slocum asked. "Don't the ladies find you attractive?"

The barkeep preened, twirling his mustache to even tighter points. When he grinned, he showed even, white teeth under the dark mustache.

"Good of you to say that, but don't go spoutin' it too loud. If my wife ever thought I was lookin' at another woman . . ." The bartender ran his finger across his throat and rolled his eyes.

"Jealous?"

"And mean, but a good woman nonetheless. She's a fine mother to our brood—five kids."

The barkeep rambled on about his family, but Slocum's attention drifted to the nude stretched along the wall and the two women in the general store. They had been decent enough looking, and it had been a long spell since he'd had feminine companionship. He wasn't sure those ladies wanted exactly what he did, though. Looking around, he didn't see any pretty waiter girls or cribs where they might take paying customers. The Prancing Pony was a drinking establishment and nothing more.

"We have a card game or two, but that's all," the barkeep said, as if reading his mind. "In a town where the women outnumber the men, not by much but some, there's no call for a soiled dove. The ones what lit here fluttered away soon enough on their way to Durango or Santa Fe."

Slocum reflected on how different life was in Heavenly compared to other towns he had drifted through. Even in Denver, the number of women was considerably less than that of the men. For whatever reason, Heavenly earned its name. He wasn't the settling-down sort, but a longer stay as foreman of the Bar-S looked mighty appealing.

"Howdy, Doc," called the barkeep. "Come on over. You know Mr. Slocum, don't you?"

The portly doctor came into the bar and dropped his black case on the bar where he could keep an eye on it. He dropped his bowler onto the table and ran both hands through thin gray hair.

"Matter of fact, I do." He thrust out his hand. Slocum shook it. Dr. Gainsborough's grip was strong and the calluses showed he was no stranger to hard work, although he must have been pushing sixty.

"The doc and me talked a while back," Slocum said. "He and his wife were out on the road while I was chasing down some rustlers."

"You and Nora? The three of you? You got along?"

The barkeep's eyes threatened to pop out, making him look like a frog with a mustache.

"No reason why not," Slocum said, wondering at the man's reaction. "I tried to get Doc Gainsborough over to see Wimmer, but it never worked out."

"Jackson is a pigheaded old fool," Gainsborough said. "Wouldn't even let me into the house."

"You and Nora went over and he chased you off?" The bartender swallowed hard and then walked off, shaking his head.

"There something I don't know?" Slocum asked. The barkeep's reaction was peculiar. "Don't you usually make house calls?"

"Me and Nora was returning to town after tending a woman up in the hills. She was all alone and needed some comforting. Gave birth to a baby boy. So, yup, I make house calls."

Slocum frowned. He heard something more in Gainsborough's words, but couldn't figure what it might be.

"You ought to come over to the house sometime when you're in town," Gainsborough said. "Nora fixes up a mean plate of beans." He laughed at this. "She never learned to cook too good, but she's got a powerful lot of other talents."

"Being a nurse," Slocum suggested.

"That, too," Gainsborough said, chuckling. "She's mighty pretty and pretty good in bed."

Slocum tried not to react. It was unusual for a medical man to brag on how good his wife was in bed. But then everything about Doc Gainsborough, Nora Gainsborough, and Heavenly seemed odd.

"Got to go. Nora's not fixing dinner tonight, but we'll be eating in bed, if you catch my drift." Gainsborough slapped Slocum on the shoulder and walked out, whistling. He carried his black bag slung over his shoulder and his bowler tilted at a jaunty angle. Barely had he disappeared than the batwing doors swung inward.

"Seamus, come get yourself a drink," the barkeep called to the newcomer. "You know Mr. Slocum?"

Slocum nodded in the young man's direction. While out tracking outlaws, Slocum had crossed Seamus Murphy's spread. It adjoined the Bar-S and was about a tenth as large. Murphy had not been too accommodating, accusing Slocum of trying to rustle his beeves. It had taken some persuading before the young rancher had let Slocum continue after the actual rustlers.

"I know him. He works for Wimmer."

"Don't get on him like that, Seamus. Mr. Slocum is a right pleasant fellow." The barkeep poured a drink. Murphy cradled it in both hands and knocked it back fast. He choked on it, then set the glass down for another. The bartender silently poured.

"Anybody workin' for that son of a bitch can't be good."

"What's your feud with Wimmer?" Slocum asked. "I haven't been around these parts long enough to know all the details."

"Ask him."

"Wimmer hasn't been too alert since he got shot."

"If he got shot through the heart, that's about the only place where it wouldn't hurt him much. He ain't got a heart."

"Any quarrel you have is with him, not me. Let me buy you a drink."

Seamus glowered, and for a moment Slocum thought he was going to decline. Then he nodded once. The barkeep was quick to fill the rancher's glass.

"To good prices for our herds," Slocum said, lifting his glass.

"I can drink to that," Murphy said. "Don't expect me to drink to Wimmer. Won't do it. Never do it."

"Never ask you to," Slocum allowed.

Seamus finished the drink and left on unsteady legs, never looking back. As he disappeared, the bartender leaned over and whispered, although they were once more alone in the saloon.

"There's been bad blood between him and Wimmer since Seamus took over that dinky spread of his. Truth is, Wimmer's done all he can to drive Seamus off. If Seamus doesn't get top dollar for his herd, he might not make it through the winter. Winters can be fierce here and a lot of feed's needed for the breeders."

"So I've heard," Slocum said. He considered another drink, then decided it was high time for him to collect the goods from Gutherie over at the general store and get on back to the Bar-S. The whiskey had been good, even if the conversation had been peculiar. Small towns kept their secrets close to the vest. Between Seamus Murphy, Doc Gainsborough and his wife, and Jackson Wimmer, there seemed a powerful lot was being hidden. As a newcomer, he wasn't privy to it. Truth was, Slocum wasn't much for gossip, though all this could affect how he did his job on the Bar-S.

"No more? You want me to put that on a tab, Mr. Slocum? You can settle up when you get into town next time."

"That's mighty neighborly of you," Slocum said, fishing in his pocket for a few greenbacks, "but I don't know when that might be. Keeping after the rustlers looks to be a full-time job, along with being foreman."

"Anytime you want, you come on in to the Prancing Pony," the barkeep said. He leafed through the greenbacks, peeled away what he needed, and returned the rest to Slocum.

As he stepped into the street, Slocum heard the heavy pounding of hooves. Colorado Pete Kelso was bent low over his horse, whipping it something fierce until the horse's lathered sides heaved. Slocum wondered if the top hand had galloped the horse all the way from the Bar-S. From the way it staggered, that cruelty wasn't out of the question.

"Slocum, Slocum!" Kelso yanked back savagely on the reins and caused the horse to set all four hooves down hard into the dust so that it skidded several yards.

"What's the all-fired trouble?" Slocum went to the man. He felt the heat boiling off the horse. If it had to walk another ten steps, it would collapse under Kelso.

"Back at the ranch. It's him. Mr. Wimmer!" Kelso was as out of breath as his horse.

"Calm down and tell me what's wrong."

"Slocum, he's dead. Mr. Wimmer's dead."

Slocum stared hard at the seedy man, waiting for the rest of the message to be delivered.

Kelso took a deep gulp of air and blurted, "He's been murdered!"

4

Slocum got back to the Bar-S before Colorado Pete because the top hand's horse had been run into the ground reaching Heavenly. Slocum took the steps leading up into the house three at a time. He stopped on the front porch and frowned. Something struck him as odd, then he realized what it was. The cowboys were going about their business as if nothing had happened.

"Hey, Cookie," Slocum yelled. "Anything wrong around here?"

"Yeah, Slocum, and you know what it is. You fergot to bring back the flour."

Slocum waved off the cook and stared at the door into the house. It was closed. Had Kelso played some kind of joke on him? Slocum knew Kelso was likely to think such a thing would be fun, but he had been too distraught for that. The way he had almost killed his horse told the real story. Nothing might be wrong, but Kelso truly thought Jackson Wimmer was dead, and had ridden his horse into the ground to let Slocum know.

His steps tentative, Slocum went to the door. He started to knock, then opened the door and went inside without announcing himself. The stench in the house hit him like a fist.

He started breathing through his mouth, as he had so many times out on the battlefield where the dead had piled up in the hot noonday sun. He knew the scent and this was no joke. Someone had died.

Slocum closed the door behind him and went into the parlor. Nothing appeared out of the ordinary in the small, cluttered room. When he went to Wimmer's office, he found the opposite. Everything was wrong. Jackson Wimmer was sprawled in a chair behind the desk, head lolling at a crazy angle. Blood from the wound in his temple had spattered across the desk in a fan of now dark red.

"You got here fast, Slocum." Behind him, Colorado Pete Kelso was pressing close. The top hand never noticed as Slocum pushed him away. "My horse was so tuckered out I couldn't keep up. See? That's him. Wimmer. He's dead."

"I noticed," Slocum said sarcastically. The expression on Kelso's face was unreadable now. The distress he had shown in town was completely gone. It might have been the ride giving him time to think, or possibly it was knowing somebody else had the responsibility for taking care of Wimmer now. Slocum just couldn't decide what thoughts ran through Kelso's head. Then he shrugged it off. Kelso wasn't the problem.

He studied Wimmer closely, but there was no horror written there on his face, or much of anything else. His features were entirely slack and his eyes were closed. A curious thought crossed Slocum's mind. For the first time since meeting him, Wimmer looked at peace.

"Damn," was all Slocum could think to say.

Everyone on the Bar-S was likely to be on the trail, looking for a new job soon enough. Slocum had never heard Wimmer mention any relatives, and no one seemed likely to take over the operation of the Bar-S. That meant the county was likely to seize the place for taxes.

Slocum ignored that concern for the moment. He was more interested in what had happened. He skirted the pool

of blood on the floor around the chair and looked closely at Wimmer. A six-shooter lay on the far edge of the desk, butt away from Wimmer. Leaning over, Slocum pressed his fingers into the dead man's throat. The flesh was cool, but not yet as cold as it would be eventually. There was no pulse beating in the old man's chicken-thin neck, but with the hole in his temple, there wasn't much chance of life persisting. Still, Slocum had to check. Wimmer had proven to be a tough old bastard and might cling to a thread of life, even with so much of his blood spattered across the desk and drained onto the floor.

A roar outside in the yard diverted Slocum's attention. He went to the door and saw Colorado Pete Kelso on the porch addressing the gathered cowboys.

"I recognized the pistol on the floor," Kelso shouted. "It wasn't Mr. Wimmer's."

"Whose was it, Pete?" Whoever shouted from the back of the tight knot of men attracted Slocum's attention. He stepped to one side and tried to see who had asked the question.

"I recognized the six-gun," Kelso said, holding up his open hand to forestall more questions. "It wasn't Mr. Wimmer's, no, sir! It was Seamus Murphy's!"

"How do you know that?" Slocum asked. He craned his neck to get a look at the men at the rear of the crowd. He wanted to know who had set up Kelso to answer a question most of the cowhands weren't likely to ask. Whoever had shouted it out was now moving through the small herd of eleven cowboys.

"I seen him with it in town," said Kelso. "That's Murphy's gun. He musta shot our boss. Murdered him!"

"Why'd he do that?"

Kelso turned on Slocum and glared at him.

"You're new around here, Slocum. Seamus Murphy and Mr. Wimmer have locked horns ever since Murphy started running beeves on his spread a year back. He lets 'em eat Bar-S grass, then brags on it in town. He's even been breedin'

his cattle with Mr. Wimmer's prize bull and thinkin' nobody noticed."

"That's true, Slocum," said a man in the front of the crowd. "Murphy took a swing at Wimmer a couple months back. I saw 'im do it outside the Prancing Pony. Ain't no love lost between the pair of them."

"Murphy killed our boss," Kelso said. "What are we gonna do about it?"

"String the Irish bastard up! I'll get a rope!"

The gunshot froze everyone in their tracks. Slocum lowered his Colt Navy and let the muzzle purposefully rove around the gathered cowboys until he had their complete attention.

"Murphy didn't shoot him," Slocum said. "That might be Murphy's six-shooter on the desk. I don't know about that, but I was drinking with Murphy about the time Jackson Wimmer died."

"You was drinkin' with that son of a bitch?" Kelso sounded ugly.

"We were having words," Slocum said. "He's an argumentative cuss, that I'll give him, but we were under the same roof back in town. I don't recall seeing him with iron slung at his side either."

"That's 'cuz he dropped it here when he shot Mr. Wimmer!"

"Why'd he leave it behind?" Slocum knew that logic meant nothing to them. Their boss had been murdered, and they wanted blood. Slocum knew most of them hadn't liked Jackson Wimmer all that much, and doing something about his death would put a dab of balm on their guilty consciences.

"Who knows what goes through a killer's head? He panicked. Is that a good enough reason, Slocum?"

"No, it's not. Murphy was hot under the collar when I talked to him, but he didn't have the look of a man who had murdered anyone and panicked."

"Might be you and him . . ." Kelso's words trickled away

to nothing when he saw the look in Slocum's cold green eyes.

"Go fetch the marshal," Slocum said. "I don't reckon you thought to do that before you rode back."

"He won't care. Him and Wimmer weren't on friendly terms."

"Wimmer wasn't on friendly terms with much of anyone," Slocum said, thinking of what Dr. Gainsborough had said about Wimmer always refusing medical help, no matter how serious it was. Slocum had almost gotten his head bitten off when he suggested that he fetch the doctor to look after Wimmer's gunshot wounds.

"We kin jist bury him," suggested a cowboy. "No need to rile up folks over in Heavenly."

"Get the damned marshal," Slocum said. "Now!"

Kelso jumped a foot, then snaked down the steps and went to get a fresh horse. Slocum waited until Kelso disappeared down the road in a cloud of dust before addressing the mumbling crowd of cowboys.

"You all have work. Get to it."

"Murphy's been a real pain in the ass. We oughta—"

"You oughta do your work and let the law worry about this," Slocum said, drowning out the man's protests. The hands mumbled a few more seconds, then went off in twos and threes arguing over what Wimmer's death meant and what they should do.

Certain that he was not going to be bothered, Slocum went back into the house. The stench staggered him. He opened the windows and left the door standing wide. It was getting cooler as the sun slipped behind the mountains to the west, but inside the house it was still hot enough to bake the dead man's flesh and get it rotting.

Slocum was no expert, but touching Wimmer's throat again convinced him the man had not been dead all that long. He went over all that Seamus Murphy had said to him in the saloon and how long afterward Kelso had arrived with

the news. There was no way Murphy could have killed Wimmer. Slocum picked up the six-shooter from the desktop and opened the gate. Slowly turning the cylinder, he saw that a single shot had been fired. He put it back on the desk where he had found it, then looked more closely at Wimmer.

The bullet had gone into Wimmer's right temple and blown most of the left side of his head across the desk. Even if the initial shot had not killed him, the copious blood gushing from the wound had killed him within seconds. Slocum peered at the entry wound and found a ring of unburned gunpowder. The muzzle had been close enough to the man's head to burn some of the wispy white hair there. Slocum had seen men with belly guns cram them into their foe's gut and fire point-blank. The bullets hadn't killed the intended victims, but setting fire to their clothing had.

Murphy's six-gun had been no farther than an inch or two from Wimmer's head when it was fired.

Slocum tried to figure out how this could have happened. Did the murderer threaten him and Wimmer mouth off? An infuriated man might squeeze the trigger and send Wimmer to the Promised Land. If Wimmer and whoever had killed him argued, why wasn't Wimmer shot in the front? And why drop the gun onto the edge of the desk, on the side opposite from Wimmer's head wound?

It didn't make a whole lot of sense.

Slocum pawed through the papers stacked to one side on Wimmer's desk, but saw nothing remarkable there. A few drops of the rancher's blood dotted the papers, but from where Wimmer sprawled in his chair, it was quite possible the blood had spattered this far.

Slocum sank down into the chair opposite the desk and leaned back, staring at Wimmer. He shook his head sadly.

"You crazy old coot. Not a friend in the world and about everyone you ever met turned into an enemy." Slocum leaned back, laced his fingers behind his head, and stared up. For a moment he wasn't sure what he saw. Then he stood and

looked closer. He finally climbed to the desktop and examined a hole in the wood ceiling beam.

He pressed his index finger into the hole.

"About .45 size," he decided. "How'd a slug get shot into the ceiling?" He rubbed the area around the hole, pushing away a few splinters. The hole was recent and the wood as yet untouched by air and dust. Whether it had been made today or last week, he couldn't say. With only one bullet fired from the six-shooter, this round was something of a mystery.

He hopped down and prowled about the room, not sure what he was looking for. Something struck him as wrong, but he couldn't put his finger on it. Although he hated to admit it, the situation was pretty much as Kelso had said. Somebody had come in, drawn the six-gun, and killed Jackson Wimmer.

"Using Seamus Murphy's six-gun," Slocum added.

Slocum left the room and went to sit on the porch to wait for the marshal. What had started as a pleasant day had turned ugly mighty fast.

5

"Damn mess," muttered Marshal Zamora as he walked around, carefully avoiding the dried pool of blood soaked into the rug. The portly lawman shook his head in disgust. "Glad I'm not havin' to clean up the blood. The whole damn carpet's probably ruined. Expensive, too."

"You didn't much like him, did you?" Slocum asked.

"You always ask questions you know the answer to, Slocum?" Zamora started to spit, but couldn't find a cuspidor. He went to the window, stuck his head out, and decorated a plant below with a brown gob of chaw. He took his time coming back, pointedly ignoring Wimmer to stare at the gun on the desktop. "That's Seamus Murphy's gun. I remember him waving it around a week or two back. I took it away from him."

"What'd you do with it?"

"Gave it back the next day. Kelso bent my ear the whole way out here about how Murphy's the killer. Got to admit he might be right. That's Murphy's piece."

"I was in the Prancing Pony with Murphy about the time this happened," Slocum said.

"Time's a crazy thing when you're drinking. Downright loco," the marshal said, finally pushing his hat back on his

39

forehead and taking his bandanna to wipe away sweat. When he finished that chore, he dabbed at a drop of tobacco at the corner of his mouth. "Damn hot in here. Not a breeze blowing outside to get rid of the heat." Zamora coughed. "Or the stench. Damn, but he's stinking up the place."

"What are you going to do?" Slocum watched Zamora turn Murphy's six-gun over and over in his hands, looking at it from every possible angle as if it might give him some clue not obvious to a casual observer. He finally tucked it into his belt when nothing new came to him.

"Need to find the bullet that blew out Wimmer's brains," Zamora said. "That about finishes what I can do here."

"He didn't go far from where he's sitting," Slocum said.

"Think he might have been standing when he was shot and then fell into the chair?" Zamora looked at the chair legs.

"Doesn't look like it. If he fell back that hard, the chair would have tipped over," Slocum said. "Besides, he's behind the desk. Mighty hard for him to move around. When I found him, his legs were up underneath, as if he was sitting when he was shot."

"Or flat out collapsed. This rung's loose and the back leg's cracked." Marshal Zamora pressed down on the straight back of the chair and it suddenly collapsed, sending Wimmer heavily to the floor. Zamora jumped away in surprise.

"You figured that out pretty good, Marshal," Slocum said. "He was already sitting down." Slocum came over and sighted along an imaginary line where Wimmer's head would have been. Even turning a little after being shot, the bullet wouldn't have gone far. Slocum looked back at the bullet hole in the ceiling. There was no way Wimmer could have been in the chair and had the bullet end up in the wood beam. Before Slocum could ask the marshal about this, Zamora let out a yelp of victory.

"Got it." Zamora drew a knife from a sheath at his belt and worried away at a cabinet. From the wood he dug out a

slug and held it up. "Can't say for sure, but it looks like it's got blood on it."

"It went into the wood at about the right level if Wimmer was sitting down when he was shot, too," Slocum said. He stepped off the distance. The bullet had bored its way into the cabinet only six feet from the body.

"That's all I need from here." Zamora matched the slug with the bore of Murphy's six-shooter. "It fits."

"There are close to a dozen men here at the ranch who might have shot him," Slocum said. "But none of the cowboys even heard the shot."

"I talked to a few of them. As loco as it sounds to me, they were actually working. You whipped 'em into shape, Slocum. I'll give you that."

"They knew which side of the bread their butter was on," Slocum said. "Nobody on the Bar-S profited from Wimmer's death."

"Most all of them hated his guts, but you're right," Zamora said. "I know men like your cowboys. If any of them had plugged Wimmer, they'd be in California by now."

"What do you do now?"

"Reckon someone could have sneaked in and put this slug into his head who wasn't Seamus Murphy," the marshal said. He said the words, but did not harbor any doubt that Murphy had been the gunman. "I'll hie on back to town and ask some questions."

From the way Marshal Zamora held the six-shooter responsible for the killing, Slocum knew what that meant.

"Murphy?"

"Have to ask how his gun came to be the murder weapon," Zamora said. "You don't think he did it?"

"I already said I was with him about the time Wimmer was killed. His alibi can't get much better than that."

"I'll still need to find out why him and his six-gun weren't together," Zamora said.

"I'll ride with you."

Zamora looked a bit sour at this, but said nothing as he left. Slocum mounted and rode alongside the lawman, but there wasn't much talking all the way into Heavenly. Both were lost in their own thoughts, but Slocum's kept rolling in big circles like a wheel without getting anywhere.

Zamora dismounted in front of the tumbledown shack that served as the town jail. From its condition, Slocum guessed there wasn't much call to lock up the citizens of Heavenly.

"I saw him at the saloon when I passed by," the marshal said. "You can come along but keep your tater trap shut. Understand, Slocum?"

"All right," he said, trailing the marshal to the Prancing Pony. Zamora hitched up his gun belt and went in, not bothering to see if Slocum followed.

Slocum edged into the saloon in time to see Zamora bump up against Seamus Murphy, forcing the young rancher back against the bar. The marshal's considerable belly held Murphy in place when he tried to slide first one way and then the other.

"I got questions," Zamora said.

"I didn't do anything," Murphy said, his words slurred from too much booze. The owner of the general store and bar stood at the far end, watching what went on. Slocum looked around for the regular barkeep, but didn't see him. Gutherie obviously looked after his interests in the bar by working here if things got slow at the general store.

"How'd your gun get out at the Bar-S then?"

"I lost it. Maybe it was stolen. I don't wear it much and keep it hung on a peg near my front door. Anybody could have swiped it."

"And who might that have been?"

Zamora glared at Murphy while he kept him pinned against the bar.

"How should I know? Maybe it was Wimmer. He hates me."

"And you hate him, don't you?" The lawman was coming to a decision Slocum didn't like. For whatever reason, Murphy didn't see what it was.

"I hated him as much as he did me."

"I think you plugged him, got scared at what you'd done, dropped yer six-shooter, and hightailed it back to town to pretend nothing had happened."

"He's not that good an actor, Marshal," Slocum said.

"Why are you sticking up for him?"

"I don't have a dog in this fight. I just don't see any way he could have killed Wimmer and ridden into town so close to the time Wimmer was killed." Slocum looked hard into Murphy's bloodshot eyes. The man was on the point of passing out from too much whiskey. He might be trying to drown his guilt, but Slocum thought the binge was due to something else. "You leave your horse at the town livery?"

"I don't have money enough for that," said Murphy.

"Then there'd be about everyone in town seeing that his horse was lathered from galloping here so fast. When Kelso came to tell me, he damn near killed his horse pushing it all the way from the Bar-S. Wimmer hadn't been dead more than an hour when Kelso left the ranch to tell me."

"I'll ask around," Zamora said. He backed off, letting Murphy breathe a little easier. The respite did nothing to stop the young rancher's smoldering anger.

"You hate me, just like Wimmer did. You all do. Every damn one of you in town hates me."

"Not much to like, is there?" With that, Zamora swung around and left.

"You got a reason for tying one on?" Slocum asked when the marshal was gone.

"I feel like it. What's it to you, Slocum? You think you can do Wimmer's dirty work for him and steal my ranch and cattle? I'm not going to give up that easy."

"Wimmer's dead. Are you so soused you didn't hear what the marshal said?"

"Yeah, right, he's dead. Between the ears. And in the heart. The man isn't even human."

Murphy tried to catch himself against the bar and missed, landing heavily on the sawdust-covered floor.

"He's drunker than I thought," Gutherie said, peering over the top of the bar. "He told me to cut him off when he ran though the ten dollars he dropped on the bar. Reckon I ought to stop settin' drinks in front of him?"

"He drink it all up?"

"Yeah, surely did," the bar owner said. He looked at Slocum and nervously wiped at his lips. "You think he killed Wimmer?"

"I told the marshal I didn't think so. He was in here about the time Wimmer was killed. Your barkeep can back me up on that. You think Murphy can be in two places at once?"

"Well, I dunno," Gutherie said. "No good askin' after Bennett. He lit out with Lulu Garston. Left his wife and five young 'uns." Gutherie looked puzzled. "Why he'd leave with a woman like that is beyond me."

"Might be he got tired of his wife and brood," Slocum said, not caring one whit about that. He remembered how the barkeep had said his wife was stepped-on-rattler mean. "When was the last time you saw Murphy?"

"I been tryin' to remember if I saw him wearin' his six-gun when he came into town earlier. Can't rightly say, one way or the other. He might have been packin' then."

"He wasn't," Slocum said. He stared at Murphy, heaped up on the floor. There was no reason for Slocum to get more involved than he already was. "To hell with it," he said, bending down and getting his arm around Murphy. He heaved and pulled the rancher to his feet. Murphy grumbled and cursed the whole way outside into the cool afternoon wind blowing down from the north.

"There's the varmint! Lynch him!"

For an instant, Slocum thought the men from the Bar-S had come to town and picked up their refrain again. Then he

saw a dozen of the Heavenly townsfolk shaking their fists at Murphy and working themselves up into a killing rage.

"Hold on," Slocum said, dropping Murphy into a chair on the boardwalk. He started to slide out. Slocum grabbed him by the collar and pulled him upright. "Does it look like he's in any condition to kill anybody?"

"He's in plenty good condition to swing for killin' Jackson Wimmer!"

Another in the crowd shouted, "He's drunk so he won't have to face hisself. That means he's guilty as sin!"

"It means he's drunk," Slocum said, stepping between Murphy and the crowd. "He was with me in the saloon when Wimmer was shot. From all I can tell, he never left, and got himself likkered up till he can't see straight."

"The marshal said his gun killed Wimmer."

"That doesn't mean *he* killed my boss," Slocum said. Logic meant nothing to the crowd. Zamora had not been too politic about asking after Murphy's whereabouts and had given them the idea there was only one suspect—the man whose gun had killed Jackson Wimmer.

Slocum considered which of the men to shoot first if it came to that—he was not going to turn Murphy over to a lynch mob, even if he had thought the man was guilty.

A couple of men in the front saw the resolve in his eyes and the steadiness of his hand resting on his six-shooter. They backed up into the crowd and created enough of a disturbance that the rest of the men began thinking of other things. When they did, the mob began to dissolve into individuals, and Slocum saw that the threat was over for the moment.

"Go on about what you're doing. Go into the Prancing Pony. Gutherie's got plenty of good booze in there waiting for you. Or go home. Just go somewhere else."

A few grumbled but the crowd dispersed, leaving Slocum with a very drunk Seamus Murphy. The rancher muttered and thrashed about, fighting unseen demons in his stupor. Slocum grabbed him by the collar and heaved him to his

feet. Murphy stumbled and went forward. Slocum did nothing to slow his progress over the railing and into the watering trough. Two horses reared and tried to pull away as the man splashed into the water.

"Wh-whatsit?"

"Go home," Slocum said.

"Who're you to dunk me like that?" Murphy tried to get out of the trough and fell back. Only then did he realize he was sober enough to complain and still too drunk to do anything about it. "Help me out, will you?"

Slocum grabbed the young man's arm and pulled, getting him to his feet in the street. Murphy dripped water and created a tiny mud puddle around him.

"You stood up for me, didn't you, Slocum?"

"Let everyone in town cool off. Not a one of them even liked Jackson Wimmer, but all of them were willing to string you up."

"I'm glad he's dead," Murphy said.

"I don't much care if that's the liquor talking or some truth boiling up from your miserable soul. Shut your mouth and go about your business. Marshal Zamora will figure out what happened."

"I didn't kill him."

"I know," Slocum said. But in spite of all he said, he was beginning to wonder if Murphy might somehow have plugged Wimmer, then made it into town to argue with him. He shook his head. It didn't seem possible.

But as he watched Murphy stumble off, his gait uneven from too much whiskey and his cursing of Jackson Wimmer slurred, Slocum had to wonder if Kelso and Zamora and the rest of the town might not be right.

6

"Pleasant day for a plantin'," Colorado Pete Kelso said.

"No day's a good day to be buried if you're the one going six feet under," Slocum said. He wished Kelso would ride with the rest of the cowboys from the Bar-S and not bedevil him with his observations on life and mortality.

"Fer Wimmer, it's a good day. Fer us, it is, too. I never cottoned much to the way he treated me. I'm surprised you got along so well with him, Slocum. You look to have a nasty temper."

"I understood him," Slocum said.

"How's that?"

Slocum looked at Kelso and silenced the man. He'd had enough of the endless rambling. He hated going to funerals and, even more so, hated attending this one. Nobody in Heavenly had much liked Wimmer, but Slocum had gotten along with him because he refused to take any guff off the old man. There had been a grudging admiration between them that could never have blossomed into friendship, not that it mattered now. Wimmer was dead and, as foreman of the Bar-S, Slocum was responsible for seeing that the funeral went smoothly. That it took every last penny he had been paid during his stint as foreman on the Bar-S mattered

47

less to Slocum than having to listen to some preacher's platitudes about Wimmer going to a better place.

As they rode toward the small cemetery on the far side of
Heavenly, Slocum saw a small knot of people already gathered
inside the knee-high stone-walled enclosure. Off to one side
stood Marshal Zamora, arms crossed and his big belly jutting
out over his broad, hand-tooled gun belt. Standing at the
grave was the preacher, nervously flipping through pages in
his Bible, probably trying to find a passage that summed up
what a son of a bitch Wimmer was without actually saying
so. Slocum was moderately surprised to see Gutherie in the
small crowd of other merchants. They talked with much waving of arms and hand motions to the undertaker.

Slocum tried to remember the man's name and couldn't.
That might have come from his distaste of funerals, or the fact
that the undertaker didn't have much of a personality. All he'd
done was nod, smile, and write down whatever Slocum said.
He might not have said more than a dozen words, and those
were all insincere, practiced words of sympathy. Slocum
would have admired him more if he had come right out and
said what he thought of Wimmer. After all, there was no family to coddle or friends to insult.

Slocum pointed to the side of the cemetery outside the
wall where the Bar-S hands could leave their mounts. Some
of them would have ridden right up to the grave, their horses'
hooves digging at the other graves. For all that, some of the
cowboys would have downed a pint of Gutherie's whiskey,
then pissed on Wimmer's pinewood coffin.

"Shall we begin, Mr. Slocum?" The unctuous undertaker
folded his hands in front of him. "The day's turning mighty
hot, and I'm certain you don't want folks to get heat stroke."

"Do you?"

"What?" The question took the undertaker by surprise. "I
don't understand what you mean."

"If some folks keeled over from heat stroke, they might
die and you'd get that much more business."

"I take it that you don't want pictures," the man said, dropping his oily tone and glaring at Slocum.

"Not of the corpse, not of the people here, not of anything," he said. Slocum motioned for the cowboys to gather around the grave. It took several seconds for them all to realize they ought to remove their hats. Only when they had did Slocum give the preacher the signal to begin the service.

Slocum's attention began to drift when the preacher got to the part about "I am the resurrection and the life." Slocum looked around and wondered who the nattily dressed man crowded close to the marshal was. He wore a tie with a headlight diamond the size preferred by tinhorn gamblers, a jacket of fine linen, and tiny eyeglasses that pinched down on his nose. There was no hint of watery eyes peering through those lenses, though. His blue eyes were bright and sharp and fixed on Slocum like a hawk might examine a rabbit on the run.

Soon enough, the service ended and the preacher gave the undertaker the signal to begin shoveling dirt into the grave and on top of Wimmer's coffin. Every spadeful of dirt echoed and made Slocum wince just a little. He turned and told the cowboys, "Take the rest of the day off. There's no need to get back to the ranch before dawn, but you'd better not be so hungover you can't do a day's work tomorrow."

They let out a whoop and tore off for the two saloons. Gutherie grinned at Slocum, tipped his hat, and hurried off. He had customers to get drunk.

"Mr. Slocum, I'd like a word with you. And with Mr. Kelso also." The well-dressed man's manner was brusque and all business. That suited Slocum just fine. He wanted to partake of some of Gutherie's whiskey and get the taste of dirt and death out of his mouth.

"This here's Mr. Longmont," the marshal said. "He's the only attorney in town."

"Must make for a hard life, having to sue yourself all the time."

"I always win in court that way, Mr. Slocum."

"Seems like the opposite would be true, too."

"Please come to my office for the reading of the will. I want Mr. Kelso to hear it, too."

"Will?"

"Mr. Wimmer's. You knew that he had registered a new will only last week, didn't you?"

"I didn't know he had an old will, much less a new one," Slocum said. "Don't make no never-mind to me, one way or the other." He rubbed dust off his lips. The ride into Heavenly had been a dry one, and standing around in the late summer sun had worn him down, just as the undertaker had predicted. An entire bottle of whiskey from behind the bar would suit him just fine, and Longmont was keeping him from it.

"Better do it, Slocum." Marshal Zamora fixed him with a cold stare.

"Come on, Pete. The sooner they have their say, the sooner we can drink."

Colorado Pete grumbled, but followed along behind. Slocum set the pace just a little faster than Longmont or Zamora could keep up with. He wasn't sure where the lawyer's office was, but Heavenly wasn't big enough for there to be many places to hide it.

When he saw Doc Gainsborough and his wife, Nora, down the main street, he headed for them. His instincts were right because the sign over the door behind the doctor verified that this was the lawyer's office.

"They got us all rounded up, I reckon," Gainsborough said.

"You weren't at the funeral," Slocum said. "Don't like seeing a patient put underground?"

"Jackson was hardly Ben's patient. That old galoot refused all treatment, though it was offered more than once," Nora Gainsborough said tartly. She started to continue her defense of her husband and his doctoring skills as Longmont

came up, key in hand. He pushed past them and opened the office door.

"Please, come in. I hope I have set out enough chairs."

"I kin stand," Kelso said. Slocum wished he had spoken up first. If he stood near the door, he could be the first out and on the way to the Prancing Pony Saloon when the lawyer was done with his speechifying.

Slocum found himself seated across the huge oak desk from the lawyer, with Ben Gainsborough and his wife to his right. To his left, Marshal Zamora shifted restlessly in the straight-backed wooden chair.

"Mr. Wimmer made a new will shortly after you became Bar-S foreman, Mr. Slocum." Longmont cut open an envelope that had been sealed with wax. He spread it out on the table in front of him. "I certify that this is a legal document, duly witnessed and executed by Jackson Wimmer's hand and of his own free will."

"Get on with it, will you, Longmont?" Marshal Zamora was as antsy as Slocum, but the lawman appeared to know what was coming.

"The Bar-S is a prosperous ranch and worth a hundred thousand dollars, more or less."

Slocum nodded. He wasn't the sort to tally up values like that, but the extent of the land and the number of cattle running on the range were easily worth that amount. If he had to put a value on it all, he might have guessed it was worth even more. With attention to actually running the ranch, it could be twice as prosperous in a few years.

"There's a lot of legal mumbo jumbo, but it all comes down to this. Wimmer left the Bar-S to you, Mr. Slocum. In its entirety."

Nora Gainsborough shot to her feet and stormed out of the office. Ben Gainsborough clapped Slocum on the shoulder and said, "Congratulations. This makes you a rich man, Mr. Slocum." He quickly followed his wife from the office.

Marshal Zamora left without uttering a word. Colorado Pete Kelso simply said, "Shit."

Slocum had to agree with the top hand.

His top hand.

7

John Slocum stood on the porch of the ranch house and stared into the sunrise. He had returned from Heavenly having had only two shots of whiskey all night long. He had moved his gear from the bunkhouse into the house and stared at Wimmer's bed when he got back ahead of all the ranch hands. He could have taken the mattress and fine Irish linen off the bed and replaced them so he wouldn't be sleeping in a dead man's bed. Instead, he had paced around the house, avoiding the office where Wimmer had died, and eventually settled on the porch. He had watched the stars fade away as the sun rose, and then simply stared at the new day.

"New day," he mused. "What do I do with a ranch?"

Slocum spoke aloud as if expecting an answer—and he heard the voice deep within saying this might be his last, best chance to settle down. Heavenly was filled with lovely ladies. He was the most prominent rancher throughout the area now, with holdings making him unbelievably wealthy. That he had done nothing to earn it rankled, though. Wimmer must have known Slocum would worry over that. It was one thing to put in a day's work as foreman and earn his keep. It was another having it all handed to him on a silver platter held by a dead man's hand.

But the trail got lonely year after year, and settling down had its benefits. His parents had been content all their lives at Slocum's Stand, up until they had died while he was away at war. He had returned and been the sole owner. Slocum touched the watch in his vest pocket. That was the only legacy his brother Robert had left him. He had always assumed the two of them would split the family farm and live out their lives after the war.

Robert had died during Pickett's Charge, and Slocum had returned to recuperate after getting gut-shot by Bloody Bill Anderson for questioning how their commander, William Quantrill, had ordered every male of fighting age slaughtered in the Lawrence, Kansas, raid. He had needed quiet to regain his strength, but a carpetbagger judge had taken a shine to the farm and wanted to raise thoroughbreds on it. No taxes paid during the war, he had lied. Forged documents backed up the demand. Pay up or get out.

When the judge had shown up at Slocum's Stand with a hired gun to enforce the eviction notice, the man had indeed taken ownership of the farm, but not the way he'd intended. Slocum had left two fresh graves by the springhouse and had ridden west without so much as a backward look. The wanted poster on him for killing a federal judge, even a corrupt one, had dogged his trail for years.

The Bar-S was his chance to settle down and become part of a community that would not care about a Reconstruction judge's death so many years earlier.

"Mine," he said, looking at the land now lighting up with warmth as the sun rose. All that the sun touched in his sight was his because a cranky old coot had bequeathed it to him.

But it wasn't his. He had done nothing to earn it. Running off a gang of rustlers hardly counted as enough of a deed to merit the Bar-S as a reward.

He'd sell the ranch, split the money equally with all the cowboys, and then move on. It was the right thing to do.

"Slocum, I want a word with you."

"What is it, Kelso?" Slocum saw how Colorado Pete's gait was a bit unsteady. He and the rest of the hands from the Bar-S had about drunk the Prancing Pony dry, and it still showed.

"I want a cut."

"What are you talking about?"

"The ranch. The goddamn ranch! You don't deserve to git it all. I want a share. A big one. I been here for two years and you ain't even worked the range for two months."

Slocum said nothing and let the man rant on. It was true he had been at the Bar-S for a short time, but he had run off the rustlers. Slocum wasn't sure Kelso had ever tried. The man lacked the spine for such a chore.

"Might be you ought to split it with me right down the middle, you and me partners," Kelso said.

"What about the rest of the hands?"

"What about 'em? This is somethin' me and you have to thrash out."

"Don't start thrashing, Kelso," Slocum said softly. "You won't like the way that turns out."

"You can't git the whole damned ranch and not let me have some of it. Ten thousand dollars. That sounds fair. The Bar-S is worth a hell of a lot more 'n that."

"What'll you do if I don't give you a cut? Quit?"

"Gimme what I'm askin' for or you'll regret it!"

Slocum paused as he stared into Kelso's bloodshot eyes. A smile curled his lips. It wasn't a friendly smile.

"I'd regret it if I gave you more than your salary. Truth is, I regret giving you that much since you don't do much to earn it."

"I'm top hand here! I—"

"Mr. Slocum! Mr. Slocum! We got big trouble!" A young cowboy stumbled up, out of breath. "Me 'n Jenks was up in the high meadow countin' steers. They're back. They came back!"

"The steers? What are you sayin'?" Colorado Pete turned

too fast and almost lost his balance. Slocum knew if he had been a step or two closer, he could have heard the liquor sloshing around in the top hand's belly.

"Shut up, Kelso. Ryan's trying to say that the rustlers are working our herd again." Slocum fixed his cold stare on Kelso. "The rustlers are stealing *my* cattle. You have a problem with that?"

Pete Kelso looked confused. He started to speak, and then clamped his mouth shut.

"Good. Ryan, get a half dozen men who can ride without falling out of the saddle and be sure they've all got rifles. Be here in the yard—*my* yard—in ten minutes. We're going to get ourselves some scalps. Rustlers' scalps."

"Yes, sir!" Ryan dashed off, leaving Kelso behind.

"You still working for the Bar-S or are you going to pack your gear and leave? Your choice, Kelso. I want you to have made it by the time I get back."

"You ain't doin' me out of a good job, Slocum, any more 'n you can do me outta my share of the Bar-S."

"Then ride with me while we're hunting down the outlaws. I don't want to lose one more steer to rustlers."

Kelso walked off, grumbling. Slocum fingered his six-shooter, considering how easy putting a slug into the man's back would be to end all the bickering. He had decided to sell the Bar-S and split the money among the cowboys until Kelso had demanded a share. Running a going concern like this ranch wouldn't be all that hard, and settling down might not be such a bad idea. Succeeding at running the ranch would spite Colorado Pete Kelso.

Slocum ducked into the house, found a rifle with ammunition, and then went to saddle his roan. It was time to start defending Bar-S property. *His* property.

"They was o'er yonder," Ryan said, standing in the stirrups and pointing across the grassy valley. "Jenks, he saw 'em cuttin' out a dozen head and herdin' 'em up the far side."

Slocum sat stock-still as he listened and watched and considered where the rustlers might have taken the stolen beeves. Where Ryan pointed wasn't their likely destination. The canyon walls rose sharply not a mile beyond. Unless the cattle thieves had found a pass through the mountains, there was no way of driving the cattle much farther. More likely, they had headed due north with the small herd, thinking to get out of the valley to sell it in North Park. The few days on the trail would give them plenty of time to run the Bar-S brand.

"What you thinkin' on, Mr. Slocum?" Ryan's eagerness was matched by that of his partner, Jenks.

"Which way would they go?" Slocum said aloud as he worked out the trail in his mind and the best way of catching the rustlers.

"It'd be like he said, Slocum," Kelso piped up. "They'd head due west."

"You know a way out of the valley and over the mountain?"

"Well, there's got to be one. Sure, there's one over there," Kelso said, arm waving vaguely in the direction of the towering hills.

"They went north," Slocum said. "Kelso, you and Jenks find where they rounded up the cattle and follow the trail. North."

"And me, Mr. Slocum? What about me?" Ryan asked.

"We'll cut across the valley and try to head them off," Slocum said. He wished Ryan had roused a couple more men from their liquor-induced stupor. Even if there were only a handful of rustlers, two men fighting them would be a chore. Depending on Kelso for any help was out of the question, but he didn't want to send the top hand off by himself to get into any mischief. While he didn't know Jenks as well as he did Ryan, he thought the young cowboy would keep Kelso honest. Or as honest as possible.

"What if we come up on 'em?" Jenks sounded eager for a fight.

"Wait for us to come in from the other side. More likely, we'll find them first. You come running when you hear gunfire," Slocum said. "Now you and Kelso get moving. I don't want to track them varmints in the dark."

Jenks and Kelso rode away at a brisk trot. Slocum settled his hat and made some guesses as to how far and how fast the rustlers might have traveled. Then he took off at a gallop, Ryan close behind.

As he rode, Slocum called out to Ryan, "How did you decide to come up here? Weren't you and Jenks celebrating?"

"Truth is, Mr. Slocum, neither me nor Jenks drinks."

"Didn't find yourselves a filly or two for celebrating with?"

"That wouldn't be right either, not till I get married. It's ag'in my religion."

"Glad you decided to look after the cattle. You probably saved me losing a hundred head or more."

"We're just doin' our job, Mr. Slocum."

By the time his roan began to flag, Slocum saw the trail leading northward. He drew rein and dismounted, studying the ground carefully. His finger traced out a hoofprint.

"They came from the north sometime last night, but they haven't come back this way. We got in front of them."

"Then we got 'em," Ryan said eagerly. He drew his rifle from the saddle sheath and cocked it. "What are we waitin' for? Let's git 'em!"

"Settle down," Slocum said, getting back into the saddle. "Our horses are tuckered out. We'll walk them for a spell. Keep a sharp eye out for the cattle. Might be the rustlers are having problems with them."

"They're only cows," Ryan said.

"After I ran off Gilley, what remained might not be as good when it comes to rustling," Slocum said. He had swapped stories with others around Heavenly, and had come to the conclusion whoever was rustling from their herds now was likely more comfortable robbing a stagecoach than stealing beeves.

"I hear 'em!"

"Quiet," Slocum said. He heard the lowing cattle, too. The faint puff of wind wouldn't carry sound far. That meant the rustlers were less than a half mile off, probably working the herd up through a stand of pines.

"What do we do, Mr. Slocum?"

"Keep your rifle ready and let's go." Slocum pulled his own rifle out and laid it across the crook of his left arm as he rode. He brought the rifle up and aimed the instant he saw two heifers pop out of the wooded area.

"Where're the rustlers? All I see are them cows."

Slocum waited as he sighted down the barrel of his rifle. At this range, he could choose which eye he wanted to shoot out of a rustler. But nobody rode after the twenty head of cattle that eventually meandered from the woods and stopped to graze on a juicy patch of grass.

"I wasn't wrong. Me and Jenks, we saw men stealin' them cows, Mr. Slocum. I swear it." Ryan sounded so insistent that Slocum had to believe him.

"How many men did you see?"

"Not more 'n four or five. It was hard to tell, but there was more 'n me and Jenks wanted to handle on our own. We're not cowards. We—"

"You did the right thing," Slocum said, cutting him off. He waved Ryan ahead toward the left side of the herd while he circled around the right. The cattle looked up incuriously, then went back to their afternoon snack. Slocum reached the rear of the herd before gesturing for Ryan to join him.

"You stay with the cattle. I'll backtrack."

"You think Jenks and Mr. Kelso already got 'em?"

Slocum wasn't sure what to think. The rustlers had simply abandoned twenty head of cattle for no good reason. There hadn't been any gunfire to signal a tussle between the Bar-S cowboys and the outlaws, but Slocum had to find out for sure.

"If I'm not back in an hour, come looking for me," Slocum said. "Do it quietlike."

"What if I hear shootin'?"

"Stay put. You might drive the cattle back out into the center of the valley where we can keep a better watch on them. Otherwise, you stick close to them."

Slocum plunged into the dark, cool stand of pines and followed the winding trail. The lack of light made it hard to see the hoofprints in the dirt, which was littered with pine needles. He wanted to find the spot where the rustlers had stopped herding and had lit out.

On the far side of the copse, he drew rein when he saw two mounted men a quarter mile off, face-to-face and arguing. Their words got swallowed by distance, but the way they gestured told him this was not a friendly meeting. Slocum pulled his field glasses from his saddlebags and trained them on the men.

He recognized Colorado Pete Kelso right away. The man he argued with had his face turned so Slocum couldn't get a good look, but from the condition of his clothing, he had been on the trail for a long time. Just as Slocum thought he would finally see the unknown man's face, the rider trotted away and rounded a bend in the trail that took him out of sight.

Slocum tucked his field glasses away and faded back into the forest, finding a spot a few yards off the trail to sit and wait as Kelso rode toward him. The top hand passed within ten feet without noticing him. Slocum started to follow, then changed direction and rode back down the trail. Kelso wasn't going to cause any trouble, but the mysterious man he had argued with just might. Until he found where Jenks had gone, Slocum wanted to keep in the shadows as much as possible.

He reached the spot where Kelso and the other rider had exchanged their heated words. A quick look at the ground all torn up by horses' hooves told Slocum they had been here far longer than he had watched. He used his reins to switch his roan into a trot. It was dangerous riding a trail with as many bends and blind twists in it, but an urgency built in his gut.

If he caught the man Kelso had talked to, answers might come pouring out.

He had barely ridden another quarter mile when he saw a horse drinking from a brook running near the trail. He rode over to it and saw blood on the saddle. Slocum thought this nondescript nag was Jenks's horse, but he couldn't be sure, until he pawed through the saddlebags and found a letter addressed to the cowboy.

Slocum reached down, snared the horse's reins, and tugged the nag away from the stream before it bloated. Pulling hard on the reins until it trotted easily on its own accord, Slocum continued back down the trail, more alert than ever. The unknown rider could not have done anything to Jenks without Slocum hearing. That meant whatever had happened to the young cowboy had taken place earlier, maybe right after he and Kelso started on this trail.

"Ohhh," came the moan. Slocum turned, his rifle swinging around. The sound came again, this time accompanied by rustling in some undergrowth near the trail. He dismounted and advanced slowly, alert for a trap. All he found was Jenks, on hands and knees, his bare head caked with blood. Slocum knelt and pulled the cowboy around so he sat on the ground.

"What happened?"

Jenks had a hard time focusing his eyes. Slocum saw that the pupils were different sizes, showing how hard the man had been hit on the head. With gentle probing, he found a two-inch-long gash in the back of the man's head. The size matched pretty well with a pistol barrel.

"Slugged. From behind. Tried to . . . I don't remember what I tried to do. Mr. Slocum?" Jenks collapsed. Slocum let him fall to the ground so he could listen for the other rider. Wherever the rustlers had gone, they must have passed Jenks—or Kelso.

Without a word, Slocum got his arm around the cowboy and got him to his feet. Jenks struggled to walk. Seeing that Jenks would never be able to ride without tumbling from the saddle, Slocum heaved him up and over his horse belly-down.

He looked like a sack of meal, but he proved harder to lash into place. There wasn't any easy way to throw a diamond hitch on the young cowboy to keep him from falling off.

Slocum decided to let the man Kelso had argued with ride on so he could get Jenks cared for. He turned north and led Jenks's horse with its burden back to where Ryan and Kelso circled the milling cattle.

"Mr. Slocum!" Ryan called. "Is he all right?"

"Got clobbered from behind. Otherwise, he's in good enough shape," Slocum said.

"Who hit him?"

Slocum looked hard at Kelso.

"Who was it, Kelso? Who hit Jenks?"

"How should I know? We started out together, but he rode off. Never said a word to me what he was doin'. Just lit out like he had a wild hair up his ass."

Slocum considered asking about the man Kelso had argued with, then decided that it was better to stay quiet on this. For the moment. It might have been only a pilgrim passing through, but it was more likely one of the rustlers.

"You didn't see any trace of them? The rustlers?" Slocum asked.

"Nary a trace," Ryan said. "Is he gonna be all right? Jenks is lookin' kinda pale."

"Why don't you and Kelso get him into town and let Doc Gainsborough poke and prod him some?"

"What are you gonna do, Slocum?" Kelso was not—quite—belligerent.

"The rustlers got off somewhere. I'm going to try to track them down."

"That's mighty dangerous, Mr. Slocum, doin' it all alone. I kin git Jenks into town by myself. You and Mr. Kelso can—"

"Better hurry," Slocum said to Ryan. "Your partner's not going to heal draped over the saddle like that."

"Yes, sir," Ryan said. He was more concerned with his friend than anything else. But Colorado Pete Kelso kept

glaring at Slocum, until he finally wheeled his horse around and trotted after Ryan and Jenks.

Slocum waited awhile, then set off after the three men. Finding the rustlers would do him no good. There was nothing to prove they had ever tried to steal any Bar-S cattle, and he had no stomach for going up against an entire gang of rustlers.

But he did want to know what Kelso did once he thought he was out of sight. Slocum left behind the cattle as they grazed, knowing they would find their way to water eventually, where they could be rounded up and moved back into the main herd. As he rode, he wondered about Kelso and how Jenks had come to be laid up the way he was.

The answer seemed obvious.

8

It was well past sundown when Ryan and Kelso got the injured cowboy to Heavenly. Slocum wanted to ride up then and tell Doc Gainsborough that he would see to the bill, but Colorado Pete veered away from the doctor's office and rode to the far end of town, leaving Ryan to deal with Jenks by himself. Slocum remained in shadow as he watched Kelso ride off. He knew Ryan wouldn't let up until the doctor tended his partner, so he rode slowly after his top hand.

Slocum wasn't sure what he expected to see. If Kelso had tied up with the man out in the valley, that would have been about perfect for Slocum. A quick draw, get the drop on the two men, and then take them to Marshal Zamora to find out what they were up to. The Bar-S had lost close to fifty head of cattle since Wimmer's death. Slocum reckoned a good talking-to with Kelso and any of the men he thought to be rustlers would recover most of the beeves.

Again, Kelso surprised him. The man rode along until he saw a woman dressed in a shimmering white dress hurrying along the boardwalk. Like the needle of a compass, Kelso veered from his course and rode to where he could call out to the woman. Slocum got closer so he could overhear.

"You can't go on denyin' you want me, sweetie," Kelso

called. "Come on. Jist you 'n me. We can find a place real private where nobody could see us—"

"I want nothing to do with you, Mr. Kelso," the woman said angrily. "Leave me alone."

"What'll you do, honey buns? What *kin* you do? If you'd jist say 'yes,' I'd take real good care of you."

She turned so that a ray of light from inside the Prancing Pony shone on her face. Slocum had seen pretty women in Heavenly, but none held a candle to her. Her raven's-wing dark hair glinted with almost blue highlights. Her bow-shaped lips pursed as she worked on what to say to the cowboy. Slocum wasn't able to hear what she did say because it was pitched too low and a considerable ruckus from inside the saloon drowned out her words, but Colorado Pete reared back as if he had been scalded.

"You li'l bitch. Nobody says anythin' like that to me!"

"I did, sir. Leave me alone."

She turned, her white skirt swirling about her ankles. Slocum rode closer, ready to intervene when Kelso jumped to the ground and went to her. His filthy hand left sooty marks on her white sleeve as he spun her around.

She stepped closer and Kelso backed off, hand dropping from her arm when she kneed him in the balls.

"Leave me alone. Can a man with even your small . . . brain understand that?"

"You ain't seen the last of me," Kelso said. He growled like a wild animal, mounted, and galloped away.

Slocum was torn between following Kelso and going to the woman to apologize. She took a deep breath, causing her breasts to rise and fall delightfully under her starched white bodice. This might not have been all that decided him, but it was enough. He dismounted and went to her.

"Ma'am," Slocum said, taking off his hat. "My name's John Slocum, and I saw what happened just now."

"Did you? Is spying on private citizens what you do? And whoever would pay you for such a thing?"

"I . . . work out on the Bar-S Ranch." Slocum saw her stiffen and reach into her purse. The glint of light off a der-ringer told him what had run off Colorado Pete Kelso—other than being kneed in the groin. She had closed the distance between them and thrust the pistol into Kelso's belly before kicking him. The worst marksman in the world could not have missed at such range with her target being in-capacitated.

"It figures," she said.

"No, it doesn't," Slocum said, taking her meaning. Any-one working with Kelso had to be just as boorish. "If he bothers you again, I'll fire him."

"You're foreman at the ranch?"

"I was hired for that very job," Slocum said, not elaborat-ing. If she had been in town, she would have known both his name and that he was the new owner of the Bar-S. For some reason, Slocum thought telling her all that would scare her off. He wanted her to stick around.

"I apologize. It's so seldom I find anyone from the Bar-S with even a speck of civility." She smiled. Just a hint, a small curl of those perfect lips, but her bright blue eyes danced also, telling Slocum she no longer put him in the same box as Colorado Pete Kelso.

"It's me that has to apologize," Slocum said. "Kelso is hardly housebroke, but that's no excuse for bad manners."

"Thanks," she said. "Now, if you'll excuse me, I have to go." She smiled a little more at him and then pushed past. He caught a hint of her perfume. His nostrils flared even as his imagination ran wild. Slocum turned to see her get into a buggy parked in the alley alongside the saloon. She expertly took the reins and snapped them to get her horse moving. With another jerk on the leathers, she headed down the main street in the direction opposite to that taken by Kelso.

He stepped out into the street and watched her disappear into the night. Only when she had gone did he realize he had not asked her name.

"Hey, Mr. Slocum, what're you doin' out in the middle of the street?" Gutherie stepped out from the Prancing Pony. "All the fun's inside. All the whiskey, too."

"Did you see the woman who just passed by?"

"I did," Gutherie said cautiously, as if Slocum intended to trap him into some confession of misdeed.

"Who is she?"

"If you got any sense, you'll give her a wide berth. She's not—well, jist say she's not your type."

"You do know her. What's her name?"

"That's Suzanne Underwood," the barkeep said as if the name burned his tongue.

"She live around town? I haven't seen her before."

"She don't live in town that I know of, and I would if she did. She travels a whole lot. Now, come on in and I'll set you up with a drink. On the house."

Slocum looked sharply at Gutherie. The man was a friendly sort who aimed to please customers. The friendly rivalry, which may not have been all that peaceable at times, with the other saloon counted some toward the offer, but Slocum thought the bar owner only wanted to keep him away from Suzanne Underwood.

"I've got other business to tend to. Thanks."

"Make that a rain check. You come in any time tonight 'fore midnight, you get the free shot of whiskey."

Slocum nodded. Gutherie looked almost fearfully in the direction Suzanne Underwood had driven, and hurried back into the saloon. Slocum stared into the distance, wondering where Kelso had got himself off to—and wondering about Suzanne Underwood. He finally shook his head. Small towns developed likes and hates as if they were people. Whatever Suzanne Underwood had done—or not done—had made at least one of the townsfolk scared to even talk about her.

"A man could get into a powerful lot of trouble with a woman who looks like her," Slocum said to himself. He wondered how much trouble he was willing to get into.

Slocum mounted and swung his horse around to ride past the doctor's surgery. Gainsborough's wife, Nora, stood outside. She smiled at him as he rode up.

"Coming to check on your cowhand?"

"Reckon I am. How's he doing?"

"Ben got the cut all stitched up. Didn't look too fearsome, but you know how head wounds tend to bleed. You got him to help in time."

"Glad to hear that. Would you tell Ryan to stay with Jenks, if that's all right with Doc Gainsborough?"

"Ryan didn't say anything about you coming to town. He said he left you out in the high meadow running down rustlers."

"Got tired of that," Slocum said. "Or maybe not." From the corner of his eye, he saw Kelso riding past in a mighty big hurry. "Much obliged for looking after Jenks." Slocum touched the brim of his hat and tore out after Kelso.

The man rode so hard that Slocum lost him within a half mile of town. Rather than keep chasing him and maybe lose him in the dark, Slocum veered off the road and went to higher ground. He might spot a dust cloud and get some idea what had gotten Kelso so fired up.

It took the better part of an hour to make his way through the rocks and onto a ridge looking out over the road leading from Heavenly into a small valley on the other side. The almost full moon had risen, giving the land a silver aspect that made it about the most beautiful thing Slocum had ever seen. A coyote howled in the distance, but the animals moving close by betrayed the abundant life in the area. There was the slither of a snake and the thump of a rabbit running, the heavier tread of a fox and maybe even the soft snarl of a mountain lion. It was all there, mingled with the smells of things growing and cattle grazing.

Slocum traced out the main road the best he could in the dark, but Kelso was nowhere to be seen. He turned his attention to the valley, wondering who grazed their cattle here.

A small herd, hardly twenty head, moved fitfully in the night. They might be searching for water, or there might be some other reason to get them moving.

Slocum worked his way down the slope. The mountain lion might be hunting for a late-night dinner—or there might be two-legged predators on the prowl. If the rustlers couldn't make off with Bar-S cattle whenever they wanted anymore, they might move on to other spreads.

It didn't matter to Slocum whose land he rode on if he bagged a rustler or two.

He made his way down the slope opposite to town, finding this less rocky. By the time he reached the bottom of the ridge, he had found a narrow, winding road. He turned in the saddle, spotted the Big Dipper with its pointer stars, and finally located the North Star to orient himself. With the moonlight so bright it was almost like riding on a cloudy day, he turned to ride deeper into the valley. Then he heard a horse coming from behind, probably from town. He had never noticed the turnoff from the main road onto this one because there had been no reason to come this way before.

Might be that Colorado Pete Kelso had found some reason, since Slocum couldn't figure anyone else who might be out riding at this time of night. He trotted off the road to a shallow arroyo where he could watch for the approaching rider. Less than five minutes passed before he saw a solitary horseman. The man had his hat pulled down and was all hunched over, and Slocum couldn't identify him. It might have been Kelso, but it as easily could have been President Grant out for a midnight ride.

The rider suddenly halted and looked around, seemingly staring straight at Slocum. Wheeling about suddenly, the rider rocketed away. Slocum considered the matter for a moment, then his curiosity got the better of him. If this was Kelso, he wanted to ask his top hand what he was doing here. If it was a rustler, Slocum could eliminate one more of the

bastards. And what man out for honest reasons would hightail it like that?

Putting his heels to his roan's flanks, Slocum got out of the arroyo and onto the narrow road. It was not as smooth as the main road because it didn't have as much traffic, but Slocum could rely on the bright moonlight to avoid any prairie-dog holes or potholes that might cause his horse any trouble.

He urged his horse to a faster gait, watching the road for trouble.

He should have watched alongside the road for snipers. The shot tore past his face so close he felt the bullet's hot breath against his cheek. Involuntarily, he reached up and touched the heated spot, expecting his hand to come away bloody. The bullet had not even broken skin.

Slocum pulled back hard on the reins and got his horse to stop. He studied the terrain for a likely spot for the sniper to hide. He saw nothing, but heard pounding hoofbeats going away. Rather than pursue blindly, Slocum rode ahead a few yards, wary of a trap. He had seen one rider. If the man was a rustler, he might have several cronies with him. All of them could be lying in wait.

The thunder of the hooves faded in the distance, and Slocum heard nothing else but the soft wind blowing across the valley. He inhaled deeply. Grass. Cattle. Good earth. The scent of things alive and flourishing. But it carried no scent of men.

Slocum touched his cheek again and winced. The slug had not broken the skin, but it felt as if it had burned a path. He snapped the reins and brought the roan to a gallop. Bending low, Slocum intended to present the smallest target possible if he did ride into another trap.

But after another mile down the road, he had not been on the receiving end of any more gunfire. He thought the rider he had spotted was also the unseen sniper. Not only did the man want to keep his identity a secret, he was willing to kill, too.

As his horse began to tire, Slocum slowed. As he came to

a trot, he caught a flash of silver out of the corner of his eye. Slocum bent lower and slowed his horse more, swinging it around in a wide circle. He approached the spot from the far side. Shadows and the confusion of shapes made it difficult to tell what he had seen. Slocum jumped to the ground and drew his six-shooter as he approached.

A buggy wheel turned slowly, spun by the rising wind. When he realized this was what had caught his attention, he walked faster. Details fell into place. A buggy had over-turned on the road and rolled over completely at least once to end up on its side. The contents of the buggy littered the slope all the way to the road.

Of the buggy's horse, he saw nothing.

But as to its driver, he saw her pinned under the broken driver's seat.

Slocum knelt beside Suzanne Underwood and pressed his hand against her throat. Her pulse was thready and her breathing shallow.

She was alive.

9

Slocum got a grip on the edge of the buggy and lifted it away from the unconscious woman. Suzanne Underwood moaned enough to let him know she wasn't close to dead yet. He worried that a broken piece of wood from the side of the buggy might have impaled her. Getting his feet squarely under him, he heaved and threw the buggy onto its wheels. It tottered for a moment, and then ran on downhill a few more feet before stopping. The back wheel slanted at a crazy angle and the seat was entirely out of kilter.

Kneeling again, Slocum cradled her head. The woman's dark hair carried streaks of dried blood. He smoothed those away from her face. In the moonlight, she seemed more dead than alive, but her lips, appearing black, moved as she muttered something. He bent over and listened, but could not understand what she said.

"Come on," Slocum said, getting his arms around her so he could lift her from the ground. He staggered a little on the slope and went to his horse. The roan smelled the fresh blood and shied away, forcing Slocum to put Suzanne down and catch at the reins so he could drag the horse back toward him. He unlooped his canteen from the saddle and dripped water

on her lips. They looked deathly black in the moonlight, but he knew that any red turned this shade. He had seen more than his share of blood this color at night.

"Umm, what . . ." She tried to sit up, but he gently held her down.

"You rolled your buggy over. Lie still. You've got quite a bump on the side of your head."

Slocum watched her reaction closely. Some men with as hard a blow as Suzanne had sustained never woke up. She was lucky.

"You're from town. Mr. Slocum?" Again, she tried to sit up. He pushed her back down. "Oh, posh, let me go. I'm not a one to be coddled."

Slocum rocked back and let her struggle to her feet. She was shaky, but managed to take a few steps without falling over.

"What happened?"

"I . . . that's not too clear." Suzanne touched the side of her head and winced. Even this light touch reopened her wound. "I was driving along and hit a rock. The wheel wobbled. I remember that. The buggy veered, my horse began bucking, and the next thing I remember clearly is seeing you." She smiled wanly. "Thank you."

"I might be able to fix your buggy and get you on your way."

"My horse ran off."

"Horses don't run too far, even scared ones. If the buggy will roll along without the wheels falling off, finding the horse will be easy enough." Slocum cocked his head to one side and judged that sunrise was only an hour or so away. Finding her horse wouldn't be too difficult then. He hadn't passed the horse, so it must have either run back in the direction Suzanne had come from, or taken off to one side of the road or the other.

They went back to her buggy. Slocum grabbed her around the waist as she stumbled.

"Thank you again, Mr. Slocum. I don't seem as steady on my feet as I had thought."

"That was quite a bump you got," Slocum said. He saw the swollen lump oozing blood through the tangle of her dark hair. "We need to find a stream and get it washed off."

"My buggy first," she said. In spite of her insistence on this, she didn't pull away from Slocum, so he kept his arm around her. She made a tidy bundle, her hip bumping against his as they looked at the buggy's damage.

"I can get that wheel nut tightened," he said, shaking the right wheel. "I don't have the tools, but any rancher would have them. Where were you heading?"

"Seamus Murphy's ranch is the closest," she said.

Slocum wondered why she was going there, then realized she had not said she was—not exactly. Her knowledge of the countryside was better than his, although he had been in Middle Park for some time now. The times he had ridden across Murphy's ranch he had been chasing after rustlers.

"Might be just as good to go back to Heavenly and get the tools there," he said.

"I can wait for you," she said, but her tone implied that wasn't what she wanted to do. She looked around, just a touch of consternation on her lovely face.

Slocum had his own problem with her remaining alone. The rustler who had taken a potshot at him was still roaming around, possibly with several others of his gang. Leaving Suzanne Underwood alone was a foolish thing to do in her condition.

"I can look for your horse, but it might be for the best if you'd just ride behind. I can get the tools, fix your buggy, and track down your horse while you rest up in town."

"That's not the sort of place for me to rest. Not after—"

"After what?"

"You're about the only one in town who'll even speak to me, Mr. Slocum."

"Why are they bound and determined to treat you like an outcast?"

"I'd rather not burden you with my tale of woe, sir," she said.

From the set to her shoulders and the way her lips thinned to little more than a razor slash, he knew prying the information from her would be difficult. Although curious, Slocum didn't care that much about small-town gossip and small-minded gossips.

He swung into the saddle and reached down so she could take his hand. With a smooth motion, he pulled her up behind him. She settled down and put her arms around his waist. It made being shot at worthwhile.

"Next stop, Heavenly, Colorado," he said. His roan tiredly plodded away. Slocum decided he was in no particular hurry since he enjoyed the feel of Suzanne so close behind him. She laid her cheek against his back as they rode. He felt her even breathing, and wondered if she had fallen asleep after a couple miles.

Slocum fell into the easy rhythm of the horse, warmed by Suzanne's arms around him and her body pressing tightly against his. The shot that sang through the still, early morning took him completely by surprise.

"Hang on," he called to Suzanne. She lurched and almost tumbled from horseback as he bent forward and put his spurs to his horse's flanks. Barely had the horse run a dozen yards when another shot rang out.

Slocum went sailing through the air, Suzanne still clinging to him. His horse's front legs crumpled and its head hit the ground. After that, Slocum was not sure what happened. He skidded along the road on his belly with Suzanne clinging to him. By the time he came to a halt, Slocum was torn up and bloody and madder than hell.

He stood and the dark-haired woman slid to one side, sitting in the dirt and staring numbly at him.

"Stay down," he snarled. Slocum slapped leather. His Colt

Navy came easily to his hand, but he could not find a target. He slowly turned to his left, hunting for the spot where the sniper had fired. Nothing moved in the dim light of predawn. Knowing it was foolish, Slocum fired several times at clumps of vegetation likely to hide a rifleman. Dust and dried leaves were kicked up, but nobody was flushed from hiding.

Knowing better than to continue firing wildly, Slocum reached down and grabbed Suzanne's hand. He dragged her upright.

"Go," he said. "Run. I'll cover you."

"Who's shooting at us?"

"Go!"

A foot-long tongue of orange flame licked out from a spot not fifty yards away. The distance was too great for a handgun, but Slocum emptied his six-gun and succeeded in driving the sniper back under cover. He backed away, then untied his saddlebags and slung them over his shoulder. His spare ammo was inside, as well as a spare pistol. Only when he had reloaded did he go after Suzanne. The woman had run farther than he expected. She was either more scared than he had anticipated, or she had taken his warning to heart.

"Go higher," he ordered. "Into the rocks. We can get under cover there."

"I . . . I'm out of breath." He heard a rasp that sounded as bad as if she had tuberculosis.

"You'll be out of breath forever if you don't keep going." Slocum swung about and damned himself for not bringing his Winchester along, too. He aimed at the bushes where the sniper had been, adjusted for the fitful wind, and elevated his muzzle to arc his round into the vegetation. His first shot missed by yards. His second took off a twig at the side of the bushes. A third shot hit dead center. Slocum stopped firing and waited.

This time he was met with a volley of rifle fire from three different positions. The men were all bad marksmen, but

they threw enough lead in his direction to force him back, again cursing that he had left his rifle behind.

"John, are you all right?"

"Keep moving. Go higher. Into the hills. There are at least three of them after us."

"Three?" Suzanne said weakly. "Who are they?"

"Probably rustlers," he said. "It doesn't much matter who they are. All I need to know is that they shot my horse, and if we don't keep moving, they'll shoot the both of us."

Slocum hung back as Suzanne made her way through the rocks. Tracking her progress was easy because of her labored breathing. He shifted position, expecting the rustlers to come after them. The more he thought, the more he reckoned that these were some of the varmints still remaining on the range to steal his beeves. Not only his, since they were on the wrong side of the mountains, but Seamus Murphy's also.

He waited close to ten minutes, letting the first blush of sunrise scrape across the eastern sky. He peered into the rising sun and then went after Suzanne. He did what he could to cover their tracks. She had left a trail a blind man could follow. After a half hour, he stopped and stared at a sheer, stony face with three caves in it.

He looked for tracks, but she had left none across the rocky ground. Unerringly, he went to the cave on the right.

"Suzanne, how deep's the cave?"

"How'd you know which I picked? There are three."

"This was the only one with a bear in it," he said.

She let out a yelp and rushed out. He caught her in his arms and spun her around. Her feet fought for traction, but he held her off the ground.

"Bears! I didn't know. We can't—" She looked into his green eyes and got mad then.

She hit him with her fist as she said, "You're joshing me!"

"Was a bit of fun, I admit," he said, putting her back onto the floor of the cave.

"You scared me."

"There's no bear in here," Slocum said.

"How'd you know I'd pick this one? I didn't even look at the other two."

"Folks tend to bend to the right when they choose. Get lost in the desert and you'll walk in circles, always heading to the right and never knowing it."

"I didn't know that," she said, "but then I've never been lost in the desert. I prefer land with more contours." Suzanne sat down on a rock and looked up at him. "Are they going to find us? The men who shot at us?"

"I waited to see. They might have decided killing my horse was good enough for the night. If they are rustlers, they're probably not too inclined to face a man when they shoot at him. Too much chance he'll shoot back. I made it clear that I wasn't going to let them simply murder me."

Her bright blue eyes drifted to the six-gun in its cross-draw holster.

"You have the look of a man who's accustomed to using his six-shooter."

Slocum dropped his saddlebags and then sat on the floor of the cave opposite Suzanne. He paused a moment before saying anything. It had been fun getting his arms around her, just as hers had been around him during their short ride. She was a mighty fine-looking woman, even with her black hair all mussed and dirt smudges on her face. The way she sat, her skirt was hiked up so he could see her ankles and even some of her bare legs.

She noticed his attention, and pulled her skirt up a mite farther, giving him a flash of her inner thigh.

"You think they'll be here any time soon?" She pulled her skirt up even more. "So we would have enough time?"

"Enough time for what?" Slocum felt himself getting harder, thinking about how he would while away an hour or so.

"For me to thank you. You saved my life."

"Maybe not. You took quite a bump on the head, but—" Slocum didn't get any further. Suzanne rose, gathered her skirts, and stepped forward, putting her feet on either side of his legs. She lowered herself slowly, swishing the skirt about seductively. Her butt settled down on his upper thighs.

Their faces were only inches apart. Slocum reached up, laced his fingers through her tangled hair, and pulled her face to his for a satisfying kiss. Their passion built until they were devouring each other. When her red lips parted just a little, Slocum's tongue worked its way into her mouth for a bit of erotic dueling. She was moaning softly now, and her breasts heaved under her bodice. Without breaking off the kiss, Slocum slipped his hand from the back of her head and pressed it into her breasts. Even through the thick cloth he felt her nipple hardening. He squeezed down until she sobbed aloud with need.

"Oh, John, John," she whispered hotly. "I want you so."

She rearranged her skirt and reached down to find the buttons on his fly. By now he was achingly hard. His erection finally popped up long and proud when she pulled open the last of his buttons. They both gasped when she rose slightly, positioned herself, and then lowered her hips. His erection slid into her hot, slick core.

She cried out at the intrusion. Slocum fought to keep from getting off like some young buck with his first woman. She was tight around him, and when she moved about, it pulled and squeezed at him in delightfully new ways.

She began moving, rising, twisting about, lowering herself in a back-and-forth swish of her hips. Every time she took him fully, she tensed around him, paused for deliciously long moments, and only then did she begin to rise. He slid in and out with increasing friction that burned and boiled.

He pushed away her bodice and exposed a breast. He took it firmly into his mouth—as much as he could cram in. The marshmallowy flesh yielded slightly as he pressed his tongue into the hard nub until it pushed back. Then he caught only

the coppery nip between his lips and sucked powerfully as she continued to rise and fall around his hardness.

They each gave as good as they got. Suzanne sped up. Slocum stroked over her back and cupped her buttocks. His mouth explored her breasts and the deep canyon between them. And then they could not restrain themselves a moment longer. She might have got off before he did. Slocum couldn't be sure—and it hardly mattered. Locked together, they struggled to share even more of one another, and then Suzanne sank down on his lap, her head resting on his shoulder. Her hot, ragged breath came in his ear as she whispered, "You went limp on me."

"Wasn't for lack of trying to keep it up longer."

She laughed and sat back. Her eyes danced.

"It's *my* turn to josh you. That was wonderful, John. I need you saving my life more often so I can reward you again."

"Don't need one to get the other," he said. She laughed at this and got off his lap, sitting beside him in the cave. Their arms pressed together; then Suzanne lifted her leg and draped it on top of his before laying her head on his shoulder.

"I wish we could just stay here like this forever."

"Forever's a long time," he said.

"You really own the Bar-S?"

The question took him by surprise. All he had told her was that he worked there as foreman.

"Reckon so. Don't know what made Wimmer give it to me, but he did. I've never owned a spread that large or profitable."

"The son of a bitch," she said. Acid dripped from every word as she gripped his arm hard. Her fingers dug into his flesh until he wondered how badly he would be bruised.

"You didn't cotton much to Jackson Wimmer? Doesn't seem that many in Heavenly did. I'd think you and the townsfolk would have that in common."

"I hated the ground he walked on."

"I'm the one walking on it now," Slocum said. Her death grip on his arm lessened. "What did you have against Wimmer?"

"How'd he die?"

"There's some debate going on about that. Colorado Pete Kelso found a six-shooter beside the body but that gun wasn't Wimmer's. That makes it look to be murder."

"Murder? I'm not surprised."

"Kelso and, I reckon, Marshal Zamora think it was a rancher out this way named Seamus Murphy who did it."

"No!"

Slocum considered her angry denial.

"He didn't do it," he finally said. "He was getting drunk with me in the Prancing Pony about the time Wimmer got himself shot."

"Are you and Mr. Murphy drinking buddies?"

"I wouldn't call it that. He has a powerful lot of anger dammed up inside for anyone to be his friend." Slocum considered how alike Seamus and Suzanne were in this regard. The mere mention of Jackson Wimmer set her off.

"Who do you think killed him?" she asked.

"I can't say, but I have my suspicions."

"Kelso," she said firmly. "It was Kelso. He's as much a bastard as Wimmer. Well, not that much. He's got a mean streak, too, but he's not evil down deep where it counts."

"You seem to have them pegged pretty well. What did you have against Wimmer?"

Slocum couldn't ask any more directly than that, and again Suzanne Underwood edged away from directly answering. She slipped down so she lay on the cave floor, her face in his lap. Slocum wasn't about to press for an answer when her lips were put to a better use than answering foolish questions.

10

"Are you still dizzy?" Slocum asked. He watched as Suzanne Underwood tried to stand. She had to brace herself against the cave wall, and even then her legs proved wobbly.

"I don't know what it can be. I was fine last night."

"You were more than fine," he assured her. They had remained in the cave throughout the previous day, waiting to see if any of the rustlers tracked them down. Slocum had watched from a vantage point higher up on the mountainside and had seen no one in the peaceful valley where they had been ambushed. Even so, he had decided it was better to lie low and let Suzanne rest. The bump on her head refused to stop oozing blood, no matter what he did to stanch the flow. He had seen wounds like that before, and they usually took care of themselves with rest. Having to hike back to Heavenly was not going to help her in the least.

In spite of his determination to have her do nothing but rest during the night, their activities together had been anything but restful. In a way, he was glad he didn't have to mount up and ride off right now since he was a mite sore. Clambering over the rocks proved strain enough.

"Thank you, John. You—oh!"

He caught her as she slipped and fell. She would have

landed facedown if he had not swung her around and eased her to the cave floor.

"You're going to have to rest up. I'll go on into town and get the tools I need to fix your buggy."

"That's a long walk."

He considered this, and remembered all he had seen while he had been atop the butte looking into Murphy's pastureland. Another way might exist that wouldn't require him to leave her for as long as a trip into Heavenly would take.

"It's closer for me to keep going over this mountain and get onto Bar-S land. If I'm lucky, I can find one of my cowboys and ride with him to the ranch house." The words rang true but odd to his ears. He was the owner of a vast ranch. He was more used to being the one riding the range for someone else.

"That sounds better. I'm not sure anyone in town would give you the time of day if you told them what you wanted the tools for."

"You don't like those people much, do you?"

"It's mutual."

Slocum almost asked why again, and then held his tongue. Even being straightforward with his questions about Jackson Wimmer and how Suzanne lived and why she didn't get along with the townspeople produced no answers. She flat out would not answer, and he saw no reason to pursue it now.

"I don't like leaving you, but I don't have much choice. Can you use a six-gun?"

"I can." Suzanne did not hesitate with her answer. Slocum took that to mean she was being truthful. He rummaged about in his saddlebags and found his spare Colt Navy. It took a few minutes for him to check its action and to load it before handing it to her. She expertly checked the chambers again, then lowered the hammer slowly.

"It's a good idea you have, letting the hammer rest on an empty chamber," she said. He nodded in agreement. She had done more than pretend to make certain the six-gun was in

good condition. She had actually examined it and understood what she was doing.

With a quick kiss, he left her. The sun poked above the eastern horizon again, today promising rain. Leaden gray clouds floated in the distance, coming off the Rockies and swooping westward toward them like misty soldiers to a battle. For the moment there wasn't much to worry about, but as the day warmed, the rain would begin pelting down.

Slocum hitched up his gun belt and began the hike. He kept his bearing as true as he could when he topped the ridge and worked down on the far side. By noon he recognized the sprawl of a meadow—his meadow.

He took a deep whiff and caught the odor of wood smoke and coffee. Homing in on it like a hawk to a rabbit, he found two of his hands enjoying a midday meal.

"Howdy, men," he said, flopping down across from them. "You got a cup of coffee for the boss?"

"Yes, sir, Mr. Slocum. Didn't hear you ride up."

Slocum took the proffered tin cup filled to the brim with barely drinkable coffee. It was too hot and too bitter and tasted as good as anything he had ever drunk. After he finished, he told them what had happened.

"You want us to git on over the hill and chase them varmints down?"

"No, I need to get back to the ranch house and scare up some tools to fix Miss Underwood's buggy," he said. One of the men frowned. The other looked more concerned with the rustlers. Slocum had to ask the one who frowned, "You been in Middle Park long?"

"Came to Heavenly more than a year back."

"So you know what the trouble is between Miss Underwood and the people in town." The words were hardly out of his mouth when he realized the cowboy wasn't going to tell him anything either. For such a friendly small town, the residents clammed up when it came to what ought to be gossip shared freely.

Slocum rode double with one of the hands, and got back to the ranch by mid-afternoon. He looked around for Kelso, but did not see him. Rather than ask, Slocum found a horse to replace his roan, again marveling that all the horses in the corral behind the barn were his, then threw tools into a buckboard and hitched up a double team. He remembered to fetch a rifle and ammo from the house before leaving.

The hands loitering around the ranch watched him leave. Some whispered among themselves, having heard his story from the two men he had ridden back with, but the others stared at him with something approaching anger. Slocum knew that Colorado Pete had been sowing the seeds of discontent, inciting them to anger over not having the ranch put up for sale and the proceeds divvied up among the lot of them.

He made good time down the main road and along the spur running off it. This portion of the trip was enough to knock his teeth out. Rocks and potholes in the narrow road forced him to drive slower than he liked, but he soon got to where Suzanne's buggy had taken a tumble down the verge of the road. He jumped down, gathered his tools, and worked for twenty minutes straightening the wheel by tightening the nut holding it. He unhitched one horse from his team and put it to the buggy, and got back to the road without having to exert himself any more than necessary.

Slocum wiped sweat from his face as he studied the mountain where he and Suzanne had taken refuge. He tied the horse pulling the buggy onto the rear of the buckboard on the far side from his new horse, a gelding that stepped along with an assured gait. He preferred the roan, now dead some distance back along the road, but the gelding would serve him well.

Driving with one eye on the grassy expanse around him, he reached a spot at the foothills. He heaved a sigh. It was a long climb up and if Suzanne had passed out, it would be an even longer trip back down. He wrapped the reins around the brake and started to get down when he heard the click of

pebbles tumbling down the slope. Without seeming too obvious, he grabbed the rifle and kept turning, dropping to the ground. As he turned, he cocked the rifle and brought it to his shoulder. He sighted in on Suzanne Underwood slipping and sliding down the slope.

"You made good time," she said. She struggled with the canteen and his saddlebags. "Want to help me? You must carry gold bricks in here." With a heave, she got the saddlebags off her shoulder. He saw how she was still shaky on her feet.

"I would have fetched you."

"You make it sound like I'm a bone to be retrieved by some hungry dog," she said tartly. Another step and she sagged. He caught her and got her into the back of the buckboard.

"I need to get my gear, then we can head for town."

Suzanne didn't answer. She had drifted off. He made her as comfortable as he could, turned around, and drove to where his dead horse lay gathering flies. It took the better part of twenty minutes to pull his gear off the dead horse. He was less interested in the saddle and rifle as he was the saddle blanket. The saddle provided a pillow for Suzanne and the blanket cushioned some of the shock driving over the rocky road. He finally reached the road into Heavenly, and drove in just past sundown. Even so, people came out and watched. It was as if he had a sign saying he and Suzanne Underwood were riding together.

They might not see her, but they recognized her buggy. Slocum drove straight for Doc Gainsborough's office. He was relieved to see a light still burning in the window. A knock on the door was answered promptly. The doctor looked tired, but a faint grin crept to his lips when he recognized Slocum.

"You bringin' me more patients? I declare, Slocum, since you took over the Bar-S, my business has about doubled."

"In the back of the buckboard," Slocum said. Ben Gains-

borough went out with him. When he saw his patient, he looked sharply at Slocum.

"She agree to letting me tend her?"

"She's not in much condition to agree to anything. She took a whack to the side of the head." Slocum related how her buggy wheel had come loose and sent her tumbling down the side of the road into an arroyo.

"That's not her horse."

"Mine. I had to hike back to the Bar-S for the buckboard and horses after my horse got shot out from under me."

Gainsborough waited as Slocum related even more of the story. All Slocum held back was how he and Suzanne had spent the previous day and the previous night in the cave.

"You might consider opening an account with me," Gainsborough said. "You're trying to triple my business, not that such a thing would be hard, considering."

Slocum looked curiously at the doctor, wondering what he meant. There wasn't another doctor between here and Montrose. Ben Gainsborough must tend about everyone in town. Before he could ask, the doctor gestured impatiently for Slocum to help him.

Together, they wrestled a limp Suzanne from the buckboard and into the surgery. As they laid her on the examination table, Nora Gainsborough came in.

"Oh, no, what happened?"

"You can tell her, Doc," Slocum said. "I'm going to get some medicine of my own."

"Knock back a shot or two of Gutherie's medicine for me, too," Gainsborough said. As Slocum left, he saw the doctor take his wife by the arm and steer her to the corner of the room, where they exchanged words in a whisper. Nora Gainsborough forced her way past her husband, and went to the table and placed her hand on Suzanne's forehead. Slocum closed the door and stepped into the cool Colorado night. It had been a hell of a couple days and he didn't have much to show for it.

Other than a delightful day and night spent in a cave with about the most beautiful woman in this part of Colorado.

"And the most mysterious," he said to himself as he went into the Prancing Pony.

"Hey, Mr. Slocum, you're too late fer that free drink," Gutherie told him.

"That's all right. I'm willing to pay for a shot or two."

"Or more?" Gutherie winked at him. Slocum nodded. He took a half bottle, went to a table at the side of the saloon, and sank down. The chair creaked almost as much as his joints. He wasn't used to walking so far, and he was even still a tad sore from his and Suzanne's lovemaking.

As he worked on his second shot, the saloon doors opened and swung shut behind a short man with a nose that twitched and a wispy mustache that made him look like a San Francisco wharf rat. He surveyed the room, then came straight for Slocum.

"I got a proposition fer you, Mr. Slocum."

"You've got the advantage on me. You know my name. Who're you?"

"Robertson, Rupert Robertson, but my friends call me Roop."

"You have many friends, Rupert?" Slocum saw how the question that should have irritated most men only sailed past him. Roop Robertson was intent on something more than conversation as he sank down into the chair opposite Slocum. He leaned forward, elbows on the table. Slocum was no spring daisy after all he had been through, but the smell from Robertson's lack of bathing almost gagged him.

"You're the new owner of the Bar-S." The way he said it didn't require any response from Slocum. Robertson hurried on, as if trying to say everything before he forgot it. "I want to buy the Bar-S. I'll pay a fair price fer it."

"Do tell."

"We kin git the town clerk to draw up the papers and—"

"I don't want to sell."

Robertson blinked as if the dim light from the coal oil lamps around the room was too intense for his weak eyes.

"But I'm willin' to *pay* fer it. You didn't even hear my offer."

"Doesn't matter. The Bar-S isn't for sale."

"I'll make it worth yer while. Real money. Cash money."

"No." Slocum saw Robertson's shocked reaction. The man started to argue and Slocum again said, "No." This time he drew his six-gun and laid it on the table to punctuate his answer.

"You'll regret it. Mark my words, you'll damn well regret it."

Robertson shot to his feet and stormed out of the saloon. Slocum watched the doors swing, then slowly poured himself another drink. Life was certainly different being the owner of a big ranch.

Slocum reached for his pistol when the doors opened again. He relaxed when he saw Doc Gainsborough come in. The man made a beeline for him and sat in the chair Robertson had just vacated.

"A drink?" Slocum pushed the bottle in the doctor's direction.

With a curt shake of his head, Gainsborough declined. He put his forearms on the table and leaned forward so no one could overhear. Somehow, Slocum didn't mind the old doctor doing this. When Robertson had tried to be all private with him, he had wanted to punch the man's ratlike face.

"She's going to be all right," Gainsborough said without preamble, "but you've got to get her out of town."

"Folks don't take much to her, do they? Neither does your wife."

This shocked Gainsborough. He straightened and started to say something, but no words came out. Slocum wondered at the shock.

He wondered even more when Gainsborough asked, "Are you selling the Bar-S?"

"Seems to be a subject that's getting a whole lot more discussion than it's worth," Slocum said. "A fellow just offered to buy it. I turned him down. Are you wanting to buy it, too?"

"No, of course not," Gainsborough said, his hand flying through the air in a dismissive motion. "In fact, I hope you don't sell it. You really ought to—"

"Hold on to your thought," Slocum said. "Looks like the marshal's joining us." Louder, Slocum said, "Evening, Marshal. You want a snort?" He held up the whiskey bottle. Zamora's eyes fixed on the bottle and he licked his lips, then shook his head about the same way Gainsborough already had.

"Heard you were back in town, Slocum," Marshal Zamora said. He hooked his thumbs in his gun belt and hitched it up under his bulging belly. "Also heard you were out at Murphy's place. What'd the two of you talk about?"

"Never saw him, Marshal. Got shot at, probably by rustlers I haven't run off yet."

"He did it, Slocum. I want you to be on guard. Seamus Murphy killed Wimmer."

"Just because his gun was found by the body?" Slocum had no desire to go over his alibi for the young rancher since Zamora had already heard it and obviously dismissed it.

"The two of them had a blood feud going. Never saw two men hate like they did. It was murder, pure and simple, and Murphy did it."

"Can't help you prove that, Marshal," said Slocum. "In court, I'd have to testify against your theory."

"Might be you and him are in cahoots. You knew the will had been changed so you get him to murder Wimmer. You and him gonna divvy up the spoils?"

Slocum sighed and then said, "The barkeep can testify we were both in the Prancing Pony about the time Wimmer died."

"Bennett's nowhere to be seen. Might be he didn't run off with Lulu like everyone thinks. Might be you or Murphy

killed him since he could say you and Murphy wasn't drinking together in the bar."

Slocum closed his eyes, took a deep breath, and then stared straight at the marshal. Arguing with a man whose mind was as set as Zamora's was wearing him down. He tried a different argument.

"I didn't know the will had been changed. Wimmer never told me. And if there was such bad blood between the two of them, Murphy would have been the last to know that Wimmer had changed his will."

"You're right. Maybe he just shot Wimmer out of spite."

"You have any other suspects?" Slocum watched the marshal carefully and read the answer before the lawman spoke.

"Don't need no one else. Even if I believe what you say, Murphy did the deed. All I need to do is prove it. He's as clever as he is mean."

"Mighty careless of a man doing so much planning to leave behind the murder weapon," Slocum said.

"Panicked. It's not as easy to kill a man as it seems."

"No, it's not," Slocum agreed. This rocked Zamora back. Their eyes met, and the marshal finally broke off.

"Don't go leaving town, Slocum, not till the trial."

"Are you arresting Murphy?"

"I'm gatherin' the evidence now. Don't have it all yet, but I will."

"I'll be at the ranch," Slocum said. "I don't intend to sell out any time soon."

All this garnered from the marshal was a scowl. He hitched up his belt again and left.

"It has been quite a day," Slocum said, pouring another shot and knocking it back. He had downed another and was beginning to feel the effect now. Accumulated aches and pains faded into distant memory and comforting warmth crept through his body and brain.

"I don't think Murphy killed him either," Gainsborough

said unexpectedly. "There wasn't any call for that because he was dying anyhow."

"Come again?" Slocum tried to push the buzz in his ears away. His thirst had gotten the better of him and now he was hearing things.

"If you can leave the bottle for a few minutes, come on over to the undertaker. I want to show you what I mean."

Slocum got to his feet and trailed Doc Gainsborough from the saloon after shouting at Gutherie not to touch the remainder of the bottle. He and Gainsborough walked in silence to the undertaker's parlor. The doctor went around to the side, rapped twice, and then went in. Slocum followed. The smell of embalming fluids made him a tad dizzy.

"Evening, Lowell. I want Slocum to see what you got from poor old Jackson's gut." Gainsborough went to a shelf and took down a jar with a blackened, withered blob in it.

"You want that, Ben? Ain't no way I want to keep it here. If anybody saw it, it'd be plenty bad for business."

"That's an undertaker for you," Gainsborough said, holding up the jar with its ugly burden. "Doesn't mind dead folks, but things he takes out of them make him squeamish." He handed the jar to Slocum.

"What is it?"

"What's left of Jackson Wimmer's belly."

"Was Wimmer your patient?" Slocum asked the doctor.

"Jackson? No, he was too stubborn for that. Refused to see me or any doctor. But I suspected what Lowell here found out when he was digging around inside, getting him ready to be worm food. Cancer. Wimmer was dying of stomach cancer."

"That would have killed him for certain sure," Lowell said, tapping the side of the jar and stirring the tumor within.

"How long would he have lived if he hadn't caught a bullet in the head?" Slocum asked.

Gainsborough and Lowell exchanged looks. Finally, the doctor said, "Months at the outside. Probably only a couple weeks. Whoever killed him did Jackson Wimmer a favor."

Slocum stared at the jar with the remains of Wimmer's stomach, then put it back on the shelf. In spite of what the undertaker said, he thought the man was going to keep the tumor-riddled stomach as a souvenir. All Slocum wanted to do was return to the saloon and finish his bottle of whiskey. It had been one hell of a couple days.

11

Slocum perched on the top rail of the corral, watching the horses mill about. He had come here to pick another horse. The gelding lacked the stamina Slocum needed for protracted riding out on the range. He had chased two men he thought were rustlers, only to have the gelding tire quickly. Slocum had lost the men.

While they might have been riders on their way south and just happened to cross his property, he wasn't so sure.

"Damn me, I'm jumping at shadows," Slocum said to the horses in the corral. They shied away and gathered in a tight knot of horseflesh at the far side. Although all were saddle broke, the horses chose to reject human contact and preferred the company of others of their kind. Slocum understood how they felt.

He stared at the horses, but hardly noticed them since his thoughts were flying far beyond the corral. Suzanne had been patched up and had left Heavenly the next day, according to what Doc Gainsborough said. Slocum had wanted to see her before she disappeared, but that wasn't in the cards. Neither the doctor nor his wife knew where Suzanne was heading. Considering the scarcity of towns in this part of Colorado, he doubted she had gone too far and figured she

would be back eventually. In spite of traveling in her buggy, she lived like a gypsy, always on the move and never lighting for long. He didn't understand her or why the people in Heavenly acted the way they did toward her. In spite of this mystery, Slocum had other things on his mind.

What worried at him like a dog with a bone was selling the Bar-S. It was lagniappe that came from a totally unexpected source. Jackson Wimmer had been an old cuss and, from all that the townspeople said, one who delighted in causing a ruckus. Giving Slocum the entire ranch had done that as surely as a royal flush swept the pot every time. Colorado Pete Kelso wanted Slocum to sell. That disreputable rat-faced man, Rupert Robertson, wanted to buy. The only problem lay in Slocum not knowing what he wanted to do about the ranch.

The Bar-S was profitable, and getting the herd to the railhead and market in a few weeks would put a considerable roll of greenbacks in his pocket. But selling meant he would move on, always chasing after the clouds on the horizon, hunting for that which had no name. Slocum was satisfied enough doing that. After so many years, it suited him. But if he settled down, it could be with a woman like Suzanne Underwood. It did not matter to him that she was on the outs with the entire town of Heavenly. He was the largest rancher in the area. If he and Suzanne married, the fine citizens of Heavenly would have no choice but to deal with her.

Slocum let out a snort of self-derision. What made him think Suzanne would marry him, even if he was rich? But there were other fine-looking ladies in town. That had been the first thing Slocum noticed when he had ridden into Heavenly. Most towns sported two or three women of marrying age, usually uglier than a mud fence. Although none of the women he had seen in town could hold a candle to Suzanne, they were hardly so ill-graced that they were forced to wear flour sacks over their heads.

Rich, important to the entire commerce of Middle Park,

married. None of those had been more than fleeting dreams for Slocum.

"Slocum, I want a word with you."

Turning, Slocum saw Colorado Pete stalking toward him. Every time Slocum had seen him lately, the man was angrier than before. Slocum wished he had been able to follow him and find where he had gone when Ryan took Jenks to the doctor after getting buffaloed by the rustlers. Suzanne Underwood had caused him to take a different road. While he wasn't inclined to look poorly on their meeting, he wished he knew more about where Colorado Pete Kelso went when he rode off. It certainly wasn't to round up strays or look after the herd.

"You finished patrolling the upper meadows?" Slocum asked.

"Got Ryan and Jenks out there to do it," Kelso said. He scowled so hard, the lines seemed to etch themselves permanently into his face, cutting fleshy arroyos around his eyes and furrowing his forehead better than any Kansas farmer could plow a line. "When are you sellin' the Bar-S?"

"I've been thinking on that very idea," Slocum said.

"If you sell it right away, we can split the take and me and the boys can move on before snowfall. It gits mighty cold here along the western slope."

"If I sell, it's not going to be right away. No reason I shouldn't take my time."

"What? You have to sell, Slocum. Like I said, the snow. The cold. We'd have to weather another long winter to git our share. That ain't right!"

"The Bar-S is mine to do with as I see fit," Slocum said. The more Kelso argued for him to sell, the more Slocum dug in his heels.

"You gotta sell."

"Why don't you go out there with Ryan and Jenks? Maybe take a couple of the other boys. See if you can't track down some of those rustlers." Slocum watched Kelso closely. The

man's anger was already in full blow. If there had been any trace of guilt, it was well hidden.

Kelso sputtered and spun around to storm away. Slocum considered firing the top hand then and there. Ryan would make a better worker, but Slocum's pa had always told him to face his enemies so he wouldn't have to worry about his back. Calling Colorado Pete an enemy might be stretching things, but Slocum couldn't be sure.

Slocum waited for Kelso to ride out. It wasn't lost on him that the top hand left by himself. Standing on the corral rails, Slocum watched Kelso start for the high meadow, then abruptly veer away and head to the south. If he followed that trail, he would eventually circle back onto the main road into Heavenly.

Tracking Kelso seemed more productive of his time and effort than anything else. For all the work required to run the Bar-S, Slocum found himself at loose ends now and again. He preferred being out with the cattle, but owning the spread forced him to deal with all the cowboys and the paperwork, not to mention planning for the drive to the railhead and a dozen other things.

Unable to decide on another mount, he saddled the gelding and went directly for the main road. If Kelso doubled back toward Heavenly, he had to pass Slocum. If he went on south, Slocum could catch up in an hour or two and find where the wrangler went.

Slocum rolled himself a smoke and puffed silently on it, continuing his thoughts from when he had perched like a crow on a fence. This time he found it hard to focus. The more he tried to concentrate, the more chaotic his thoughts became. It was with some relief that he saw Kelso coming up the road, heading for town. From his vantage point, he watched until Kelso disappeared around a bend in the road.

Only then did Slocum start his slow pursuit. Kelso had been riding fast, but if he stayed on the road, Slocum would get to town an hour or so after him. That was plenty of time

to have a drink and ask around. He could even find Doc Gainsborough and talk some with him. Of all the people interested in the Bar-S, Ben Gainsborough was the only one who had advised him not to sell. Somehow, Slocum doubted it was because the doctor had taken such a liking to him that he wanted him to stay.

Slocum rode past the cutoff going toward Seamus Murphy's spread. As he'd done so many times before, he would have kept riding, hardly noticing the narrow road winding back into the hills before opening onto the lush valley. This time, however, he drew rein and then dismounted to study the soft dirt at the edge of the road.

A narrow-wheeled buggy had cut down into the grass and left distinct tracks recently. Slocum rubbed along the side of the groove and watched it crumble. The buggy had come this way only an hour earlier—or less.

The only person he had seen driving a buggy in the area had come this way before—and once more traveled along the road. Slocum looked down the road toward Heavenly and then into the hills. He could always find Kelso later. Suzanne Underwood proved a more fascinating diversion for his tracking skills.

As he rode, he considered the possibility that he might talk with Seamus Murphy. The man's ranch lay somewhere farther along the road. Slocum wanted to know more about this part of the countryside. If he saw a few rustlers here, that might mean they had their hideout nearby. With the mountains unexpectedly rising and turning into odd valleys all over the landscape, the outlaws might hide about anywhere. But if they hid, they still had to move the stolen cattle to get paid for their crime. Slocum doubted Marshal Zamora would ever be bribed into allowing stolen cattle into Heavenly. Other towns were miles distant. It would pay for Slocum to explore a bit more and find out if the marshals and sheriffs in those towns were inclined to look the other way as herds of stolen cattle were sold.

He passed the spot where Suzanne had driven off the road
that night. Then he came to his dead horse. The buzzards and
bugs had almost picked the carcass clean. He patted the nervous gelding's neck and said, "Don't worry. That's not going
to happen to you."

He brought the horse to a trot, then slowed after another
half mile when voices drifted to him. It took him a while to
locate the source. Two people stood under a scrub oak fifty
yards off the road. Even at this distance he could tell they argued by the way their arms flailed about. He didn't need the
field glasses in his saddlebags to know one of them was
Suzanne. Her skirt flared as she turned from side to side and
raised her hand high. She shoved the man back a step, but he
did not retaliate.

Slocum heard their muffled argument but could not figure
what the fight was about. He reached back, pulled out his
binoculars, and brought them up to get a better look at the
man.

Somehow, he was not surprised to see Seamus Murphy.
The young rancher whirled about, his back to Suzanne, and
faced Slocum's direction. She shoved him again but Murphy
stood stolidly, arms crossed on his chest and looking as if he
had been carved from stone.

To ride closer, Slocum would have to reveal himself. That
wouldn't be too bad because Suzanne and Murphy were
about at the end of their argument. Her pose duplicated the
man's. They stood back to back, arms crossed and now silent.
Slocum lowered the field glasses and tucked them back into
his saddlebags. Slowly, he urged his horse toward the pair.

He had no warning as a bullet tore through his pants leg.
The slug was quickly followed by another and another, and
Slocum was falling to the ground.

12

The gelding jerked to the side and reared, throwing Slocum to the ground. He landed hard enough to knock the wind from his lungs. Through the bloodred haze cloaking his eyes, he saw the horse stagger away. He lay still, struggling to regain his wind. The pain subsided. Careful tensing and relaxing of his muscles convinced Slocum he had not broken a rib falling, no matter how much it felt like it with every breath he sucked in. Turning his head slowly, he tried to find where the sniper who had shot him lay hidden. The best cover lay a couple dozen yards off the road in a clump of weeds.

Hand moving gradually, he slid over his belly and wrapped his fingers around the butt of his Colt Navy. He waited for any movement, but nothing came. When he was sure he was strong enough, he jerked to his right and then rolled left as fast as he could to end up in the shallow ditch beside the road. Slocum wiggled along on his belly until he got closer to the weeds. He reared up, six-shooter clutched in his hand. He was still shaken from the fall, but his hand was steady enough to fire.

If there had been a target, he would have squeezed off a shot. All he saw were broken weeds where the rifleman had

lain in wait for him. He got to his feet and approached warily. The ground was hard enough to make tracking by boot
prints difficult. He found a spent, shiny brass shell casing.
Other than this, he saw nothing. Whoever had ambushed
him had lit out like his ass was on fire.

Slocum slid his six-gun back into its holster and then
looked for his horse. His heart almost exploded when he saw
the horse on its front knees, struggling to stand. Hurrying
over, he saw that the bullet tearing through his pants leg had
gone into the gelding's side. Pink froth came from the
horse's nostrils. Slocum drew his six-shooter and fired a
single shot into the horse's head. It let out a cry of pain and
surprise before dying.

"Damn you," Slocum cried. "That's the second horse of
mine you've killed! I swear, you'll pay for it!" He looked
around for any trace of the unseen gunman, but he might as
well have been the only human in a dozen miles.

Then he remembered what had lured him in this direction
in the first place. Suzanne Underwood and Seamus Murphy
had been arguing not a hundred yards away. Trudging through
the weeds, he reached the small stand of junipers and looked
around, but they were gone. One set of hoofprints headed due
east. He followed the small footprints that had to be Suzanne's
to a spot where she had climbed into her buggy and driven off.
Any help he might have gotten from either of them had evaporated.

Trudging back to his dead horse, he stripped off the saddle
and other tack, heaved them onto his shoulder, and started
back for his ranch house. It got farther every time.

When Slocum returned to the Bar-S ranch house, all the
hands were gone. He reckoned they were out tending the
herd and getting it rounded up for moving to the railhead.
This was an especially dangerous time for both the cowboys
and the herd. Rustlers could kill several cowboys in a simple
ambush and not have to work to round up most of the cattle.

That sort of worry could wait. Slocum was dog tired. He

dropped his gear on the front porch and went inside to find a pitcher and some water. He gulped the water straight from the pitcher and then splashed water on his face to get some of the dust off. Only then did he realize how tired he was. His feet hurt something fierce and his legs threatened to snap under him like toothpicks.

He went into Wimmer's study—*his* study now—and sank down into the chair where the old rancher had died. Slocum leaned back and closed his eyes, but he opened them slowly to stare at the bullet hole in the ceiling. It was fresh. He could tell because the wood splinters around the hole were not discolored. How it had come to be there was beyond him since only one round had been fired from the six-shooter found on the floor.

Seamus Murphy's six-gun.

Slocum closed his eyes and started to drift to sleep. Something niggled at the back of his mind, like a feather tickling his throat, but it went away when he heard the front door creaking open. In one smooth motion that belied his tiredness, he was on his feet, six-shooter drawn and pointed at the door of the study as . . . Suzanne Underwood came in.

"Oh," she said, her hand going to her mouth. "I didn't mean to startle you."

"It could be deadly," he said, returning the pistol to its place on his left hip. "Do you always barge in without knocking?"

"But I did knock. Twice. Didn't you hear me? When I found the door open, I thought I'd come in and—"

"And?" Slocum saw a sly look come to her bright blue eyes.

"And see if I might talk to you."

"Talk?"

"It's something we haven't done much of," Suzanne said. "Not that I mind."

"Seems we had plenty of chance to talk," Slocum said. "And a mite more."

"Oh, John, it was hardly what I'd call 'a mite more.' It was a considerable amount more."

Slocum tried to read something in the young woman's face and couldn't do it. Her eyes fixed on him like a snake following a bird, but there was no lust there. Discounting what she said, he tried to figure out why she had actually come to the Bar-S.

"I was riding earlier, hunting for strays," he said. "I thought I saw you and Seamus Murphy talking."

"Did you now?"

"More like you were arguing. How is it you know Murphy?"

"Who doesn't know him? For all the miles of rangeland, the area around Heavenly is mighty small. Or should I say, there aren't many folks on it."

"You mosey about a lot," Slocum said. "What is it that brings you out my way?"

Again he saw the light in her eyes, but it wasn't for him. Not exactly. He wondered if there was any way Seamus Murphy could have been the shooter. If so, that meant Suzanne knew about the man's murderous ways since she could not have ridden away fast enough to avoid seeing the attack. He had seen her and the rancher together, then been shot at. Slocum shook his head. Unless Murphy was made of smoke, he could never have reached the patch of weeds fast enough where the sniper had lain in wait.

"You're shaking your head, John? Are you telling me to leave? That you don't want my company?"

"Seems like me and Murphy are about the only two in the whole of Colorado who want your company," he said. The way she reared back like he had struck her told him he had touched a nerve.

"That's not a nice thing to say."

"But it's true," he said.

"They don't approve of my upbringing." Suzanne stood stiffly, eyes fixed on the far wall where no picture hung. The

play of emotion told Slocum she was reliving an unpleasant past. "My pa was not very likable, and he treated me like dirt."

"Seems that would make folks cotton more to you."

"My pa," she went on, as if she had not heard, "threw my ma and me out. Drove us off like we were nothing more than dogs. Nobody in town would have anything to do with us because he would have taken it out on them if they had helped." A sneer came to Suzanne's lovely lips. "They're all cowards, each and every last one of them. I hate them as much as I do my pa, but for a different reason. I hate him for what he was and them for what they aren't." The words were cold and flat, and warned Slocum to drop the question. Whatever bad blood there was between her and the citizens of Heavenly had to remain hidden. For a while longer. Slocum could and not imagine how the entire town could turn against a woman and her daughter after being turned out by a tyrant.

Before Slocum could say another word, he heard the pounding of hooves outside. He swung around and faced the door as Ryan burst in, out of breath and face red from exertion.

"Mr. Slocum, you gotta come quick like a fox. We caught 'em. We caught a whole damned passel of 'em."

"Rustlers?"

"Must be six or eight of 'em. Shot it out with a couple, winged one. Got some more trapped in a box canyon."

"You can stay if you like," Slocum said to Suzanne. He was not certain if he wanted her to be here when he returned, but she settled the matter.

Stiffly, she said, "I will not remain here one instant longer." Suzanne spun and flounced off. Ryan started to say something, then looked at Slocum and clamped his mouth shut.

"Let's ride," Slocum said. He pushed past Ryan and hefted his gear on the way to the corral. A quick look at the horses nervously moving about there convinced him a dun mare was

his best choice. In minutes, he had saddled and ridden after an anxious cowhand.

"Tell me what happened," Slocum said.

"It was like this, Mr. Slocum. Me and the others was rounding up the cattle when they tried shootin' it out with us. They didn't know four more of us was on the way back to camp. We outnumbered 'em two to one. Lead flew and horses were rearin' and—"

"Anyone hurt?"

"None of us, Mr. Slocum. No, sir, we surprised them outlaws and even winged one of them. They lit out with us on their tails. Drove 'em into Blue Rock Canyon. You know the one?"

Slocum didn't and said so.

"Box canyon. Colorado Pete, he chased 'em and then stopped when he got to the mouth to wait for us. When we get enough firepower, we kin go on in and flush 'em."

Slocum frowned. Colorado Pete Kelso wasn't the sort of man he expected to lead the attack against the rustlers. If anything, he would hang back and let others, like Ryan and his partner, take the lead—and the bullets.

They rode hard for twenty minutes before Slocum heard sporadic gunfire. From the sound, only a couple men were firing.

"Sounds like we got ourselves a fight goin' on," Ryan said. He licked his lips and looked apprehensive.

"You ever kill a man?"

"No, sir, I never have, and that's the gospel truth. Gives me the willies thinkin' 'bout it, but ever since Jenks got his head bashed in, it's been worryin' at me like a burr under a saddle blanket."

"You'd kill to save Jenks?"

"Reckon so. And 'bout any of the rest of the boys. They're a good crew, Mr. Slocum."

"Keep your pistol in its holster unless you've got something

worth shooting at," Slocum said. He galloped ahead and drew rein near Jenks. The man was bent over in pain, but he looked as eager as Ryan to get on with capturing himself some rustlers.

"Colorado Pete's got 'em all bottled up," Jenks said.

"You shouldn't be riding yet," Slocum said. "Didn't Doc Gainsborough tell you to put in some bunk time?"

"Cain't make money layin' about," Jenks said. Bandages that had been white once poked out from under his Stetson, giving mute testimony to his earlier injury.

More gunfire from within the canyon echoed out. Slocum's keen ear picked out only one six-shooter firing.

"How many rustlers are in there?"

"Cain't tell, but Colorado Pete's gone after 'em."

This struck Slocum as odd, but he might have misjudged Kelso entirely.

"You watch the mouth of the canyon. Don't shoot just because someone's coming out—it might be me or Kelso. If it's not us, try to capture them."

"How hard?" Ryan asked.

"Not so hard you put your lives in danger," Slocum said. He snapped the reins and moved his horse onto the narrow trail leading into Blue Rock Canyon. As he entered, he saw why it had gotten the name. The rocks weren't blue, but had a greenish tint to them that would appear blue near sundown. He wasn't much of a geologist, but there might be turquoise in the canyon walls, or maybe copper ore.

Several shots came in rapid succession, then nothing. Slocum galloped ahead, reaching for his six-gun as he rode. Not twenty yards ahead he saw that Kelso had the drop on a man half hidden by vegetation.

"Kelso, don't shoot him!"

Slocum's sharp command caused Colorado Pete Kelso to jerk around. His pistol rose, as if he intended to fire on Slocum. Then he swung back and aimed.

"He's surrendering, Kelso. Don't shoot a man with his

hands in the air or, I swear, I'll see you in jail for murder!" As much as Slocum wanted to end the miserable life of every single rustler in central Colorado, he wanted this one alive. Dead men couldn't give him information about where the rustlers camped or how many head they might have made off with already. Even more important, Slocum wanted to know how many outlaws he faced.

"He's a low-down, no-account sidewinder," Kelso said. He aimed and was going to fire, but Slocum rode forward and then jerked hard on the reins, causing the dun mare to dig in her heels. A cloud of dust rose between the cowboy and the rustler.

"Damn it, Slocum, I had him."

"He's not going anywhere," Slocum said. He saw a dead horse off in the brush. Some of the earlier gunfire had claimed yet another animal. If this kept up, there wouldn't be a single cowboy in all of Middle Park astride a horse.

"He ambushed me," the man in the brush called. "He opened fire on me and there was no call for him to do that!"

"He's a rustler," Kelso said, moving to get a shot.

Slocum dropped to the ground and drew his Colt Navy. This brought Kelso around when he saw who the six-shooter was aimed at—and it wasn't the rustler in the bushes.

"You got the wrong damn man in your sights, Slocum."

"Put the gun in your holster, Kelso." Slocum waited until the top hand reluctantly obeyed. Only then did Slocum turn and call to the hidden man. "You come on out. Keep those hands grabbing clouds."

The man slowly came from shadow and stepped into the sunlight angling down over the canyon rim.

"You shoulda let me shoot him, Slocum," said Kelso.

"I'm no rustler."

"You've got a powerful lot of explaining to do," Slocum said to Seamus Murphy. The young rancher glared at him, but had the good sense to keep his hands high in the air.

13

"You got no right to hold me," Seamus Murphy said. His jaw thrust out and his eyes flashed angrily. The instant he started to lower his hands, Kelso reached for his gun again.

Slocum moved fast, grabbing Kelso's wrist to keep him from drawing.

"We got him," Slocum said. "Back off."

"You're the one what wanted rustlers cut down. This is one of the worst. We caught him red-handed."

"What are you doing on Bar-S land?" Slocum watched Murphy closely. Somehow, he could not believe the young rancher was out rustling. He was such a hothead, he wouldn't last ten minutes with a gang. He would anger the wrong outlaw and get shot in the back. The only possibility was that Murphy was hunting for strays to move to his own herd. Even a few cattle from the Bar-S herd might mean the difference between surviving and having to turn his ranch over to the bank in foreclosure.

"Some of my cattle strayed here. I was lookin' for 'em."

"Liar! You were stealin' Bar-S beeves!"

"Shut up, Kelso," Slocum said. "He might be telling the truth." If Slocum expected any gratitude from Murphy, he

would have been wrong. Murphy glared at him as hard as he did at Colorado Pete Kelso.

"Go on, murder me. You won't believe anything I have to say. String me up! That'll make you feel good, won't it? You can brag on it around Heavenly."

"Let Marshal Zamora sort it all out." Slocum waved to Jenks and Ryan, who had ridden up and watched in silence. "Get him into town and tell the marshal what happened."

"I'll go with them. They'll let this bastard get away, sure as the sun rises." Kelso's fingers tapped on the butt of his pistol.

"Go on," Slocum said. "And you," he said directly to Kelso, "get on back to finding rustlers. We're too close to rounding up the herd for them to bother us now."

Kelso spat at Murphy, swung around, and stalked to his horse. He jumped into the saddle and galloped off.

Slocum watched Ryan and Jenks ride off on either side of a defiant Seamus Murphy, then turned his attention to the trail taken by Kelso. He wondered if Suzanne Underwood waited back at the ranch house, but he doubted it. She had acted as if every step into the house had been barefoot over hot coals. Slocum wondered if it was a coincidence that Suzanne had shown up about the time Murphy was out riding on Bar-S rangeland. He shrugged it off. He had something else eating at him even more.

Once out of the box canyon, he stepped down from his horse and examined the ground for traces of Kelso's horse. Wherever Kelso rode, it wasn't back to the high meadow where most of the herd milled about, waiting for the cowboys to move them north. Slocum found the trail and followed it cautiously.

After twenty minutes, he caught sight of Colorado Pete ahead. He halted and reached for his field glasses. It took a few seconds for him to figure out what he was seeing. Kelso remained on his horse some distance from a ravine. Movement at the edge of the ravine caught Slocum's attention,

and he sat a little straighter when he caught sight of the crowns of two battered hats. Kelso talked with the men hiding in the deep arroyo, but Slocum could not get a good look at them other than to see that one hat had a cut alongside the crown and that it had, at one time, been a bright Kelly green. Sun and wind had faded it to a shade Slocum could not put a name to. After five minutes, Slocum lowered the binoculars and tucked them away, never having seen the faces of the men in the ravine. Kelso rode off, heading due west.

Slocum waited, hoping to catch sight of the men who had remained hidden, but they used the steep banks to mask their departure. Slocum could not even tell which way they left. He considered tracking them, but knew he would be stirring up a hornet's nest. If he poked around too much by himself, he was sure to run afoul of what had to be a new gang of rustlers. He had been the target of too many rustlers' ambushes since coming to Colorado.

Retracing his trail, Slocum came to the fork in the road, one branch leading to the Bar-S ranch house and the other to Heavenly. He chose to ride into town.

It was after dark by the time he reached Heavenly. He licked his lips and tasted dust, but rather than head for the Prancing Pony and Gutherie's quick pour from a bottle of decent whiskey, he went to the marshal's office.

"What you want, Slocum?"

"Pleased to see you, too, Marshal," Slocum said. He dropped to the ground and wrapped the reins around a hitching post.

"Don't go thinking you own the town."

"What gossip have you been listening to?" Slocum faced him squarely.

"What do you want, Slocum?"

"My boys brought in Seamus Murphy. You have him locked up inside?" Slocum waited as Marshal Zamora

thought on the matter before nodding once. "You mind if I talk to him?" Zamora shook his head. "Thanks, Marshal."

Slocum pushed past the lawman and went into the small office. A pair of cages at the rear were empty. The third held an angry, pacing, cursing Seamus Murphy. The rancher looked up sharply when Slocum came closer.

"What do you want? To put the noose around my neck?" Murphy reached up and tugged at the orange bandanna he wore. He slid a finger under it and lifted, mocking the way a noose would tighten.

"That what's going on in town?" Slocum grabbed a chair and pulled it where he could sit down and look at Murphy. "They going to lynch you?"

"You put me in here," Murphy said. "It's all your fault."

"The way folks think about you has nothing to do with me," Slocum said. "Why do they hate you so much?"

"Go to hell."

"Does it have something to do with Suzanne Underwood?" Slocum wished he were playing poker with Murphy. The expression on the rancher's face was too easy to read. "Why does everyone in Heavenly hate her? For all that, why does she hate *them*?"

"You leave her out of this. The marshal's the one talkin' 'bout charging me with Wimmer's murder."

Slocum considered this and discounted it. Zamora must have thrown that into the stew pot to get Murphy to confess to something else. Rustling cattle was nowhere near as bad as murder, though both might get a man strung up.

"Unless the marshal thinks I'm in cahoots with you, I gave you an alibi for the time Wimmer was killed." Slocum remembered how Marshal Zamora had toyed with this notion. If the lawman had moved on, giving in to facts rather than reflexive dislike for Murphy, all that had to be dealt with were the rustling charges.

"Why'd you bother? You hate me like the rest of these . . ."

Murphy began sputtering incoherently. His anger was so great, he couldn't even think up an appropriate insult. Considering the colorful language Slocum had heard as he came into the jail, that was almost unbelievable.

"I like to know the truth. You were drinking with me when Wimmer was shot. But that doesn't mean Suzanne Underwood might not have something to do with it." Slocum remained impassive as Murphy smashed hard against the iron bars, fingers groping for Slocum's throat.

"You get back or I swear I'll shoot you like a weasel in a trap," Marshal Zamora roared. Slocum had not heard the lawman open the outer door. He pointed his six-shooter directly at Murphy to make him obey.

"There's no call to shoot a man already in jail," Slocum said. He doubted anything more would come from Murphy's lips but curses. Without another word, he left the jailhouse, stepping into the cool Colorado night.

Slocum took a few seconds to wonder why he didn't leave Murphy to his fate, much of it caused by the young rancher's own hotheaded deeds. He could do that, but it wouldn't be right. With some reluctance, he passed the open doors of the Prancing Pony and the gaiety inside and headed down a side street until he reached Ben Gainsborough's office. He knocked on the door.

"Why, good evening, Mr. Slocum." Nora Gainsborough held the door as if she expected to slam it, and relaxed only when she saw him.

"Were you expecting someone?"

"Ben's out on a call. Mrs. Fiarino's having a baby any time now."

"Mind if I come in?"

She had relaxed, but now she tensed and looked as if she wanted to bolt and run. "No, come on in. Could I get you some coffee?"

"That'd be fine." Slocum doubted a cup of coffee, even if Nora Gainsborough fixed it to perfection, would do anything

to cut his real thirst. Whiskey would do that, not coffee. He settled down in a chair and watched as she bustled about, reaching for a coffeepot on the Franklin stove at the side of the office.

"Tell me about Seamus Murphy," Slocum said as she turned with two cups. She hesitated, then handed one cup to Slocum.

"Why do you think I know anything about him?"

"Nobody in town will talk about him or Suzanne Underwood."

"Is that so? I know nothing about them that would interest you."

"All sorts of things interest me," Slocum said, sipping at the coffee. He nodded in her direction to show his approval. He had drunk better coffee, but it still went down well. "I wouldn't mind hearing about Jackson Wimmer either." This time she could not maintain her stony facade. Her lips thinned and the vein on her left temple began pulsing visibly.

"It's no secret that I found the man despicable. Most all in town did. He was crude, had a sharp tongue, and did not mind sharing his low opinion of all things living with anyone unable to escape quickly enough."

"Being the richest man in Middle Park gave him license to say anything he wanted?"

"The way he treated people, he could have been the richest man in the whole world and it wouldn't have been right. I'm surprised someone didn't take a gun to him earlier."

"Do you think Suzanne Underwood might have been capable of shooting a man like Wimmer?"

Nora Gainsborough sat straighter and put her cup down on a low table.

"It's time for you to leave, Mr. Slocum. Mind you, I bear you no ill will because Jackson Wimmer chose to give you the Bar-S. My tolerance for discussing him is very small."

"Sorry if I offended you, Mrs. Gainsborough," Slocum

said. "One thing you could probably answer. How did the ranch come to be named the Bar-S?"

If Slocum thought she had been pissed off before, now he saw hatred in her eyes. He couldn't tell if it was directed at him or Wimmer or even someone else.

"I cannot comment on that. Good evening, sir."

She opened the door and tapped her foot waiting for him to leave.

As Slocum started to leave, he almost bumped into Ben Gainsborough. The doctor wore a smile ear to ear.

"Slocum, good to see you." Gainsborough looked past and said to Nora, "It was a girl. She's naming it Catherine Marie. Both mother and daughter are doing fine, though the baby's a little on the light side, but it was a difficult pregnancy." Gainsborough dropped his medical bag by the door and slapped Slocum on the shoulder. "Join me in a drink. That's why you came by, isn't it?"

"Ben, he—" Nora Gainsborough chewed her lower lip and looked uneasy.

"I have to be on my way."

"One drink, Slocum. Good whiskey. Special bottle. I keep it for celebrations."

"I don't know that a baby being born is such a thing to celebrate," Slocum said.

"You sound positively Irish. Cry at births, laugh at funerals. Well, I'm not Irish and I want to celebrate my upcoming marriage."

Slocum stared at Gainsborough, thinking he had misheard him. He glanced at Nora Gainsborough and then back. Her expression was unreadable.

"Whose marriage?" he asked.

"Mine and Nora's. I thought that was why you came by, to congratulate us."

"But you're married already. I don't follow what you're saying." Slocum saw the flash of confusion on Gainsbor-

ough's face as he held out a water tumbler generously filled with whiskey. Hardly realizing he did so, Slocum took it. He kept his eyes fixed on the doctor.

"You aren't a local, so you didn't know. Nora and I, well, we haven't gotten married. We just shared a roof."

"And a bed," Nora Gainsborough said sharply. "There's no need to be coy. We've lived as husband and wife. We finally decided to make it legal."

Slocum started to ask if there wasn't a judge or preacher in town, but he knew there were two ministers. For whatever reason, they had not chosen to marry.

"Congratulations," Slocum said, thrusting out his hand. Gainsborough shook it. "I shouldn't have called you Mrs. Gainsborough," he said to Nora, "but I thought . . ."

"That's all right. You're new to town and no reason for you to inquire."

"How long?" Slocum bit off the question. It was none of his business.

"A few years," Nora said quickly.

"Why now?" Slocum asked. "If things were working for you as it was, why tie the knot?"

"I finally decided to make an honest woman of her," Gainsborough said, looking at Nora. Slocum saw her looking daggers at him, and knew there wouldn't be an explanation beyond what he had gotten.

"When's the shindig?" he asked.

"We'll set a date in a few days," Gainsborough said. "There's a lot of planning to do."

"There's very little remaining to do," Nora said. "I've had it planned ever since . . . for years."

Slocum considered all the couple said and couldn't make head nor tail of it.

"This isn't much, but it ought to go a ways toward your wedding," Slocum said. "What do I owe you for patching up Jenks?"

"No charge," Gainsborough said, obviously too happy with delivering a healthy baby and telling Slocum of his up-coming nuptials, but Nora had no such qualms.

"No charge for rooming for the day he spent here," she said quickly. "Five dollars for bandaging him up."

"Sounds reasonable," Slocum said, fishing in his vest pocket. He found four single dollar bills and added a silver cartwheel to the pile on the table beside his coffee cup. "I hope I don't have to pay you any more for repairing my cowboys."

"From what I hear, you just might," Doc Gainsborough said. "Going after the rustlers the way you are is going to cause lead to fly."

"I'll keep my head down," Slocum promised. He touched the brim of his hat in Nora Gainsborough's direction and then downed the remainder of the whiskey in his glass. He left quickly.

The door shut behind him and he heard Nora's muffled voice rising in anger. Slocum wondered what had sparked it, but if he had to bet, he would place all his money on his visit and the questions asked about Seamus Murphy—and Suzanne Underwood.

It was time for him to get a few more whiskeys under his belt. He headed for the Prancing Pony and a half bottle of Gutherie's best liquor.

14

Slocum settled down with his bottle of whiskey at the corner of the Prancing Pony bar so he could watch the sporadic coming and going of the patrons. Gutherie enthusiastically served four cowboys from another spread, keeping them drinking by reciting any of a dozen timeworn tall tales. He was more comfortable here than he ever had been in the general store. While it might have something to do with the whiskey Gutherie sampled now and then, Slocum reckoned the man preferred the company in the bar to that of the store.

Letting the liquor slide down his gullet and puddle warmly helped Slocum think on what had been said over at Doc Gainsborough's office. The more he thought, the more he realized that other citizens of Heavenly skirted Nora Gainsborough—or whatever her name was. They had to deal with the doctor and tolerated her, but they did not shun her the way they did Seamus Murphy or Suzanne Underwood. For all the initial friendly appearances when he had ridden into Heavenly, Slocum realized now that the undercurrent in the town was one of suspicion and outright scorn. What Suzanne and Murphy had done to earn it, he was at a loss to say. An unmarried woman living in sin certainly explained everyone's attitude toward Nora.

He knocked back another shot and stared at the door. For a moment, he thought the whiskey had clouded his vision. Then he sat straighter and stared hard. His eyesight was as sharp as an eagle's. Moving back and forth just above the tall swinging doors, a tall-brimmed hat captured his attention completely. He had seen that hat before, with a notch cut out of the crown and a peculiar color green.

"One of the men Kelso was talking to, the one hidden down in the ravine," Slocum said aloud. Two gamblers at the next table glanced in his direction, then hastily turned back to their game when he glared at them.

He picked up his bottle, still sloshing with a good six or eight drinks left, and set it down on the bar.

"Gutherie, do me a favor and save this for the next time I come in."

"Sure thing, Mr. Slocum. It's got your name on it," the bar owner said jovially. From the way he worked the four cowboys bellied up to the bar, he was having a profitable night and no request would have been too outrageous. The usual way would have been for Slocum to take the bottle with him or simply leave it. Any number of other bar patrons would have pounced on it the instant he left. Saving it for later was a service that no barkeep wanted to catch on.

Slocum was out the swinging doors and looking around before Gutherie recorked the bottle and stashed it on the back bar. Slocum looked up and down the main street. A slow smile came to his lips. In front of the darkened barbershop, Kelso and the man with the peculiar hat pressed close together, whispering. If ever he had seen men up to no good, it was these two.

When they hurried off, Slocum found his horse and mounted. He waited a few minutes to be sure they weren't riding toward him, then headed down the street in the direction they had taken. He urged his horse to a long trot, and soon spotted the riders ahead. From this distance in the dark, he couldn't be sure he followed Kelso and the man

wearing the cut-up green hat, but who else would be out for a nocturnal ride?

The riders cut off the road and headed into the hills. For more than an hour Slocum followed, falling back when he had to be sure they did not spot him. When he caught the scent of a campfire and cooking beef, he slowed and eventually stepped down from his horse and advanced on foot.

In a hollow, six men crouched around a fire, helping themselves to sizzling steaks. Slocum didn't have to see anymore to know where that beef had come from. The six were on Bar-S land, and in the distance he heard the mournful lowing of cattle. His cattle. He had found another gang of rustlers.

Before he retreated, he spied on them, trying to identify Colorado Pete Kelso. When he realized it wasn't possible in the dark, Slocum reluctantly left, found his horse, and galloped back toward town. He was out of the saddle and running a few steps when he reached the jailhouse.

He tried the door, but it was locked.

"Marshal! Marshal Zamora! Let me in. I found some rustlers."

He heard grumbling inside the jail. The bar locking the door scraped free and a crack appeared. Both a bloodshot eye and the barrel of a shotgun poked out.

"I tracked down a half dozen rustlers," Slocum said. "They're bedded down for the night by now not all that far away. Get a posse and we can catch them red-handed."

"Damnation, Slocum, don't you ever sleep? I busted up a fight tonight and sent two cowboys back to their spread, flat on their backs in a wagon."

Slocum stood his ground. The marshal could not simply return to bed. Zamora grumbled some more, opened the door, and motioned for Slocum to come in.

"Lemme get my pants on. Six of the varmints, you say?"

"A couple hours' ride from here, right on the edge of the Bar-S."

"So they stole your beeves? You offerin' a reward?"

"You can't claim any reward."

"Not for me. Who in their right mind's gonna traipse out in the middle of the night after outlaws likely to ventilate them 'less there's money on the line?"

"Twenty dollars for every man," Slocum said, realizing the lawman was right.

"That's a princely sum. Sure you want to go that high?"

"I want to make certain no rustler thinks of the Bar-S as easy prey."

"Not that, not since you showed up. You've done a right good job of running them bastards to ground—or stringing them up," Zamora said. He opened a drawer and grabbed a box of shells for his shotgun. "You get on outta here while I round up some men."

Slocum glanced into the cell where Seamus Murphy lay. Murphy was not asleep, but he wasn't sociable enough not to pretend to be asleep.

Slocum left, Zamora right behind him. The lawman started to say something, then thought better of it. Insulting Slocum by suggesting he was leading them on a wild-goose chase to break Murphy out of jail wouldn't accomplish anything.

Slocum mounted, and waited impatiently for the marshal and four men to join him. From the way the four wobbled in the saddle, he guessed Zamora had found them all in a saloon.

"Will they be sober enough when we get there?" Slocum looked at them and wondered if a couple might not fall out of the saddle before they left Heavenly.

"Only way to find out is to get there," Zamora said. "Lead the way, Slocum."

Because of the drunks, it took closer to three hours for Slocum to get back to the spot where he had spied on the rustlers' camp earlier in the evening. The fire had died down and six dark shapes were arrayed around it.

"Nobody on guard?"

"Don't see anyone," Slocum said. He elbowed the marshal when a cow let out a mournful cry.

"That's good enough for me. If those aren't your boys, then they're moving cattle across your land. Trespassing at the least."

Slocum was glad to see that the combination of the cold night ride and the sudden fear of the outlaws had sobered the four men with them. Two waited nervously while Zamora went with another in one direction and Slocum circled with the remaining posse member. Walking softly, he made his way down the slope into the outlaw camp. Slocum drew his six-shooter and waited for his partner to catch up. The man's hand shook as he held his own six-gun.

"I ain't never kilt nobody."

"No need to start tonight. If shooting starts, get under cover and stay there. Don't even think of firing your gun," Slocum cautioned. He knew he would be safer with only rustlers shooting at him. A frightened man behind him was likely to kill him by accident.

Slocum walked with a confident stride into the middle of the camp. He saw Zamora and the other newly deputized drunkard coming from the other direction.

"You're all under arrest for rustling," Slocum shouted.

The sleeping men stirred, then sat bolt upright. One went for a six-gun. Slocum kicked it away and covered the man. The others had even less presence of mind, being awakened from a sound sleep.

"Tie 'em up. Make sure the ropes are secure," Zamora ordered. The marshal snorted and shook his head. "So much for the wicked sleeping with an uneasy head. We could have taken the cattle back and they'd never have known."

Slocum saw the four deputies were feeling their oats now, pushing the rustlers around and acting like cocks of the walk.

"I want to see the cattle," Slocum said.

"Me, too. Hate to think I nabbed innocent men."

"Whoever they are, they're not innocent," Slocum said. And as they went down into the arroyo where close to twenty head of cattle were penned, he saw the Bar-S brand on more than one rump.

"Whose brand is this?" Slocum ran his fingers over the brand. "Looks like Circle M."

Zamora spat and said, "Murphy. That's Murphy's brand."

Slocum peered at the marshal through the dark; then a slight smile came to his lips.

"So he might have been telling the truth about hunting for his cattle on my land."

"He's rotten through and through."

"Disagreeable?"

"That," Zamora agreed.

"Just like Jackson Wimmer?"

"Get his damned cattle cut from your herd. I'll release the son of a bitch and tell him where he can find his beeves."

"I'll get my men to run the Bar-S cattle back into the pasture. I'll drive these back to Murphy myself."

"He doesn't appreciate anything anyone does for him."

Slocum said nothing to that as he made his way through the herd, swatting bovine rumps and forcing six cattle branded Circle M away from the rest. Nobody in Heavenly had done much for Murphy to appreciate. Even if they had, Murphy was not the sort to appreciate it. Slocum reflected on how it took a man a considerable amount of practice to accept generosity from others.

Like driving the six cows back onto Circle M land.

Slocum saw that the four deputies had their prisoners bound and on horseback, ready for the trip back to Heavenly. He studied each face closely, but Kelso was not among them. He stopped in front of the man with the faded green hat.

"You aren't rustling all by your lonesome. Who's helping you?"

"My partners here. Nobody else."

Slocum knew he had no way of forcing the man to talk. The man in the green hat was hardly the brains of a gang, but how much did it take to gather a few drifters together to rustle cattle? Figuring out an innocent reason for Kelso to meet twice with rustlers proved more than he could dream up on the spur of the moment.

"There might be others," Slocum told Marshal Zamora. "Keep a close eye on these six."

"Nobody's getting out of my jail unless I let them out," the marshal vowed. Slocum hoped Zamora wasn't blowing smoke.

The posse rode off with the prisoners while Slocum started Murphy's cattle on a trail leading toward the spot where he reckoned a ranch house might be situated. The cattle wanted to dawdle, and Slocum was half asleep in the saddle. It had been a hell of a long day, he hadn't eaten, and the whiskey sloshing in his belly made him a tad giddy. Still, knowing he had gotten Murphy out of jail and had even found the reason for the man prowling around on Bar-S land satisfied him.

Just before sunrise, he ran the cattle up to a small one-room cabin set in the middle of a stand of junipers. Murphy had done a fair job in proving his land. A small vegetable garden behind the cabin showed he had a little talent as a farmer, but his barn consisted of nothing more than a lean-to.

As Slocum shooed the cattle out to a pasture behind the cabin, he spotted a buggy still hitched up to its team. He rode closer, and noted that his repair work on Suzanne's buggy was holding up well. He tied his horse to the buggy frame and went to the cabin. From inside came sounds of things being thrown about.

Slocum drew his six-shooter and went to the door. He pushed it open with the toe of his boot. He lowered his gun when he saw Suzanne Underwood kneeling on the dirt floor, pawing through a box of clothing.

"You reckon Murphy has something that would fit you?"

Suzanne jumped as if he had touched her with a red-hot

poker. One hand went to her throat and the other burrowed about in the box.

"John! You startled me. What are you doing here?"

"I like that," he said.

She looked at him quizzically.

"The question you just asked. I like it so much I'm going to ask you the same one. What are *you* doing here? Robbing a man locked up in jail?"

"No, nothing of the sort." She struggled to find a plausible answer. "I was hunting for something that might exonerate him. Nobody in Heavenly likes him. They're going to railroad him, and I want to help."

"Because nobody in town likes you either?"

"Yes," she said. The word sounded as if a snake had spoken. It came out more as a hiss than a human sound.

"What would there be in there that would get him sprung from jail?"

"I don't know. That's why I was looking. A receipt perhaps, or a deed or something."

"He's not a rustler, but you know that," Slocum said, watching her reaction closely. Suzanne did a better job now of hiding whatever she felt. "I brought back a few head of his cattle that had gotten in with mine."

"You herded them back yourself?"

"Been a cowboy a long time," Slocum said, "and I know my way around a cow."

"That was mighty neighborly of you," she said. She licked her lips so that the pink tip of her tongue slid out and over her lips. Watching the small gesture caused emotions to stir within Slocum's loins. "Seems as if you ought to get a reward for that."

"Doing the right thing's reward enough," Slocum said. He knew he was lying. Suzanne was a lovely woman and he wanted more than the satisfaction of returning stolen cattle to their rightful owner. He wanted her.

Two sure steps took him across the room to her. His arm slipped around her waist and drew her in close. She molded easily to his body. Her eyelids drooped just a little as her lips opened. He kissed her.

One instant she had been pliant, almost boneless. Now she was more than an armful. She clutched him as hard as he was holding her. He felt her breasts mash down against his chest and her tongue come questing into his mouth. He let his hand drift lower until he could cup one firm buttock. He pulled her in even harder to his body. Her legs parted and she curled around one thigh where she began rubbing up and down faster and faster.

She broke off the kiss, panting hard. "I want more than this, John. I want you. In me. I want this."

He groaned as she gripped at his crotch and squeezed down. He was already hard. This made him want to explode.

"Wearing all these clothes isn't going to get either of us where we want to go," he said.

She moved her nimble fingers over his gun belt and let it fall to the dirt floor. Barely had it crashed down when she worked on the buttons of his fly. As she struggled to free his erection, he began working on her blouse. He caught his breath, as much from the feel of Suzanne's hand around his naked hardness as from the sight of her perfectly formed tits spilling from her blouse.

He bent over and kissed first one and then the other. Every time his tongue raked over the rubbery tip on each, she squeezed down hard on him. He had to struggle to keep from getting off too soon.

"Damn, but you're beautiful," he said as he buried his face between her breasts. He kissed and licked and then sucked in her left nipple to press against it with his tongue. This caused her to stumble a mite. Her grip on his manhood lessened as desire racked her trim body.

Slocum used the respite to slip off her blouse. She was

naked to the waist and this was not enough for him—for them. Together, they unfastened her skirt so she could step out of it. Clad now only in her high-button shoes, she was a vision of loveliness that made Slocum even more aware of how lucky he was.

"You're overdressed," she said accusingly. Working together again, they got Slocum's coat, vest, and shirt off. It took more work getting his pants off. He had to kick free of his boots for that.

"We're both as naked as jaybirds," she said. "Except for my shoes." She turned away from him, looked teasingly around as she bent to begin unbuttoning them.

"Don't bother," he said, moving in behind her. "I like the way you look, wearing nothing but them."

"How much do you like it?" Her voice was ragged with desire.

"This much," he said, stepping up so his crotch pressed into the firm roundness of her buttocks. He thrust forward between those half-moons and aimed down lower. He slipped along her nether lips and felt how ready she was. She reached back and caught at him, guiding him inside.

Slocum thought he was prepared for the slow entry into her core. He was wrong. It was new and wonderful and exciting as he slid slowly balls-deep into her tightness. He put his hands on her hips, but Suzanne lost her balance and rocked forward.

She caught herself on the edge of the bed and started to climb onto it.

"No, this way," Slocum said. Sweat beaded on his forehead now. He reached around so his forearm clamped firmly on her belly. With this for leverage, he pulled her back into his groin as he thrust forward. He had thought he was as deep as he could go. He was wrong. They both gasped in delight when, fully hidden, he began rotating his hips around. No spoon in a mixing bowl had ever felt finer or more fulfilled.

"Fast, John, do it faster. I want it hard."

"It's hard, all right." Slocum burned all the way down into

his balls. When Suzanne shoved her hips back as he drove forward, he knew he was losing control. He began pistoning faster, sinking deep and hot and hard.

He was vaguely aware of her crying out. He was too lost in his own sensations to notice. When he spilled his seed, he pulled her back into his crotch so hard he lost balance. They turned, still locked together, and he sat heavily on the bed where Suzanne had been leaning.

She straddled his legs as he sat, moving herself up and down furiously until there was no more reason to do so. Suzanne rolled to one side and finally crawled into the bed. Slocum lay half under her, feeling the sleek skin, her soft, hot breath, the way she moved lazily now.

"Will you, John?"

"Again? I'm plumb tuckered out. You do that to a man."

"Not that," she said, moving closer. He felt her still rigid nipples rubbing against his back as she scooted around. Her hand snaked over his body and worked lower to cradle his limp organ. One leg lifted over his so she could strop against his thigh.

"What then?"

"You'll help Seamus? He's in a world of trouble."

Slocum could only nod. He had done what he could to help the rancher—more than anyone else in Heavenly, he had done what he could. Somehow, he wasn't overly surprised that Suzanne wanted to help Murphy, too.

15

Slocum got back to the Bar-S ranch house by late afternoon the next day. He had spent a considerable amount of time with Suzanne Underwood, pleasurably so, but he felt a growing tension between them the longer they were together. Waiting at Murphy's small cabin for the man to return had not seemed a good idea, but Suzanne had insisted. Slocum wondered what Seamus Murphy's reaction would have been if he had found the two of them intimately engaged.

Shrugging it off since it never happened, Slocum went into the study and sank into Wimmer's chair. He heaved a deep sigh. This would always be Wimmer's chair since he had been sitting in it when he died. And this was Wimmer's office and, Slocum reluctantly admitted, the Bar-S was Wimmer's ranch. Jackson Wimmer had put his indelible brand on everything. Thought of selling it all off once the herd was sold and safely on railcars heading back East danced in Slocum's mind again.

Being tied down as a ranch owner didn't bother him as much as he thought it would. Inheriting the Bar-S worried at him in ways he had never considered, however. He had been *given* the ranch and had not earned it. The few weeks he had worked it as foreman hardly counted. Finding a twenty-dollar gold piece was one thing. Being handed a working, profitable

128

ranch was another. It galled him that he saw no way of putting his own imprint on it. Even changing the name from Bar-S to something else made no sense. He could claim the brand as reasonable, him being Slocum and all. But Wimmer's Bar-S wasn't likely to ever be Slocum's Bar-S.

Even the notion of finding a filly in Heavenly and settling down faded after his tryst with Suzanne. None of the women in town could match her—and she wasn't going to let him throw a bridle on her and claim her as his own. He doubted any man could, but if one came close to getting her into his corral, it would be Seamus Murphy. Suzanne Underwood had never said as much, but Slocum knew she was sweet on the fiery Irishman.

He leaned back in the chair and stared at the bullet hole in the ceiling. Again came vague notions drifting across the edge of his mind like thistledown against his cheek. Just as quickly, the wind blew away any conclusion to the chaotic thoughts. Slocum reared back and clasped his hands behind his head. He looked around the spacious, well-appointed room, but for some reason his eyes came to rest on the blank wall to the side of the desk. This was the spot Suzanne had stared at so intently and that had caused such anger.

He groaned as he stood. He could ride all day and not feel this sore. Suzanne was a powerful lot of woman. Slocum went to the bare wall and looked closely at it. By catching the afternoon sun against the wall in just the right angle, he saw that a picture had hung here long enough for the wood around it to fade. A quick look around convinced him the picture had not been knocked down or otherwise fallen. Whatever had been here was gone.

Too many mysteries stalked the Bar-S for him to ever be comfortable here. Slocum came to his decision. He would sell the place after roundup. First, he needed to know what it was he was selling.

Going through the cabinets in the office revealed a ledger with Wimmer's crabbed writing and careful numbers all

lined up in columns. Slocum dropped this onto the desk. He needed to study it and try to figure out how the old man had kept his books. If he wanted to sell the Bar-S, he needed to know exactly how profitable the place was and the full extent of the rangeland.

The rest of the cabinet revealed nothing of interest. Slocum moved to a low table just under the bare spot on the wall and found a drawer. He opened it and found a diary with Wimmer's name embossed on the cover in gold lettering. Slocum started to take it out, then stopped. Reading another's diary was worse than spying. Whatever Jackson Wimmer had thought would be recorded inside, Slocum wasn't sure he wanted to know. He hesitated again, then opened the cover. The diary dated back several years, making him wonder if there were earlier volumes all filled and filed somewhere. With sudden resolve, Slocum slammed shut the cover and pawed through the other items in the drawer. He had never thought Wimmer was the type to collect small broken wood toys and odd-colored rocks, but they were all in the drawer.

Slocum shut the drawer on Wimmer's peculiar treasures. There was only so much one man ought to know about another, and poking through this drawer gave him too much information about the crusty old galoot. The people in Heavenly might have hated Wimmer's guts, but Slocum had developed a certain respect for him, if not actual liking.

He had other matters to attend to instead of figuring out why Wimmer had saved the relics he had.

He pulled back the chair behind Wimmer's desk and sat. On the desk lay the ledger book taken from the cabinet, silently inviting him to use some skull sweat figuring out the financial details of the Bar-S. He rested his hand on the cover, and had started to open it when a pounding at the outer door echoed through the ranch house.

"Come on in," Slocum called. He leaned back. His hand drifted to his belt buckle so he could go for his six-shooter if trouble walked through the door.

Trouble like Colorado Pete Kelso.

Slocum was surprised to see his visitor was the gent from Heavenly.

"Slocum?" The man stood in the doorway, looking around as if he hunted for a rat hole to dive into.

"Mr. Robertson," Slocum said in greeting. He did not move his hand from the butt of his Colt Navy. "I didn't expect to see you again."

Rupert Robertson came into the room, eyes darting about suspiciously.

"You alone?"

"Only you and me, if that's what you call being alone," Slocum said. He rocked back, taking his hand from his pistol when he saw that Roop Robertson was not likely to gun him down. From what he could tell, the man was unarmed, though he might carry a small pistol in a shoulder rig. As Robertson approached, his jacket billowed out from his body. If he carried any weapon, it had to be up his sleeve or in his boot.

"I want the Bar-S. I'm willin' to pay up for it."

"It's not for sale." Slocum would have sold to Robertson if the man had come to him only ten minutes earlier. Or maybe not. Something about the weasel of a man irritated Slocum. He had no real bond to the Bar-S, but the ranch deserved to be in better hands than those of Roop Robertson.

"I'll offer you more 'n you could ever hope to get from anybody else."

"Who the hell are you?"

The question took Robertson by surprise. The man's mouth opened and closed like a trout flopped up on a riverbank. Robertson finally got his wits about him.

"Just a body who knows a value. The Bar-S is a good ranch. You're not the ownin' type."

"And you are?" Slocum looked the man over and knew, whatever Robertson did for a living, it was not ranching. The closest this potential buyer had ever come to a cow was sticking a fork in a steak at some restaurant. The more Slocum

looked, the more he wondered if Robertson had ever had enough money to even buy a steak. His clothing was thread-bare, his boots unpolished, and it might have been a while since he had eaten a square meal.

"'Course I am. I . . . I got plenty of money to buy the ranch off you."

Slocum stood and went around the large desk. Robertson backed away as he came. Even expecting Slocum to attack him, Robertson was too slow by half. Slocum grabbed the man by the throat and lifted until only his toes dragged along the carpet.

"Who are you working for? You don't have two nickels to rub together, and you've never worked a herd in your life."

"Me, I work for me." Robertson gurgled as Slocum squeezed tighter.

"How much is he paying you?"

"Fifty dollars. This ain't worth no fifty dollars. He said you'd sell right off. Kelso never said you'd try to kill me!"

Slocum dropped the man. Robertson fell to the floor, gasping for breath. He wasn't surprised that Robertson had named the real culprit behind the clumsy attempt to purchase the ranch.

"Where'd Kelso get money to buy the place?"

"I don't know. I don't know!" Robertson cowered as Slocum advanced on. "He paid me twenty and said I'd get the rest when you sold. That's all I know!"

"Get off my land. If I see you again, that twenty riding in your pocket ought to be enough for a decent pine coffin."

Roop Robertson scuttled away like a spider, got to his feet, slipped, and then found traction. He raced out the door and less than a minute later, Slocum heard a horse galloping away. A deep breath settled him a mite. He made sure his six-gun slid easily from his holster, then went hunting for Colorado Pete Kelso.

He found him in the bunkhouse, lounging back and swill-ing from a pint of whiskey.

"I just ran him off," Slocum said. He watched Kelso closely to be sure the man didn't have a pistol hidden under a blanket near his hand. If Kelso so much as twitched, Slocum was going to gun him down. He had reached the end of his rope with his top hand.

"Figured you had from the way Robertson run off like a scalded dog," Kelso said. Slocum was glad the man didn't feign ignorance and irritate him further.

"On your feet."

Kelso downed the rest of his liquor and then tossed the empty bottle at Slocum. He followed the bottle in a rush, fists flying. Slocum dodged the bottle, but could not avoid a heavy fist smashing into his upper arm. He staggered back, trying to get his balance. Kelso kept coming as he pressed his advantage. Slocum caught another punch on his cheek that snapped his head around.

By now cowboys from all around came to see what caused the ruckus.

Slocum put his head down, took a couple more punches to his shoulders, and then charged like an angry bull. He slammed his shoulder into Kelso's belly and lifted the man off the floor. Colorado Pete continued to hammer at his back, but Slocum was beyond feeling the slight damage. He spun Kelso around and heaved him outside. Kelso sprawled in the dirt in front of the bunkhouse.

"Don't," Slocum said, when he saw how Kelso was reaching under his coat. "If you pull a gun, you're dead."

Ryan and Jenks nudged each other, then came over. As Ryan held Kelso down, his partner pulled Kelso's six-gun out and tossed it away.

"So you and your gang gonna murder me?" Kelso glared at Slocum.

Slocum unbuckled his gun belt and handed it to Ryan. A crooked grin came to Kelso's lips. He got to his feet and squared off. This was the last decent expression he would ever have. Slocum unloaded a haymaker that caught Kelso

in the center of his face. His nose broke and a spray of bright red blood geysered out. The man staggered and grabbed for his smashed face.

Slocum gauged distances, stepped up, and swung with the full power of arm and body behind the blow. He buried his fist wrist-deep in Kelso's belly.

The man folded like a bad poker hand.

Stepping back, panting harshly, Slocum looked down at his fallen opponent kicking feebly on the ground.

"You're fired," Slocum said. To his surprise, the gathered cowboys all cheered. He looked at Ryan and saw a wide grin on the young man's face. Jenks clapped him on the shoulder, and others crowded in to shake his hand. Slocum had to pull back because he thought he might have cracked a bone or two in his hand with the punch to Kelso's face.

"That sidewinder deserved it," Ryan said. "I was thinkin' on leavin' the Bar-S if I had to put up with him much longer."

"You're the new top hand," Slocum said. "I need a ramrod for the drive to the railhead. You up for it?" He looked at Jenks. If he had thought Ryan's smile was big, it was nothing compared to his partner's.

Slocum bent down and grabbed a handful of shirtfront and pulled Kelso to a sitting position. He knelt and shoved his face close. The smell of blood made his own nostrils flare and his heart beat a little faster again.

"You can keep the horse," Slocum said. "Everything else will be divvied up among the men."

Kelso made some inarticulate sound. Slocum shook him until the man's eyes cleared, and he stared straight at him.

"You and the rustler with the green hat were in cahoots. I don't know if you were part of that gang or if you just happened to tell them where to find Bar-S cattle. It doesn't matter. They're locked up, and maybe you ought to be. There's no proof, but I reckon you've been selling Bar-S cattle to the rustlers. Is that where Robertson's money to buy the Bar-S came from? My own cattle?"

"I'll kill you, Slocum. I'll kill you!" Kelso's threat came amid a new shower of blood as he tried to exhale through his nose.

"Don't make me shoot you, Kelso. I will. You won't be the first—or the last." The coldness of Slocum's words and the steely green eyes fixed on Kelso made the former top hand look away.

"My gear. I want my gear."

"Fetch his saddle, Ryan. Get his horse ready."

"No, no, my gear in the bunkhouse!"

Slocum stood and dragged Kelso to his feet. With a strong shove he got the man walking toward the corral.

"You can't steal my gear," Kelso cried.

"Were you in cahoots with George Gilley, too? Seems rustling dropped off when I ran him out of Colorado, then started again a few weeks later about the time the green-hat gang showed up. You responsible for more than twenty head of Bar-S cattle being stolen?"

"You haven't seen the last of me, Slocum."

"I doubt that. A man like you'd try to shoot me in the back."

"All ready to go, Mr. Slocum," called Ryan. He led Kelso's horse from the corral.

"One minute," Slocum said. "That's all the time you got to make yourself scarce."

Kelso had taken off his bandanna and used it to stanch the flow of blood from his nose. He clumsily mounted and rode away, muttering to himself as he galloped off.

"He's a mean cuss, Mr. Slocum," said Ryan. "You better watch yourself real close. Me and Jenks and the rest'll do what we can."

"I think we've seen the end of rustling," Slocum said, watching the dust cloud settle. Kelso was gone, but he had ridden in the direction of Heavenly. That meant he wasn't likely to go too far. He would belly up to a bar, get himself roaring drunk, and find some Dutch courage in bad whiskey.

Slocum knew he would have to finish the fight started in the bunkhouse sooner or later.

"You reckon he was responsible fer it all?" asked Jenks.

"He probably told the rustlers where to take our beeves so they wouldn't get caught. What we've got will probably fetch a decent price. That means all the more for you boys to share," Slocum said.

A new cheer went up from the cowboys.

He looked at them and said, "I'm not paying you to lolly-gag. Get to work. Get them to work, Ryan."

"Yes, *sir*."

Slocum waited for his cowboys to disperse and get to their chores. It took a lot of work to keep a ranch in good shape. Without Colorado Pete Kelso, the work would be done a lot quicker.

He walked back to the ranch house and promised himself a long, hot bath to get rid of all the aches. After all he had done in the past couple days, he deserved it.

16

"How many?" Slocum stared in disbelief at Ryan. The young cowboy's grin was huge.

"O'er a thousand, Mr. Slocum. We rounded up o'er a thousand head of cattle, all with the Bar-S brand on their rumps."

Slocum let out a long, low whistle of disbelief. He had worked on Wimmer's ledger, but could not make head nor tail of it. The man had kept meticulous records, but they were all in some code only he could decipher. Or maybe Slocum simply didn't have the book learning needed to figure out the full extent of the Bar-S holdings.

"You're not out rustling cattle to add to the count, are you?"

Ryan laughed and shook his head. "No, sir. That there's the best count we can make. The Bar-S covers a lot of country. Took me and Jenks and the boys a whale of a long time to scout it all. Without any more rustlin' goin' on, why, we have quite a herd."

"Quite a herd," Slocum repeated softly. He was richer than he had ever considered. Louder, he said, "Half of all the profit will be divvied up between you and the rest."

"Half? That'd make us all rich," Ryan said. "Leastways, it'd make us a damn sight richer 'n we are now."

"You all deserve it, sticking with me the way you did."

"Nothing to it. You're a good boss, Mr. Slocum. It's gonna be our pleasure to work fer you as long as you'll have us. And if you keep payin' bonuses like that, you might need a stick to pry us loose. We'll hang on tighter 'n a blood leech in a Louisiana bayou."

Slocum looked across the broad grassy stretch of the high meadow where most of the Bar-S cattle grazed. He imagined three or four other expanses equaling this. There had to be that many if he had a herd so large.

"We ain't seen him either," Ryan said.

"Kelso? Heard tell he was making trouble in town, but when I went in last week, he was gone."

"He's like steppin' in cow shit. No matter how you scrape, there's always some stink left behind. He's not gone too far, mark my words."

"Get the herd bedded down for the night," Slocum said. "We need a decent map to find a trail to the railhead at Montrose that won't work off all the meat on their bones."

"I went on the drive last year," Ryan said. "I think I remember the trail purty good."

"We'll talk it over at chuck," Slocum said. "Are there still strays to the west of here?"

"Saw a few. Not more than ten or so."

"You keep the herd all quiet. I'll see if I can't find those strays." Slocum climbed into the saddle and rode west, the sun bright in his face. The past couple weeks had been close to perfect for him. The rustlers were gone, Kelso had disappeared, and even the fuss about Murphy murdering Jackson Wimmer had quieted down, though Slocum still felt the undercurrent in Heavenly when he went in for supplies at Gutherie's store and to take a nip or two of Gutherie's booze. Life was as good as it had been in a passel of years. The only thing Slocum missed was seeing Suzanne Underwood, and he reckoned she was spending her time out at Murphy's Circle M.

Slocum rode down into a ravine, then followed it around to come out near a clump of trees where a spring burbled up. He smelled the sulfur in the air and cursed. He didn't want his cows drinking from a hot spring. Too much mineral made them sickly. He had seen some cattle drinking from sulfurous ponds, then the cows just upped and died. Not that he was getting greedy, wanting as many cows as possible to be driven into the stockyards, but he didn't like seeing any animal sicken and die.

His nose wrinkled as he neared the spring. The rocks were stained bright yellow from the sulfur and more than one small, picked-clean carcass near the edge of the pond told him how dangerous drinking this water was. A larger animal might not die, but it wasn't healthy no matter the size. He had heard tell that on the other side of the mountains, over in Manitou Springs, people from back East paid huge sums of money to bathe in sulfur water. Taking the waters was supposed to cure what ailed them, from arthritis to ague and tuberculosis, but they weren't drinking the water.

A lowing from farther west caused him to turn his horse's face in that direction and away from the sulfur spring. He was glad that the cattle had either not found the sulfur spring or had left it behind. Slocum put his spurs to his mare's flanks and got the dun moving at a trot.

He saw a dozen head of cattle grazing peaceably in a narrow draw not a quarter mile ahead. As he rode, Slocum worked through numbers in his head. He could sell off a fair number of cattle, make a profit, and still have enough head left to get a good start on the next year's herd. The Bar-S was going to be successful for a long, long time at this rate.

"Bar-S," he said to himself as he guided his horse down into the narrow channel leading toward his strays. "Where'd the name come from?"

Jackson Wimmer was the kind of man who would have named the ranch after himself. The Bar-W maybe, or the J-Bar-W. Slocum decided this was just one more thing

about Wimmer and his legacy that would never come to light. He had never asked, but Wimmer might have bought the ranch from an earlier owner. If so, changing the brand might have been more trouble than it was worth, though after a couple seasons, running a pair of brands would no longer be necessary.

"Come on, you mangy cows," Slocum shouted. He unfastened his rope and played out a ten-foot length. Whirling the end around his head made a whistling sound that got the attention of the beeves. They looked up from their afternoon meal with dull brown eyes.

Then all hell broke loose. Slocum was forming them into a smaller herd to get moving when a half dozen more cattle came thundering down the draw from higher up on the hillside.

The frightened run of the other cattle spooked the ones Slocum was working. He looked from side to side, and knew he had no room to get out of the way of the stampeding cattle. That left only one thing to do. He swung about and raked his spurs along the dun's sides, leaving bloody streaks. The frightened horse lit out like its tail was on fire. Slocum hunkered down, head next to the straining horse's neck.

"Come on, run, run!"

The horse's hooves pounded hard on the ground, but Slocum felt new vibration. Thirty head of cattle came closer and closer behind. He heard them and smelled them and felt their panic. The fear transmitted itself to his horse and caused it to balk.

"Not now, run, run, run, damn you, run!"

Slocum did not quite regain control of the horse, but did get it galloping along. He was content to give the horse its head—for the moment. It remained in the narrow channel cut by years of heavy spring runoff from higher elevations, but Slocum realized he had to get out fast when his horse began to flag. With every step, the animal weakened. Its terror grew and it started to toss its head about.

Slocum chanced a look over his shoulder. The cattle were so close he could almost feel their hot breaths. He did see wide bovine eyes completely ringed by white. Their fright was not lessening and neither was their headlong stampede.

Swinging his weight and using his right knee to press into the horse's flank turned it enough for it to stumble up a slope. The dun scrambled onto the lip of the draw and stumbled a few more paces. Slocum drew rein and halted its panicky run. The horse's flanks heaved as its mighty lungs sucked in air. Slocum patted the horse's neck and calmed it the best he could.

The stampeding cattle had raced on down the ravine, and had come to a spot where the high walls turned lower, allowing the cattle to spread out. As they did so, their panic eased.

"That was a close shave," Slocum said. He pushed his hat back and mopped at his forehead with his bandanna. He remained where he was, not bothering to herd the cattle. They headed in the right direction. Ryan or another of his hands would spot the beeves and get them into the main herd.

Slocum wanted to do a bit of exploring. It took some doing, but he got his horse back down into the draw and started uphill again. When he reached the spot where he had found the cattle grazing, he studied the ground. It had been so badly cut up by the cattle's hooves he could make out nothing more than that the cattle had eaten all the grass there. He rode slowly farther up the draw, and found where the other cattle had come charging down to spook the cattle he had first found.

He stepped down and examined the ground more carefully. His finger traced around a deep hoofprint in the soft earth. He could still make out where the horseshoe had been nailed on. Slocum looked around, but whoever had ridden here was long gone.

Refusing to simply ignore his brush with being trampled, he prowled about restlessly, getting the picture of what had happened. The cattle in the draw were a lure for him. A

lone rider had stampeded another dozen cattle and caused the tide of frightened beef that had almost overwhelmed him. The conclusion was inescapable. Someone had tried to kill him.

"Who might that be?" Slocum asked himself. He had a score to settle with Colorado Pete Kelso because he couldn't think of anyone else inclined to do such a thing. As he started to mount, something colorful fluttering nearby caught his eye. Pulling his foot back out of the stirrup, he went to the low thorn bush and tugged the bandanna free from the nettles.

Holding it up to the light to see it better, Slocum turned it over and over. He recognized the distinctive orange kerchief as the one Seamus Murphy had worn when the marshal had clapped him into jail. Slocum started to cry out about the stupidity of the Irish rancher. Trying to kill the only man who had tried to get him free of the law seemed monumentally stupid. Then Slocum calmed a mite.

It *was* stupid. There was no reason for even a hothead like Seamus Murphy to kill Slocum. Even if he carried a grudge, it was hardly the biggest or worst. Slocum could see Murphy gunning down the marshal or taking on half the town for what they said about him, but there was no point in putting Slocum at the head of the list.

Unless . . .

The uneasy crawling in his gut warned Slocum that he might have trespassed, on property Murphy considered his own. Had Suzanne Underwood let slip that she and Slocum had spent time together? That would set off most any man, being cuckolded. Worse, Slocum could see Suzanne holding it over Murphy, telling him she was going off with the richest man in Middle Park. That would be a double sting to a touchy man's pride.

Slocum tucked the bandanna into his coat pocket, and set out to track the man responsible for driving the cattle down into the draw and causing the stampede. At first, the trail was confused by the cattle trampling the dirt. He cast out a bit

farther and found a single set of fresh hoofprints going away from the draw.

Buoyed by the sight of such distinct tracks, Slocum rode faster. Now and then he lifted his gaze to the horizon to be sure he wasn't riding into an ambush, but from the way the rider had whipped his horse to a gallop, Slocum knew he was following a man who wanted nothing more than to get the hell away from the scene of his crime.

His would-be crime. Slocum touched the butt of the pistol slung at his left hip, then rode faster. It was almost dusk when he lost the trail. The rider had gone across a broad stretch of rock. In daylight, Slocum might have found bright scratches where steel horseshoes had nicked the rock, but in the twilight, such a pursuit was impossible.

Stretching, he looked around. It was quite a ride, but he could get over a ridge of mountains and drop down on the far side—onto Seamus Murphy's land. Slocum knew he should have told Ryan or another of his cowboys where he was headed, but he felt an itch to settle scores.

He crested the ridge and worked down a trail on the far side, and eventually came to the narrow road leading to Murphy's cabin. The stretch of road ahead had been nothing but misery for Slocum, but he rode on. This time he didn't get his horse shot out from under him. He halted and stared at the cabin when he came to the clearing. A wispy curl of wood smoke rose from the chimney, but Slocum knew better than to assume Murphy was inside. His caution paid off when he heard grunting and sloshing.

Murphy made his way from the spring some distance away, lugging two fully filled buckets. In the darkness, Murphy did not see him. Slocum dismounted and walked closer. He made certain the leather keeper had been slipped away from the hammer of his Colt Navy. If the need arose, he could slap leather and get his six-shooter blazing in the wink of an eye.

The Irishman whistled between his teeth as he dumped both buckets of water into a barrel beside the front door. He

started back for the spring when Slocum called out his name. Murphy froze.

"Slocum?"

"I want a word with you. Turn around real slow and keep both those buckets in your hands. Go for a gun and you're a dead man."

"Go on, cut me down. You might as well shoot me in the back. It's what the rest of you people want to do."

"Who's that?"

"Anyone in Heavenly. Everyone. They keep hopin' I won't be able to pay the mortgage on the ranch so they can run me out. They won't do it! I'm not givin' up!"

"Heard tell that you were behind in payment to the bank, but you haven't been foreclosed on yet."

"They're thinkin' on it."

"You've got a chip on your shoulder."

"And you've got the drop on me. Either shoot me in the back or get off my property."

Slocum dropped the reins and walked around to where Murphy could see that he had yet to draw his six-shooter.

"You been over on my land today?"

"That's none of your business."

"I'm making it mine," Slocum said. He pulled the orange bandanna from his pocket. "This yours?"

"Looks like the one I lost. Don't see many that color, so, yeah, reckon it's mine."

"Where'd you lose it? I saw you wearing it when you were locked up."

"For a trumped-up rustling charge!"

"Where did you lose it?"

Murphy dropped his water buckets. He thrust out his chin truculently, as if daring Slocum to take a swing at him. The way Slocum felt at the moment, it wouldn't be his fist smashing into the young man's face. A single bullet would serve his purposes better. But he held back.

"Where did you lose it? I'm not going to ask again."

"I don't know. I had it when Zamora let me out of jail. I got back here and took it off, thinking to wash it."

Slocum ran his fingers over the grimy cloth. It hadn't been washed in a month of Sundays.

"Did you?"

"I must have dropped it. I took a bath and washed my clothes. But I couldn't find it." He shrugged. "Thought the wind had taken it. I'd just piled my clothes out front while I was rootin' around inside the house huntin' for other things to wash."

"What else?"

"Bedsheets. That was it."

Slocum stepped closer. Murphy's bravado cracked, and he took an involuntary step back. His eyes went wide when Slocum took a deep sniff.

"Show me your bed."

"I ain't—"

"Show me."

"All right, Slocum. You're not going to—"

Slocum shoved him into the cabin and went to the narrow bed. All he had to do was touch the sheet to know Murphy had been telling the truth. It had been washed recently.

"You been here all day?"

"I've been here since I got out of jail, if it's any concern of yours."

Slocum pulled the orange bandanna from his coat pocket and tossed it to Murphy.

"Needs cleaning."

Slocum left the rancher with his mouth gaping and a hundred unasked questions on his lips. He mounted his dun mare and rode away, thinking hard. Somebody had gone to a bit of trouble to frame Murphy. If Slocum had been killed in the stampede, his ranch hands would have found the bandanna and probably recognized it. Whether they went to the marshal or simply strung up Murphy wouldn't much matter. Both Murphy and Slocum would be dead.

Something made Slocum even more curious, though. If he had not asked some questions, he might have gunned down Murphy. Was that good enough for whoever had stampeded the cattle? Killing Murphy looked to be the result, no matter what happened to Slocum.

That was more than curious. It was downright diabolical.

17

"There might be a couple strays still in the high pasture, Mr. Slocum, but fetchin' 'em in for the drive's not gonna matter one whit." Ryan took off his dusty Stetson and banged it against his thigh. A cloud of brown trail dust billowed up. He slapped it once more and then settled the hat squarely on his head, the brim touching the tops of both ears.

"We'll need some supplies from town," Slocum said, "for the drive. Otherwise, we're ready."

"Counted close to eleven hunnerd cattle," Ryan said. He looked sheepish and said, "Jenks counted 'em. I'm not too good at cipherin'."

"Have him teach you. I don't want a top hand who can't count higher than the total of his fingers and toes."

"That'd be eighteen," Ryan said. Seeing Slocum's reaction, he added, "Froze two toes off last winter."

"Least you know how many you've got," Slocum said, laughing. He was pleased with the roundup. He had cattle he had not found listed in Jackson Wimmer's ledger—and all carried the Bar-S brand. They were his cattle to do with as he saw fit.

That posed something of a problem for him. He could sell all the cattle and make a few extra dollars, or leave some

in the pastureland for breeding next year's herd. If he did that, it meant he intended to stay and become a full-time rancher.

"You thinkin' hard on something, Mr. Slocum? I found that there map of the trail to Montrose. I kin read maps a whole lot better 'n I do books. This will be a trail I've ridden before."

"Last year," Slocum said, his mind wandering. How many cattle to keep back? It would have to be the prize heifers, some calves, and maybe a pair of bulls.

"Who you want to send into town for the supplies?"

Slocum shook himself out of his reverie. It took a couple seconds to remember what had gone on.

"Who deserves a break from riding herd?"

"Reckon we all do. But it wouldn't be a good thing to let ever' one of us go into town. Those saloons are a big attraction when you have a couple dimes in your pocket."

"I'd get back a dozen drunk cowboys, is that it?"

"You'd have to bail us all out of Marshal Zamora's lockup. I don't cotton much to bein' the only sober one crammed into one of them cells with drunks," Ryan said. "But if any of the boys got into a row, I'd hafta go to his aid."

Slocum laughed again. It felt good not to be tense and on guard all the time. It felt good to be a rancher and to be looking at a powerful lot of money from a decent herd.

Slocum heard himself saying, "Send a couple boys into town for the supplies. You and Jenks get back to the herd and cut out three hundred of the best to use as breeding stock for next season."

"Yes, *sir*," Ryan said. He let out a whoop and tossed his hat high into the air.

"Why so excited?"

"I just won a twenty-dollar bet with Jenks. He said you wasn't stickin' 'round next year. Yippee!" Ryan raced off to spread the news. Slocum settled back on the front porch of the ranch house—his ranch house. He looked across the yard to the bunkhouse and the barn and the corral filled with

horses. All his. It was quite a responsibility, but that part had never gnawed away much at Slocum. His entire life had been filled with doing what was right. This seemed right, even if it meant giving up his wandering to find what lay just beyond the horizon.

"The Bar-S is what lay at the end of the trail," Slocum said. He rocked back in a chair and listened to the flies buzzing, the horses moving about in the corral, and all the other comforting sounds of a ranch.

Ryan and Jenks rode to the high pasture to select the stock for next year. Slocum would check, but doubted either man would go far wrong in his choices. A few minutes after that, the buckboard with three other men rattled off down the road toward Heavenly, intent on fetching supplies for the trail drive. The smaller sounds Slocum had heard before now became the only ones reaching him.

Until he heard something moving inside his house. Without hurrying, he reached across his belly and laid his hand on the ebony handle of his six-gun. He turned his head a little to get a better look at the front door. It had blown open in the weak breeze stirring around. Through the opening he caught a quick reflection in a mirror and an indistinct body moving across the far window, now lit with noonday sun.

Slocum rocked forward and got to his feet. He slid his six-shooter from its holster and went to the door. Using the toe of his boot, he pushed it wide open and lifted the muzzle to sight in on . . . Suzanne Underwood.

She jumped when she saw him in the door, his gun pointed at her. A hand fluttered to her throat and she let out a tiny gasp.

"Oh, John, you scared me. It seems like you're always pointing that thing at me."

He dropped his pistol back into his holster, went inside, and kicked the door shut with his heel. Looking at the woman was about as delicious as sitting on the porch and realizing everything he saw was his personal property. Suzanne had on

a new floral print dress made of thinner fabric than the white
one he had seen her wearing that first time long ago in Heavenly. The day was warm and she had sweat a mite. The cloth
plastered itself to her chest and made her breasts look as if
they had been upholstered. The nipples were visible and so
inviting, it was hard for Slocum to take his eyes off them.

"You came in the back way."

"I didn't want your men to see me."

"If you drove your buggy, they saw it when they left for
town."

"I . . . sold it. All I have now is a horse to ride." She
rubbed her backside. "It's been a while, and I'm not used to
long miles yet."

She saw how he stared at her as she ran her hands over
her curvy hindquarters, and smiled.

"Am I amusing you?"

"Can't say that," he admitted. "More like giving me quite
a show."

"A show? Whatever can you mean?" Her hands left her
pert rump and dropped to her sides. Fingers curling, she
grabbed double handfuls of cloth and began raising her skirt
off the floor. Her high-button shoes and trim ankles appeared. But she did not stop as she lifted more and gave him
a look of bare calf.

"If you give me much more of a show, I'm not certain
where I should sit to watch it."

"Sit anywhere you like, but I don't want you only watching," Suzanne said. Her tongue slipped between her ruby
lips and made a slow circuit. "No, John, I don't want you just
watching. I want you to be *participating*."

She moved slowly toward him, lifting her skirt even
higher so he could see bare legs. When she was about arm's
length away, she widened her stance and kept pulling up her
skirt with a soft rustle. Slocum hardly noticed the sound. He
was too intent on her bare skin and that she wasn't wearing
any underwear.

"I knew I'd see pretty vistas when I came to Colorado," Slocum said. He unfastened his gun belt and laid it on the desk. Then he reached out and ran his fingers over the sleek curves of her breasts. She had been sweating more than he thought. His fingers turned slick. He caught one nipple through the cloth and twisted it slightly. Suzanne closed her eyes and moaned softly.

"I want more, John," she said. "I want only what *you* can give me."

She gasped when he began giving both breasts the same treatment. Then he slid his fingers under the cloth and peeled it slowly off her skin. Unbuttoning her blouse took a little doing, but feeling her heat and silken skin made it worthwhile. He tossed her blouse to the floor, leaving her naked to the waist.

"How do you want me?"

In answer, Slocum put his hands around her slender waist and lifted. She let out a cry of surprise as her feet left the floor. Then she landed hard on the edge of the desk. She put her hands on her breasts and began massaging them.

"What now?"

Slocum ran his hands up her calves and slid her skirt away, just as he had stripped her of her blouse. When her skirt bunched around her waist, she looked more naked than dressed. He dropped to his knees and let her dangle her legs over his shoulders. This brought his face in close so he could lick and kiss her nether lips.

She leaned back, supporting herself on her elbows. Of their own volition, her knees rose until she placed her feet on the edge of the desk. Her knees parted, letting him have full access to her most intimate region.

Slocum drove his tongue forward and tasted the salty tang of an aroused woman. Using his tongue, he dipped and dived, sucked and slid it all around, until she trembled like she was seized with a fever.

"More, John. This is so good, but I want more. I want *you*."

He was in no hurry. He continued to kiss across the thick dark bush and moved upward slowly to her belly. His tongue repeated with her navel what it had done lower. He felt her stomach quiver at his damp touch. Then he skipped over the thick wad of skirt and found the deep canyon between her breasts.

"Oh, don't stop, John. I want this. Oh, how I want this!"

She laced her fingers behind his head to hold him down at her breasts. He spiraled up one snowy mound, toyed with the hard pink nipple he found, then skied down into the deep valley to repeat his action on the other side. When he caught this nipple between his lips, he sucked hard and drew it across his teeth. She arched her back and then flopped weakly onto the desk.

"More," she gasped out. "More, more."

Her legs were still draped over his shoulders. He reached up and drew her closer. His crotch pressed into hers.

"Free you, get you out." She reached around and hurriedly unbuttoned him. He snapped free of his cloth prison—and sank immediately into her heated center.

Legs over his shoulders, she was bent double. As he thrust forward, he pressed her upper thighs down into her breasts. She recoiled, pushing him back. He slid from her.

"No, not that. No!"

He slid back into her heated tightness. The moisture he had tasted now made his erection slick. He moved faster. The friction built until the carnal heat erupted like prairie fire. It consumed him and then it consumed her. Slocum was not sure of anything but the intense sensations that ripped through him and then left him panting for breath.

He backed away, letting her legs drop to either side of his hips. Suzanne wore a smile of pure delight. Her eyes flickered open and the smile grew even more.

"So nice, John. You know exactly what I need."

"Maybe sometime we can do this in a bed. I've got a big one in the bedroom." The instant the words left his lips, he

saw the change in her. She looked away and whatever residual bliss there had been evaporated.

"Yes, that would be nice," she said, sitting up. She still did not look him in the eye as she moved off the desk and tried to smooth her skirt down over her legs. She was still bare to the waist. When he handed her the discarded blouse, she took it, still avoiding his direct gaze.

He watched her complete dressing with a mixture of loss and curiosity. If he had ever entertained any notion of settling down with Suzanne, it was gone now. But why? It wasn't anything he had done, but he couldn't see why mentioning making love in a bed would turn her so cold so quickly.

Slocum strapped his six-shooter on and waited until Suzanne completed her toilet.

"You came by for something. What was it?"

"Why, I thought we just did it," she said, but there was no passion in her words. It was as if she read from a prepared text.

"That was icing on the cake. What's the cake?"

"Oh, John, you can be so vexing. Why must you always get down to business so fast? You're just like—" Suzanne cut off her sentence abruptly. He waited for her to finish. He wanted to know who he was like, but she changed her tack. "I need a favor."

"Money?"

"No!" Her sharp retort put roses into her cheeks and fire into her eyes again. Then she took a deep breath. Somehow, the sight of those magnificent breasts rising and falling didn't move him the way it once had. "I want a favor from you."

"Seamus Murphy?"

Anger flared for a moment, then she softened. "What you must think of me," she said. "Yes. Seamus Murphy. Nobody in Heavenly likes him."

"From what he says, they all want to string him up."

"They think he killed Jackson Wimmer. He'd never do that."

"Any crime seems to have his name written on it," Slocum said, thinking of how Marshal Zamora had been so eager to brand him a rustler. The notion that Murphy might have tried to kill him with the stampede also rose in Slocum's mind, but he was good at reading men. He had made money playing poker for years and knew bluffs from the truth—most of the time. While Murphy might have gulled him, Slocum thought the young rancher was telling the truth about losing the orange bandanna. That meant someone was trying to frame him.

"He works hard on his ranch," she said. "He knows what he's doing. It's just that he has never gotten a chance to prosper."

"The bank is threatening to foreclose," Slocum said. "That's why I thought you wanted to ask me for money."

"To give to Seamus?" Suzanne shook her head. "He's too proud to accept a gift. Or even a loan. His pa had reason to hate bankers, and it rubbed off on Seamus."

"What's your part in this?"

"I . . . after what we did, it seems wrong . . . I—"

"Never mind," Slocum said. He knew that Suzanne Underwood would do whatever she could for Seamus Murphy. Although he had never seen the two of them together when they weren't arguing, it went along with what he knew of Murphy's character. He was as rough as a dried corncob. And Suzanne was smoother than silk.

"He needs your help, John. I'm begging you for it."

"Might be he should pull up stakes and go somewhere else," Slocum said. He waited for her reaction. It didn't take but an instant and he was not disappointed.

"We'd never do a thing like that! Why, this is his home. He's worked hard to prove that ranch. He's not the sort to give up because the going got tough."

Slocum nodded slowly. This was what he had hoped to hear—and matched what he had seen in Seamus Murphy. Too often the West provided enough space for a man to keep

moving to run away from his problems. They always caught up, but the open horizons let him keep going. That Murphy was willing to dig in his heels and fight for his ranch and a place in the community set well with Slocum.

"What do you want me to do that I haven't already? I got him out of jail after he was arrested for rustling, and you said you don't want money to pay off the bank."

"The murder charge against him," Suzanne said. She looked as if she had bitten into a persimmon. "You know he didn't kill Wimmer, but someone did. If you can catch his killer, that will clear Seamus."

"It doesn't seem that Marshal Zamora is going to work too hard to find anyone other than Murphy," Slocum said. He looked up at the hole in the ceiling. Where had that come from? His eyes drifted to the bare spot on the wall where a picture had hung. Somehow, those went together, but he had no idea why.

"Nobody in town will believe Seamus didn't kill Wimmer, but with someone on trial for the crime, that'll go a ways to easing Seamus's mind," she said.

Slocum looked at her sharply. That made no sense. What did Murphy care who killed Wimmer and why would finding the real murderer ease his mind?

"Kelso," he said. As if the pot had finally come to a boil and that name rose to the churning surface, he knew.

"The son of a bitch," Suzanne said. "He wouldn't leave me alone. He loved me, he said. I'd sooner go to bed with a diamondback rattler."

"He was sweet on you, and you're sweet on Murphy. Kelso wanted to frame Murphy for whatever he could. He was the one who got the drop on Murphy and accused him of rustling." Slocum's mind raced. It had been a while since he'd laid eyes on Kelso. There was no telling where he had ended up.

It might well have been out in the west pasture so he could stampede part of the herd in Slocum's direction.

"How'd Kelso get Murphy's bandanna?"

"What?" Suzanne's eyes went wide in surprise. "I didn't know that he had it."

Slocum quickly explained what had happened to him.

"Seamus would never do a thing like that. If he wanted to kill a man, he'd walk right up to him and have it out."

"I believe you're right. His temper tells me he's not the sneaky kind."

"If that's a compliment, thank you," Suzanne said. She looked at him skeptically.

"Kelso left his gear in the bunkhouse. I want to see what's there."

They went to the empty bunkhouse. It took Slocum a few minutes of poking around to find the box where Ryan had shoved it. Suzanne sat on a bunk as Slocum knelt and began rummaging through what was mostly junk.

"There, John, that's Seamus's spare spoon. It's got his brand etched into it. He lost it after I—" Suzanne looked hard at Slocum, then summoned her courage. "He couldn't it find after I spent the night with him for the first time."

"You used the spoon?"

"I don't understand what that has to do with anything."

"If Kelso was following you and saw, he might have stolen the spoon to have something of yours. Something you used."

"He could have stolen Seamus's six-shooter to frame him! And his bandanna! There's no telling what else he might have taken."

"All of it to remind him of you and to get back at Murphy. If he got Murphy convicted, he'd be free to court you."

"Never in a million years!"

"When a man's crazy in love, things like that don't matter," Slocum said. "I suspect Kelso is both crazy in love and just plain loco."

"Do you think he murdered Wimmer?"

Again Slocum heard the bitterness in her voice, but knew better than to try to find its source.

"He had reason enough to do it and then frame Murphy. If Murphy and I hadn't been in town together, it might have worked."

"Prove it, John, please. Prove it." Suzanne chewed her lower lip, then stood and went to the bunkhouse door. She turned and started to say something, thought better of it, and rushed out.

Slocum kept pawing through the box and found a framed picture buried at the bottom. He pulled it out. It was about the right size to have been taken off the wall in Wimmer's office. Holding it up, he looked at the faded photograph of a much younger Jackson Wimmer and a girl who could not have been older than five or six.

He pushed the box back where Ryan had stored it, but he took the picture to the ranch house and hung it where it had once been proudly displayed by a crusty old curmudgeon.

The frame neatly covered the unfaded area on the wall. This was the picture that had been removed by Kelso, probably when he had killed Jackson Wimmer. Now all Slocum had to do was prove it.

18

"Shore thing, Mr. Slocum. We got this here herd ready to move," Ryan said. "Don't go worryin' your head over it none."

"You're doing good," Slocum said. The cattle filled the pasture. As far as the eye could see, brown and white and black movement told of the huge herd ready to drive to market. Ryan had selected well for the start of next year's herd also. Slocum felt safe in letting the young man keep order in camp until he got back.

"You be gone long?" Ryan asked.

"Don't think so," Slocum said. He looked up the draw where he had almost been killed by the stampede. He had been distracted before by Murphy's kerchief. Although it had been a while, he thought he could find the trail of the man who had tried to kill him—Colorado Pete Kelso.

He and Colorado Pete had some serious talking to do, and it wasn't just about the stampede.

"We got a week, maybe two before the weather changes on us," said Ryan. "This high up in the mountains, the weather's always a bitch. Can't predict from one day to the next."

"I won't be more than a day. If I am, take the cattle on into Montrose and wait for me there."

SLOCUM'S BAR-S RANCH 159

"I'd have to feed them in Montrose. Feedlot prices are mighty steep, and I can't negotiate the price for you. You're the owner of the Bar-S, after all."

"I'll be back," Slocum said, slapping Ryan on the shoulder. He appreciated the way his new top hand worried about the details. Swinging into the saddle, Slocum turned toward the west and headed out. It took less than an hour to find the draw, and two hours to convince himself he had found a faint trail leading not to Seamus Murphy's ranch but farther westward.

The notion that he might be following a ghost trail worried him a little. Then he saw how the trail circled around and headed for a pass that would put him onto the road leading into Heavenly. At this point, Slocum stopped studying the ground and started riding harder. His dun pony protested a mite, but kept him heading toward his target. Heavenly was as likely a place for Kelso to go as anywhere else since Slocum doubted he would stray far from Suzanne Underwood. The man was obsessed with her.

As he reached the road and turned toward town, Slocum wondered how far that obsession would take Kelso. Kidnap? Murder? Either was likely for a back-shooting son of a bitch like Pete Kelso. He had tried to get Murphy hanged rather than facing his rival for Suzanne's affection man-to-man. Slocum turned grim. Kelso would do anything to get the woman. Anything.

Thinking about Suzanne caused a knot to form in Slocum's belly. He was taken with her, but she was devoted to Seamus Murphy and would do anything for him that she could. Slocum saw the two of them as standing against the townspeople of Heavenly, but what drew them together was more than that. If he disengaged his emotions enough, he could see that Seamus and Suzanne were quite a pair.

"Lucky bastard," Slocum said, a rueful smile on his lips. His horse turned its head and looked up at him quizzically. A quick pat reassured the mare that all was well.

All he had to do was track down Kelso and ask a few simple questions. The answers would put Colorado Pete in jail for a long time, if they didn't get him a noose.

As Slocum rode into Heavenly, he passed the courthouse. A flash of movement caught out of the corner of his eye made him draw rein and look more carefully at low bushes under a window. The movement there did not come from a vagrant breeze. Slocum turned his pony's face toward the side of the courthouse, and was quick enough to duck when a man popped up like a prairie dog and opened fire on him.

Slocum struggled to get his horse under control. By the time he did, the gunman was gone—and a new danger presented itself. The bushes flared high with a greasy smoke and orange flame that licked at the side of the building.

"Fire!" Slocum shouted. "Ring the alarm. Fire!"

Seconds later came the clanging of the fire bell from the far side of town. Fire was more to be feared than anything else. It struck fast and could consume every building in Heavenly within minutes. Most of the structures had been built leaning against each other with no thought to safety. Materials were dried and flammable, and if the fire spread to either of the saloons, all that could be done was evacuate everyone to a safe distance and watch the town burn.

Horses neighed loudly and a smaller bell rang furiously. Slocum saw a pumper truck careening down the middle of the main street, the driver half dressed and the team almost out of control.

"Where's the fire? Where's the danged fire?"

"Courthouse," Slocum shouted. "You got water in that tank?"

"Hell, no. Need to run the hose over to the creek."

Slocum lashed his horse securely to a hitching post and helped the volunteer fireman uncoil the thick canvas hose.

"Where's the stream?"

"Yonder," the fireman said, pointing. "Hurry it up. The whole damn side of the whole damn building's on fire!"

Slocum slung the hose over his shoulder, leaned forward, dug in his toes, and started pulling. The heavy hose snaked out behind him as he sought the creek. A line of vegetation drew him. He couldn't hear the murmur of water as it cascaded over rocks due to the tumult in town now. Worse, the crackling of the fire threatened to drown out even fervent shouts of encouragement.

Slocum gave one last tug and dropped the hose to the bank. He found a deep pool, waded in, and pulled the hose after him.

"Start pumping!" His shout might have been heard, or the fireman could have figured there was no harm beginning the steam pump. The hose bucked about as it drew water. Slocum fought to hold it underwater. His arms ached from the effort, and finally he found a way to wedge the hose between two large rocks and pile others atop it to hold it in the stream. Sloshing, he climbed from the water and ran back to the fire.

Three men held the hose attached to the pump. The man who had driven the pumper rig stood next to the steam engine, cursing, kicking the balky machinery, and sometimes making small adjustments with a big wrench. Whether it was the wrench or the cursing, Slocum didn't know, but the engine kept turning and the pump provided a powerful flow of water.

He watched as the water arched up into the air and crashed down on the side of the two-story courthouse. The whitewashed wall had turned a sooty black and in some places the fire had burned through, but the prompt arrival of the pumper had prevented fiery disaster from destroying the building and the town.

"What happened, Slocum?"

He looked around to see Marshal Zamora. The man stared with wide, frightened eyes at the dwindling fire. Slocum had seen horses with the same look before they turned and galloped back into a burning barn.

"I saw a man in the bushes. The next thing I know, he took a shot at me and the fire started. I didn't get a real good look at him."

"Everyone out of the building?"

Slocum stared at the courthouse. Water continued to extinguish smaller fires that popped up.

"Don't know."

"Better go look." Zamora strode off with forced courage. Slocum reckoned the man was afraid of fires. He couldn't much blame him. He had been in more than one wildfire in his day, and they were nothing to take lightly.

"Damn me," Zamora said, pulling open the front door. A cloud of black smoke billowed out. "This is enough to make me get a decent job."

"I'll go in," Slocum said. He pushed past the marshal and went into the smoke-filled lobby. Four rooms led off the small area. Stairs at the rear went to the second floor where there would be more rooms. Eyes stinging from the acrid smoke, Slocum bent low and saw a pair of boots toward the rear of the lobby.

"Can you get to him, Slocum?"

The lawman squatted down and peered under the layer of thick smoke. He had seen the man, too.

"I'll get him out." As Slocum started to go to the rescue, the man rolled over and he got a good look at his face. "Murphy!"

Calling his name galvanized Seamus Murphy into motion. He rolled back onto his belly and wiggled like a snake to get out the back way. Slocum followed and burst out the back door and collided with Marshal Zamora.

"The son of a bitch lit out 'fore I got around," the lawman said. "I'll have his hide nailed to the barn door for this."

"Why? He was caught in the fire."

"He set the damn fire," shouted Zamora. "There's no other reason for that worthless cayuse to be in the courthouse."

Slocum said nothing as he wiped soot from his face. Zamora shouted to the volunteer firemen putting out the last of the sparks threatening to jump to other roofs. In a few minutes, Zamora came back holding a hat. He shook it at Slocum.

"See? See?"

"You've got a hat that's been burned. So?"

"It's Murphy's hat. I recognize the hatband made from those crazy Irish knots. It was in those bushes where the fire started. He's a firebug as well as a murderer."

"He didn't kill Wimmer, and he didn't set the fire. The man I saw in the bushes had his hat pulled down low when he took off running."

"You keep your nose out of this, Slocum. I don't know why you're stickin' up for that varmint, but you'll swing beside him if you don't watch yourself."

"Don't threaten me, Marshal."

"It's not a threat as long as I'm wearing this badge." Zamora tapped the battered star on his chest. "I have to keep the peace. Killing Wimmer might be somethin' nobody cared much about, but burning down the courthouse goes too far." Marshal Zamora swung around and shouted for volunteer deputies.

Slocum saw that the lawman intended to put a posse onto Murphy's trail, only it looked less like a posse and more like a lynch mob as the angry men gathered. Old hatreds had bubbled up and consumed them, making Murphy's lynching a certainty if they caught him. He stayed at the edge of the mob as Zamora whipped up their passion against Seamus Murphy. Saying a word in defense of the rancher would have gotten him strung up, so Slocum moved away and looked around the bushes where he had seen the man who had set the fire.

The shrubs were burned to bare limbs and provided no evidence. The ground had been turned to mud from the deluge from the pumper truck. Slocum went into the courthouse and poked around. The stench of burned wood choked him, but he kept looking and finally stood where he had seen Murphy.

The door to the county clerk's office stood open. Slocum went in.

On the floor lay a ledger. He stepped over it and looked for some reason Murphy might have come here. This wasn't the land office. If there had been a problem with his land deed, he would not have come here. Hardly noticing, Slocum bent and picked up the ledger and returned it to the counter.

He blinked as he saw Murphy's signature on the bottom line. Slocum closed the book and muttered to himself. Seamus Murphy had come to the courthouse to get a marriage license. Knowing that the evidence of why the rancher was in town would mean nothing to Zamora, and even less to a mob all riled up and ready to stretch Murphy's neck, Slocum knew what had to be done. He had to find the arsonist and make him confess.

Finding Murphy's hat where the fire started told Slocum who had set the fire. Colorado Pete Kelso had tried to frame Murphy before. Several times before, unless Slocum was completely mistaken. Kelso must have taken Murphy's gun and used it to kill Wimmer, then had left the young rancher's bandanna to implicate him in the stampede. Now he'd tried to frame Murphy for the fire, probably not only because Murphy loved Suzanne, but also because the young rancher wanted to marry her.

Kelso had a lot to answer for.

Marshal Zamora had finally gotten the mob mounted and headed out of town in the direction of Murphy's ranch. Slocum hoped Seamus had the good sense not to return to his cabin. He sucked in a breath, wondering what Zamora would do—or allow—if his posse found Suzanne Underwood at the cabin. Hanging a woman was not something even a blood-crazed mob would do lightly, but it was a sorry event that could not be discounted.

This made Slocum all the more eager to find Kelso and force a confession from him. Nothing less would save

Murphy from the hangman's noose or Suzanne from what the posse might do to her.

Slocum fetched his horse and rode out of town following the posse. Tracking Kelso wouldn't be possible, but figuring where the owlhoot might go was easy enough. He wanted the posse to go after Murphy, and the likely place they would find the rancher was on his own property. Slocum remembered a hill looking down into Circle M land that might give a good view of the cabin. Kelso would want to see Murphy's heels kicking in the air because that would complete his revenge for Suzanne choosing the wrong man. In his head, Kelso might even think this would leave Suzanne open to him courting her again.

It suddenly occurred to Slocum how he himself might turn this to his own advantage. Let the marshal string up Murphy, and Suzanne might fall into another man's bed— his. Barely had the idea blossomed in Slocum's head than it withered. He would never do that to get a woman. Though he had not quite come out and promised, he had assured Suzanne that he wouldn't let anything happen to her lover. More than this, any fire that might have blazed between him and the lovely woman was now turned to ashes.

"The man signed the county ledger to get a marriage license," Slocum mused.

He urged his pony into a trot, cut off the road, and struck out across the countryside, finding hilly land fast. The horse struggled to get up the steep slope, but Slocum eventually came to the top of a ridge looking down over Murphy's rangeland. It would be a while before the posse reached Murphy's cabin, giving Slocum time enough to hunt for Kelso.

While the narrow trail he had followed to this overlook was the quickest he knew, Slocum realized Kelso had explored every inch of the land and knew the terrain better than about anyone else. If the man had been in cahoots with the rustlers, he had followed every ridgeline and knew every

hollow in these hills where strays might gather. Riding slowly, Slocum hunted for sign that Kelso had passed by recently.

He didn't find it. But he did see that he had been wrong about the spot where Kelso intended to watch the hanging. Some distance behind the cabin, in a stand of junipers mixed with taller cottonwoods, Slocum saw a flash of light reflected off metal. Using his field glasses, he waited until Kelso showed himself so he could be sure he wasn't seeing one of the posse lying in wait for Murphy.

Slocum studied the cabin and wondered if Murphy had already returned. There was no sign of anyone there, which heartened him. Putting away his binoculars, Slocum rode down the steep side of the hill and circled to get behind the grove where Kelso waited. It took longer than he thought, but Slocum didn't feel the pressure of time yet. Zamora and the posse hadn't shown up, nor had Seamus Murphy. Only when those two forces met would there be fireworks.

Dropping to the ground, Slocum let his horse wander away. He drew his six-shooter and advanced as silently as any Apache brave, slipping into the cool shadow of the trees. Every step had to be tested to be sure he wasn't breaking a twig or crunching down on dried leaves, which would warn Kelso. He need not have worried about alerting his former top hand. Kelso perched on the lowest limb of a cottonwood, intent on the cabin and nothing else. All Slocum had to do was aim and fire. He couldn't miss.

As quiet as a shadow slipping over a shadow, Slocum came up under where Kelso let his legs dangle down off the limb. His gun back in its holster, Slocum reached up and grabbed Kelso's boots and pulled as hard as he could. The man let out a loud cry of surprise, and grunted when he hit the ground hard. Lying facedown, Kelso had had the wind knocked out of him.

"You can roll over whenever you've got a mind to,"

Slocum said. "I've got you covered." He plucked Kelso's six-gun from its holster and tucked it into his belt.

"C-can't breathe."

"You won't be breathing much longer either if they lynch Murphy for something you've done."

"Ain't done nuthin'."

"You framed him for Wimmer's death."

"You cain't prove that."

"You set fire to the courthouse and tried to frame him for that, too."

"What's all this to you, Slocum? You got your big fancy ranch and a thousand head of cattle. What's it all to you if Murphy is lynched?"

"You really think getting rid of Murphy will improve your chances with Suzanne Underwood? She doesn't want a thing to do with you."

"So that's it," Kelso said, gasping hard. He sat up and glared at Slocum. "You figger you'll let the marshal hang Murphy, then pin all that on me so you'll get her. It won't work, Slocum. Suzanne loves me. She's just a mite confused, and you and Murphy are doin' it to her."

Slocum laughed harshly. Of all the people he had come across, Suzanne Underwood was hardly the one he would call confused. She knew what she wanted and would do anything to get it—even sleep with another man if it saved her beau. Slocum was slow to realize that Suzanne had been with him because she sought his help protecting Seamus Murphy, not because she found him desirable. That hurt bad, but Slocum appreciated her reasons. She had no friends and little else to offer to get a defender for Seamus Murphy.

Women had done far worse. And Slocum was looking at a man who'd certainly committed worse crimes to get what he wanted.

"Any reason I shouldn't plug you? You're not going to see Murphy hanged, one way or the other. If I can't stop the

lynch mob, then I'll rob you of the pleasure of knowing your scheme worked."

"Go to hell, Slocum."

"Not before you." Slocum aimed his pistol and then looked up. Marshal Zamora and his men were riding up to Murphy's cabin.

"He's in there. I know he's in there, and the marshal'll get him. I'll die knowin' that I succeeded, not failed!"

Slocum stepped up and swung his pistol, laying the barrel alongside Kelso's head. The man went out like a light. Slocum hurried to the man's horse and got his lariat. It took several minutes to tie him up and lash him to the tree so he faced away from the cabin.

Then Slocum ran to the cabin, worried that Kelso might have told the truth for once. Seamus Murphy might be in the cabin and at risk of getting his neck stretched, unless Slocum could convince the mob he had the real culprit trussed up and waiting for them.

19

By the time Slocum reached Seamus Murphy's cabin, the posse had completely ringed it. Most had rifles or shotguns pointed at the walls, but Marshal Zamora and two others had six-shooters aimed at the only door into the cabin.

"Come on out or we start shooting," Zamora called.

"He's not in there," Slocum shouted. This got the marshal's attention, but the rest of the posse refused to budge. They kept their weapons trained on the cabin. He even heard one man grumbling about how much effort it would take to burn Murphy out. Another piped up that it would be worth doing since Murphy had tried to burn Heavenly to the ground.

"You butt out, Slocum. This is a matter for the law to handle."

"He's not there."

Zamora looked hesitant; then his jaw firmed and his lips thinned to a line. He spat a gob of chaw, held up his left hand to keep the posse where it was, then walked up and kicked in the door. The flimsy door slammed back and came off its hinges, falling down with a loud crash. Zamora jumped and almost opened fire. Then he came out of a crouch and went into the cabin.

Slocum followed. The room was empty.

"He didn't come back here," Slocum said. "He probably knew what would happen and didn't cotton much to a necktie party with him as the only guest."

"We'll find him. Truth is, he doesn't have anywhere else to run. If I have to, I can send out a dozen scouts and track him down."

"I caught the man responsible for everything," Slocum said. "Colorado Pete Kelso. He's the one who killed Jackson Wimmer and set fire to the courthouse to frame Murphy."

"Why'd he go and do a thing like that? He's a mean drunk—that I know from the times I tossed him in the clink—but what'd he gain by doing any of that?"

Slocum began his explanation, but the marshal was as stolid as the Rockies themselves and refused to believe a word of it.

Slocum walked slowly back to the tree where he had tied up Kelso. The man had struggled and had almost gotten free. Slocum took a few seconds to cinch down the rope again until Kelso complained.

"You're gonna cut off my damn hands that rope's so tight."

"You won't be needing your hands or much else when the law catches up with you," Slocum said. "All they'll need is a neck to put their noose around."

Kelso laughed harshly and said, "They're off huntin' fer Murphy, aren't they? I heard their horses ridin' off. A lot of them. You didn't turn me over 'cuz you knew you couldn't prove a thing."

"I don't much care about you starting a stampede and trying to kill me," Slocum said, looking down at the bound man. "Trying to frame Murphy for it with his kerchief is another matter."

"Nothin's illegal, even if I did it."

"You must have spent a powerful lot of time rooting around in Murphy's cabin."

"He's always out ridin' herd. That's the way it is when

you're a lone rancher. He couldn't even afford to hire a hand or two to help with the chores."

"So you rummaged through his belongings and took his bandanna and gun and hat."

"That hat." Kelso chuckled. "I thought that was a nice touch. Start the fire, leave it, then he'd get blamed. I didn't know he was inside the courthouse. That made it all the sweeter."

"How'd you know he was there?"

"After I set the fire, I watched. I considered takin' another shot or two at you, but you headed off to the creek. If you hadn't got the water pumpin', they'd have gone to see why. I needed enough time to get out of town."

"So you saw Murphy inside the courthouse?"

"Of course I did."

"Why'd you try to frame him for Wimmer's death? Because you didn't want to take the blame?"

"I had Murphy's six-shooter. Seemed the thing to do." Kelso laughed at the frame. "All I had to do was fire it."

"Into the ceiling?"

"Didn't want to shoot out through a window. I blasted a splinter out of the ceiling with Murphy's gun, then took the one beside Wimmer and hid it."

"You didn't use your own gun to kill Wimmer?"

"I didn't kill Wimmer. He was already dead. I heard the shot and went in. He was sprawled in the chair with a gun beside him. I saw my chance and took it."

"If you didn't kill him—" Slocum was cut off when Marshal Zamora pushed him aside.

"I heard enough. You got a big mouth, Kelso. I don't know if we can hang you for that, but you said enough to send you to jail for burning down the courthouse."

Kelso looked up. His mouth dropped open.

"I heard the horses. They left. You went with them."

"You thought he did," Slocum said. "I convinced him that Murphy wasn't the owlhoot he thought."

"But I wanted to make sure what Slocum told me wasn't just chin music. I've known a passel of men who could spin yarns that sounded good but were purebred lies. Not this time. You confessed of your own free will."

Kelso fought, but between the marshal and Slocum, they got him hog-tied and belly-down over his saddle.

"Reckon I ought to thank you, Slocum," Zamora said. "I got me a real criminal in Colorado Pete."

"No need to thank me, but you owe Seamus Murphy an apology."

"Well, it's likely to be a spell 'fore we see him again. If the man had a lick of sense, he's already in Wyoming and still ridin' hard."

"You said it, Marshal. If he had a lick of sense. He's got more to keep him here than the threat of dangling from a rope."

Marshal Zamora looked quizzically at Slocum, then led Kelso's horse with its human cargo back toward the cabin where his own horse was tethered. As Slocum watched them go, he chewed at his lower lip and thought hard. Kelso probably thought Wimmer had left *him* the Bar-S. With the owner dead, Kelso would be rich and powerful. And Kelso also thought that framing Murphy would be a way to get Suzanne Underwood.

Slocum walked back to find his horse, but he puzzled over Kelso's denial about having shot Wimmer. Kelso had discharged Murphy's six-shooter into the ceiling so it would look like the murder weapon, but why would he lie about killing Wimmer himself? He had boasted about every other crime he had committed. Murdering his boss would be a clever scheme in his twisted mind.

Slocum mounted and headed back down the road until he found the shortcut that led over the mountain onto Bar-S land. He had a herd to deliver to Montrose.

"We're almost there, Mr. Slocum. Another few miles and we're on the flats leading to the town," Ryan said.

"It's been an easy drive," Slocum said. "No rustlers or storms. Only the one problem."

"Cain't ever tell 'bout Colorado rivers. The Gunnison ran faster under the surface than I'd've thought for this late in the year. Still, we only lost a couple dozen head."

"Not bad for a herd of this size," Slocum said.

"You're soundin' mighty sad, if you don't mind my sayin' so. Somethin' eatin' at you, Mr. Slocum?"

"I've been thinking about the Bar-S all the way here and what I want to do," Slocum said.

"You fixin' to sell it?"

Slocum looked past Ryan to the other cowboys who had been loyal to him. They'd worked for Jackson Wimmer because he paid them. These men worked for John Slocum because they respected him. One or two, like Ryan and Jenks, he might even come to call friends—if he stayed on to run the ranch.

Being on the trail had reminded him what he liked so much. Under the bright Colorado sky he felt free. Sitting and filling out papers, worrying about bills, even with plenty of money to pay them, always sending men to do this chore or that . . . Slocum felt as if he had strung head-high barbed wire around himself at the Bar-S. The more he worked, the more he knew he belonged on the open range.

"I'm seriously considering it," Slocum said. He had no reason to lie to Ryan. "Keep it under your hat until after the herd's sold, will you?"

"Yes, sir, I will."

"I promise I won't sell to just anyone. He'll be a top-notch rancher."

"Wish I could step up and say that sounded like me, but it don't," Ryan said. "Truth is, being top hand is about all I'd want. Maybe foreman, but that's more 'n I want to think on right now."

"Right now, with the promise of a few silver dollars in your pocket, that's good enough."

"Yes, *sir.*"

Slocum laughed. He understood Ryan completely because that was the way *he* felt. It wasn't that he'd necessarily get roaring drunk, or even find himself a warm armful for the night, but he could feel that way. Ryan had his own moral code and could pass on such diversions. Slocum was free to choose whether to indulge or not. If he had a wife back on the Bar-S, he wouldn't be free to even think on such diversions after a long drive eating dust and listening to the mournful complaints of too many sides of beef on the hoof.

"Keep the herd here while I see to selling them," Slocum said.

He wanted to gallop into Montrose, but satisfied himself with a more stately walk. He looked around and saw a booming town serviced by a railroad. The people were pleasant and nodded to him as he rode, but there wasn't the friendliness that he felt in Heavenly the first time he had ridden in there. Slocum went to the stockyards near the railroad depot and looked for likely buyers.

He had expected two or three. He counted five.

On impulse, he went to the buyer with the smallest office, which was staffed by only two men. One, obviously the bookkeeper, looked as if he had not eaten in weeks. The other man looked up, gave Slocum a small grin, and came around a desk with his hand thrust out.

"Howdy. My name's Larkin. You lookin' to sell some cows?"

"I am, Mr. Larkin."

"I've got to warn you right off, I'm not the biggest shipper and I can't pay the most, but I am certainly the friendliest cuss in all of Montrose."

The bookkeeper grunted and turned back to his books.

Larkin said, "I usually say that I'm the handsomest, but my partner over there didn't like that."

"Reckon he wanted to claim that for himself," Slocum said.

The bookkeeper looked up, startled, then grinned. Larkin clapped Slocum on the back and ushered him to a seat at the desk.

"Now let's see what kind of a deal we can make to ship your beeves off to Denver."

The bargaining went on for the better part of the afternoon, but Slocum soon had twenty-five dollars a head for his cattle. After culling for breeding stock and taking into account those he had lost on the trail, Slocum pocketed $20,000. This wasn't the best price he could have gotten if he had gone to a larger buyer, but Slocum felt an obligation to do what he could to help those who were struggling to make good.

Somehow, although they looked nothing alike and their dispositions were like night and day, Larkin reminded Slocum of Seamus Murphy. Both men were tenacious and knew what they wanted out of life. He appreciated that.

He appreciated it even more when he realized he had come to a decision. He knew what he wanted out of life, too.

20

A lot had happened in the weeks Slocum had been on the trail, driving the cattle to market. Heavenly had a more cheerful aspect about it. Slocum rode directly to the marshal's office and went inside. Zamora sat behind his desk, reading a week-old copy of the *Rocky Mountain News*. He looked up when Slocum came in, and motioned toward the chair on the other side of the desk.

"Wondered when you'd get back," Zamora said.

"My curiosity got the better of me," Slocum said. He glanced toward the three cells at the rear of the jail. All were empty.

"Kelso got himself convicted of arson and a half dozen other crimes, including stealing from Seamus Murphy, and got sent to the prison over in Pueblo. Everyone was glad to see him go, though some were pissed that they didn't get a necktie party."

"They're not still thinking about Seamus Murphy for that honor, are they?"

"Nope." The marshal leaned back and laced his fingers behind his head. He looked as content as a cat with a bowl of fresh cream. "Things are real peaceful now in Heavenly. You might say the town's finally living up to its name."

"The rustlers are all driven off," Slocum said. "Other than the cattle saved over for the next year's herd, there's not a whole lot to draw the outlaws."

"Always some folks lookin' for a quick steak and easy meal, but they're nothing like a hardened rustler," the lawman agreed. "You looking for anyone in particular? The newlyweds?"

"Reckon so," Slocum said. "I wondered how long it would take for them to get hitched."

"Not more 'n a day or two after you hit the trail. I have to say, that made folks a whole lot friendlier toward them. Now maybe if somebody's got an ache or pain, they'll take it to Doc Gainsborough instead of the vet. He was gettin' mighty tired of seein' more human patients than four-legged ones."

Slocum put on his best poker face. This was not what he had expected to hear.

"Where might the happy couple be right now?"

"Over at the doc's office."

"Marshal," Slocum said, "I wish you nothing but the best in keeping the peace."

Zamora chuckled, then rocked forward so he could plant his elbows on the desk and continue reading his newspaper. Slocum left and went directly to Ben Gainsborough's office.

"Mr. Slocum, heard you were back," Doc Gainsborough greeted. "Come on in, pull up a chair, and let's share a nip of . . . medicine." He looked at Nora from the corner of his eye to see how she responded. She made a sour face and waved him to go on. "That's why I married her. She understands that a man's got to sample a taste of whiskey now and then, call it medicine or just plain camaraderie."

"You *just* married her?" Slocum took the amber liquid and sloshed it around in the water glass. Gainsborough had poured a hefty drink. With a single swift gulp, Slocum downed it. The liquor burned down to his belly and sat warming his innards.

"Slocum, you've been here for a while but you don't know squat about the people. Nora and I, we, well—"

"Get to the point, Ben. He's not a child." Nora Gainsborough looked at the whiskey bottle as if damning it for her husband's reluctance. "We were not married but lived together in sin."

Slocum knew that already. He had another question that burned the tip of his tongue as he asked.

"For how long?" Slocum saw Nora and Ben exchange looks.

"Close to fifteen years, give or take," she said. "This is why the townspeople avoided Ben when they had medical problems."

"That's why they went to the vet," Slocum said, remembering what the marshal had told him.

Gainsborough chuckled and sipped at his whiskey. "He got more business than I did sometimes. I thought about taking up his line of work. No foaling season could be as hard as working on a patient who thought I was Satan's tool."

"His bedmate," Nora corrected.

"Why'd you just get married after all these years?" Even as the words left his mouth, Slocum knew the answer. "Jackson Wimmer died," he said in answer to his own question.

"The son of a bitch refused to divorce me. He was all about controlling everyone around him. He made money from the Bar-S, as you probably know going over his books, but more than this, he never gave up power. Ever." Tears welled in Nora's eyes. She put her hand on her new husband's shoulder.

"You could have moved somewhere else where they didn't know you," Slocum pointed out.

"No, I couldn't."

"Her daughter wanted to stay near her pa, though he treated her worse than anyone else after Nora left him."

Slocum reached for the whiskey and poured another jolt as strong as the first. Only after he had swallowed a considerable portion of it did he trust himself to ask, "Suzanne?"

"Our daughter, mine and Jackson's. We left him when she was five."

Slocum remembered the picture on the office wall and how Kelso had taken it for no reason he could tell. Now he could. Kelso was obsessed with Suzanne Underwood, and had either found out or recognized her as a small child with Wimmer. He had taken the picture as a trophy after killing Wimmer, probably as a show of devotion to Suzanne.

"She doesn't have anything good to say about him. But why does she go by the name Underwood?"

"That's my maiden name. I suppose it was the only way she could think to make it seem, at least to her, that she had disowned us all."

"I saw that plainly. She acted like she was walking on hot coals the times she was in the ranch house," Slocum said.

Gainsborough's eyebrows arched. "She went there? She vowed she would never go there as long as he was alive."

Slocum went cold inside as pieces of the puzzle fell into place for him.

"She killed her pa, didn't she? She shot Wimmer."

"No!" Both Nora and Ben shouted at the same time.

"Then Kelso must have, only he didn't brag on it. A man like that would."

Again, Nora and Ben exchanged looks. Gainsborough supplied the key that Slocum lacked.

"You know he was all eaten up inside with cancer. I showed you what remained of his stomach over at the undertaker's," Gainsborough said. He studied Slocum a moment, then went on. "It's hard to prove, but I think Wimmer killed himself. He couldn't stand the pain anymore, and it wouldn't have been long before he began wasting away to nothing."

"He was already skin and bones," Slocum said, remembering how light Wimmer had been when he picked him up after the rancher had been shot. He should have realized Wimmer was sick then, but the old codger's sharp tongue had kept the conversation away from such observations at the time.

"A man like him, always in control, he could never tolerate

being beholden to someone else to feed or fetch for him because he was unable to do it himself." Nora moved behind Ben and put both hands on his stooped shoulders, as much to comfort herself as him, Slocum thought.

"So Kelso only took advantage of the situation?"

"The best we can figure, he heard the shot, found Wimmer dead, then left Seamus's gun to implicate him," Gainsborough said. "You answered why Kelso had the gun."

"A trophy. He fired the gun into the ceiling so it would have a round spent, then took Wimmer's so nobody would ask why there were two guns that had just been fired. That was a mistake. If he had left it, it might have looked like he and Murphy struggled and fought it out."

"That might get Murphy off with a self-defense plea. This way it looked as if Wimmer was murdered."

"The old son of a bitch checked out by his own hand, and Kelso took advantage." Slocum finished his whiskey. "You know about your daughter and Murphy?"

"They've made no secret of how they feel about each other," Nora said. A tiny smile crept across her lips. "Like mother, like daughter, I reckon. At first I thought she took up with Seamus just to thumb her nose at everyone in town, including me."

"You and her don't get on very well?"

"She never forgave me for a lot of things. She was young when I left Jackson, but she was a complete pariah in town as a result of me taking up with Ben. She grew up being snubbed and blamed Ben here for it because I loved him so. That might be why she and Seamus are so good together. She's with another outcast."

"They just might be like two peas in a pod," Slocum said.

"He's a hothead, and she might be a calming influence on him. Opposites, not kindred spirits."

There was a touch of wistfulness in her tone that made Slocum sit up. His mind raced as choices surfaced and sank.

"You reckon they're out at his ranch?"

Nora shrugged. Gainsborough said, "Last I heard, he had filed for a marriage license. With the fire and all, I don't know if the clerk's had time to do much about it."

"What Ben means, Seamus is still as much a pariah as ever. There's been plenty of time for them to get their records in order and they haven't done it. Suzanne didn't even come into town when Ben and me got hitched."

"Nobody showed up, 'cept the judge," Gainsborough said. "And Gutherie. He was a witness. Never expected that from him, but who's gonna cross the man who owns both the general store and saloon?"

"I might be able to speed up things." Slocum got to his feet. "Don't go off for a while. I'll be back."

Slocum went to the courthouse and saw how it had been repaired in his absence. It took the better part of an hour for him to find everything he needed, going from one clerk to another. Then he went to the bank before returning to Gainsborough's office. Slocum didn't take the offered chair or glass of whiskey this time.

He handed Nora Gainsborough a sealed envelope and said, "Don't open this until the right time."

"Right time for what?" She looked confused as she ran her fingers over the stuffed envelope.

"You'll know," Slocum said. He shook hands with Ben Gainsborough and nodded to Nora, then left.

He mounted and knew he had one more stop to make. Slocum found the turnoff from the main road and headed into the hills, using the shortcut that would take him to Seamus Murphy's cabin. He reached the lonely cabin an hour before sundown to find Murphy standing in the doorway with his six-shooter in his hand. Slocum had been spotted riding up.

"You get on outta here, Slocum. You're not welcome."

"Don't hurt yourself with that hogleg," Slocum said, stepping down from his horse. "I want a word with you."

"They sent you. I know they sent you to throw me off my land. You're not gonna do it."

"We won't let you," Suzanne said. "We're in this together, and we won't let you throw us off."

"I talked it over with the clerk. If you still want that marriage license, just ask."

"Don't meddle, Slocum. I don't need you meddling. Next thing I know, you'll be buyin' the Circle M note from the bank and giving it to me as a wedding present."

"We wouldn't accept it!"

"The thought never crossed my mind," Slocum said. "Your problems with the Circle M are yours and none of my business."

"Then get out. I got work to do if I'm gonna keep this place."

"You'd do anything to make a success of it?"

"Yes," both Suzanne and Seamus said as one. Slocum forced himself to keep from smiling as he recollected how Nora and Ben Gainsborough had answered simultaneously, too. They were as much of one mind as these two were.

"I never thought I'd ever be a rancher and certainly not own a spread the size of the Bar-S." Slocum looked hard at Suzanne and said, "Your pa named the spread after you, didn't he? Bar-S? Bar-Suzanne?"

"It was his way of keeping his thumb pressed down on me."

"Might be," Slocum allowed. "Might be he was proud of you being his daughter. But that's not what I wanted to say."

Slocum waited to build a little tension. He got it. Suzanne pressed closer to her man, and Murphy fingered his six-shooter. Both looked anxiously at Slocum.

"I'm not cut out to run a ranch the size of the Bar-S. Truth is, the longer I stay there, the more I want to just ride away."

"So why don't you do it?" Suzanne asked.

"I intend to, but getting the ranch as a legacy that wasn't mine wears down on me. I'm letting you have first chance at buying the Bar-S from me."

Murphy laughed harshly.

"There's no way I could buy a ranch that big and successful. I can't even meet the mortgage on the Circle M."

"I said I don't care what happens here. You can buy the Bar-S for five thousand dollars."

"You might as well have asked for a million dollars. That's as far out of my reach as five thousand."

"Borrow the money," Slocum said.

"Nobody in town's gonna loan me a plugged nickel, much less that much. If they would, I'd have paid off the note on my own place."

"Buy the Bar-S and I reckon you'll have the banker begging you to take out a bigger loan or even giving you a break on the one you've got. The more money you have, the more bankers want to give you money," Slocum said.

"Who?" asked Murphy. "Who has that much?"

Slocum looked at Suzanne. She recoiled and shook her head when she read the answer in his face. Murphy still didn't know.

"Your ma might have that much. Ask her."

"I won't be in her debt."

"Would that be so bad? You could pay her back in one good season and own the Bar-S free and clear. The Circle M butts up against Bar-S land. The two ranches together would be even more profitable. I've seen some of your pasture. Looks good."

"Your high pastures are better," Murphy said.

"They could be yours. You up to a challenge like that?"

"I'd need ranch hands," Murphy said.

"It'd be real hard keeping the ones that worked the Bar-S this season," Slocum said, "because I gave each of the ten a five-hundred-dollar bonus. They'd be looking for that much again, if the ranch was successful."

"If you could give them that big a bonus, why are you selling?" Suzanne stood beside Seamus now, and forced his hand with the six-gun down.

"I'll have more money in my pocket than I've ever had."

"The five thousand we'd pay you," Suzanne said. Slocum saw her turning over the possibilities in her mind.

"All the debts are paid from profit from this year's herd. You'd be starting even, except for the loan."

"From my ma."

"From your ma," Slocum agreed.

Suzanne's expression changed and she said, "You must have really itchy feet to give up the Bar-S like this."

"I do," Slocum said.

"Shake on it, Seamus," Suzanne said. "We're buying ourselves a ranch."

"If your mother has the money," Seamus Murphy said skeptically.

"She does," Slocum said.

Durango was only another day's ride ahead of him. Occasionally, Slocum fought the urge to turn around and go back toward Heavenly, but he'd resisted the first couple days on the trail, and now the longing to be on the Bar-S again was slowly fading.

He had done well for himself. Suzanne and Seamus had gone to Nora Gainsborough and smoothed over differences that were caused by pride and the need to find someone to strike out against. What Slocum had not counted on was Seamus Murphy's insistence on putting a price on the Bar-S twice what Slocum had asked. The five-thousand-dollar balance would be paid to Slocum in ten payments, deposited in the Heavenly bank over the next decade. If he ever needed money, he reckoned he could return to Heavenly once a year and then ride off again with a new bankroll.

Or he could let the money pile up. He had spoken with the banker. When Seamus and Suzanne had children, they just might find accounts in their name. Slocum knew Nora would see that the banker remained honest.

He patted the wad of greenbacks in his pocket and glanced back at his saddlebags where gold coins rested, all

in payment for a ranch he had never wanted. He might miss Ryan, who had accepted the job as foreman from Seamus Murphy, and riding land that was his, and the sight of a thousand head of fine cattle being driven to the railhead in his name, but he doubted it. Along with moments like that came fighting rustlers, stringing endless miles of barbed wire, worrying about things he no longer had to even consider.

Slocum tapped his mare's flanks and got the horse moving a little faster. He had no idea what he would find in Durango, but it had nothing to do with the hundreds of problems of running a ranch.

Once more he was free, and it felt good, damned good.

Watch for

SLOCUM AND EL LOCO

360th novel in the exciting SLOCUM series
from Jove

Coming in February!